D0722724

No Country
for
Old Gnomes

No Country for Old Gnomes

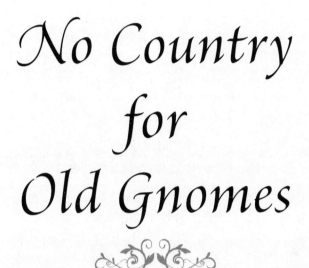

THE TALES OF PELL

DELILAH S. DAWSON
AND KEVIN HEARNE

DEL REY
NEW YORK

Copyright © 2019 by D. S. Dawson and Kevin Hearne

All rights reserved.

Published in the United States by Del Rey, an imprint of Random House, a division of Penguin Random House LLC, New York.

DEL REY and the HOUSE colophon are registered trademarks of Penguin Random House LLC.

Map by Kevin Hearne was originally published in *Kill the Farm Boy* by D. S. Dawson and Kevin Hearne (New York: Del Rey, 2018)

LIBRARY OF CONGRESS CATALOGING-IN-PUBLICATION DATA
Names: Hearne, Kevin, author. | Dawson, Delilah S., author.
Title: No country for old gnomes / Kevin Hearne, Delilah S. Dawson.
Description: First edition. | New York : Del Rey, [2019] | Series: The Tales of Pell ; 2
Identifiers: LCCN 2018051284| ISBN 9781524797775 (Hardcover) | ISBN 9781524797782 (Ebook)
Subjects: LCSH: Fantasy fiction.
Classification: LCC PS3608.E264 N6 2019 | DDC 813/.6—dc23 LC record available at https://lccn.loc.gov/2018051284

Printed in the United States of America on acid-free paper

randomhousebooks.com

2 4 6 8 9 7 5 3 1

First Edition

Book design by Caroline Cunningham
Frontispiece gnome illustration: iStock/benoitb
Title page border: iStock/jcrosemann
Title page and chapter opener ornament: Vecteezy.com
Space break ornament: iStock/mxtama

To all the unsung goth heroes:

We're singing your song.

Do not feed the gryphons
yes feede
gryphones

DÄMKÖLD SEA

The Claw

Soperki
Cheapmeat
Bigly-Wicke
Gobbleneck
Okesvaa
Chumpspittle

Jyggaly
Dyddaly
Drybbyl

Jusipert
Pavaasik
Luri
Honeymelon Hills
Koloka

YGLYK

Dismull
Bruding
Misree Hills
Pruneshute Forest
Muffincrumb
Tykkyl
Wyglyng

DOLOROUS
OCEAN

Glumlee
BORIX
Tennebruss
Tower
of Thorns
Nokanen
Caskcooper
Fyckyl

Retchedde
Sullenne
Malefic Reach
Home of the Dark Lord Toby
Dower
THE SKYR
The Toot
Towers
Toodleoo

Fort Valiant
Fort Craven

Drabbe
Dorf Bay
Pyckåbøg
Håpipøle
Figgish Fen
Meadow Verge
Bob
Skaggs Heath
Frangibull

Lårpendrånk
KÅFKØMPF
The Coxcomb
Neatcamp
CORRADEN

Grundelbård
Riverhead
Foolscap

SERPENT SEA
HERE BE MONSTERS
really specifically right
here, not kidding

Åftpümpf
Håmlett
Sküterländ
Bearded Plains
Korpas Range
Songlen
Mudskip Ferry

The Grange
Pikestaff

Proudwood
Lighthouse
Centaur Pastures
Catacombs
of Yore
Nockney
Flemme

The
MORNINGWOOD
Qul Desert
QUL
Quti
Qruditay
Quder
Fulva
Glanse

Truffle Bay
Four Skins
Ouchii Hills
Quulayd
Quchii Qu
KOLON

Humptulips
Groggÿn
Taynt

GRUNTING
Fapsworth
Llama Drama

Titan
Toothpicks
Wolward
Henghua
Jukai
Limpf
Mons Mountains

Tower of the
Sn'archivist
Petrel
Grakkel
TEABRING
Blatter

URCHIN SEA
Whimbrel
Manchaek
Sinuicho
Shih Hills
Pakreas
Seamen Cove

Malefic Beach
Khugas
Baoshu
Splien

HERE BE OTTERS
they be super cute
BURDELL
Lün
12
Zhaoteng
Liaoxing
Skrodal

Bustardo
Kakapoh
8
9
10
Broken Tooth

Cape Gannet
CHUMMY SEA
Banhai
Olonkh
AWFUL SALTY SEA

1
Khotran

2
3
4
5
6

The Seven Toes
1. Big Potatoe Island
2. Mace Island
3. Asafoetida Island
4. Cinnamonk Island
5. Sage Island
6. Thyme Island
7. Ginger Island

The Several Macks
8. Mack Guphinne
9. Mack Muphinne
10. Mack Enchiis
11. Mack Ribpe
12. Mack Elmorr

The Western
Earldoms of
PELL

Drawn by LeNarde Picklesmith
of the Bigly-Wicke Picklesmiths
for the
Dark Lord Toby Fitzherbert of
Malefic Reach, which has a
Tower Moste Tall and Thicke

BLOODY OCEAN

The Island That Has No
Name Because No One Ever
Goes There or Even Talks
About It for Some Strange
Reason but Trust Me It's
Beautiful

Map by Kevin Hearne

CONTENTS

No Country
for
Old Gnomes

1.

In a Cave Just Positively Riddled with Blood and Gecko Toes

"Look, building anticipation is great and everything, but I think the most important thing to consider is—"

—Thibault Cherkmerkin of the Cheapmeat Cherkmerkins, famously before hurling a fish in the face of his mother-in-law, thereby starting a food fight that lasted three weeks and that he ultimately lost

Enter three witches.

What they entered was not a race. It was, in fact, a cave of ominous portent, which was different from a regular cave in that it possessed a spooky lighting concept. This was achieved by kindling a fire in the cave and then covering it with the black iron bottom of a cauldron, in which something eldritch may or may not be stewed. But let's be real: No one ever bought a cauldron and installed it in a cave to make a mundane soup. It was always, *always*, going to be an eldritch stew. Especially since they'd brought the requisite bucket full of entrails, pouches of herbs, and assorted dried eyeballs.

"*Thrice* the bundled cat hath mewed—" the first witch said, in perturbed disbelief that one cat could have so much to mew about.

"Then let him out of the dang sack!" the second witch said, her exasperation clear. "You know he hates it!"

The cat in question mewed again and was thus released from his torment. He ran out of the cave like his tail was on fire. Which it was, as he'd accidentally run too close to the flames.

"It's time, sisters! It's time!" the third witch intoned, like she was somehow better and witchier and closer to the spheres than the other two witches.

The first witch sighed and rubbed her temples. "Gather 'round the cauldron, then, and let's get on with it. Magick waits for no one."

"Did you just say *magick* with a *k*?" the second witch asked. "And why would you say *'round* instead of *around*?"

The first witch looked a bit sheepish. "I read in *Better Brooms and Cauldrons* that it made things more official, and since you insist on wearing hand-knit tunics covered in kittens, someone has to put in the work at adding some ambience."

"Witches are supposed to have cats! It's right there in the handbook!"

"*One* cat," the first witch said, now on the attack and looking down her nose. "A familiar cloaked in night to do thy dark bidding. Not seventy-three strays milling about the house. Every time I visit your place, I leave smelling like an outhouse crossed with a wharf. And the hair!"

"If you can't use Malefichant's No Hair On There spell, are you really a witch?" the second witch sniffed. Her kitten-covered tunic was the requisite black, but it was coated in a thick layer of cat fur and stained a particular shade of brown that could only be called Tuna 'n' Vittles.

"Enough!" the third witch cried, clawed hands in the air. "We're running out of time!" She cleared her throat, spat a phlegmglobber into the fire pit, and began.

> *Double, double toil and mess*
> *The fire's hot and I hate chess—*

"What's that?" the second witch broke in. "You hate chess?"

The third witch drew herself up tall. "I do."

"But how is that relevant to the spell—"

"It rhymes!" the third witch spat. "Rhyming is more important than meaning."

"But you could've gone with *bless, dress, guess, less . . .*" The first witch trailed off. She was not a poet and she did know that well, but she could rhyme when the moment required it.

"If you have a better spell up your sleeve, please continue," the third witch said with that horrible sort of sweetness that suggests a punch to the schnozz might work better for all involved.

"Ahem," the first witch said. "Continuing.

> *In the poisoned duodenum throw*
> *Three fat toads and a tortoise named Joe—*

"Joe?" the second witch screeched. "But he was my favorite thatch tortoise!"

"They're a pestilence," the first witch said, her voice quite stern. "And they were warned. As I said, ahem.

> *Filet of eel and dab of butter*
> *Add salt and pepper, marinate overnight in apple juice*
> *Roast at three-fifty for an hour—*

"That's not the spell; that's a recipe for eel casserole," the third witch hissed.

"Then I'll go on, shall I?" the second witch asked sweetly. "Now, AHEM.

> *Wool of llamataur, tongue of bat*
> *Eye of newt and a fuzzy hat*

Adder's arse and gecko's toes
Into the pot the whole mess goes!

Each witch bent over to pick up a bucket, and they all dumped their ingredients into the cauldron with a hearty splash.

"Cool it with a pint of blood
Then the charm will be real good."

The third witch bent over again and held a large, red-splashed bucket overhead with a dangerously sloshy sound.

"Ye gods!" the second witch cried. "Where'd you get all that blood?"

"Er," the third witch said. "The, um, shop?"

"You did not! Liar!"

Before she could be questioned further, the third witch dumped the entire bucket of blood into the cauldron, turning it into a gooey red mess that smelled like pennies and farts.

"And that was way more than a pint!" the second witch continued. "That was absolute gallons of blood. And it wasn't nice and cool, because then it would be all coagulated, like a giant, jiggly scab, and it would've made a terrible splash. It was hot *and* fresh. It's probably not even going to cool the dang charm. It's going to make it hotter. What if the charm's not *real good*, like the spell says?"

"Then I suppose the coming war will be less warrish," the third witch said peevishly, and then muttered, "Or possibly more warrish." She shook a gnarled finger at them. "Honestly, ladies, we met tonight to try to hurry things along with this war and throw the entire country into chaos and strife, and you're more concerned about the source of random buckets of blood. It was barely a pint, if that. Got it from a sick baboon. Not a problem at all. Not even two cups. Call yourself witches."

"That's gaslighting, that is!" the first witch shouted. "You pretending like there's no problem when there's obviously a problem and then downplaying or diminishing our feelings, all to throw us off the scent of your unexplained and honestly alarming abundance of blood."

"Barely a thimbleful," the third witch said, dropping her first, far-smaller bucket into her second, enormous bloodstained bucket with a clang.

"I don't think I like Girls' Night Out anymore," the second witch whined. "We could've stayed in with a bottle of Moscato and read the saucy bits of an anatomy book out loud in funny voices."

"What's done is done," the third witch said, but she grinned in a way that reminded the other witches of sharks and used-broom salesmen. When the third witch realized the other two were staring at her, she straightened and plastered a polite smile on her face. "So, when shall we three meet again?"

"Uh, I'm busy," the first witch said.

"Yeah. My cat's sick," the second witch added.

"Which one?"

"Er, all of them. For the foreseeable future."

The silence grew very uncomfortable.

"Fine. Bye, witches," the third witch said, swinging her blood bucket as she sauntered out of the cave.

"Where'd we find her again?" the second witch whispered to the first witch.

"At the Ye Olde Meet-Up Bulletin Boarde," the first witch said. "We needed a third for the spell. But she looks different than her picture."

"Definitely more evil," the second witch agreed.

"And what was that about chaos and strife and starting a war? I thought we were doing a spell to help the Bruding Boars win their jousting competition?"

"Oh! I almost forgot."

The second witch pulled a gold-and-brown scarf out of her bag and tossed it into the now terribly bloody-looking cauldron. Al-though the spell had suggested blood would cool it down, the caul-dron now somehow seemed even hotter, the red glop inside viciously boiling and bubbling and almost growling as it cooked. The scarf twisted and twirled on the liquid's surface, briefly forming the shape of a triangle.

"What's that mean, I wonder?" the second witch said. "Almost looks like a gnome hat."

"A gnome hat?" The first witch blew a raspberry. "That's preposterous. Nobody cares about gnomes! Maybe it means our jousters will win first, second, and third place! I so hope we win. Go, Boars!"

They left together, buckets swinging, and went to find a bottle of Moscato.

Neither noticed the surfeit of portent in the air, wafting from the coppery-smelling cave, probably because the second witch smelled so strongly of cat urine.

But the portent was there nonetheless.

2.

Beset by Naked Halfling Malice

"Never trust quotes placed at the beginning of chapters as if they were diamonds of the brain. They were probably written by a halfling expressly for the purpose of deceiving you."

—Gnomer the Gnomerian, in the Fourth Gnomeric Cycle, ♭♪♏-♩♪

I n a hole in the ground there lived a family of gnomes. Not a yucky, moist, gross hole filled with worm tails and old chicken bones, nor yet a dusty, crusty, sandy hole entirely lacking modern plumbing and ergonomic seating: It was a gnomehome, and that meant tidiness and comfort.

In this particular moment, however, there was strife. There was, in fact, a Mighty Row. Onni Numminen had finally had enough of his twin brother's ungnomeric antics.

"Offi, you can't wear that thing to the Midsummer Shindig. It's ridiculous."

Offi looked down, the gaslights flashing off his glasses. "Why not? It's a cardigan. All gnomes wear cardigans. And you must admit it's tidy. I'm following all the rules." He tugged his scraggly beard in a way gnomes did when they thought they were getting away with something, which only annoyed Onni more.

"But it's black! With rabid purple bats on it!"

The very sight of the thing nearly made Onni's brain short-circuit. *Tidy sweater, never better!* was one of the very first gnomeisms every gnomelet learned in gnomeschool, but it was assumed the sweaters would be in bright colors and feature embroidered ducks, pineapples, or tulips, cheerful symbols of gnomeric togetherness. It was true that Offi had knit himself a finely crafted cardigan, but it was entirely the wrong color. What kind of gnome would wear black? And then he had gone and lovingly embroidered creepy purple bats on it, their eyes made of shiny red buttons. Offi was correct: Technically, there was nothing wrong with it. But it was obvious to anyone with eyes that Offi Numminen wasn't being . . . gnomeric.

And that was the worst thing a gnome could do, outside of stealing pudding or shaving off his or her beard.

"You can't wear it to the shindig," Onni repeated, tugging his own scruffy beard in exasperation. "I won't allow it."

Offi gave him a dark look, in part because that was one of only two looks Offi could give these days, the other being one that said that life was merely a slow trudge toward death and Offi's soul was a black repository for pain.

Onni hated both looks, and gnomes weren't supposed to hate anything, except an untidy sock drawer. And halflings. And anyone who called them "knee-high," since they had their own knees and were appropriately taller than said body parts.

"I can so wear it, and I will, and you don't get to allow me anything. I've tried to be like you, Onni, and where did it get me? Nowhere. Pretending to be happy never made anyone happy. Do you know what it's like, being me, and you being you? Knowing everyone thinks my twin is the poster boy for gnomeric youth? By dinkus, they gave you a medal that straight up says PARAGON OF GNOMERIC YOUTH on it. And I have to stare at it all the time."

He glumly glanced to where the medal hung on a plaque amidst dozens of other medals proudly proclaiming things like EXEMPLAR OF TOGETHERNESS and TIDIEST CARDIGAN and SPIFFIEST HAT and WOW, WHAT A GNOME. And then they both glanced to Offi's identical plaque, which featured only one sad, smallish medal, reading EATS PUDDING WITH MINOR GUSTO.

For once, Onni tried to see things from his brother's point of view. Onni considered himself a foine boy, and not only because he had three FOINE BOY medals. But he *tried*. He actively wanted to make his parents proud by being the most gnomeric of gnomes. He got along. He spouted the gnomeisms whenever appropriate. He did his best to be round, affable, and clean and to wear only the brightest colors.

Whereas Offi had recently slid into the darkest acceptable colors: navy blue, forest green, and a particularly virulent shade of plum just this side of a bruise. He was appropriately round and clean, but not even a curmudgeonly badger would consider him affable. He was grim. He was dour and even verging on sour. He was, in essence, Not Jolly.

Onni's twin increasingly turned away from people and sought his quiet corner of their father's workshop, where Offi put on his unacceptably greasy work cardigan and tinkered with Old Seppo's broken or forgotten machines. Why, Offi hadn't even gone to the Everybody Goes to This Dance dance! He was destroying Onni's social capital, and that was one thing Onni couldn't abide. So he tried another tactic.

"If you wear that to the Midsummer Shindig, you'll break Mama's heart."

Offi glared. "Mama loves Papa, and he's not the most gnomeric of gnomes."

Onni snorted. "That's different, by dinkus! He's a war hero. They're allowed to get peculiar. And he still wears appropriately bright cardigans. Besides, he's starting to get a reputation in town—you know that. Paranoid, they call him. Just last week at the beard salon, I heard Una Uvulaa call him Crazy Old Seppo."

That finally brought fire to Offi's eyes, a rare third look that appeared to be Characteristically Ungnomeric Rage. "Did she mention he installed one of his Halflings Hate This Heat-Resistant Hatch hatches for her? Because they may talk about him behind his back, but the foine folk of Pavaasik still rely on him to keep their homes safe from halfling firebombs." A flash of worry lit Offi's eyes, and Onni frowned at the shadows around them. By hokum, had his batty twin lined them with soot? They were all . . . soulful.

"It's getting worse, you know," Offi continued. "Pooti Pinkelsen's whole family exploded last week. The halflings' firebombs are getting worse. I heard Papa telling Mama about it. If they'd had one of Papa's hatch covers, they wouldn't have had their giblets blown up. So our love of gadgetry trumps your love of . . . getting along. You can't get along if you're dead."

Onni's hands clenched into fists, and he regretted starting the row. Gnomes were proud of their round stomachs but had little stomach for fighting.

"Look, Offi, gadgetry has its place, but the heart of our strength will always be people. As Mama always says, *Stick together, tough as leather!*"

Offi rolled his eyes, shocking Onni. For all that they were twins, identical down to their blue eyes and golden curls, distinguishable only by Offi's black-rimmed spectacles—which were honestly mostly for show—Onni was quite sure he had never rolled his eyes in such a deliberately rebellious manner. His brother was on dangerous ground.

"Onni, how do you not get it? The halflings are dropping *firebombs* into our *homes*—seemingly just for fun, I might add—and that's not going to stop because everyone wears a nice cardigan and holds hands while singing 'The Get-Along Song.' They tried that once, and everyone blew up! Everyone we know *is blowing up*! My cardigan is not the problem. Father is right. We need weaponry. And not the sort that hurls waistcoats at squirrels to hide their shame. Real machinery, like he built during the Giant Wars."

"Not this again!" Onni moaned.

"Just because you got a B in Trebuchets 101 in gnomeschool, you always look down on machinery!"

"And just because you got a D in Charisma and Charm—"

"The teacher had a natural prejudice against glasses!"

"You had oil on your cardigan!"

"You had . . . er, charm on yours!" Offi tried, pushing up his glasses and glaring at Onni.

"Not this again," Onni moaned.

And that's when they heard the BOOM!

Their eyes met.

"Firebomb!" they said in unison.

3.

BENEATH THE SWEATY ONION
FLESH OF A ROGUE

"Listen, darlings, onions are wonderful in stews and when grilled really complement a nice steak, but if you walk around smelling like them it's your own fault. Wash your hands after handling them with a bit of salt to get out the stink, then again with soap, and I promise everyone will be happier for it."

—JOOLIA CHYLDE, *The Clever Craft of Corraden Cooking*

All strife disintegrated as the brothers ran for the main hatch. Onni's heart was thumpity-thumping like mad, his brain going to terribly ungnomeric places that involved his beloved mother exploding to bits.

"Do you think—" he began.

"Don't think. Just run," Offi muttered.

They bolted through the tunnels toward the kitchen, but a shadowy shape stepped in front of them, causing Onni to skid to a halt, already drawing his belt knife.

"Die, halfling!" he shouted, lunging forward.

"Good sentiment, bad eyesight," Old Seppo said, neatly blocking the strike. "C'mon, boys. I've got the main hatch sealed, and Mama will meet us outside the lute room."

Without another word, the old gnome took off, running faster than Onni had ever seen him move. As they ran through each section of tunnel, Seppo pulled a hidden lever, and a steel-reinforced door slammed down.

"They got the kitchen?" Offi asked.

"Aye, the dinkuses. That's why Mama and I were eating our pudding in the sewing room. I pity the fool who still thinks a kitchen is a safe place to dine."

They reached the lute room, where Venla Numminen was carefully placing her two most prized lutes into a special carrying case.

"Those halflings won't be looting my lutes," she said with a frown. "Not today."

Onni had never seen his gentle mother so serious. Venla had once been a traveling chanteuse in a popular band called the Magic Morels, and all the album covers of her naked-but-for-the-artistic-placement-of-her-knee-length-hair-and-beard made it easy to forget that she had acted as a nurse during the Giant Wars. Now, faced with firebombs and evacuation of the home she'd lovingly built with Seppo, she embodied calm strength, her orange cardigan perfectly straight and her beard ribbon still neatly tied in a bow.

With the entire family reunited, Seppo opened up a new hatch, one Onni had never seen—not that he tended to notice gadgetry. The tunnel beyond was barely lit by jars of glowing green algae placed at intervals, and four suitcases waited just inside. Seppo pushed one into Onni's chest, and then they were running again, bags in hand. As they passed hidden air vents, he could hear the foul cackle of halfling laughter, far overhead, and smell hints of smoke and sausage. His step faltered, but then he reminded himself: He was a Foine Boy. He was strong, and he would continue to be strong for his family. When he tried to glance back at his twin, he saw that Offi's general woe-is-me-for-I-am-a-tortured-soul-and-I-walk-the-world-alone face had been replaced by a brand-new by-dinkus-this-is-worrisome face. Poor Offi—he just wasn't made for heroics.

The tunnel ended in an empty room, and Onni began to feel the hints of a Grand Panic. But then Offi stepped forward and gave Old

Seppo a solemn nod, and together they took hold of some sort of hokum gadgetry affixed to the floor that ran up into the ceiling. It was a mess of gears and cranks and shafts and lube—all that stuff Offi and his father were always talking about; you'd think shafts and lube were the only things in the world sometimes the way they carried on—and now they rammed it up and down, grunting as bits of icky dirt fell down onto their cardigans. It was, Onni realized, some sort of saw, and they were creating their own escape hatch by cutting out a circle of earth. Soon, Seppo pulled yet another lever, and a thick flap of soil and sod levered open to reveal the night sky.

"Where are we?" Onni asked, partially impressed by what his father and brother had achieved and partially terrified of halflings with bombs and also murderous stoats, for gnomes were a smöl people, and the nighttime was considered Quite Dangerous.

"Out beyond the goat pasture," Seppo answered, heaving a ladder into place. "You boys leave your bags with us and head to the barn for the ponies. There'll be sentries, so have your wits about you. Meet us back here when the brouhaha is over. These old bones ain't as bouncy as they used to be."

Onni gazed upon his parents, noting for perhaps the first time that they were indeed becoming whitebeards, and that their eyes were bracketed by a lifetime of smile creases. With the heaviness of the night sky overhead and their home lost forever, they looked wee and old and helpless, and he knew he had to rise to the occasion. He climbed to the top of the ladder and stood on the grass above.

"Mother, Father. Take care," Onni said, injecting nobility into every word as he squinted to the horizon. "We will return."

"By gumballs, what do you think Mama and Papa are going to do?" Offi scoffed, pulling himself to stand beside his twin. "Beat a pudding pan with a stick and say, *Hey, halflings, how's about you lob a foine firebomb me-wards,* or something? Of course they're going to be careful! And what's with all the squinting? Do you need my glasses?"

"No," Onni whispered indignantly as he started for the barn. "I was being heroic."

"Are heroes generally nearsighted?"

Onni's teeth ground together—as if Offi knew anything about heroes! "Come along and shut your pudding hole before the halflings hear us."

The brothers crept toward the barn, and Onni had to admit that his brother's woefully black cardigan was wonderful for sneaking. Up ahead, the goats were bleating and butting heads and ejecting terror pellets as smoke billowed through the barnyard, and this was quite useful, as it covered up the sound of creeping gnomes. The only light came from the moon and the pierced-tin lanterns hanging from the eaves of the barn. Onni saw two halflings standing by the fence, one telling a racist joke as the other picked his nose. Both were turned away from the goats, toward the fire and smoke beyond. Onni wouldn't let himself look at what was left of his home; the sound of cackling and bawdy songs about gnomesplosions and the scent of brauts suggested the halflings were having a by dinkum party and barbecue around the flaming kitchen hatch.

"I see two halflings, but there'll be at least one more," Onni whispered. "In the barn, probably."

"I know that! We took the same How to Be Respectfully Sneaky class. And before you ask, yes, I remember everything they taught us in the Polite but Necessary Stabbing and Smacking About the Face seminar, which we both found so invigorating."

"So this dumb gnome walks into a bar, right?" the racist halfling was saying, in that loud voice people tended to use when telling terrible jokes. "And there's a halfling and a dwarf and a giant, just minding their business, and the bartender says—urghk!"

Which Onni found strange, as he'd never heard anyone say "urghk" before.

Then he saw what had happened: Bulgy Bertram the billy goat had wisely chosen to ram the racist halfling in the crotch, driving him to the ground. While he was there, Bertram finished him off with a concussive head butt.

"Louis, what the—"

The other halfling didn't get to finish his sentence, as a crossbow bolt bloomed from his chest, suggesting that the third, hidden halfling wasn't very good at his job or was perhaps unheroically nearsighted. Now there were two halflings on the ground and being proudly plopped upon by a very self-satisfied goat.

Offi nodded his approval. "I always liked that goat."

"He gave us a couple of shields, didn't he? Let's make use of them," Onni suggested, and Offi nodded in that way the twins had of not needing to talk when picking up racist halflings whose hairy butts would serve as cover.

They squeezed through the fence and darted among the goats to heave the heavy halflings over their shoulders. Onni hated everything about the halfling: He was greasy, reeked of onions and butt musk, and was covered with coarse curly hair that made Onni's neck itch. When he felt something metal bouncing on his back, he realized that the halfling was also wearing the gold medallion of a drub: a Dastardly Rogue Under Bigly-Wicke. The halfling criminal organization had publicly denied being behind the firebombings around Pavaasik.

Onni and Offi ran for the barn door, and they'd almost made it when Onni heard the next thwack of a crossbow. Luckily, the bolt lodged in the rump of the racist halfling, and Onni wouldn't let himself consider how close it had come to his own face. For all that the smöl gnomes, burdened by odiferous halfling flesh, could only run at roughly the speed of an excited tortoise, they were almost to the barn door, and the remaining halfling was in sight.

But then Offi tripped and his dead-halfling shield flopped into the dirt.

Curled into a ball, the unprotected Offi rolled pell-mell toward the halfling assassin, who was hurriedly reloading his crossbow. Onni knew what he had to do. With every ounce of strength in his pudgy body, he threw the racist halfling at the enemy, and then everything seemed to happen in slow motion.

The halfling stepped aside, avoiding Onni's salvo of tossed rogue flesh.

The halfling raised his reloaded crossbow, his hairy finger on the trigger, the bolt aimed for Onni's heart.

But the halfling had forgotten about Offi.

Onni watched, proud and terrified, as his unathletic brother rolled up and swept the halfling's leg, just like they'd learned in their Great Ways to Run Away class.

The halfling went down hard, the crossbow flying from his fingers.

Onni saw an opportunity to employ one of the 37 Methods to Finish Him from that invigorating seminar. He picked up a milking bucket and beaned the third halfling in the noggin, hard enough to knock him unconscious and raise a goose egg on his forehead. With all three enemies dispatched, Onni put out a hand to help up his twin.

"Uh-oh, my foine lad! There's hay on your cardigan," Offi said, voice dripping with irony.

Make hay while the sun shines, bake hay pudding when it rains! Onni dutifully recited.

Offi rolled his eyes again, like he was getting used to the forbidden gesture. "Who are you underneath all those memorized sayings, brother? I like you better when you're not spouting gnomeisms."

"And I like you best when you're taking down halfling assassins before they can shoot me," Onni admitted with a smile and open arms, hoping his brother would take the olive branch and stop being so stonking difficult.

It almost worked. Offi accepted the hug, but he didn't relax into the embrace and wiggle, as happy gnomes did. He just gave a dreary sigh.

Then it was back to business. Onni kept watch at the barn door with the crossbow as Offi saddled their four fat little sway-bellied ponies and wrangled the donkey into his harness. Onni had never been more glad to see Puggyrump and Buttertum and Jellybells and

Mrs. Wicklebum and their dear little miniature donkey, Happy Mumbletoes. They were so cheerful and pudgy it was impossible for even Offi to grump around them. Soon they were leading the beasts toward the secret hatch where Venla and Seppo waited. Their father claimed the fourth pony as his own. Seppo always said she had once been a fierce war steed, and as his father tied on his bags and mounted the shaggy little beast, Onni almost believed him, for a moment.

They paused outside the barnyard to take one last look at their gnomehome. It was now nothing more than an open hatch filled with flame and billowing black smoke, a ruin surrounded by capering halflings waving sausages on sticks. Their overwhelming arsenal of incendiaries had defeated their father's booby traps. Old Seppo shook his head and held out his hand to Venla for reassurance. She grabbed it and squeezed.

"Listen to them laugh, Venla. That's our pride and sweat they're burning down. Our peace and love and joy."

"No, Seppo. I won't believe that. They can never burn down our peace and love and joy. We carry that with us in the pockets of our cardigans. *Home is where the gnome is.* Let the rogues laugh now. We've already outsmarted them and they haven't a clue. We'll come back when we're ready, and then they won't be laughing."

"No, they won't," he agreed, and he released her hand and turned his mount to the west. The old gnome glowered at the horizon, squinting, his face a web of wrinkles. "When we come back, they'll be dying."

"But where will we go?" Onni asked.

"We'll head to Bruding. Scuttlebutt says there are refugee centers there among the humans and that Lord Ergot won't allow the halflings to cause trouble in his demesne. We'll find our people, regroup, and plan our revenge."

Onni's eyes slid over to his brother's face and saw such sadness there that he felt himself welling up. They were a long way from the Grand Row they'd had earlier, when they'd had nothing more pressing than a silly black cardigan to worry about. Onni looked at his brother's chest, and his mouth fell open as he spotted something by the firelight.

"Offi, your cardigan," he said, pointing to the once-neat sweater with its embroidered bats. "It's ruined. There's . . ."

"Blood on it," Offi finished for him. "Halfling blood."

Looking off to the horizon, properly and heroically squinting, Onni added, "Get your washtub ready, brother. It will be a bloody business when the gnome empire strikes back."

"Whoa," Offi said, with feeling. "You totally just gave me chills."

4.

ACROSS THE LEA AND FUMING IN THE TENEBROUS DARKNESS

"Red sky before night, no need for a fight. Red sky at dawn, don't yawn. Halflings probably set your barn afire, so gather your war ponies, tie back their manes, and attack—then, my good gnomes, you burn them back."

—GNUTE YAKKIN, in *The Compendium of Gnomeric Resistance Rhymes*, ♭:♯

Kirsi Noogensen's parents thought she was out mushroom hunting, but she was actually hunting Onni Numminen.

Well, perhaps *hunting* was too harsh a term, for words were deeply important to her. Nothing invasive or sneaky or violent was occurring; she was merely in a public space near Onni's house, nurturing a smöl hope of seeing him.

She sat on a quiet bench in a lamplit square, admired fireflies glowing in the dark, and from time to time stole a glance at the Numminen family's main hatch, a complicated affair with more than the usual number of safety measures.

Old Seppo had installed a hatch like that on her own home. Her parents had become so controlling and fearful, especially since the halflings had gotten so ... well, openly murderous. Their favorite saying of late was *Stay inside, no one's died!* But Kirsi wasn't going to be frightened into limiting her life. The day her parents installed an alarm on the main hatch, she began digging a tunnel out of her bedroom with a spoon and kept it covered with a poster of famous stage actor Brt Frk, renowned for his glossy beard and disdain of vowels.

Kirsi had been smooshing on Onni since they were wee gnomelets in kindergnomen, and even if he'd never paid attention to her before, she was certain that he would one day—possibly today. She cultivated an elaborate fantasy in which she was sitting on this very bench, writing in her green journal beside a basket of red mushrooms, and Onni would climb out of his hatch to go for a walk because something important and red-haired was missing from his life. And then his soft blue eyes would alight on the slight, freckled gnomegirl who just so happened to be sitting outside, her luxurious beard curled around her finger, and he would fall instantly in love, and—

BOOM!

Kirsi looked up to see two halflings dancing around the Numminen hatch, giggling as smoke billowed from the gnomehome. She'd been staring off into space, twirling her beard and daydreaming, and had completely missed the very thing her parents had tried so hard to get her to fear. Her jaw dropped, her beard forgotten, and she scrambled behind the bench, out of the lamplight. Some old gnomeric instinct made her freeze in the dark. It was said that halflings sensed money, food, and drink, in that order, and that most other things could escape their notice if only one held very still and tried not to smell like flapjacks.

"Did you see that, Pascal?" one halfling said, doing the cancan with a stick of dynamite in one hairy fist and a torch in the other, illuminating them with a ruddy glow.

"Yes indeed, Aristide! Dumb little pepperheads didn't even know what hit 'em. Marquant Dique will be ever so pleased. Old Seppo's been on his list forever."

A tooled-leather portmanteau sat near the hole, proudly displaying the seal of the Dastardly Rogues Under Bigly-Wicke. Of course it was them. The rest of the halflings, Kirsi had heard, mostly just wanted to eat and smoke and drink and sit around idly, but the drubs were bad news. Their leader, Marquant Dique, was on WANTED posters all over the gnomeric sections of the Skyr.

Her fingers found her beard again and she plucked a single hair from the center of her chin. She knew what she had to do.

She closed her eyes and recalled Onni's shiny golden hair, his patchy but promising beard, his peaked woolen hat with the earflaps and the embroidered snowflakes. Now they were all so much ashes.

Also, probably, bone chunks and other gross things that gnomes, in general, did not think about.

With this vision came great focus, and with great focus came rage.

"By the mad menses of Maija the Motherlost, may your execrable chest hairs catch fire as your plans come to ruins," she whispered, narrowing her eyes at the capering halflings and holding up the single beard hair. Elaborately twirling it between her fine fingers, she crafted it into a starburst pattern and swallowed it in one tickly gulp. The power began deep down in her belly, warm and sweet, and rippled up and out of her fingers toward the gibbering monsters. "You thick-toed troglodytes!"

It wasn't long before the halflings ceased their capering and began screaming. The curly chest hair of which they were so proud had caught fire, and no matter how they beat themselves and each other—which was quite a lot, actually, and humorous to watch—the fire would not go out. Such was the nature of magic: It had its own timetable, especially when you were on the losing end of it.

Kirsi burped and stroked her waist-long beard. She often rued that she'd been born with the power to curse instead of the power to bless, but now the curse felt like a blessing. One hair, one curse: That was how it worked. She was cautious with her magic, but she still had to be careful where she plucked from. Her grandmother, a great and powerful bristle witch, had nothing left but stubble after a lifetime of meting out blessings—for good harvests, for sturdy, prosperous gnomehomes, for fat babies and fatter wives. Though she wasn't beautiful, Granny was known for her generosity and kindness. Kirsi loved magic, but she maybe loved her beard more, so she tried to keep the cursing to a minimum. Still, this time it was worth it. And after all, why did it matter if she had a patchy beard if Onni wasn't there to admire it?

Out by Onni's barn, several other screams suggested that her curse had brought pain to more halflings than she'd anticipated. Kirsi grinned. Good. Let them suffer. The halflings seemed determined to destroy gnomeric life of late. Firebombs, kidnappings, alpaca rustling, and aggravated snack theft incidents were all up across the Skyr. Kirsi couldn't even go to the Perfekt Pudding Parlor without worrying about some halfling beating her up for a spoonful of tapioca. Most tragically, her uncle Ulric had been directing traffic around a vulnerable line of ducklings when he died in a halfling attack.

As much as her emotional life centered on Onni, Kirsi had begged her parents in the past months to move somewhere, anywhere, safe. Even if it meant living in Bruding, among the silly, stupid, uselessly tall humans. The Skyr was no longer safe for gnomes, and Kirsi felt more comfortable outside than she did underground, which was considered deeply ungnomeric. But her parents were determined to die in their gnomehome.

And now, for the first time, Kirsi suspected they would. And she knew with complete certainty that she would not. She would follow Onni Numminen anywhere, but not into a sudden and explosive death.

She didn't have much on her. Just her clothes, her coat, her hat, her most capacious mushroom basket, a very nice pencil, and a green journal full of drawings of her and Onni riding a unicorn and surrounded by a heart. She had no canvas pack of provender, no waterskin. But if she went home now, she might not have a body left to carry such supplies. Since watching Onni's kitchen explode, she'd seen columns of smoke curling up from the direction of the city. This was no random band of murderers; a coordinated attack was unfolding.

Home was no longer safe.

Reaching into her cardigan's emergency pocket, she withdrew a shiny, unused automaatti bird. Her parents had pressed it upon her even before the halflings had begun their wave of terror. Invented during the Giant Wars, this bird, delicately crafted of brass, was capable of delivering just one message at a time, unlike more-advanced models that could recite poetry or argue over the proper recipe for butternut pudding. Kirsi clicked the small button on the metal bird's back, and when its eyes blinked red, she spoke slowly and carefully.

> Dearest Mama, Papa, and Granny,
>   I love you very much, and I'm sorry to leave you, but Pavaasik is overrun with drubs. Please join me in Bruding when you can. I want to live a life without fear. Or at least without fear of blowing up in my own house.
>   Nose rubs, Kirsi.

She released the button. The bird's eyes blinked green, and it flapped off into the trees, high above the reach of even the tallest troll, much less the hairiest halfling. It would go straight to her gnomehome, putter down a narrow tube, and come out in the kitchen, startling the everloving hokum out of her parents. Maybe it would startle them out of their complacency.

Kirsi turned away from the flames and smoke billowing from Onni's main hatch and hoped he and his family were elsewhere and not burned to death. She wiped ineffectively at the tears watering her beard, picked up her basket of mushrooms, and began walking toward Bruding. Or at least thataway-ish. She wasn't used to navigating by the stars, or at all, but she figured she could adjust her course as needed in daylight. Right now she simply needed to get out of town.

As gnomes were mostly homebodies, Kirsi had no idea what lay outside their neighborhood except for a general idea that the Big Road led to a terrible, dirty place called Bruding, where tall, stupid, dangerous people lived amidst miles of sewage and beer. Gnomes thrived on order and beauty, and humans apparently liked to destroy both things. They had a lord there, and an earl for Borix, and a king for all of Pell, but Kirsi suspected they weren't very good leaders if they allowed their people to live in filth. (But she should be fair: The gnomeric leaders also deserved some censure for allowing the half-lings their violent sprees.) All she remembered from Mostly Useless Geography class was that at the juncture between the Skyr and Borix, the road went from small, tidy, and nicely landscaped to sprawling, dirty, and despoiled by highwaymen and large monsters that hated knit woolen hats.

She was soon lost in the underbrush, her cardigan torn by thorns and her hat unacceptably mussed. When she stumbled over a scrubby little trail marked with a donkey's hooves and droppings, she gladly followed the path, assuming that anything terrible would still be too full from eating the donkey to eat a smöl gnome like herself.

The donkey's path crossed a creek, and Kirsi bravely sloshed into the ice-cold water. The horrid feeling of wet boots and skirt made her grimace. By the time she reached the center of the creek, she was surprised to find the water up to her gnomish waist.

And then the current rudely swept her away.

The first thing she did was shriek in indignation. The second thing she did was almost lose hold of her beloved mushroom basket, which her mother had woven with love. Thanks to a gnomeric attention to detail, the basket floated far better than a gnomelet weighed down by wet woolen clothes, so Kirsi managed to climb into the basket before the river could drag her down deeper.

The world slid by in a gurgle of water, both pretty and frightening. Banks of evening primrose loomed over the creek, their yellow heads bobbing in the nighttime wind. A curious rabbit stared at Kirsi, eyes huge and, she thought, crafty. Her grandfather had gotten into a fight with a rabbit once, and he'd loved to pull back his blue wool eyepatch to show the twist of scar where his eye had been. Kirsi had somehow forgotten that the outside world beyond tight gnomeric fences was filled with terrifying rabbits, furious hedgehogs, and towering fawns with razor-sharp hooves. She shivered and nestled lower in her basket, hoping the rabbit hadn't noticed her.

When she peeked over the basket's edge again some while later, the creek had slowed. It had carried her to a marshy area populated by cattails, but at least the current was still moving. She dozed fitfully until the basket bobbed and bucked in the waters again, gaining speed as the creek flowed out of the marsh and into an unfamiliar stand of timber. She was lost, and her basket smelled of wet wool and squashed mushrooms, but at least she knew that on this side of the Honeymelon Hills she wasn't headed toward anything with the dirty flavor of halfling society. Their cities were rickety, unbalanced things, wood and brick haphazardly slapped together by supposed architects who'd never seen a plumb line. Instead, she was in some strange new wilderness, which she hoped was a bit closer to Bruding than to Jusipert. She'd seen nothing of the Big Road, but then again, wilderness and roads kept little company. And then, wonder of wonders, her basket twirled into some calm shallows with water striders darting along the surface, and it fetched up on a sandy shore.

Before the basket could change its mind, Kirsi scrambled out and dragged it away from the creek. Her mushrooms were all broken and wet, her skirt stained, and her leather boots gummy. At least there were no gnomes nearby to see her in such a state. Once into the grasses and ferns, she stomped to shake the mud and sand from her hem. But she was at least grateful to be on the opposite shore instead of the same side where she'd started. Even better, she saw a path that ended at the sandbar, its old pavers overgrown with velvety green mosses and lit by dancing fireflies. Grinning at her luck, Kirsi stepped onto the stone path, leaving tidy little gnomeric footprints in her wake.

5.

On the Dew-Slobbered Slopes of the Honeymelon Hills

"The kill is never quite so sweet as the *anticipation* of the kill. There's an awful lot of blood involved in killing, for one thing, not to mention ropes of intestine and jiggly organs and the very real danger of wolves hunting you in turn. Consider that one can sensibly enjoy a pipe and a pint while savoring the anticipation, or maybe fondle something that's feeling ticklish instead, and one can quite happily dwell in that sweet anticipation for a lifetime."

—Bergeron Wildefeet of the Cheapmeat Wildefeets, in *The Hunting Halfling's Preference for Cake and Fortified Bunkers*

The hunter crouched on the hillside above the gnomeric city of Koloka in the early morning, dawn lighting up his toe hairs with golden rays of promise. But to the hunter—a dignified halfling named Faucon Pooternoob of the Toodleoo Pooternoobs—the weather and the pleasant vista were irrelevant and, actually, a bit incommodious. All he cared about was the promise of victory—finally—after a hunt that had stretched out for close to a year. He prided himself on keeping careful records, so he knew that this hunt had been the longest and most embarrassing of his life, each day of his bullet journal marked with a frowny face. Bagging his prize would be especially fulfilling, the more so since all others who had hunted this particular quarry had failed.

He closed his eyes and inhaled deeply of the melon-kissed air, savoring this sweet moment before he embraced a long-sought victory. He savored it so much that he toyed with the idea of another momentous inhalation, before he was inevitably interrupted by a phlegmy cough and a wash of foul breath. He looked up, nearly blinded as the sun glinted off a drub medallion.

"Mr. Pooternoob, sir, are you having trouble breathing? Perhaps a touch of indigestion?"

Faucon the hunter regarded the troublesome drub with the sort of look he usually gave to overcooked eggs at second breakfast.

"Excuse me?" he asked.

Bernaud Cobbleshod of the Gobbleneck Cobbleshods took a groaning knee next to him in the wet grass and cursed softly as the ample dew soaked right through his mustard-stained pants.

"Narsty," he hissed. "It's like somebody whizzed all over the mountain."

"Or like someone disrupted my concentration," the hunter said quietly.

"Sor-ree," Bernaud replied, not unlike a teenager who thinks adults get upset about the silliest things. "Just thought you had forgotten how to breathe right and wondered what the plan was, is all."

Faucon focused his inward eye on beautiful things—a stack of writs, a tightly phrased contract, the pleasure of a flawlessly kept ledger—to calm himself. But, alas, the sweetness of the moment had flown, pierced by the horror of the other halfling's gingivitis and bad laundry habits. He would not be able to return to that peaceful headspace now, even if he banished the drub from his presence. He would have no choice but to feel the impatient lout breathing behind him, smelling like sour milk and slowly trying to make the world smell the same. He'd be haunted by the sight of the drub's horrific feet, callused and cracked and topped with yellowed fungal toenails. That was the problem with drubs: Thinking themselves rebels, they thumbed their noses at the Handy Handsome Halfling Handbook for Hair and Skin Care. Faucon despised rebels, almost as much as he despised cheaply made exfoliant scrubs. But he would use them both to pursue his goals, if he had to. He might as well proceed with the hunt. For Faucon was cut in the cloth of the more traditional halfling gentleman, and, unlike the messy newfangled drubs and their foul ilk, he would finish what he'd started.

With a hum of determination, Faucon considered the thatched roof perched on the hillside below him yet still far above Koloka and its frustratingly gnomeric avenues of escape. For although the gnomeric city looked pleasant and tidy enough topside, well did Faucon know that the ground underneath was actually riddled with unplotted tunnels, supposedly built to code but never mapped, intentionally designed to befuddle pursuers. Faucon shook his head. Gnomes were, without doubt, the most deceptive peoples on Pell. They presented an orderly society to the world, but a deadly chaos lurked beneath their well-groomed façades, a rebellion and sometimes a carelessness that could lead—that *had led*—to the untimely death of one he loved well. Plus, they called him rude names.

Squashing down his past like a particularly well-stuffed club sandwich, Faucon pointed to the east, where the morning sun filtered through the canopy of the Pruneshute Forest.

"I need approximately half of your men to spread out along the tree line to prevent escape into the woods. They need to be quiet getting there, but I want them to be seen once they are in position. In fact, I want them chucking firebombs at the house from that direction. The other half of your men need to circle around below the house and prevent any chance of escape to the city. That will leave my prey two choices: Run uphill here to me, where I will have the high ground, or flee to the west and into the plains, where there will be no protection."

Cobbleshod squinted at the house and then at the hunter. "I don't understand. You're going to let them run?"

The hunter held on to his patience, but just barely. "The last year has demonstrated that we cannot prevent them from running. They are extraordinarily good at it. This, right now, is the closest we have ever been. So our priority must be to control *where* they run. Having them in the open will allow us a particular advantage."

"It will? Pretty sure they can run faster than us."

Faucon pinched the bridge of his nose. "They can, yes. They have proven that time and time again. But we have a friend now, if you recall, who can cover great distances rather quickly and who will have little trouble capturing what needs to be captured."

"The new recruit? Jean-Claude Ungumption? He only ran fast that one time because his foot was on fire—"

"Not the new guy. *My friend*."

Cobbleshod gave Faucon a look of grave doubt. "You have friends?"

Faucon exhaled a weary sigh and pointed up. "Just one."

A crooked brown-toothed grin split the drub's face as he scratched idly at his greasy whiskers. "Ah, I got it now. Your friend. Your good friend with the claws 'n' wings 'n' such. Marquant Dique will be pleased. And so will we, when we get paid, eh?" He looked like he was considering smacking Faucon on the shoulder in a friendly sort of way, and Faucon's glare suggested that if he did, he would regret it. So Cobbleshod scratched his crotch instead, the witnessing of which Faucon considered only a slight improvement over an insufferable assault on his personal space.

"Yes, well, we must finish this first. Did you secure the ingredients I requested?"

Cobbleshod nodded eagerly. "Aye, the boys just put 'em in your tent. Although I don't understand why you'd need ladybugs. Never thought of them as a gourmet item."

"Never mind that. How is our guest?"

"Your . . . friend? She's awake and hungry."

"Perfect. Then let us begin, Bernaud. Silently move your men into position and wait for my signal. And please ask our guest to join me here."

The drub backed away silently with the gait of a practiced thief, and Faucon's lip curled at his departure. Working with these drubs was a necessary evil if he wanted to destroy his prey—and he did want to destroy it. He also desperately wanted to bathe and wash the stink of these dastards off him before rejoining respectable halfling society. He looked down at his hands and worried that his rich umber skin had taken on some unsightly ashiness. He was malnourished and in need of a paraffin bath and a seaweed wrap and a good multivitamin with a shot of wheatgrass. His own feet, while in much better shape than Cobbleshod's, still required a pedicure and a good bit of shaving with a sharpened rasp. That was the making of a true halfling: a sincerely dignified set of toes. No one could deny he deserved some rest and relaxation. And maybe some of those little cranberries covered in yogurt. His personal supply had run out weeks ago.

And then, once he took Marquant Dique's dirty money and had spent a sufficient sum on some much-needed self-care, perhaps he'd spend the rest of his earnings on taking down the drubs themselves—starting with their leader. He didn't know how Marquant Dique of the Bigly-Wicke Diques had become the leader of the Dastardly Rogues, but he did know that his methods had been underhanded and that the Skyr had been worse off ever since it happened. Faucon the hunter would hunt them all, hunt even his own kind, until there was no further lawbreaking in the halfling lands. There would be justice and peace and even a uniform building code. Only then would the blood stop flowing.

"Give me building codes or give me blood," he breathed, toying with the idea of making it his motto. Despite the false dichotomy it presented, he thought it worked because of course people would prefer to adhere to building codes rather than suffer grievous personal injury. His primary concern was justice, and it began with proper laws, which could only be made in buildings with solid foundations and the appropriate number of fire exits.

Clearly, blowing up the gnomes one by one wasn't working—for anyone. The murderous little busybodies could only be taken down through diligent research, paperwork, and proper zoning laws. Just thinking about it made Faucon drool a little and crave cranberries. First the drubs, then the gnomes. It was the only way regular law-abiding folk could find peace. And Faucon dearly ached for peace. And time to properly grieve the loss of his love, whose passing was still fresh in his mind.

Movement to his left caught his eye. That disgusting Cobbleshod was leading his corps of rogues down to the tree line, the halflings' fine leather portmanteaus—the only agreeable thing about them, really—bulging with explosive ordnance; a few archers carried full quivers at the ready.

A whisper of movement behind him caused Faucon to pull his sword and spin, and he had to stifle a cry of terror and remind himself that his dangerous guest was not interested in his flesh. At least, not at present. He bobbed his head at her, and she returned the gesture and then sat in the wet grass next to him on the hillside, folding up her wings.

"I hope the campsite is to your satisfaction?" Faucon said. They had bivouacked on the other side of the hill to prevent their quarry from sensing their approach, and he was sensitive about the fact that the area was furnished with the sharp-edged and pokier sorts of rocks, not at all elegant for four-legged creatures whose sitting position left their rectums covered in sand.

It will suffice, the answer came. The voice in his head carried an undeniable tone of regal puissance; it was the cultured voice of a queen. *What do you require?*

"The hunt will begin soon. Our prey is in the house you see below. I would like you to follow from above when they try to escape, secure the gnomeric construct when possible, and bring it to our camp."

Describe this construct.

"It will appear to be a golden person. A sort of smallish yellow biped."

And the creatures guarding this construct? Might they also be gold-enne?

"No. They are more . . ." He grimaced as he said the word. "Fuzzy. You will have no trouble distinguishing the target from the guardians."

Excellent. And once I bring this construct to you, then there will be breakfast?

"Yes. We will all have breakfast then."

With the ingredients you promised? Her tone edged toward wistful desperation, and Faucon marveled at her desires. She could devour him and all the drubs too, and they could do nothing but scream as she tossed them about like puppets and feasted upon their livers. But she had demanded a very specific reward and needed his help to make it happen; such was life without opposable thumbs. Thus they had an arrangement.

"Yes, it will be as I promised."

Let it begin, then. I am hungry and would be satiated.

Faucon turned his gaze downhill and saw that Bernaud's rogues were already in place along the tree line. He had to wait an excruciatingly long time for the remainder of his force to spread themselves between the thatched hut of his enemy and the city of Koloka below. When they were finally ready, he raised a hand above his head and twirled it, signaling Bernaud to begin. The halfling copied the gesture, and the rogues all whooped, pulling firebombs from their satchels and hurling concentrated death at the hut.

Faucon twirled his mustache and grinned. His quarry would not evade him—not this time. He abhorred murder, but, oh, how he loved legally permissible violence.

6.

Aclatter with a Surfeit of Brooms in a Strategic Mobile Habitat

MAINTENANCE INSTRUCTIONS FOR AUTOMAATTI,
MODEL PIINI:

1. Do not attempt to repair unless you are a Certified Gnomeric Gearhand.
2. Do not under any circumstances remove the Automaatti Crystalline Power Unit.
3. Avoid submersion in water and/or tar pits. Automaatti are not designed for aquatic use.
4. If you have questions, ask.

—Etched on Piini Automaatti's lower back, along with a butterfly and some barbed-wire swirls

Arms spread wide, Agape Fallopia stood her ground.

Sure, said ground was a little shaky. Wooden boards under cloven hooves weren't the best footing for any sort of fight. And ovitaurs like Agape weren't well suited to fighting, considering they had a human head and torso and a sheep's woolly legs but also a sheep's flat, expressive ears, which tended to flap overexcitedly during confrontations. After all, the only things sheep ever really got in fights with were rocks, streams, and holes in the ground, and they were mostly known for losing such fights. Agape had trained in self-defense but didn't want to actually hurt her parents. Fortunately, steps one through four suggested trying to find some way to de-escalate or run away, five through nine were mostly a descent into aggressive bleating, and only at step ten was it suggested that maybe trying to kick something would be a good idea as a last resort.

But just now Agape was feeling more human than sheepish. She wasn't going to back down this time.

This particular ovitaur family argument had been brewing for many moons, and Agape had been mentally practicing the very many ways it could go. She had envisioned reasonable talks around an unlit campfire or the hearth of a pleasant dwarvelish inn that smelled of lavender, while she sipped at a cool glass of wheatgrass juice. She'd hoped for passionate but fact-based discourse.

She never dreamed she'd end up using her body as a shield as her parents approached, her mother waving a frying pan in a menacing sort of way, her father holding a pair of pliers.

"Move, laaambykins," her father barked.

"No!" Agape barked right back.

"You're young," her mother said with fake sympathy, waggling the frying pan. "You haaave so much life ahead of you."

"Is that a threat, Maamaa?"

"No. Yes. Kind of. Just baaack off, please?"

Her father gave it a try. "Don't do what we did. Let us free you from this insane servitude. It'll only take a moment. Won't hurt a bit." Her dad made a feint, but Agape pivoted to intercept him. "Come on, laaambykins. It's for your own good. Piini's just ... well, he needs to be put out of his misery."

Agape glanced at the tarnished metal man standing behind her, the crystal still glowing faintly in his forehead. He didn't look miserable. He looked inert. If only he would wake up, show any signs of life other than shambling around where he was told to go. If only he would rise up and defend himself, they wouldn't be in this predicament at all.

But he wouldn't. He *couldn't*.

"Piini Automaatti, take the frying paaan away from my mother, Fedora Fallopia," Agape said in the loud, clear voice her parents had schooled her into using when speaking to the family golem. It hadn't worked for her yet, but it was worth a try.

The metal man behind her squealed in protest as his body lumbered forward with little grace to snatch the frying pan from Agape's mother, who baaed in protest. Although he had once been gold, so the story went, Piini was now layered in years of grime and something like rust. His joints squeaked, his feet creaked, and he'd recently become little more than a piece of junk. Agape remembered playing with him when she was small and her father had ordered him to babysit. She'd loved Piini then. Even though he couldn't talk, he could play endless games of cards, tic-tac-doe, and hide-and-get-lost. She'd tried Red Rover once and lost, badly, but he'd still been her favorite and only playmate. These days, he could only respond to the simplest of commands, and only if they were spoken very loud and with utter clarity. Until this day, however, he'd never responded to Agape's command.

Her parents were agape, and so was Agape.

"There. See? Piini is fine. He's just older. Different. You caaan't kill him," she said, secretly pleased by the command in her voice.

But her parents weren't done.

"He's a machine, laaambykins. It's not killing. It's . . ."

Her father seemed to struggle with the right word as her mother picked up one of the many brooms rattling around their current hideout, a cottage they'd rented from a witch at a very reasonable rate, thanks to its recent haunting by a somewhat stubborn poltergeist.

"It's a mercy, shutting him down. It can't be fun, being traaapped in that raaattly, gummed-up old body," her mother finished.

"Then we find someone to fix him. We find a Certified Gnomeric Gearhand, like it says on his baaack. Someone has to know what he was made for and why Great-Great-Great-Great-Graaandmother

Alkmene was taaasked with guarding him. He's important. That's what you always told me. Aaand I believed you."

Agape's faather shook his head but did not put down the pliers. "No one knows what he does. It's all just rumors, legends. We've been to every corner of the globe, hiding thaaat fool machine, protecting him from who-knows-whaaat, and no one has ever known anything about him—and the gnomes won't even talk to us, much less tell us where to find a gearhand! But we're done. Done scurrying and camouflaging our caaamps and going without fires when it's cold outside to avoid drawing attention. Your mother and I—we're putting our hooves down. We're shutting it down and taking you to Dizzyworld to ride rides and eat churros and guzzle slushy ice."

"He's not aaan *it*!" Agape bleated. "You caaan't just dehumanize Piini because he's suddenly inconvenient for you. We're supposed to guard him, and I will continue to guard him, even if that means I'm guarding him from you. Piini." She spoke loud and clear. "Please give me the frying paaan."

The metal man gently put the pan in her hand, and she marveled at how heavy it really was. Would her own mother have brained her just to pluck the jewel from Piini's forehead and kill that spark of life, no matter how dim, that kept him marching after the Fallopia family, step after step, across the world? Agape had seen everything Pell had to offer, as she'd been taught it wasn't safe to stay in one place for more than three days. The High Mountain Home of the windsong dwarves, the underground caverns of the outcast dwarves, the labyrinthine cities of the humans, the emerald valleys, the bounteous fields, the stiff and quivering glories of the elvish Morningwood. The gnomes scattered and shuttered their hatches as soon as the ovitaurs drew near, but she'd walked among all the other peoples of the Skyr. Of course, she hadn't given them her real name or attempted to become friends with anyone, as her parents promised her that friends would one day turn on her, whether for profit or mutton. So she'd been lonely, perhaps, but there was always Piini, who would never leave her. Who would see the whole world with her again and again.

She figured one friend was all she needed to live a pretty charmed life.

It was odd, realizing that all this time her parents had felt trapped.

"Sweetie, you wouldn't hurt us," her mother said, holding the broom menacingly.

"And you shouldn't hurt me. So let's put down our weapons and taaalk."

Agape watched her parents meet each other's eyes and nod. Her own eyes narrowed. Her mother's broom fell to a more sweepish and less smackish angle. But her father kept angling, hoof by hoof, toward Piini, the pliers gripped in his dark-brown fist.

"Sure, honey. Come on over to the hearth, and we'll sit around whatever foul potion's bubbling in the cauldron and taaalk."

Grim but determined, Agape took a step toward the hearth. She wasn't surprised when her father lunged toward Piini, eyes mad and pliers outstretched, but she was ready. With one quick rap of the frying pan, she smacked his hand and knocked the pliers away.

"Ow!" her dad cried, rubbing his hand.

"I'm not a child. Lying to me won't work anymore." She held out the frying pan, blocking her father from his fallen pliers. "Piini Automaatii, put your haaands over your gem and don't let anyone remove it."

The metal man put crabbed hands that couldn't go completely flat anymore over the gem in his forehead, his dim eyes unblinking.

But Agape's father's eyes went over crafty. "Piini Automaatti," he said in his most commanding voice, "remove the gem."

Piini's hands didn't move.

"Piini Automaatti, by the blood of Alkmene Fallopia, I hereby order you to remove the gem in your forehead," he said, even louder and more clearly, with the sort of precise pronunciation that makes other people wince.

Still the metal man's hands didn't budge.

Agape's father deflated a little, looking far more middle-aged. "Honey, ewe want to try?"

Her mother shrugged and rubbed her temples. "He never did listen to me. You're the one with the Fallopia blood. I guess it's finally haaappened."

"What haaappened?" Agape asked.

Her parents stepped forward, arms out, but this time they didn't go for Piini with their landlord's kitchen gadgets. They engulfed her in a warm hug that she couldn't help nuzzling into. They hadn't hugged her as much lately, as she'd grown her first adult wool and also bosoms.

"You have become the Vartija," her father said gently. "The burden of guarding Piini Automaatti is now yours. He's attuned to your voice. We have completed our taaask."

Agape's mother and father stepped back, and her father pulled a much-worn sheaf of papers from his camouflage jacket. With great dignity, he held the packet out to Agape, who took it, feeling as if a golden light surrounded and suffused her, formally acknowledging her place as the anointed guardian of Piini Automaatti and the last in a long line of ovitaurs who had fulfilled their tasks.

"Does this mean . . . ?" Agape started but was too overcome with emotion to continue.

"That we're free!" her father shouted, capering around the room like a new lamb.

"That we can settle down! And have a fire every night! And buy a sturdy duplex in a quiet suburb with an attentive HOA! And wear a color besides camouflage!" her mother added, wiping away a single tear and joining her husband in a proper frolicking.

Agape could only stand there, stunned, frying pan in hand. She gently returned it and the pliers to the stone mantel, where they'd been hanging before her parents had turned somewhat murderous. She turned to look at Piini, but he remained entirely unchanged, his hands firmly over his gem and his face utterly expressionless. Why did she remember him smiling when she was younger? He didn't even seem to have a mouth now. But he was hers in the way that anyone agreeing to a life of servitude is actually the owner of their destiny.

"So you guys are just . . . ?"

"Leaving. We haaave this little place picked out in the outskirts of Grakkel. Made a down payment years ago and haaave been counting down the days. I can't wait to not haaave a job!" her father crowed. "And a yaaard! I'll need to buy a ruler and make sure the graaass is exactly three inches taaall!"

"I'm going to stay in the house for weeks without opening the curtains, and I'm going to obsessively sweep the front porch and waaatch the neighbors through the closed windows and listen to the weather reports all day and never ever traaavel again!" Her mother kissed her on the cheek, and it felt very final and strange.

Agape watched, silent and oddly empty, as her parents gathered their belongings and stuffed them into their familiar packs. Her mother shed her camouflage sweater, tossed it in the fire, and brandished a caftan in a floral print bright enough to flag a bull. As she slipped it on, she grinned more brightly than Agape had ever seen. Following her example, Agape's father tossed his own camo jacket into a corner of the cottage, where a flurry of ensorceled brooms swept it under the bed. He, too, had been keeping secrets, as he pulled a white turtleneck and a brown corduroy jacket from his pack.

"Oh, thaaat feels better. I feel more like myself than ever."

Agape could only shake her head. "It's like I don't even know you guys. I thought you loved traaaveling."

"I loved it when we had that caaaravan wagon," her mother said. "But camping out, seeing new things, meeting new people? Ugh. I waaant to know every intimate detail about aaall my neighbors and sometimes get their mail and read it before returning it."

"You can join a book club. Subscribe to magazines." Agape's father drew her mother in for a nuzzle. "And play bridge. And do something with turquoise. We can go to town haaall meetings and shake our fists. Be a part of the raaabble and get roused."

"Bliss," her mother agreed.

Agape felt like one big shrug. "So whaaat do I do now?"

Her parents gave her a pitying smile, and her mother chucked Agape's chin.

"You take care of Piini Automaatti. Just like we did. You know the drill. Don't stay anywhere for more than three days. Keep your camp-site camouflaged. Always give a fake name when renting a room. Beware of water haaazards. Don't taaalk to strangers. Don't make friends—they'll just betray and abaaandon you. Trust no one. Haaave a child at some point, raise them like we did you, then in twenty years you caaan retire, just like us!"

Before, rebellion had felt exciting and dangerous, but now Agape looked into her future and saw . . . ye gods. Caftans and corduroy? But no. She loved traveling, always had, and that wouldn't change. She loved sleeping on a bed of leaves, loved seeing new trails, loved bathing in streams, loved trading bits of cheese to fairies to light her lanterns. The only difference was that now she was the one plotting the course. They could go anywhere, she and Piini. This was what she'd wanted, wasn't it?

Looking back at the tarnished gold man, still and silent, she was filled with hope and the tiniest bit of anxiety. She was the Vartija now, and that job came with certain dangers. She would be hunted, from now until the title passed on.

"Write us, laaambykins!" her father called. "I hear the new Pellican Postale Service is faaantastic!"

Agape had been frozen, lost in thought, but her parents were al-ready at the door, packs on their backs, pointing to a postcard leaning against the mantel and showing palm trees.

"Good luck, daaarling!" her mother called. "We'll aaalways love you! The guest room is utterly open for you as long as you don't stay longer thaaan two days!"

And then the door slammed. And they were gone.

Agape turned in the sudden silence, her heart an aching chasm. "They're gone. For good. I guess it's just you aaand me, Piini."

Before the metal man could respond, the door slammed open, bouncing off the wall and making Agape bleat in surprise.

It was her father, his pack stuck full of arrows.

"It's the drubs," he gasped. "They finally found us."

7.

Inside an Oven Disturbingly Full of Bones

"Few gnomes appreciate how stonking big the culinary accoutrements must be to feed the taller folk. More than one gnome has mistaken an oven for cozy guest quarters, only to discover that it's a box of deadly fire."

—Sonni Somnambulist, in *How I Survived Twenty-one Terrible Places to Sleep*

Dawn broke winsomely, and Kirsi skipped along, certain that something lovely was just around the corner. The few trees she'd seen by the creek were quickly left behind as the path led her through golden fields filled with bright songbirds and into a little wood—well, actually, a very large wood, for Kirsi was comparatively smöl. When a snug cottage with a gently puffing smokestack appeared, Kirsi's steps quickened. Whoever lived in the cottage had to know where this path went and if it was, in fact, a good way to go.

Pushing open the picturesquely crooked gate took quite a bit of effort. It was a very large gate, and Kirsi began to wonder what sort of person the gate belonged to. Not a gnome, but also most likely not a halfling. Anything bigger than a halfling was, to her, Quite Big, which encompassed dwarves, elves, humans, trolls, and giants. She had no way of knowing what sort of Quite Big person might live here, but she had to assume they were kind: Many attractive candy motifs were worked into the cottage's design with a gnomeric flair. The siding resembled chocolate bark, the windowsills were striped red and white like the peppermints in old people's pockets, and the shingles resembled flattened cinnamon buns.

She could smell something lovely dancing on the air now—that sort of baking that involves eating lots of dough and licking frosting off the spoon. She skipped up the path, careful not to leave wet, smeary footprints on cobblestones that glimmered in pastel candy colors. The door had to be six times as tall as she was, but she was a gnome, and gnomes were proud things, so she was not afraid to rap her knuckles against it. She knocked three sharp knocks and waited, smiling. The door swung open to reveal a hideous old woman with a twisted cane, her back bent and her nose equally bent and also burdened with bulbous, hairy warts. The woman's scraggly black hair struggled over a spotted pate, her wispy black clothes giving off a dangerously heavy odor of mothballs and cold porridge with a slight undercurrent of old blood and cat urine.

Looking around, the old woman scowled. "Darned sales-elves," she muttered. "Think they can get away with anything, what with their luminous hair and shapely buttocks. Well, if I ever catch them—"

"Greetings from down here!" Kirsi called.

When the old woman looked down, Kirsi gave her best curtsy and waved. Instantly, the old woman's face went through several changes, from irritation to craftiness to something resembling a smile that somehow failed, possibly because she didn't have quite enough teeth and the ones she did have were rather pointy.

"Oh, hello, dear!" she crooned, bending over as much as her back would allow. "How nice to have a wee visitor! It's been a long time since a gnome braved my gate. What brings you to my abode?"

"Oh, I'm lost," Kirsi said. "I'm headed for Bruding. Would you happen to know the way? I wish I still had some nice mushrooms to offer you, but . . . well . . . I fell in the creek." She held out her basket to show the mushy mushroom mush in the bottom.

The woman laughed. "That's all right, dear. I only eat sweet things. I've been baking today. Would you like a little treat to help fatten you up?"

Like all gnomes, Kirsi was always hoping to get a little rounder, and she nodded, pleased. "That would be lovely, thanks. I only wish there was something I could do to return the favor."

"That's right, that's right. You gnomes are such polite and honorable creatures. I could most certainly use a little help around the house, and I think you're just the right size. But first, please come eat until you're perfectly stuffed."

Kirsi skipped inside, and the old woman led her to a gnome-sized table and chairs, where she laid out a delicious repast of sugary treats, from macarons to macaroons and tarts to tartlets. As Kirsi ate, the old woman clucked at her, complimented her fine cap, and encouraged her to keep nibbling. It was lovely to feel full again, and Kirsi soon dabbed the crumbs away from her beard with her handkerchief and stood.

"Thank you. That was delicious. I'm ready to help you now."

"Are you sure you wouldn't like to eat some more, dear?"

"Oh, no. I'm very full."

"But wouldn't you like to be just a little more full?"

Kirsi shook her head and burped. "I ate some hair earlier and don't want it to come back up on me. I'm good."

"Very well, then. First of all, there seems to be something wrong with my oven. Something stuck in the back, preventing proper heating and ventilation. I can't imagine what it is. Could you just crawl in there and see?" She swung the oven door open and bowed.

With a professional nod, Kirsi removed her peaked hat and inspected the oven, which was rather large and still a bit warm from baking. She pulled over the gnome-sized chair and clambered up onto the oven door. Peering inside, she squinted.

"It's very dark in here. Could I have a light, please?"

"Of course, dear," the old woman said, bringing Kirsi a lit wax taper.

Swinging the taper from side to side, Kirsi walked deeper into the oven.

"Keep going, dear," the old woman said. "I think it's in the very back, whatever it is."

Kirsi kept walking, her boots skittering over burned sticks and charred black chunks and crunching on brittle bits of something.

"Maybe a little deeper," the old woman suggested.

Suddenly, the oven door closed, and Kirsi screeched. Even with her candle, the oven had gone quite dark, and it felt quite hot, here at the back. She looked toward the door, hoping the old woman would open it again, which she didn't do. But not to worry—Kirsi had a job to finish, and a little hot darkness didn't change that. She held up her taper to light the back of the oven and found what looked like fresh scratch marks. Pulling out a hard crescent that felt oddly like a fingernail, she tossed it on the oven's floor.

"Weird," she said, holding the candle up.

Outside the oven, the old woman began to cackle uproariously.

"What?" Kirsi called.

"Oh, nothing, dear," the old woman responded. "I just read a funny 'Barfield' comic. You know, the one about that hilarious talking bear?"

"Yeah, that's a good one," Kirsi replied. "Oh, wait." She picked something up, held it under the candlelight, and laughed as she walked to the oven door and knocked.

"What's that, dear?" the old woman said. "I can't hear you."

"I found the problem. Please open the oven door."

"What?"

"Please let me out now!"

There was a long pause before the old woman said, "I'm afraid I can't do that."

Despite the heat making her sweat, Kirsi went cold. A few beats passed before she was able to ask, "Why not?"

The old woman cackled again, longer this time, before answering.

Her voice sounded very, very far away.

"Because I'm soaking my bunions and there's a cat on my lap and I can't reach the oven door. Hold on, dearie; this might take some time."

Kirsi felt sweat trickle down her back as the taper wax dripped over her hand, making her hiss at the pain. Outside, something clanked several times in a distressing manner. The oven seemed to be getting warmer now, and she was just about to start banging on the door when it opened. Kirsi had to blink against the bright light as she held up the candle and the object she'd found.

"Sorry about that." The old woman pointed down at her feet, which were still in an old washtub surrounded by puddles. "I thought it would take you more time to fix it. Hard to hop over here during my daily Bunion Hour."

"That's okay. My granny has Bunion Hour too. But look! Here's the problem." Kirsi held up the round, charred mass. "Feels like a skull, maybe?"

The old woman took the object in both hands and considered it, then cracked it open, flecks of carbon sprinkling to the floor. "Oh, that's not a skull, though this oven has seen more than one brain cooked in its original casing—carbonized sheep bones keep my ink black. No, that's a cinnamon bun that fell off the baking sheet. I wondered where it had gotten to! I do declare, what a helpful girl you are!" True enough, the thing was charred to a cinder outside but all tan dough inside, with crispy swirls of blackened cinnamon that hinted at the lost possibility of deliciousness.

"Always glad to help," Kirsi said, stubbing out the candle and hopping down from the oven door to smooth her red hair and demurely replace her hat. "What's next on your list?"

"Why don't you eat this shiny red apple first?" the woman said. "You look hungry."

Kirsi struggled under the weight of the apple, which was the reddest thing she'd ever seen and glistened more than usual. She took a huge bite, finding its flesh sweet and delectable.

"I could do this all day," she said. "You're really very generous."

"It's rare to have such help in the deep, dark woods. What brings you here, anyway, if you don't mind me asking?"

"Halflings. The drubs, I mean. They're throwing firebombs into gnomehomes in Pavaasik. I saw my smoosh's hatch catch fire. I don't know if he's alive"—Kirsi's bottom lip trembled at the thought—"or burnt like that bun in the back of your oven."

"Oh, my dear, I am so sorry! Those awful drubs! You can be sure that if any of them ever visit me, I'll cook them up with bay leaves and thyme and bury their greasy bones in the pumpkin patch."

"I beg your pardon?"

The old woman chuckled and winked at her. "Halflings can be quite tasty if you slow-roast them."

"You eat them?" Kirsi took a step back. "But you don't eat gnomes?"

"Oh, no, dear, I would never. Gnomes are too salty and bitter. But don't let your pretty beard get knotted up about that! It's not your fault that you taste wretched, now, is it?"

Kirsi wondered briefly if she should be upset to learn that her flesh was revolting but soon decided that it was a net positive.

She helped the old woman with several more tasks, including fetching a pair of red slippers and spinning straw at a spinning wheel, and noticed that neither of them ever asked the other for a name. Normally, introducing oneself was the polite thing to do, but somehow it never came up. After a filling lunch and a delightful conversation about local wild mushrooms and their relative levels of tastiness and poison, the old woman filled Kirsi's basket with baked treats and tasked her trio of tame flying monkeys to carry Kirsi to the Big Road at the border of Borix, where it was only a short journey farther to Bruding, even with little legs.

It was very fortunate, Kirsi thought, that she'd come across that wee snug cottage.

8.

Afoul of the Fearful Cabbage Pastor of Misree

"For a quick death via blunt-force trauma, find a dwarf on Mead-schpringå and suggest they'll spend the rest of their life working in the mines. Or tell them bees are dumb."

—Kerttu Kettunen, in *Ninety-nine Diverting Ways to Be Destroyed in Pell*

It was another disappointingly beautiful day in the Misree Hills, confounding all expectations of Båggi Biins. The hopeful young dwarf had come to the most wretched part of Borix to have his mettle tested, his honor besmirched, and his beard soiled—but only under perfect conditions. And all he'd found was a lumpity bumpus toad who appeared to be an exceptionally good listener.

"Much as I would wish otherwise, my friend, I simply cannot return to the high mountain retreats of the Korpås Range and take tea with the wind and stone until I have expunged the violence within my soul—a singular goal, to be sure, since I'm rather certain my soul is of the nonviolent kind. Still, the dwarvelish custom of Mead-schpringå dictates that I must seek an outlet for whatever anger might be hiding in my bones before I can settle into the calm, ascetic life of an adult." As he said this, he stroked his oiled beard and admired how it fell upon his fine woolen tunic, but not in a proud sort of way that suggested he was better than a toad, for Båggi truly believed everyone his equal or better.

He offered a bit of honeycomb to the toad, and when the toad politely turned his head away, Båggi patted the fellow on his warty head and gobbled the honeycomb himself.

"So here I am. I had thought, by coming to the washed-out north—not that these dismal skies are your fault, ha ha!—that I could achieve my goals somewhat differently than most of my brother and sister dwarfs, whose songs now bear a weight of sadness since they returned home. Their voices deepen, you know, which is considered quite a boon during a cappella competitions. But me? I wish to sing with unburdened conscience, no matter the difficulty of achieving it."

The toad gave him a soulful and understanding sort of look, and so Båggi pulled his knitting out and settled in, needles clicking.

"Groggit?" the toad said.

Båggi shook his head. "No, my sister's name is Tåffi, but you're right—she took a different path. On the first day of her Meadschpringå, Tåffi popped her bunghole—that's the spout of the cask, you know; people get confused sometimes and think it means something else. She popped it open when the sun reached its zenith, poured a flagon and passed it round, then promptly headed south from Sküterlånd to the Centaur Pastures to pick a fight. She won that fight, slaying a centaur, and as expected—indeed, as intended—it filled her with remorse and she never wished to be violent again. Why, she wouldn't even pinch a flea! And the sad thing is that for all she is bereft of violence, it's as if something in her heart broke that day. When my violence leaves me, I want to be a better dwarf than I was before, not a lesser one. I am determined to do some good while I wear my lowland boots, and I simply cannot do that by hunting centaurs or picking slapfights with elves."

The toad, again, said only, "Groggit," and then he bounded away, but in the sort of way that suggested perhaps he'd learned something wise. Båggi looked down at the half-finished toad hat on his needles and made a little humming noise before spying a robin pecking at a worm nearby. He bum-scooted over, tossed her a few crackers, and when she was near enough to hear him without his having to yell, he continued his knitting, although now, he'd decided, it was a *robin* hat.

"As I was telling Mr. Toadly Groggit, my brother Såggi was the only one of my siblings to never come back from his Meadschpringå. The well of violence within him was bottomless, as it turned out, so he remained abroad in the world and took employment as a guard in Malefic Beach, slaying trolls and the like at the behest of a witch. A witch! Can you imagine? His letters say she's quite generous, though, and does great good in the community."

The robin had run out of crackers and chirped querulously, wondering why there wasn't any more, so Båggi tossed down yet more morsels. "You're right. It was disappointing, but at least my dear brother didn't bring shame to the family by going down into the mines for a worldly fortune, chipping away at his own goodness with every swing of the pickaxe and giving all dwarvelish people a reputation for avarice. That's only for outcasts, you know, ha ha! I still miss my brother, and also his cat, Dåggi, who went with him and must've likewise discovered untold depths of violence in his heart. Do you think, perhaps, I should go visit Såggi while on Meadschpringå?"

The bird gave him a quizzical look, cocking her head and fluttering her feathers.

"Sweet unbuttered biscuits, you're right! I do wish to avoid the south. So the north it is, I suppose. I thank you for your wise counsel."

And with that, Båggi snipped and tied off the last bit of yarn and attempted to put the hat on the bird, which she took as a personal affront and flew away. He wrote a tiny note, stating, "This Hatte is for Anyone who might have a great Yearning for such a Hatte," and left them both on a rock. Then, carrying his cask and picnic basket and Telling Cudgel, his mind much clearer after these edifying discussions, he stood and turned to the north.

The first town he had visited in Borix, aptly named Dower, was a spiritless place full of mostly pale humans and some other folk, including a goodly number of halflings and a few gnomes. People noted his cask and cudgel and were extraordinarily polite. He did not know if they were customarily so or if they were making a special effort for him, attempting to keep his incipient violence at bay. Everyone respected a Telling Cudgel, the old dwarves said. Regardless, it became abundantly clear after a couple of days that Dower would give him no honorable way to expunge his violence, but he heard that Lord Ergot in the north was a disagreeable sort and all manner of trouble might be found in Bruding.

That suited him fine: He had wished to explore the Misree Hills anyway for the herbs and wildlife rumored to live there. Some rare ingredients for medicines and tonics were said to thrive in its crags and valleys—some so rare that a single bulb would provide a year's comfort in room and board and mead. Båggi would settle for a collection of prongroots, a vital ingredient in the popular dwarvelish tonic for men, Ol' Chub's Tubby Nub Elixir for Potent Virility.

Båggi did not walk the lonesome road winding north from Dower to Bruding, but he did keep it in sight. People on lonesome roads tended to get robbed by highwaymen. Such a confrontation might force him to defend himself, and then he'd be no different from his sister, Tåffi, who had provoked the centaurs. And the herbs and roots he sought weren't going to be on the road anyway.

After a breakfast of foraged berries and his last baked doughballs of assorted nutmeats carried from his home, Båggi reached the summit of a slope he'd spent most of the previous day climbing. He anticipated seeing more of the same—a wooded valley in between the hills—and he was mostly right. But nestled in the valley below was a winsome farm astraddle a river. It had a waterwheel, a tidy barnyard, hayfields and cornfields for the livestock, and a more-than-ample garden for the farmer. Båggi even saw rows of herbs, both culinary and medicinal, and it made his heart happy and his belly hungry. Such a farmer would know the value of what Båggi had collected in his travels. Perhaps he could trade for some fresh provisions—dried legumes and root vegetables, the sorts of things that would travel well.

Something didn't seem right to Båggi, however, so he did not immediately descend. Instead, he took a knee, leaning on his cudgel, and watched the farm until his conscious mind could latch on to the disturbing but elusive element his subconscious had identified.

The problem, Båggi realized, was a surfeit of lettuces.

Beyond the farmyard and garden was a troublingly vast tract of what appeared to be lettuce. The farmer must really be into salad. And what was worse was that no one was tending to the lettuce patch—or to anything. That was what bothered him: ideal working conditions at a beautiful time of day, and not a single person working on a significant operation like this.

Perhaps they were inside the blue-trimmed white farmhouse, having breakfast; Båggi had only recently finished his own. His best hope for trade, then, would be to approach the farmhouse and give the farmer no cause to think he intended to steal anything.

Rising to his feet, he sang a traditional dwarvelish tune for luck as he began to pick his way downhill.

"My boots have brought me to a merry meeting;
I clasp my hands before you in greeting.
Sing bee-bum, pond scum, biddly-o!
Let us have biscuits with our cups of tea,
And trade stories of you for stories of me.
Sing mouse nose, squirrel toes, biddly-o!
Let us speak of our troubles and our joy
And the motley crafts we are wont to employ.
Sing puppy paw, bunny jaw, biddly-o!
But if I do disturb I will make amends;
I'll take to my boots and we'll part as friends.
Sing fawn fur, kitten purr, biddly-o!"

Båggi called out to the farmhouse as soon as he thought he might be heard. "Hello, good neighbors! Hello! May I trade with you today? Might we have a cup of tea together in peace?" He did not receive an answer or any indication that anyone was home until after he had climbed the steps to the front porch and rapped upon the door, calling out a friendly greeting again. At that, a voice bellowed in return.

"Stay awhile!" a man's high tenor said, and Båggi replied that he would and backed up from the door to pose no threat. He placed his cudgel in the crook of his arm and clasped his hands together in front of his chest.

There was some crashing and stomping around inside, and then the door whipped open to reveal a rather surprising farmer.

Like dwarves and gnomes and halflings, humans tended to walk the world in many kinds of skin, but Borix was primarily populated by the pale variety. This human, like Båggi's family, had warm reddish-brown skin. That was only a mild confounding of expectations; of much greater significance was the human's clothing. It was not that of a farmer. It was clearly some sort of ecclesiastical gear, somber black except for a couple of pinpoints of color. A bright-green enamel pin was affixed to a white kerchief wrapped around the man's neck, with a matching one in the middle of a truly bizarre hat. The pins and the hat were both shaped like a head of lettuce, and Båggi wondered if the field he'd spied earlier might not have some significance to this man—this pastor?—other than mere food. It must have, because he could conceive of no reason why one would otherwise voluntarily wear such a strange hat—not that he would ever say so, as Båggi firmly believed that everyone had a right to enjoy their headgear of choice, no matter how peculiar.

"Yes, hello?" the man said. He had grown out his dark beard on both his face and neck, Båggi noticed, except for a narrow, shaved strip directly under his nose, down his chin, and extending down the middle of his throat. Båggi guessed it must have some significance, like the hat, but he couldn't imagine what. A dwarf would never disfigure their beard so.

"Good morning, good sir! I am Båggi Biins from the mountain homes, traveling north to Bruding. I wondered if perhaps I might trade for provisions, since you seem amply supplied."

"Trade?" The man cocked his head to one side, nearly toppling the hat off his head, which he threw up a hand to steady. "It would depend on what you have."

"I've been collecting herbs in the hills."

The man narrowed his eyes. "Have you any pink-petaled dewlaps?"

"I do, and much more besides."

The man smiled, displaying a sizable gap between his upper front teeth. "Then I would be happy to trade. Welcome, Båggi. I am Brother Bo Boffing. Please call me Bo." He clasped his hands, mirroring Båggi's traditional dwarvelish greeting, and the herbalist was so grateful for the familiar gesture he almost gave Bo his pink-petaled dewlaps for free.

Bo stepped onto the porch, closing the door behind him, and hooked a thumb to the left. "Let's go to the barn. I have a worktable there where we can spread your flowers and enjoy a casual dicker."

"Your farm is quite impressive," Båggi said on the way there. "Bless my bees, I've rarely seen one more attractive."

"Thank you. We think the ideal farm is aesthetically pleasing as much as it is fruitful. It pleases the cabbage."

Båggi began, "The ca—" but shut his mouth firmly, realizing that he had nearly walked into a dangerous trap.

Now it all made sense. The field wasn't lettuce at all, and neither were the hat and pins. It was cabbage, and that wasn't good. Båggi knew instinctively that he should leave as soon as possible, before the subject could be raised again. Had he possessed sufficient victuals for the days ahead, he would have simply run away. But since he had a mighty appetite and still needed to trade, he tried a different gambit to keep the conversation friendly.

"When you say 'we,' do you mean your family, Brother Bo?"

"Oh, no, I mean my brothers and sisters."

"But . . . are not your brothers and sisters your family?"

"Only metaphorically speaking. They are my brothers and sisters in cabbage."

"I see," Båggi replied, though he didn't, once again refusing to inquire about the cruciferous death field. "Are they off somewhere else today?"

"Yes, there's an ongoing brouhaha in Bruding betwixt the gnomes and humans. My brothers and sisters have gone to render what aid they can. In the form of cabbage."

Båggi again steered the conversation elsewhere. "Gnomes? That's truly surprising. I never thought they were warlike."

"Oh, they're not. They are refugees, running away from halflings in the Skyr. Apparently it's the halflings causing the trouble, firebombing their gnomehomes up and down the earldom. But Lord Ergot doesn't want the gnomes coming in such numbers to Bruding. They're fixing things, and that's annoying."

"I beg your pardon?"

"Well, the gnomes are terribly clever, you know. They can't sit still but must improve upon whatever they find."

"Yes, I do know that. We learned such in dwarfery school. But why is it annoying if they fix things?"

Bo sighed deeply. "It lets the people there know that there is a better way to live and that Lord Ergot is a rather terrible shepherd of his metaphorical flock. Understandably, he'd prefer the people to believe his stewardship is the best they can hope for. But it turns out they're realizing they preferred the earl who slept for several years."

"An earl slept for several years?"

The human shot the dwarf an aggrieved look. "How did you not know this? It was shouted from the throats of all the heralds."

Båggi spread his hands. "I just came down from the mountains for the first time. I heard in Dower that there's a new king in Songlen, the Goode King Gustave, but I heard nothing about the Earl of Borix having a longish snooze."

Brother Bo shrugged. "It was a strange curse on his castle, but it's been lifted and he's awake now. A bit of tension has grown between the earl and Lord Ergot, though. Honestly, they're both rubbish. It's why we like to live out here. Now, let's see what you have." They were in the large red barn now, and while it was spotlessly tidy, everything else about it was disturbing. Large, crude paintings of cabbages adorned the walls, and, in addition to the usual bins of foodstuffs, the shelves ranging around the walls held the wrong sorts of items: bricks, jars of viscous red fluid, and far too many scythes to keep a body comforted. Still, Båggi needed supplies, and here he was.

The trade was soon accomplished, and Båggi tried to hide how anxious he was to leave that horrible barn. He could find his own fresh greens, but a dwarf used up a lot of food, and he needed those dried beans, spices, and some flour for flatbreads.

"Want a cabbage to go?" Bo asked as the dwarf stuffed his pack full and fastened it closed. "Totally free."

"Oh, no," Båggi begged off, trying to contain an involuntary shudder. "I'm not fond of cabbage because it disagrees with me, but thank you."

Brother Bo grinned. "Nonsense. You just haven't had *our* cabbage yet. Best in the world."

"I don't doubt it. All your produce is high quality. But it is still cabbage and it will destroy my digestive system."

"Oh, I assure you, our cabbage would never do that. It told me so."

Båggi knew well his blush turned his cheeks apple red. "All cabbage would do that, Bo. I am not sure how much clearer I can be without lapsing into crude language. It is a vegetable that detonates dwarvelish bowels. We cannot coexist. We avoid eating it because we want to live."

Brother Bo frowned. "You're speaking literally? You will die if you eat it? I have never heard that before."

"How many dwarves have you had visit your farm?"

"You're the first," Bo admitted.

"Please believe me, then. Dwarves do not eat cabbage. We cannot stomach it."

"Okay, I believe you, but come on," Bo said, picking up a short chopping blade. "You don't need to eat one of our cabbages to appreciate how remarkable they are."

Båggi remained still as Brother Bo Boffing began walking toward the field. He turned around after a few steps and beckoned with the blade. "Come on. I promise you'll be interested. These are special." When Båggi did not move or respond, he added, "Please. Indulge me."

The dwarf sighed and trudged unwillingly after the human. Bo smiled that gap-toothed grin. "Thanks," he said. "These really aren't your normal cabbages."

"How are they abnormal?"

"They are vessels of prophecy, Båggi. Futures soaked up and coiled, wrapped tightly and evergreen until we harvest them."

"Evergreen? You mean they remain fresh throughout the winter?"

"Indeed they do. They remain fresh for years. There's a healthy cabbage out there that sprouted before I was born."

"How is that possible?"

Brother Bo smirked. "It is not mere soil and sun and water, I can tell you that."

Båggi felt that he should probably take his leave now, but he was intrigued, for something arcane must be happening if Bo spoke the truth.

"Are you . . . cabbage wizards?"

Bo laughed. "Oh, no! But that's delightful. No, we're seers of a holy order. Our formal name is the Serene Prophets of Revealed Death in Cabbage."

"That . . . doesn't sound all that serene, if you don't mind me saying. I mean, it begins serene, I'll grant you, but I think it rapidly degenerates from there, ha ha!"

Brother Bo chuckled. "I understand, believe me. But the serenity is found in our meditations and prayers."

"And, uh . . . to whom do you pray?"

"We worship the perfect cohesion of space and time and nonlinear probabilities represented by cabbage."

"Wow, that's . . . yeah."

They arrived at the edge of the cabbage field and Brother Bo squatted down next to the nearest one, which looked quite healthy and eminently capable of exploding Båggi's intestines. "I will show you their peculiar qualities. Will you place your boot against the side of this cabbage, stepping on this leaf on the periphery here?" Bo pushed down a leaf and Båggi shrugged, not seeing what harm it could do. He stepped on the leaf, his ankle resting against the green sphere in the middle, and Bo made encouraging noises.

"Yes, yes, that's it, just remain there while I consult." And then he rested his hand on top of the cabbage, closed his eyes, and spoke a stream of mystical gibberish. Båggi wondered how he could politely extricate himself from this nonsense and take his leave.

"Interesting," the pastor said, eventually returning to intelligible speech. His eyes flicked up to Båggi's accoutrements. "I see you are carrying a cask and a Telling Cudgel. Does this mean you are on your Meadschpringå?"

"That's correct. You've heard of it before?"

"No, the cabbage just told me. And it also told me you have quite a bit of violence to exorcise."

Båggi scoffed. "Why, that's a load of backroom boom-boom! I enjoy long walks on the cliff face, brewing elderberry mead, crafting homemade poultices, and butterfly kisses."

"I have no doubt that is all true. But it is also true you will employ that Telling Cudgel soon and end many lives." The seer's hand shot out, pointing across the field. "There, you see? Six rows across and ten down."

"See what? A cabbage?"

Brother Bo leapt up and high-stepped over the rows, then scooted down one until he had found a particular specimen. "Yes, but not just any cabbage! Do you see? It quivers and shakes! It longs to tell us something!"

Båggi could see that the leaves of the cabbage that Bo pointed to were moving without the aid of wind. He didn't know if he would describe the movement as longing, however. It was more like a child that desperately needed to visit the privy.

The prophet sank to his knees before the cabbage, left hand spread over the vegetable, small machete in the right. His eyes closed in ecstasy. "Reveal to us, Sacred Cabbage, the first death that will be caused by the dwarvelish herbalist Båggi Biins!"

"Hey, what?"

Brother Bo's blade chopped down into the base of the cabbage with a hollow thunk, and at the same moment Båggi felt his heart clutch in his chest, a strange pain blooming there. The seer ripped the cabbage free and something red sprayed from the base, which Båggi thought odd.

"Behold the blood of one of your victims!" Bo cried. He turned the base to his face and peered at the core, which Båggi realized might resemble a spine traveling up into the base of a skull. The harvested portions of cabbage were described as heads, after all. "A halfling! Father of two! Loves his dogs!" Bo tossed the cabbage aside and shook his head as he got to his feet. "Oh, Båggi. How much rage must live inside you to kill such a person?"

"That's not funny," the dwarf said, feeling shook. "It's horrifying."

"I agree. Revealed Death is no joke." A rustling noise, a couple of rows closer but farther north, drew their attention. "Another cabbage longs to speak of the future!"

"What? No. Great galloping gallberries, stop this!" Båggi said, even as Brother Bo rushed to the spot. "Please."

The prophet ignored him, once more kneeling and repeating the ritual, and Båggi again felt a punch in the chest when the machete chopped into the vegetal head.

"A second halfling! Beloved brother and uncle, caretaker of an elderly hamster. Collects porcelain figurines of frogs." Bo tossed this cabbage aside and fixed the dwarf with a reproving glare. "Honestly, what kind of demons do you keep caged in those ribs?"

Båggi didn't know how to answer. His breath came in short gasps, and he was sweating even though it was a pleasant day. Brother Bo was clearly deranged, yet he also had some kind of strange power that caused real pain. A new rustling in the rows beckoned, faint but discernible. Bo turned to find the source and then stared at Båggi, agog.

"No, please," Båggi whimpered.

Bo waggled a finger at the flailing vegetable. "That's the oldest cabbage in the field. Growing here long before my arrival, waiting all this time for you! What will it reveal?"

"Your unkindness, no doubt," Båggi replied, but the pastor was already sprinting to the spot. The dwarf labored after him, wondering why his legs felt so leaden and his lungs couldn't seem to fill properly. "Brother Bo! Stop! I insist!"

"I cannot stop the Revealed Deaths once they begin! Every one of these cabbages foretells the violent death of someone at the hands of our visitors!"

Båggi did not say aloud that this had to be one of the most inhospitable ways to treat visitors apart from actually poisoning them or killing them, but he thought it. He also thought it shouldn't continue. And as Brother Bo knelt beside the ancient cabbage, his machete raised high, ignoring his guest's pleas to desist, Båggi felt some new emotion stirring within him, his skin flushing, his teeth clenching. He gripped his Telling Cudgel in both hands, knuckles whitened against the base, and he saw peripherally that it was beginning to transform from a simple gnarled piece of wood into something far more deadly, with spikes protruding at all angles like a wakening porcupine. The Telling Cudgel always told the world when a dwarf was angry and when he was at peace, and it would also tell Båggi when he had purged the violence from his spirit.

He began to raise the cudgel above his head just as Brother Bo's machete thwacked into the old cabbage, and he was staggered by the impact, once again, at his core. The pastor inspected the head and intoned, "A middle-aged troll who enjoys croquet. Imagine what a rare creature he must be! But not for long, eh?" He clucked his tongue against the roof of his mouth a few times. "You're a monster, Båggi Biins."

The herbalist gasped at the insult and felt a new wave of anger wash through him. He hefted his cudgel, and the pastor gave him a soft smile, throwing his arms wide. "Yes! Strike me down among the cabbages, that my blood may mingle with theirs!"

Båggi dearly wanted to, but he would not be baited. He remembered that he was not obligated to stay there a second longer; only his good manners had brought him to the cabbage field in the first place. With his unprecedented rudeness, Brother Bo had released him from any need to be polite. So Båggi pointed himself north and ran, his picnic basket thumping against his back, not bothering to issue a farewell. As soon as he cleared the cabbage patch, his lung capacity returned and his Telling Cudgel slowly, meekly, slid and scraped itself back into an innocent bough of gnarled hardwood with a mead cask and pint glass etched into the grain.

He hoped the cabbage prophecies were all nonsense—he could not imagine ever slaying innocent halflings—but whether or not their visions were true, Båggi understood now why he needed to go out on Meadschpringå. It turned out he had plenty of violence lurking inside his spirit, patient and waiting, and it had only needed the right person—or cabbage—to coax it forth.

Perhaps, Båggi thought, this Lord Ergot was another such person. He began trudging toward Bruding, hating cabbage more than ever.

9.

CALCULATING THE AIR-SPEED VELOCITY OF A LADEN CHICKEN SHACK

"Thatch tortoises lead intensely interesting lives. For example, they . . . No, I'm sorry. I can't pretend anymore. After decades of research and an epic waste of time, I've no choice but to conclude that they are intensely boring creatures. What am I even doing with my life?"

—MANG ROVE, in an introduction to the shortest doctoral thesis ever, which reads in its entirety, "Please see title," which is called, *Thatch Tortoises Are Just Tortoises That Slowly Eat Your Roof and Occasionally Lay Eggs: and No, I Can't Explain How They Got Up There in the First Place Even Though I Observed Them Closely for Thirty-five Tedious Years*

In the space of a heartbeat, Agape's life went from contemplating a future of independent freedom to taking care of her wounded parents. Her father fell inside the shack and turned to pull Fedora in behind him. Her beautiful caftan was torn and burned in several places, but they both seemed mostly unharmed.

Mad cackling erupted outside, along with several loud explosions— the hallmarks of a visit from the dreaded halfling drubs. The thatch overhead caught fire, and then something deeply strange happened.

The cottage lurched upward with a terrified cluck.

"Wait," Agape gasped, stumbling to catch herself against the mantel. "Are you saying those chicken legs weren't just ornamental?"

As if in response, the cottage clucked again and began to run on its long orange chicken legs, which had definitely appeared to be a fun quirk to a cheap rental. The lease they'd signed had included a deep discount in case of "abrupt relocations," something labeled the "Chicken Run Clause," and suddenly it all made sense. The realtor, who in retrospect had seemed very witchy, had definitely lied to them on multiple counts—and also tsked at their hooves. At the time, Agape thought it was because they'd scratch the floors, but now she understood it was because the witch was well aware that they'd be sliding all over the dang place if the house took to its feet. Agape might've been mad, but considering the drubs outside, she rather thought having a mobile home was useful in this instance.

On her belly now, brooms clattering all around her, Agape crawled to Piini and put a hand on his heavy golden foot.

"Piini Automaatti," she said, recognizing her role as Vartija. "If we get separated, take my parents to Bruding. I'll meet you there. Keep them saaafe!"

As the running house canted side to side and bumped into trees and bushes, and as the halflings outside whooped and cheered, tossed more firebombs, and gave chase, the metal man's head inclined slightly. His hands came down to his sides as the gem in his forehead flared briefly with a warm and understanding glow. Did Agape imagine that Piini nodded? Probably. It didn't matter. After all this time on the run, they'd finally been found by the halfling hunters.

Her first hour as the Vartija was already a failure. She could only hope the witch's house could outrun the drubs. Crawling to the fireplace, she took the frying pan back in hand. She couldn't help noticing the postcard of Grakkel her father had left behind as the contents of the house skittered madly and fell to ruin all around her.

"Wish You Were Here," it said, and their new address was scrawled beneath it.

Yeah, well, Agape wished they were anywhere else. The house, it seemed, shared that desire. But the drubs must've expected that the Fallopia family would run. They were not only half sheep—and running away was a primary instinct of sheep—but that was what the Fallopias had always done to protect Piini, especially in this last year of unusually dogged pursuit. Although Agape couldn't see out through the filthy and cobwebbed windows, she could feel each lurch when the house's direction was forced to change, and it was all too easy to imagine halflings herding them one way or another with arrows and firebombs.

"Is there any way to control the house?" she asked her parents, who merely huddled together near the open door.

"This is baaaad!" her mother bleated as if she'd lost all sense.

"I can't staaaand the haaalfling maaafia!" her father moaned.

Crawling over to them, frying pan in hand, Agape gently nudged her cowering parents away from the swinging door and slammed it shut, catching a glimpse of a dozen halflings pursuing them with homemade bombs in their tooled leather bags.

The chicken shack must've found a gap in the halfling line, however, as it first surged forward and then slowed to a sustainable pace without too much zigging and zagging. The gentle gallop, accompanied by not-so-gentle clucking, was easy enough to ride, almost like a boat in choppy seas. Still, Agape knew the limitations of hooves on wood, especially with dozens of brooms rolling about. She crawled over to the desk and opened the drawer, looking for the usual helpful information provided when one rented an edifice. Unfortunately, all she found was a curse to keep tortoises out of the thatch, which would've been far more useful before the thatch had caught fire.

Still, perhaps she could save one life.

"Bubble, bubble, toil and poof, get this tortoise out of my roof!" she cried. The first thatch tortoise nearly concussed her as it fell from the ceiling. But then she thought of holding the frying pan over her head as the rest rained down. Once the plopping had stopped, she grabbed a broom and scooted them all under the bed like giant hockey pucks as the shack sped up again.

Forced to look at the roof, she had to concede that it was really and truly on fire, and a pan of water and a rag could not handle it. No wonder the shack was in such a hurry. She could hear the drubs shouting and cackling nearby, but she wasn't sure she wanted to rub clean a patch of the dirty window glass to see where they were headed. If it was in the direction the halflings wanted them to go, it wasn't going to be pleasant.

Not that occupying an ambulatory dwelling was pleasant. Especially when it exhibited aeronautical ambitions. In a paroxysm of panic that sent them all sprawling to the floor, the house sprang out into space and hovered for just a moment before dropping like a stone.

"Daaaaang!" Agape cried in unison with her parents, and worried about the impact that would surely come when the house landed, for although they'd noticed the supposedly ornamental chicken legs, nothing had been said of secret wings. Chickens were not renowned for long-distance flights, and chicken wings laden with the weight of architecture, furniture, and ovitaur occupants were even less likely to deliver a nice long glide. Sure enough, her stomach nearly fell through her throat as they plummeted. Nothing could've prepared her for the heavy smack of impact, and she'd barely begun to celebrate being alive when water started to ooze through the cracks in the floorboards.

The flaming chicken shack had cleverly jumped into a lake. And here Agape had always assumed that chickens were dumb.

She crawled back to her quaking parents and shook her father's shoulder. "Daaad? Maamaa? The house is sinking. We've got to get out."

"Aaaaaaghhh!" her mom wailed.

But her parents dutifully stood, clutching each other and watching Agape with wide eyes. It seemed to her that they'd aged decades in the span of an hour.

"Piini Automaatti," she said, using her commanding voice, "get out of the water safely. Stay with me. Do you understaaand?"

The metal man strode to the door, feet clomping through the rising water, and punched a hole in the ancient wood.

That woke Agape's father up enough to mutter, "There goes our deposit."

Agape immediately understood that they weren't going to drown—it was just a little fen. Perhaps chickens weren't as smart as she'd given them credit for. The water destroying the floor wasn't anywhere close to putting out the fire on the roof. But there was still danger, of course. Squeezing through the hole in the door after Piini, she didn't see any halflings, but she knew they were on their way. With each step, the metal man sank deeper in the bog, but he didn't get stuck, and Agape was able to shepherd her parents out in his wake. Soon they all stood among the cattails, looking out at the golden plains beyond while the poor chicken house, struggling in the muck, burned down behind them. It clucked irritably and tried to shift out of the quagmire, but it had entirely the wrong sort of feet to effect any sort of escape. Agape would've felt bad for the unlucky clucker if she hadn't been fully aware of the still very real threat of the drubs.

"What do we do?" she asked her parents.

Her father looked at her in puzzlement. "You're the Vartija now," he said. "It's up to you."

Agape considered the perverse logic at work. When she'd woken up, her parents had been in charge. Then, for a brief and magical moment, she'd been independent, as her parents moved on with their lives without giving her a single thought. Now she was soaked to the hocks in bogwater and cauldron contents, surrounded by broken brooms and confused tortoises, in charge for the first time. And not only responsible for Piini but also her parents. Their survival and her destiny, it appeared, were up to her.

She sighed. To the east they could only expect more halflings. There were hills to the north and south. The nearest help was in Bruding, and it was also the easiest terrain to cross.

"We head for Bruding," she said.

10.

Through a Cold Blü Sky Bereft of Fluffee Egges

"Alternate spellings for some words—typically colors and other sensory adjectives, but also some nouns—are asserted by gryphons and other beings who insist that their heightened perceptions reveal an extrasensory reality. Alternate spellings, therefore, will be marked in the dictionary with an asterisk and indicate that the word's definition is essentially the same as the common spelling but also includes the additional nuanced understanding of such beings. In short, gryphons are weird."

—*EDITOR'S NOTE IN* Lexi Conn's Dictionary of the Pellican Language, *42nd edition*

Skies have different temperatures and textures, Gerd reflected, and in that sense they were very similar to egges. Skies could be cold and hard, or hot and moist, or any number of other things, and so could egges. As a gryphon, Gerd could fly right through all manner of skies, and in a way, all manner of egges flew right through her. It pleased Gerd that her two favorite things—skies and egges—had so much in common. Sometimes skies thundered and boomed with anger, for example, and sometimes egges made her backside thunder and boom as well.

Though there was no danger of thunder at the present. Gerd

doubted she had ever seen a sky so blü as the one she shot through right then, hunting the goldenne man for Faucon, the unusually kleen halfling. A clear day, a brilliant day, and a rare day, for this region north of the Coxcomb, her old high home in the rocks, was so often glümee with clouds. Her wingtips sliced through the air, her beak a breaker streaming wind past her eyes, the goldenne fur on her flanks rippling in the breeze. Below her, the targets moved slowly and bleated in dismay at her approach, which made Gerd feel a pang of guilt.

She did not mean to be so frightful and did not wish anyone ill. She certainly did not want to eat any ovitaurs. Humans tasted terrible, and anything that was part human was therefore at least part terrible. Gryphones left centaurs, llamataurs, minotaurs, and ovitaurs alone as a result. Gnomes were too salty, halflings tasted rotten, and dwarves required so much salt that one might as well not bother. Elves were delicious, though; a nice elf butt roast was an exquisite delicacy, and one that Gerd had only tasted once, at the funeral feast of her grandfather. Elf butts were infamously hard to come by, however, attached as they were to elves who lived in the Morningwood, that being a place very difficult to fly through and see well. There was so much blasted glitter in the air, sparkling and winking in harsh tones of blü and yellö and redde, that gryphones could go blind in mere minutes. Indeed, many gryphones had gone blind in pursuit of the world's most delicious meat. If anything should be taboo for gryphones to eat, Gerd thought, it should be elf butts, because that would save the eyesight and even lives of so many hunters. But no, instead it was taboo to eat egges: glorious, harmless, tasty egges, which could be made into fluffee omlets. The world did not make sense.

Gerd wanted to reassure the ovitaurs that she meant them no harm, but she could not use her vocal cords to make the kinds of noises most folk would understand. Her assorted whistles, gurgles, and screeches were perfectly comprehensible to gryphones, but other creatures typically interpreted them as terrifying. So she used the peculiar talent of gryphones to think aloud, which, she was told, sounded to thinking beings like someone speaking in their own language, except in their heads.

Hello, she thought aloud to the ovitaurs. *Please be calm. I am not here to eat you.*

Instead of being grateful, the ovitaurs baaed and bleated and shrieked in terror. The youngest and most supple one shook her wee fist and demanded that Gerd go away.

I will go away, Gerd assured them as her talons locked on to the shoulders of the shiny yellö man. *I just need to take this fellow with me. There are egges at stake, you see.*

Faucon had promised her four very special omlets—the fluffee ones with gourmet ingredients—if she brought back the yellö man. She had been told he was goldenne, but he wasn't really shiny, now that she'd seen him in person.

He was not really a man either, Gerd discovered. For one, he didn't have skin. He was made of very hard metal, and her talons could only scrape and scratch the surface without getting any real purchase. Faucon had called him a construct, and now she understood. She lowered her rear legs, the strong lion ones, and grasped the hips while her scaled front claws tried to lift at the shoulders. The yellö man strangely made no sound or any move to protest this, but perhaps he saw no need, since Gerd could not move him at all. He was far too heavy, or else there was some kind of magic at work. Meanwhile, as Gerd flapped and strained to lift something immovable, the ovitaurs were throwing rocks at her, and some of these rocks were creating ouchies.

She screeched at them, and they cringed, and for good measure she thought aloud, *Stop that. I will defend myself if necessary.*

They resumed after a few moments, however, and she still could not move the dull-yellö metal man. Faucon would be displeased and she might not get any fluffee omlets.

But perhaps, if she could not figure out the mystery of this man, one of these ovitaurs could supply answers. She let her target go and flapped her wings to lift straight up, thereby avoiding another volley of rocks, and then swooped down to catch one of the ovitaurs, which was quite agreeably movable.

"Piini Automaatti," the ovitaur shouted, "keep my paaarents safe!"

The creature struggled in the grip of Gerd's talons, and the other ovitaurs screamed and threw more rocks, but these missed Gerd completely as she banked around to head back to Faucon. The yellö man, left behind, made no objection.

Hello, I am Gerd, she thought aloud to her selected quarry. *I will not hurt you on purpose. I just want you to speak to Faucon. If you stop struggling, you will not be accidentally sliced up by my talons. I am being as gentle as possible.*

The ovitaur stopped her wriggling, though it may have been because they had climbed to such a height that she would plummet to her death if she won free.

"Faucon will kill me," the ovitaur said. "You are taking me to my death."

Gerd considered this. *I suppose that is possible. Faucon has killed people before. But I have not heard him say he wants you dead. He wants the yellö man.*

"You mean the yellow man?"

That is who I mean, but yellow with a w is insufficient to describe him. He is truly more yellö with an umlaut.

"What?"

Gryphones can see more than most creatures. We perceive layers of color and texture that you do not, and our language reflects that. This beautiful sky we fly in right now is not blue with an e; it's blü with an umlaut. You must respect the umlaut.

"Umlauts are not high on my list of priorities aaat the moment," the ovitaur said.

Nor are manners, apparently. You still have not shared with me your name.

"I beg your pardon, Gerd. I am Agape Fallopia, Vartija of the Elder Laaaws."

Startled, Gerd craned her neck down to look at her captive more closely. Yes, there it was: the telltale lambent glö about her head that certified Agape was a true Vartija. Gerd shuddered with awe.

When Gerd had been a hatchling and then a fledgling, her mother had told her stories of the Vartija, creatures specially selected to protect artifacts of great and sacred purpose. There was nothing so honorable in the world as a Vartija, and there were few gryphones who didn't wish to become one at some point. Gerd's own uncle Lurp had made the entire family proud, protecting a sacred shoehorn once used by that long-dead great ruler and uniter of Pell, King Barthur. But the possibility of becoming a Vartija no longer existed for Gerd: As a disgraced outcast from the Coxcomb, a base eater of egges, she could never be presented to the Solemn and Cloaked Convocation of Elders as a servant of the laws.

It is my honor to meet you, Agape. What is your charge?

"I am to protect the automaatti."

I do not know what that is.

"The yellow maaan you tried to steal. He is the automaatti."

Gerd's stomach rumbled with a mixture of hunger and disquiet. Not only was she unable to become a Vartija, but now circumstances had turned her against them. Which meant, she supposed, that she was on the wrong side here. And which meant that Faucon might not be as noble a halfling as she had hoped. He didn't wear the drub medallion or smell of sour milk like some of the others, and she had told herself that spoke well of his character, but she wondered now if she had not been seduced into something that smacked of evil simply because he made such fantasticke fluffee omlets.

Gerd hootled in wry amusement. No wonder Faucon had been having such trouble tracking down these ovitaurs: They were honking Vartijas! She didn't know why the automaatti was important to the Elders, but she knew she wouldn't help Faucon pursue it anymore, not for all the egges in the Skyr.

I still think you should talk to Faucon, she told Agape, *but you should tell him that you're a Vartija. I will confirm the truth of it.*

"What difference will thaaat make?"

I don't think Faucon knows. I certainly didn't know. And it makes a difference to me, even if it doesn't to him or the drubs working for him. I will protect you and return you to the automaatti. I swear it by my nest and keep.

The creature in her grasp fidgeted as if she didn't quite believe Gerd, or perhaps she merely found it uncomfortable being carried thousands of feet away from the earth. "Okay, thanks, Gerd. But why aaare you working for him anyway?"

. . . I have no nest or keep.

"Oh. Thaaat makes your oath a bit suspect, doesn't it?"

I do not know any other way to swear, but I promise I am sincere. The gryphones no longer consider me one of their own, but I still consider myself a gryphone and abide by all their codes, except for the one about egges. You can rely on me to keep my word.

"I appreciate thaaat."

Gerd spied the camp the halflings had made, saw the smoke rising from the cookfires, and her belly growled again. She was really hungry.

Spiraling down, she saw some of the drubs point up at her, and one of them went to fetch Faucon out of his tent. He was waiting for her when she landed with Agape, and he looked unhappy, with his hairy arms folded across his smart but slightly undersized pin-striped suit. His scowl deepened when the drubs came to take Agape away and Gerd enfolded her wings around the diminutive ovitaur, screeching defiance.

Back away. She is under my protection, Gerd thought aloud. The drubs obeyed. They did not want to mess with that beak or those talons.

"That is not the golden man I asked you to bring me, Gerd," Faucon said. "That is a scrawny, useless leg of lamb."

She is not useless, Gerd said.

"I'm not scrawny," Agape muttered. "I have supple flaaanks."

"I have no use for supple flanks, so please explain," Faucon replied.

I will. But first, that promised breakfast. Four fluffee omlets with gourmet ingredients.

Faucon shook his head. "That was the promised reward for the golden man."

This ovitaur is better, Gerd countered, *and we'll all be in better moods after we eat.*

Silence stretched between them while Faucon reassessed the situation and Gerd waited patiently. She could see him calculate that everyone was hungry, and if the ovitaur really was useless, all he'd lose were a few egges. Whereas if the gryphone was hungry and denied said egges, she might reconsider her stance on eating halflings, or at least popping their heads off like berries from a bush. Finally he threw his hands up and gave her a grim nod of respect.

"Perhaps you are right. Skipping breakfast is not the halfling way. The fire is ready, so please excuse me as I make my preparations. If anyone troubles you"—he looked around sternly at the drubs—"you have my permission to eat them. But you do understand that the prisoner must be restrained."

Gerd's eyes narrowed. *But not painfully so.*

Faucon's eyes narrowed more. "For now."

When he nodded at Bernaud Cobbleshod and the drubs, they hurried forward and tied the ovitaur to a chair. For her part, Agape struggled and bucked and lashed out with her hooves, but one young ovitaur was no match for a dastardly gang of halfling rogues, who were almost of the same size but had infinitely better balance.

Once Agape was trussed, Faucon ducked back into his tent, but Gerd remained on high alert. The drubs had regarded her with indifference before, but now that she had stood up to Faucon, they looked less than friendly. And she did not know what preparations Faucon had truly gone to make. Perhaps, since she had defied him in front of his minions, he would seek physical violence. She supposed she did not truly trust him now that she realized he might be more sympathetic to the drubs than to the law. At least he couldn't stop her from eating the drubs, even if her taste buds urged her not to.

One drub took a step toward her, his hand stealing toward his pocket, but then Faucon emerged from the tent with what passed for a winsome smile and two jars held above his head, which he shook to catch the sun glinting off the glass.

"My half of our bargain," he said. "Crickets and ladybugs! To be sprinkled on four gourmet omelets."

Gerd would have smiled if her beak were capable of such elastic exercise. She could hear him add the extra syllable to *omlets* and suspected he wasn't saying *ladybugges* with the proper number of *g*s, but she didn't correct him. She and Faucon might have a serious disagreement after this; she would not allow him to hurt the ovitaur, and even seeing the creature tied with strings caused Gerd pain. They might as well have one last fluffee, crunchy meal together before their tender truce was shattered.

Gerd unfolded her wings and sat back, making a pleased sort of purr. But the ovitaur did not look hungry or pleased. She looked quite glüm. Despondent. As Agape's browne eyes filled with tears and Faucon twirled his mustache, Gerd knew she had done the right thing, helping this Vartija. If what the ovitaur said and what her aura told Gerd were true, no number of egges was worth giving the goldenne metal man into the hands of the drubs. Gerd would eat, and Faucon would speak with Agape, and then they would see.

It was fortunate, Gerd thought, that her own senses went beyond, for she suspected that the future had just shifted course. Hopefully for the better. And the batter.

11.

Spread-Eagled Uponst a Divan of Questionable Provenance

"It is the rare leader who actively tries to improve the lives of his most vulnerable people. The usual condition of monarchs is to take bribes, reign over a slow tumble into chaos, and deflect blame."

—Arno Tuutti, in *The Unexpected Insouciance of Anarcho-Syndicalism*

ORDER YE NOW AND RECEIVETH HALF OFF. PLEASE TIP THY 'ZA COURIER. COURIERS CARRY LESS THAN SEVEN FICKELS AND THREE TURNIPS. DELIVERED WITHIN THREE HOURS, OR YOUR MONNEY SHALT BE RETURN-ED!

—Pamphlet advertising Ye Olde Hutte of Pea-za

Goode Kingge Gustave the Greate—for that was the way his mail was addressed—drooped over a cushy divan, enjoying the many bonuses of being human and able to control his bodily functions. He'd once been a goat, but he got better. A bowl of flawless cherries sweated over ice in a bowl nearby, while a flagon of Kolonic wine sat untouched by his elbow. Try as he might, he couldn't get a handle on the benefits of a good Kolonic and vastly preferred the effects of a piping hot cup of kuffee. It moved something deep within him, almost reminding him of the giddy, carefree life he'd led when he was just a winsome goat kid, plopping his way through life before a rogue pixie and a magic boot had unceremoniously turned him into an awkward human and sent his pooboy, Worstley, on a quest. For a goat, there were no responsibilities, no worries.

But as a human, he was, as his friend Argabella would say, Brimful of Concerns. As much as he enjoyed receiving mail—and he did, for he'd turned the Pellican Postale Service into a veritable symphony of productivity, and now he was all but rolling in mail of all sorts—he'd noticed that much of it was in fact not the good sort of mail but, rather, the bad sort of mail. Which was fun, at first—especially the hate mail, which he enjoyed peeing on to practice what the humans called "aim." But these days, as his tutors caught him up to speed, he was beginning to get a sinking feeling, something that his adviser, Grinda, called "guilt." It twisted up in his stomach like a bad boot, and the more he read this one particular letter, the more terrible he felt. The square of paper was quite small, and the handwriting was pleasantly perfect and loopy. He'd expected it to say something quite cheerful, and he'd been horribly disappointed.

Dear Goode Kingge Gustave the Greate,
     Please send Helppe to we Gnomes of Soperki in the Northe. The Halflings Hereabouts do daily Harry oure People with Murder Moste Foule. Why just Yesterdaye, a Mollotop Boozebomb was tossed into the Gnomehome of my Uncle Hoopi, and we did find him in Severale Moiste Pieces. He is not the Firste, nor will he be the Laste. We Industrious, Peaceful Gnomes wish only to Enjoy our Pudding and contribute our Taxes to your Grande Pleasure without being Unceremoniously Blowne Uppe in our Owne Gnomehomes.

Most Desperately,

Floopi Nooperkins

"Well, that's distressing," Gustave said to himself. "Puts me off pudding when I think about it, really."

He picked up the next letter, which was human-sized, slit it open with a child-safe letter opener he'd received as a gift, and unfolded the creamy paper. It was another missive from that slimy Lord Ergot of Bruding. Ergot wrote Gustave every other day, congratulating the king on the Foine Jobbe he was doing and bragging about how well his own lands were run and how he should most definitely be invited to the castle for some sort of cabinet appointment, award, or what he called "bro-times on the town," followed by a winky face. But he also wanted to discuss a persistent problem with gnomes flocking to his city and wantonly improving his infrastructure without permission.

Gustave had not yet met Lord Ergot in person, and he definitely did not wish to enjoy "bro-times," with or without a winky face—not on the town, not anywhere. Although Gustave had been made to understand that his job was to get along with earls and lords and not hate them, he recalled with distaste that it had indeed been Lord Ergot who'd killed Bestley, the older brother of his old pooboy, Worstley, who was also dead.

Perhaps it was not a good omen, Gustave thought, to have a name that ended in -tley.

This question of gnomes and halflings had come up before; the first letter from Lord Ergot had arrived during his birthday celebration a couple of weeks ago, and at the time he'd decided they should go to the Skyr and settle it. But events had conspired to distract him from mobilizing, what with a constant stream of questions coming in to ask how his policies differed from the late King Benedick's and the need to respond to a troll uprising in Songlen.

"Ick," he said, tossing that letter down into a growing pile that his Officiale Pooboy would eventually haul away, declaring as he did so, "Time to compost the poste!"

He picked up the next letter in the stack, this one smaller and slightly grubby and written in a careless, childish hand. There was a large grease stain at the bottom of the page, together with an actual piece of honey-glazed bacon that had no doubt created it.

> Deare Greatte Kinggge Gooodee Gustave,
>   Alle is wellle here in Chumpspittle. We Halflings are a Quiet and Studious people who never bother nobody nohow. Anything bad you hear from those Terrible Nastye Noe Goode Gnomes is Gosh Darned Dirty Lies. We just thought You should Know.
>
> Signed,
>
> THE HALFLINGS (all of them)

"All the halflings?" Gustave muttered to himself. "Literally all of them? Do they write letters by committee? Grinda and I can't even agree on breakfast, much less the wording on a letter."

"What's that, your highness?" Grinda swept into the royale maile room in her official Adviser's Uniform, which was an elegant arrangement in seafoam green that included a cloak and turban.

Gustave turned to face her. "Halflings: good or bad?" he asked.

Grinda was one of the few people Gustave trusted completely. Although he'd once considered her a distinct threat, even aside from the age-old fear that anything on two legs would eat a goat given the slightest provocation or excellent tenderizing marinade recipe, he'd since grown to care deeply for the wise old witch. They'd long ago agreed that there were no stupid questions when a billy goat suddenly found himself human and the ruler of a large kingdom, even if sometimes his questions were a bit peculiar.

Grinda frowned, the lines of her face melting a bit. "Halflings? To eat, or as employees, or what?"

Gustave considered. "Just in general. See, I have this letter from 'the halflings'—all of them, apparently, if letters are to be believed— and then there's this other letter from a single gnome who tells a very specific tale about halfling violence against his people. And then Lord Ergot assures me that all is well except that gnomes are flooding into his city and improving it without a permit. Oh, and a flyer that promises our next pea-za will be delivered within three hours or Our Monney Shalt Be Return-ed. We like peas, right?"

Using his hands, which he still considered quite a parlor trick, Gustave picked up and held out all the papers in question. Grinda took them and sorted through them one by one, her eyebrows drawing dangerously down as she read the letters. When she tossed down the pea-za flyer, Gustave muttered, "Hey!"

Grinda sighed the sigh she used when Gustave did something horribly and unavoidably goatish. He pre-winced, just to be ready when he learned what he'd done wrong.

"This is a problem," she finally said.

"Pea-za is a problem?"

"Not that."

"My hands? I used them wrong?"

"No, Gustave, it's—"

"I swear I'm not 'watering' the indoor plants anymore."

Grinda sighed even more loudly, which was Gustave's signal to shut up.

"The problem is not you, your highness. It's as you've said. Whatever is occurring between the halflings and gnomes isn't good, and it would seem our Lord Ergot is rather anxious to cover up how bad it is or at least ignore it, so long as it raises his tax base."

"What's he got against gnomes? Aren't all people welcome everywhere in Pell?"

"Legally, yes, that's supposed to be the case. In practice, we have groups of people who like to isolate themselves from others. They welcome people who look like them and make anyone who's different feel unwelcome. The elves in the Morningwood, for example, don't allow anyone to stay; all must pass through."

"Right, I knew about them. Well do I remember our sudden and explosive expulsion from the Morningwood. But why won't Lord Ergot help these gnomes?"

Grinda shrugged. "It may simply be a strain on his resources. He's not really supposed to be in charge of those people."

"Who is, then? Who's in charge in the Skyr? Didn't we have an earl come here for my crowning ceremony?"

"The Skyr sent the halfling portion of the kanssa-jaarli."

"The halfling portion of, uh, what was that, a dessert?"

"The kanssa-jaarli is an Alphagnomeric term for the leadership of the Skyr. Two earls—one gnome and one halfling—ruling in tandem."

"And Alphagnomeric is . . . ?"

"The language of the gnomes. Very difficult to learn. They do speak Pellican as well, of course."

Gustave's head was spinning, and not just with hunger for pea-za. "Okay, great. I know that I've seen at least one gnome and one halfling before, but I just thought of them as tiny humans who would still eat me if given a chance. There's more to it than that, isn't there?"

"Indeed, there is."

Sashaying across the room, Grinda selected a book from a shelf and brought it back to the divan. She sat beside Gustave, who no longer considered this a predator's attempt to cunningly lure him into complacency before sticking a fork in his rump. Opening the book and flipping to the page she wanted, Grinda pointed to a cheerful and round-looking person in bright woolen clothes, standing beside a watering can, which was about the same size.

"This is a gnome. Gnomes are about knee-high, before they put a hat on, and they are known for being tidy, industrious, hardworking, and deeply concerned with getting along and gadgetry."

"He looks spiffy."

"That's a woman. Female gnomes have beards, you see."

"Just like goats! I like them already."

Grinda turned the page and pointed at a lankier person with a mop of curly hair echoed on fuzzy fingers and excessively large bare feet. "This is a halfling. Halflings are supposed to be a friendly and creative people interested in fine foods, bespoke tobacco, and copious amounts of ale. Harmless hedonists who write excellent poetry. But we've since heard stories that the halflings of the Skyr have developed a—"

"Festering boil?" Gustave added helpfully, as he'd been very surprised when it had happened to him.

"A problem with organized crime," Grinda finished. "You see, after the Giant Wars of 882, the gnomes and halflings worked together to build a crevasse to keep the giants out. The gnomes are excellent architects, and the halflings are excellent labor, provided they're fed nineteen times a day, so they were able to complete a marvel of the world with their combined talents. Without the threat of being turned into appetizers for giants, however, they've gradually turned into uneasy neighbors in the Skyr rather than staunch allies. This is not the first whisper of unrest to rustle through the castle."

"I wouldn't call it a whisper. I mean, the halflings blew up Floopi Nooperkins's kin Hoopi."

"Allegedly," Grinda murmured, her fist on her chin, the book forgotten.

They sat there in companionable but frustrated silence for a moment, and Gustave greatly missed the practice of chewing his cud, which had once been very relaxing. Grinda had since informed him that the word *ruminating* applied both to regurgitating food and to thinking about something with a sort of grindy feeling in the brain, and he vastly preferred the chewing option.

"Somebody needs to do something," Gustave finally said.

Grinda turned to look at him, unblinking. "That would be you, sire."

Gustave stared at her and her eyes widened as she realized she'd made a mistake.

"I mean sir! Sorry, I forgot." Gustave didn't like the idea of being anyone's sire, even in a metaphorical sense. He put up with *your high-*

ness and *your majesty* and other such nonsense, but he'd made it clear that he preferred to be addressed as *sir*, just like any common person worthy of respect. He just happened to be the one sir who had to make big decisions, and Grinda never hesitated to remind him of that. "You're the king, and it's your kingdom."

"I know. But what do I do? I mean, this greasy letter says it's from 'the halflings,' but even with our carefully selected, well-trained, and nicely paid postale service, I don't think they'd know how to deliver a letter addressed to all of them. And this Nooperkins guy seems Quite Foine, but how do I find him if he's fled to Bruding, and what do I give him to make up for the fact that his uncle got exploded?"

Grinda held out her beringed fingers. "Here is your first test, your majesty. Two people in one place. Each wants something different. Violence is involved. How do you propose to solve this problem?"

Gustave reached for a cherry, trying not to think about the Nooperkinses. Chewing helped him think, even if it wasn't a delicious boot or a patch of luscious grass.

"What I need to do," he said slowly, his eyes rolling in opposite directions and his ears drooping a bit with muscle memory from his caprine days, "is to go over to the Skyr and sort this out personally."

Much to his surprise, Grinda beamed.

"Excellent, King Gustave. I'll set it up."

"Set up what?"

"The meeting."

"With who?"

"Whom?"

"What?"

"The meeting."

Gustave let his head fall into his hands.

"Cud was so much easier than grammar," he groaned.

"I'll set up a meeting with the kanssa-jaarli and make it clear that the halfling and the gnome must both attend. We should invite Lord Ergot too, since he has an interest in resolving this. We'll have to research the historical documents governing the, er, governance of the Skyr. Beyond the title of kanssa-jaarli, which was created after the Giant Wars, I'm unfamiliar with how they run things, I admit. But we must know where the law stands, discover where each side stands, and consider where you, the king, wish to stand."

"Maybe I should stand behind a large number of armored soldiers if there's going to be violent bits."

Grinda put a hand on his shoulder, which was no longer bony and furry. He leaned in to her a little bit, and she gave his shoulder a scratch. When he'd magically transformed from goat to human, Gustave had changed a great deal in body but not in mind and heart. Some of his old comforts still remained, although very few people knew about them. The castle staff was paid very well never to mention the midnight bleating.

"Standing around doing nothing would be nice, I'm sure, but that's not how it works anymore," Grinda said gently. "We may not know what's going on yet, but I suspect there is much good you can do in the Skyr. It won't be easy, but most things worth doing aren't."

Gustave sighed and stood. Gently toppling the tower of mail, he couldn't help noticing how very many smallish, square, tidy letters he saw neatly addressed from the sorts of places that just flat out sounded gnomeric. Lots of Ks and Ps. He plucked up several and fanned them out toward Grinda like a deck of cards.

"I bet these are chock-full of Woe," he said darkly.

"Woeful indeed, I'm sure, your majesty. Let me get started on the details of your trip."

Grinda swept out of the mail roome, and Gustave took up his letter opener and selected a small, square envelope with a return address in Nokanen. He had research to do. He was the king now, and his Nooperkinses needed him.

12.

SURROUNDED BY DISTRESSINGLY BEARDLESS CHINS AND THE GRUMBLES OF THE ELDERLY

"Ping-Pong balls spend more time on Pell as metaphors than they do as necessary components of a sport."

—ZHOU SANCHEN, in *The Secret Lives of Balls*

Offi all but fell through the human-sized door, his pack tumbling from his callused hands onto a nicely swept floor. Finally, the Numminen family had reached the refugee center, and for one brief moment he did not feel dismal. He only felt relief.

The road to Bruding had been dusty and lonely at first, and then Seppo's pony whickered at some familiar smell. The Numminens had found a long line of gently smoldering gnomes toting their remaining unexploded possessions toward the human town of Bruding, where, rumor had it, they could live in peace, far from halfling malice, naked or otherwise. The road, at least, was kept clean by the nightly camps of gnomes settling around well-built fire pits. Wherever the soil by the cobblestone road was rich, vegetables and flowers grew in neat rows, which told Offi how many refugees had passed this way, planting a seed and leaving their trash in tidy compost heaps, as was the gnomeric fashion. It felt almost like a pleasant trip, until he thought of something he needed—a favorite mechanical pencil or delicate screwdriver or his pile of hoarded black yarn made from only the most nihilistic alpacas—and remembered that he'd left all his belongings at his halfling-bombed home, save this one small pack.

The bored human guarding the gate to the city of Bruding was the first one Offi had ever seen, outside of his schoolbooks, which had pictured humans with altogether more arms and sharper teeth. The guard had ordered the caravan to divide itself into groups of twenty, with each group sent to a different refugee center to ensure that supplies were distributed fairly. The card he handed Seppo gave roughly scrawled directions to a large building of the sort humans seemed to favor: boxy, shapeless, boring, yet without a single straight line. Offi considered the sign hanging outside particularly worrisome; it read, THE LORD ERGOT LIVING MEMORIAL PING-PONG PALACE AND REFUGEE CENTER, putting much more emphasis on the Ping-Pong than on the refugees, since the last bit was scrawled in an uneven hand while the first bit was nicely printed. The door was human-sized and had no handle within a gnome's reach, but when Seppo knocked, it swung open to reveal yet another armed and towering human. The fine hairs on the back of Offi's neck prickled. If this place was so safe and welcoming to gnomes, why were there so many armed human guards?

Seppo gave his card to the human within, and the human sighed and grumbled, "Come on, then. Almost at capacity as it is. The ponies will have to go."

"To where?" Onni asked.

"The hostler or the knacker, depending on how much money you have or need," the man said, looking crafty.

Onni dutifully led the family ponies to find a hostler, and Offi did the almost-falling-in-relief thing and took the extra bags to save his exhausted mother the burden. Seppo seemed distracted and unusually quiet.

The building inside was beyond disappointing. The crooked stone walls were dirty and scrawled with Pellican graffiti, the words so high, large, and grammatically horrific that they could only be the work of humans. The man led their group down a long hallway. They passed several closed doors and a befuddled but harmless-looking dwarf—but no halflings, at least.

Finally, the human stopped outside a closed door. Pulling a heavy ring of clanking keys from his belt, the man unlocked the door and pushed it open to reveal a room lined with uncomfortable-looking human-sized wooden bunks along two walls. A window let in just enough light to make it dreary beyond all hope.

As the man turned to leave, Offi looked to his father, but Seppo seemed a sad shade of his former self. No one else stepped forward with questions or thanks. Offi wished Onni was there, with his charisma and can-do attitude, but someone had to speak up. So Offi did, for all that he felt very awkward.

"Wait, if you please, sir. Can you tell us about this place? We've heard many rumors, but our people are frightened and could use some encouragement."

The guard spat on the ground, causing all the gnomes to shudder.

"It's a refugee center. You're refugees. So you stay until it's safe to go back home. Provisions arrive once a week. Each room handles its own problems."

Still, Seppo didn't speak, didn't lead. So Offi kept going.

"But who is in charge? How will we know when it's safe to leave?"

"The government is in charge, and they'll tell you when it's safe. That's the whole point of government, innit?" Shaking his head in disgust, the guard disappeared out the door, and Offi joined his fellow gnomes in a brief Incredible Sulk, their shoulders falling and the crowns of their knit hats tipping toward the ground.

Gnomes felt safest underground or, barring that, under a nice bush. They liked the company of their own kind but definitely required a reasonable amount of privacy for beard oiling and occasional hat removal. Sleeping here, in a large stone room surrounded by other gnomes, without walls or tents or hatches between them, felt as foreign as the thought of shaving one's beard off.

"We're doomed," Seppo said, right as Onni walked in. Offi was already nodding along with his father, his brief attempt at leadership having drained him completely. He felt out of sorts in so many ways, especially since his dated bug-out bag contained only cheerful cardigans a size too small, none of the comfortable black ones he'd knitted recently. Even worse, Onni's bag held . . . identical cardigans, down to the embroidered unicorns.

But Onni did that thing he always did, the one where he put his hands on his hips and looked around as if the sun was always rising on a fine and frolicsome day, and it seemed to Offi that a golden light always shone on his brother, what with his good eyes and strong chin and the way his hair tended to make one perfect little blond curl on his forehead. Onni, he thought, would look quite good wearing a cape.

It wasn't that Offi didn't like his brother; it was just that he was realizing that Onni was like a lantern, while Offi was more like a cold, inky cave, an endless tunnel of darkness and echoes. He'd even written some poetry recently that, he felt, expanded on this metaphor in a way that a kuffeehouse full of other people in black might appreciate, if he could ever find such a magical place. He grimaced as his twin began to speak.

"We're not doomed," Onni said with great confidence. "We must stay positive. I looked in the other refugee rooms on my way in—the doors were open, after all—and it would appear we can modify whatever we want, chop up the furniture to build things of the proper size. The humans don't seem to notice much. A little building, a little trading, a little painting tulips and polka dots, and we'll have this place gnomeworthy in no time."

Venla raised her head and tugged her beard with pride, but Old Seppo's head still hung. The fiery determination he'd shown earlier to return to their gnomehome and take vengeance on the halflings had somehow been extinguished.

"Uh, sure," Offi said, trying to be supportive for the sake of his parents. He wasn't accustomed to seeing them gloomier than he felt, and it was rattling.

And then, as usual, Onni decided what was needed was a good old-fashioned quote from the *Book of Gnowledge*.

"If your life's not feeling that zing, an impossible project is just the thing!"

When Seppo didn't respond and none of the other, older gnomes took charge, Onni pointed at one of the bunks and asked, "Well, who has a saw? Let's get busy making some walls. Mother, perhaps you'd like to set up your cookpot by the window and get a pudding going? And, Offi . . ." He looked at his brother, and Offi hunched his shoulders and glared, fairly certain that Onni was about to turn him into an errand boy. "Why don't you investigate the building and see if there are any additional resources? Provisions, or wood we can build with, perhaps?"

"Fine," Offi grumbled, because arguing with Onni just now would leave him up to his ears in gnomeric aphorisms and clever rhymes about *zep* and *pep*. Around him, the Sulk became a Coalescing. The gnomes looked up, one by one, smiling, reaching for their saws and mallets and pudding spoons. Although Offi's instinct was to trade a lemon-yellow cardigan for some black yarn and find a quiet corner in which to start knitting until he felt like himself again, Onni clapped him on the back and shoved him toward the open door, so out the door Offi went, adjusting his large glasses so that he wouldn't stumble. He wanted to get away from his brother—from everybody, for privacy had been impossible on the trail and all the gnomes were too fond of square dancing—so he stepped into the hall and set about exploring the rest of the facility, although he silently committed to not enjoying it.

He passed two more closed doors but was too short to open them and see if they contained yet more aggressively large beds. The first open door he found led to the largest room he'd ever seen, big enough to fill with every gnome and donkey he'd ever met and still have room for an entire forest and his own black heart. This room was approximately half full of Ping-Pong tables, each as tall as two gnomes and painted a virulent green. So now he knew where they could get more lumber, at least. Running calculations, he returned to the hall-way and headed for the next open door. That one held a break room of sorts, with four generally unkempt and impossibly identical humans playing cards and drinking a foul brown brew from wooden cups. Offi was scandalized at their lack of beards and had to purposefully look away from their clammy chins and nude throats, some peppered with a shocking fuzz of stubble. Thank goodness his mother wasn't there to see it.

"What're you looking at, shrimp?" one asked with a sneer.

Offi had never been challenged by a human before and was nearly too surprised to respond.

"I'm looking at four humans loafing about," he answered, telling the truth because he assumed that they could smell lies, the way snakes and foxes could.

The human who had addressed him—he thought? They were so similar—stood, his chair falling with a dangerous clatter.

"I'll stomp you into the ground for that, you little frog!" he boomed, and Offi took off running before the man could fulfill his promise. Humans, apparently, took offense easily. Perhaps their naked necks made them overly sensitive.

As quick as his legs could take him, Offi bolted down the hall, terrified at every moment that he would hear the giant boots pounding behind him, the human's foul drool raining from above as he scented his prey. Wait—could humans smell their prey, or did they sense movement or heat? Offi hadn't paid much attention in his Taller-Folk Biology class. He dove into the next open door, rolled into a ball, and hoped he'd fetch up behind a convenient Ping-Pong table. Instead, he slammed into something big and warm that swayed like a tree in a storm but did not fall over, and someone blurted out, "Oh, my sad unbuttered toast, I do beg your pardon!"

Another voice, and a very familiar one, laughed joyously. "Offi Numminen, what do you think you're doing? And is that a yellow cardigan?"

What he found when he uncurled and stood up was so bizarre

that he completely forgot about the angry human clamoring for his blood. First, there was the confused dwarf he'd seen earlier, as wide and thick as a boulder, standing around twice the height of a gnome, sporting a fine and bushy beard, and smiling shyly. And beside the dwarf was Kirsi Noogensen, grinning at him, a basket of fresh mushrooms at her feet.

"Kirsi? But how?"

Instead of responding, she hug-tackled him, squeezing the breath from his lungs and making him squeak in an undignified manner. It was the closest Offi had ever been to a girl he wasn't related to, all squashed together down the front, and a confusing tumult of feelings tumbled through him. He'd noticed Kirsi in class, of course—she was sprightly and good-natured, round as an apple, with a lovely red beard—but he'd never expected to be on the breathless receiving end of one of her hugs. Her woolen cardigan was especially attractive, navy blue with embroidered pine cones. But then he realized he probably shouldn't be looking at her pine cones and he blushed and looked away.

"Oh, Offi! I can't believe you're alive! When I saw the bomb go off, I just—"

"Wait," he interrupted, untangling from her and stepping back. "What do you mean, when you saw the bomb go off?"

At that, Kirsi's cheeks reddened and she fiddled with her beard. "I was walking past your place, and I saw the halflings bomb your main hatch, so I . . ."

"Ran away?"

"Cursed them."

"Oh."

Kirsi was watching him carefully to see how he took this information. Offi knew Kirsi's grandmother was a famous bristle witch, and it was whispered that Kirsi might've inherited some of her magic, but thus far she hadn't made her powers public. It was rather a surprise to find out her magic was of the cursing sort rather than blessing, as bristle witches could generally only do one or the other. No wonder she'd kept it quiet. Some people would've drawn unwelcome conclusions and treated her differently because of her curses; if there was one thing gnomes hated, it was being different. Except for Offi, who actively liked things that were different. His estimation of her went up a bit, and he tried to imagine her in a black cardigan with embroidered poisoned apples. Darkly winsome, it would be.

"So what did your curse do to them?" he asked.

Kirsi brightened for a moment before a pall of rage narrowed her eyes. "Well, I thought they'd killed your whole family, didn't I? So I sort of set their chest hair on fire. But if you're alive, that means Onn—I mean, your whole family is safe?"

Offi shrugged. "Safe, if unsettled. My father's given up hope. But Onni went to work, getting everyone motivated to make the space bearable. You know how he is. We just got here, you see. And then I met some humans, and . . . well, one of them mistook me for an amphibian, which is an error in perception so profound I cannot explain it. I just ran."

Kirsi nodded along. "They're as big and beastly and stupid as we were taught, but with rather fewer arms, don't you think? But so rude. Almost as if they don't want us here, at our own refugee center! But, Offi, you simply must meet my new friend . . . ?"

She looked at the dwarf, who bowed and said, "Bǻggi Biins, at your service!"

"Boggy beans?" Offi said, confused, making the dwarf wince politely.

"Yes, I can see by your face you're thinking I've been named after legumes native to a bog, but I assure you my parents would never do such a thing. It is simply that dwarvelish names often have unfortunate homophones in Pellican."

That didn't clear anything up for Offi, who knew even less about dwarves than he did humans. Gnomes generally kept to themselves. Dwarves, at least, were rumored to have the normal number of teeth and arms, along with a comforting number of beards and a talent for knitting when the mood took them.

"We were just meeting when you rolled in, and Bãggi doesn't know anyone else here either." Kirsi looked down, tucking one toe tip under the other shyly. "I'm the only gnome here without a family, it seems."

That got Offi's attention, and he completely forgot the dwarf, even though he was staring straight at the stout fellow's shiny belt buckle, which was shaped like a bumblebee on a flower.

"But where's your family? They didn't get—"

He buttoned his lip before he could say the word *exploded*.

There were no words that seemed sufficient and polite for discussing what happened when one's home was at the business end of a halfling firebomb.

"I don't think so." Kirsi avoided his eyes. "When I saw what happened to your home, I ran. My parents would never leave. They're too dug in. Unwilling to change. So I sent them a missive and followed a donkey trail into the brush."

"Hey, that was our donkey, Happy Mumbletoes! And you followed us all the way here?"

"Mostly. I couldn't stay a minute more once I saw your farm get attacked."

"That sounds like a reasonable course of action."

But it didn't. Gnomes were family creatures. For a gnome to leave home, alone, was extremely ungnomeric. And when things got ungnomeric, gnomes didn't know what to do. Offi had previously pegged Kirsi as being just like any other gnome, which was supposedly a great compliment. But as he considered that perhaps she was quite different and had secretly always been so, he felt a certain kinship.

He was about to ask her how she felt about bats when the dwarf chose that moment to stick his hand straight down, grab Offi's hand, and shake it gently but vigorously.

"Hello, good friend, hello! If only we might have a cup of tea together in peace, but I fear the facilities don't lend themselves to that sort of thing." Craning his head, Offi could tell that despite his friendliness, the dwarf was as out of his depth as everyone else. "Unless you know where we might find some hot water? Or perhaps you'd be interested in a bit of honeycomb on crackers? I just really feel like eating something comforting right now, you know?"

Gently slipping his hand away, Offi gave the dwarf a smile that he hoped was comforting. "Food would be good. My father—no, my brother, actually—sent me out to see what sort of resources I could find. He was thinking of building materials, but food is a resource too, and our people will be hungry after today's long walk. Not that we have nothing—we have a pudding on. You're both welcome to join us, I'm sure, as soon as it's ready." His eyes traced Båggi's squar-ish head, lush and covet-worthy beard, and round belly, which could probably contain an entire human-sized bowl full of jelly. "If you're not too terribly hungry?"

"Oh, my spicy brown mustard," the dwarf said, eyes going wide in shock. "I would never want to leave anyone hungry. It is the dwarvel-ish way to bring more food than you take, and I have some fine dry goods from a farmhouse." Båggi's eyes took on a faraway, haunted cast. "So long as there's no cabbage, I should be glad of the company. Beyond glad, really."

"Come along, then. I'll need to finish my lap around the building, make sure I can give a full report when we return." That was another new feeling—knowing that others were counting on him. Especially with Seppo having lost his conviction, Offi wanted to do a good job for his people, for all that he would prefer to do it in black eyeliner and a black cardigan.

Offi led the way with more confidence than he felt, hoping Kirsi would see him as mature and effective, a Gnome of Certainty. He realized, as he strode down the echoing hall, that the person to whom he would be giving said report was his brother, and he wondered if his father had yet regained his wits. Old Seppo had always seemed strong, secure, and powerful to his sons, but Offi worried about what had happened to his father's spirit and abilities since they'd left their home. It was as if he'd left his old self behind in the masterpiece of his architectural career. Could one's attachment to material comforts have such a powerful hold on one's faculties? If so, the halflings had firebombed more than a mere gnomehome.

As they walked, he looked in each open door, gauging what could be taken for building purposes and what was already committed to other uses. Many of the rooms appeared to have been stripped, including an exercise room bereft of metal but dotted with human-sized mats and ropes. They passed a padded room utterly bouncing with gnomelets, watched over by some exhausted-looking gnome matriarchs with gray hair and frayed nerves. The kitchen, sadly, was guarded by a snarling human with a terrifying mace of the smacking and not the flavoring sort, and so Offi could only conclude that there would be no sharing of provisions.

Armed with the general information that the refugee center was a dismal place where they weren't so much being welcomed as tolerated, Offi led Kirsi and Båggi back toward the room, where, hopefully, Onni had lit a cheery fire under gnomeric buns and gotten everyone to work on beds and puddings and sanitation and other things a gnome needs.

But before they reached the right room, the front door burst open, vomiting forth a very strange group of people. Two of them appeared to be half person, half sheep, and all frantic, while the third person wasn't really a person at all. It was a gnomeric construct—of that much Offi was certain. The workmanship was familiar somehow, and he longed to inspect the creation himself, to see the intricate gears and carefully fitted machinery within. Here and there, small glints gleaming in a fresh nick or scratch suggested the construct was gold and that it had once shone like the sun, for all that it was now tarnished brown, its crevices gummed up with dirt and sand. A golden jewel glinted from its forehead, and even though its eyes were dark and its mouth was barely a suggestion, Offi felt as if this automaton saw him. And smiled. Something tickled the back of Offi's brain like a childhood fairy tale, half forgotten.

"You there," the sheep man said, straightening his corduroy jacket over a stained white turtleneck as he pinned Offi in a commanding glare. "You're a gnome, right?"

Offi gave Kirsi a look, but Kirsi being Kirsi, she bustled forward, waggling a finger.

"That's no way to greet someone, my good sir! You might begin with a hello, or a how-do-you-do, or at least offer a smile. *A greeting smile will go a mile,* you know."

Offi felt the slightest bit of twitterpation to hear her spouting off the usual gnomeism while scolding a complete stranger.

The man shook his head, his ears flapping.

"No time for niceties, kid. We're on a time crunch to pay escrow, and closing papers don't wait. Now, is either of you a Certified Gnomeric Gearhaaand?"

The term was unfamiliar to Offi, but his heart was seized with a Sudden Fervor. He was a gnome, that was very true, and he had very handy hands when it came to gears. Having learned at Old Seppo's side, he was confident in his skills with any gnomeric construct or gadget. He couldn't wait to get his hands on this old automaton and crack it open. And so he did a very deeply ungnomeric thing.

He lied for the first time in his life.

"Why, I certainly am, sir," he said.

"But—" Kirsi started, and he spoke right over her.

"But I didn't bring my certificate. You're right, Kirsi! It was in the workshop when my family was forced to abandon our exploded home and flee the halflings. But I assure you that if you need someone to look at your automaton, I'm the gnome to do it."

"Look aaat it?" the man bleated. "I want you to take it! Shut it down! It won't listen to me anymore, and it won't stop following me, and I would certainly write a sternly worded letter to a maaanager if I could find the right one."

"My husband used to be a Vartija," the woman whispered in the sort of loud voice that wanted to be overheard, drawing the singed edges of a colorful caftan around her shoulders with her nose in the air. "But now we're private citizens. Caaan't go play Bunko with that thing hulking behind us, caaan we?"

"I'd be glad to take possession of it," Offi said, trying to hide his huge smile.

But every time the sheep folk attempted to leave, waving and bursting with their goodbyes, the metal man followed them. No matter how loudly and rudely they spoke to him, no matter what names they called him, he kept plodding right after them.

"This is insufferaaaable," the woman moaned.

Offi cocked his head and stared at the automaton's back, which hinted at some kind of script under the muck. Although he longed to inspect every crevice of this device, it would be far more instructive if there weren't two histrionic sheep people moaning at him while he did it. And then he remembered something Seppo had taught him on his fifth birthday, when he'd received My First Futzing Kit, a toolbox full of perfect little screwdrivers and hammers and wrenches.

"All gnomeric devices have a fail-safe," Offi said, quoting his father.

"Oh, the jewel won't come out," the sheep man said. "Believe me, we've tried."

But Offi just shook his head and said, "Please keep him still."

The sheep folk froze in place, and the automaton froze in place, and Offi went to the back of its right ankle and found the three perfect little buttons hidden under the grime, their shapes chased into the design so flawlessly that no one would notice them—unless their father was a celebrated inventor who'd passed down the old ways of Alphagnomeric gadgetry.

"Control, alt, delete," he muttered, pressing all three buttons at once.

"The jewel! It's not glowing!" the sheep man said, stating the obvious as if it were surprising.

"He's suspended," Offi said proudly. "So you should be able to leave. I won't reactivate him until you've had some time to—"

He was about to say "escape," but Kirsi broke in with a far more polite "make that important meeting of yours."

"Excellent!" the sheep woman cried.

"Aaand we're off," her husband exclaimed. They hurried toward the door on clicking trotters, and the man turned back. "Oh, and if you should see a younger ovitaur girl named Agape, please tell her to remember to write us. We left her a caaard with our address."

"But we won't be ready for visitors until after renovating!" the woman called.

And then they were gone, leaving the automaton with Offi.

"Oh, my metallic mumblety-peg, do you think it's hungry?" Båggi said. "I did not wish to intrude, as such constructs are not the realm of my people, but I might have some Corti Corter's Crusty Cocoa Coins, if you think he might need sustenance?"

"He doesn't need any," Offi said, but kindly. "Very thoughtful of you." He walked around the automaton, fingers itching to pry open its chest plate and see what wonders waited inside. He'd need a ladder, or maybe some scaffolding, and a tool kit, and a very tiny headlamp, and—

"Something about this isn't right," Kirsi said.

But Offi could only gaze up at the automaton in wonder.

"You're right. He could use a coat of black paint."

13.

Under the Grim Weight of an Implacable Iron Toe Ring

"The heart of halfling art is the river city of Muffincrumb. Once you've sampled the craft of their brewers, distillers, and vintners, you will doubtless be robbed shortly afterward, either by scalawags or by the city's artisans, who charge an exorbitant premium for their work. It's best to stay out of halfling cities, honestly, if you enjoy holding on to your money or your life. Gnomeric cities are far more orderly places to visit if you want to see the Skyr and come back alive with knickknacks, woolen cardigans, and vaguely amusing anecdotes about pudding with which to bore your friends."

—Yaz Morfulgent, in *Plausibly Safe Pellish Vacations for the Unwary Traveler*

"Nah, that's all dirty lies from jealous gnomes. Come on down to Muffincrumb and find friendly faces and reasonably priced caricatures drawn by humble and mostly harmless artisans. Why, if you get killed here, I'll give you your money back, plus a coupon for one free ale at Le Backstabber Bar."

—Glaceau Soupernougat of the Muffincrumb Soupernougats, Muffincrumb Tourism Bureau

Faucon the hunter stood alone in his tent, stared at his freshly groomed feet, wiggled his well-kempt toes, and sighed. This morning he had gone to the trouble to wash his feet with LaVergne Treaclesweet's No-Soot Foot Soap and follow up with a thick application of Dr. Torrance Ocean's Liquid Locomotion Pedicare Lotion before putting on his favorite celebratory sapphire toe ring, reserved only for special victories—but he had done so all too early. Gerd had not delivered his prey.

He slipped the prized sapphire bauble off his toe, placed it in his velvet-lined ring case, and instead put on the Bland Iron Ring of Failure. The metal's chill seemed to spread up from his toe, bypassing his carefully oiled foot hair, and encompassing his heart. He did so hate to fail, and this would be his punishment, a reminder to squeeze every possible drop of information out of the ovitaur.

He settled into the routine of making omelets for the gryphon and then more for himself and the drubs, making four at once and going through several dozen eggs in the process. It was calming—all the exact measurements of ingredients, the art of flipping an egg flapjack. After he fed the throng, he set one beautifully fluffy omelet before the ovitaur, who could not even begin to eat it, tied as she was to her chair. Faucon remained pleasant throughout. First breakfast was close to sacred to halflings, constituting the end of many hours without food. Second breakfast could occasionally be skipped, but the first meal of the day needed to happen early and it needed to be filling. After second breakfast came time for a bite of something, then luncheon, with second luncheon as an encore, then snacksies or tea before apple time, then proper dinner, and finally second dinner, which was often taken at a local Dinny's chain restaurant just so a body didn't spend all day doing dishes and getting pruney fingers. A bit of a snack could happen anytime one felt peckish, which was most of the time.

Faucon left the cleanup to a few of the drubs and approached the ovitaur and gryphon, his pin-striped waistcoat stretched tight over his belly.

"Now. On to business. You have eaten your requested repast. I have fulfilled my half of the bargain. We find ourselves having a beautiful day with a gorgeous blue sky—"

It's blü, Gerd corrected him.

"As you say, Gerd." The gryphon's insistence that he pronounce colors only she could see had once troubled him, but he'd since grown to find it endearing, much like his grandfather's penchant for blanket forts.

He turned his attention to the ovitaur. She wore a camouflage tunic over her torso and a small diamond stud in her left nostril. Her skin had cool undertones to the deep umber, and she kept her hair trimmed close to the skull, with expressive lamb-like ears on either side; they were currently drooping angrily. She had the air of the hunted about her, as if she trusted no one.

As if she could not be broken.

If he wanted information, Faucon had work to do. He would start with emotion and charisma, and if that didn't work . . . well, she would learn how the drubs had earned their reputation for foul deeds. He put on a winning smile.

"Hello. We have not been properly introduced. With whom do I have the pleasure of speaking this morning?"

Ah, yes, Faucon thought. *Smooth. The charm is still there.*

"Why should I tell you, drub?"

Faucon flashed a grin. "You should tell me because you are tied to a chair, surrounded by enemies, and being glared at by a gryphon who would tear out your intestines like vermicelli."

I would not! Gerd interjected. *I told you, Faucon. She is honorable.*

"That may be," he said to both of them, "but she must cooperate if I am to judge her merits on my own. Now, what is your name?"

Please speak to Faucon, Gerd urged. *He is reasonable. He cares about the law above all else. He has a law degree in a fancy frame.*

The ovitaur looked from the gryphon to the omelet placed just out of reach on the table, and her stomach growled. "Fine. My name is Agape Fallopia." Her eyes said she was scared, but her frown said she was angry about it. "Aaand you are?"

"Faucon Pooternoob of the Toodleoo Pooternoobs." He executed a slight bow to make her feel at ease.

The girl's eyes widened. "*The* Faucon? The famous hunter?"

"The very same."

Agape's curiosity briefly overcame her caution. "How'd you find us?"

"I regret to inform you that the witch who owns that chicken shack also took payment to tell my associate of your rental agreement."

Agape snorted. "Oh. Cluck money. So it waaas betrayal that brought you here and not your skill. Good to know."

Faucon smiled, knowing that she was trying to wound his pride, but he had no doubts regarding his skills. One accepted all help in bringing down prey.

"Tell me, Agape, why is your family so desperate to protect that gnomeric automaton?" She simply stared at him without replying, and he returned it for a full minute. "Oh. Is it a secret?"

Tell him, Gerd said.

"Or else," Faucon added to maintain the proper level of menace.

"We are Vartijas of the Elders. Protecting the automaatti has been our faaamily's task for generations."

Faucon shrugged at what was largely a gabble of nonsense to him. "That tells me nothing. The Elder Annals have been lost for centuries, and therefore the laws therein cannot be debated."

"Perhaaaps you should first tell me why you want Piini, then."

The hunter looked down at his splendid feet, eyeing the Ring of Failure. It was giving him a bit of a rash, but he did deserve it. What he did not deserve, however, was an interrogation turning back on him.

"I think not. You tell me where the automaton is." He carefully pulled a small metal-toothed comb from one of the many pockets in his waistcoat. "Or else . . . THE COMB."

The drubs outside all gasped audibly, and the ovitaur looked to Gerd in confusion.

"The . . . comb?" the ovitaur asked, uncertain.

He has many tortures beyond my ken, Gerd admitted.

"The comb." Faucon held it up as if admiring it. "Nothing special. Just a dastardly little enchanted device with a penchant for tangling toe hair. Or, in your case, wool." He suddenly slammed his hand on the table before Agape, making the omelet and silverware jump. She bleated and struggled backward. "One rake from this comb, and you will never get your wool untangled. The tiny hairs will entwine permanently." He leaned in, and she flinched away, eyes shut. His mustache close enough to tickle her ear, he whispered, "You will have a wool wedgie for the rest of your life."

The moment strung out, and a tiny bleat of fear escaped the ovitaur, which pleased Faucon greatly.

"I don't know," she whispered.

He took a step back, arms crossed, careful to keep the comb away from his own wrist hair. "Do you not?"

The ovitaur shook her head. "When Gerd caaaptured me, they raaan away. My paaarents and Piini. The automaton you want. So, no, I don't know where they aaare."

"You're lying." Faucon winced, realizing he was so upset he'd used a contraction.

But Agape didn't argue the point. She looked up, her eyes glowing with rage. "Aaand what would you do with the automaton if you did find it?"

"Destroy it."

There was no gasp of shock or horror. She'd clearly expected his response, which wasn't the most fun way for an interrogation to go. "Why?" she asked.

"Because that is my task."

"You mean because someone is paying you."

"That too, perhaps. I have my reasons."

The ovitaur spat, and Faucon danced back lest her spittle touch his beloved feet.

"Just like a haaalfling, to destroy something he caaan't understaaand!"

Faucon put the comb back in his pocket and stepped forward again, as gingerly as he had first approached Gerd. Threats weren't working so well with the ovitaur, so he would try charm again. At the very least, it would leave her confused.

"Then help me understand, Agape Fallopia."

Gently, he took up the spoon on the table, cut off a corner of the omelet, and held it out to her. The ovitaur tried to resist, but as Faucon had learned upon meeting Gerd, fluffy omelets were impossible to resist, especially if one was hungry. Agape turned her face this way and that, screwed her eyes shut, flapped her ears, but eventually gave in and snarfed down the eggy deliciousness.

"Now talk," Faucon urged.

Agape chewed and swallowed and sighed before saying, "Look. The automaatti is a baaarely functioning lump of tarnished metal and gummed-up gears. He's never threatened a halfling. So why would anyone waaant him destroyed so baaadly?"

Faucon waggled a finger at her. "I was rather hoping you could tell me."

Agape shrugged. "I caaan't. We have no idea why he's important."

The halfling threw his hands wide. "Well, if it is unimportant and barely functional, why not let us take it off your hands so you can do something beautiful with your life?"

Agape glared at him. "Well, if he's unimportant and baaarely functional, why not let me go so you caaan hunt down something beautiful aaand, I don't know, take its life? Isn't thaaat what you do, Faucon the hunter?"

Faucon hated to admit it but, despite his earlier threats, the ovitaur was defying all expectation. And the truths she was revealing about the gnomeric construct were troubling. Faucon had been told it was dangerous, outfitted with numerous anti-halfling weapons of aggression, from toe stompers to depilating wands. That's why he'd sent Gerd after it. But now . . . well, if it was useless, why was it so dangerous?

"Hunting the automaton is not a personal vendetta; it is a matter of law and therefore principle. The kanssa-jaarli outlawed such automatons three years ago."

"Whaaat? But the kanssa-jaarli is one gnome and one haaalfling, ruling the Skyr together, right? So why would a gnome ever agree to outlawing gnomeric automatons?"

Faucon shook his head, his eyes narrowed and his stomach eager for a small bite of something to help him think. "Not all gnomeric automatons. Just the dangerous ones. Just the kind you are protecting."

"But why haven't I heard of such a law? I mean, we've visited cities in the Skyr during the paaast three years. We've been around plenty of gnomes too, aaand none of them ever said, *Hey, thaaat automaton is illegal now.*"

"I cannot explain what you may have heard. Ignorance is no excuse. But the law exists."

The ovitaur nodded along like they were in this together now and she wasn't tied to a chair. "So you work for the kanssa-jaarli? The government is funding you?"

"No. I am funded by—" Faucon was cut off by a noise behind him. Bernaud Cobbleshod, who'd been hovering in the background, stepped forward with a cocky grin and spoke up.

"We don't work for the kanssa-jaarli." Cobbleshod paused to belch robustly. "Our loyalty is to Marquant Dique. And we don't owe answers to you, lamb gams."

Agape snorted at Bernaud with the same sort of revulsion Faucon felt. "Marquant Dique, infamous leader of the Daaastardly Rogues, is funding a hunt for automaatti to hold up the law? Kind of makes you question the legitimacy of thaaat law, doesn't it?"

Her eyes met Faucon's, and he was only somewhat troubled to realize he was more compelled by her argument than by the promise of ample remuneration.

This law is not legitimate, Gerd broke in, and all eyes swung to her. *Agape and her family are Vartijas of the Elders. The laws from the Elder Annals supersede any law recently made by your kanssa-jaarli.*

"Bleh," Cobbleshod said. "That giant chicken is talking nonsense."

Gerd ruffled her feathers in indignation, but Faucon ignored the drub and the offensive green fuzz growing on Cobbleshod's hairy toes. "Your people have better memory of such things, Gerd. Who are these Elders, and what is a Vartija?"

The Elders led the world before your silly kings and earls and lords and kanssa-jaarli. Every race had their own Elders, and there was also a Convocation of Elders from all races that ruled the world, and their laws were the foundation of civilization. I will have you know that the Convocation of Elders made no law regarding egges and I have broken no law from the Elder Annals.

"Of course," Faucon said, sensing that it was the right thing to say. "You would never do that."

Correct. And the Convocation of Elders would never make such a shortsighted decree, not about egges and not about robottes. They took the long view—so long, in fact, that they foresaw their own decline. And they saw that there were wonders of their tyme that should survive until our tyme. Recipes, for example. Did you know that somewhere there is an archive of recipes guarded by Vartijas? Imagine the quiches and sauces untasted by modern tongues! And—

"Tell me more about the Vartijas, please."

They are guardians of knowledge and sometimes hold the keys to hidden archives and treasures. Whatever they protect is immensely valuable and should not be destroyed.

"Piini is vaaaluable?" Agape said.

"Hidden archives?" Faucon said.

"The key to treasures?" Bernaud said, hairy fingers twitching against his knife. "This ovitaur girl holds the keys to treasures? D'ye think they're in her chest cavity?"

Gerd continued as if they had not spoken. *The yellö man that I could not move was important to the Elders, Faucon. To all of them—the convocation, I mean, not just the gnomeric Elders. Otherwise it would not have ovitaur Vartijas protecting it through generations.*

Bernaud stepped up, his knife drawn, showing a rime of honey and dirt on the blade. "All I know is Marquant Dique don't care about archives or varmints, or whatever she is. He wants the treasure, and he wants that automaton. And I want to know what you mean to do about that, Pooternoob."

"My intention has not changed, Bernaud. But I must complete my interrogation. The horrible tortures will begin shortly. Please go help your men clean up the dishes from breakfast and begin chopping the mirepoix for second breakfast."

"I'll chop you," Bernaud muttered, but he obeyed.

At the word *tortures*, Agape had drawn back against her chair, but Faucon didn't move toward her. He lowered his voice, confident that the gryphon could hear him. "Would you mind telling me, Gerd, how you know that Agape is a Vartija? Are you merely accepting her word?"

No. She has the aura. I can see it. All gryphones can.

"I have an aura?" Agape said. "What does it look like?"

It is like lemon ice drizzled with mäple syrup.

"You mean maple syrup?"

No, I mean mäple. Respect the umlaut.

"And because she is a Vartija," Faucon continued, "you think the automaton should not be destroyed."

Correct. It would violate Elder Law, which is the highest law. Therefore, Faucon, I will not help you retrieve the yellö man. I will help this Vartija protect it from you, in fact.

"You will?" Agape and Faucon said simultaneously.

I will.

That changed Faucon's calculations considerably. Gryphons could be bought with rare foodstuffs or particularly nice ribbons, but they rarely committed themselves to a cause for free unless they felt it to be unimpeachably noble.

Faucon felt a turbulent flutter in his lungs, like someone had stuck a fork in there and twirled his tissue around it like strings of pasta. He knew it meant he was feeling emotions, but he didn't have a name for them yet. There were probably several of them that needed to be sorted out.

Faucon didn't particularly like emotions. He liked laws, and emotions just got in the way.

But the emotions didn't seem to care. He'd been lied to by the drubs, so there was anger. And horror that he'd lost a year of his life to a lie, thinking he was behaving righteously. Also shame that he'd not figured it out sooner, and a flailing uncertainty about what to do next. He needed to anchor himself to certainty, fast, and so he began talking, waggling his fingers about in distemper and pacing back and forth in front of the gryphon and ovitaur.

"I am one who upholds the law. I need you to understand that about me. I lost a loved one because gnomeric architects—the same ones who are so famed for their skills—did not adhere to the law and erected a statue without following specified civil building codes. It was a statue of Hedvige Hootleboop of the Toodleoo Hootleboops, renowned founder of Hootleboop Foods, which employed and fed so many halflings in our part of the Skyr." Faucon's vision blurred as his eyes swam with tears. "Remy and I were at the Caskcooper city square the day after the erection, admiring the fine bronze figure and enjoying our midday repast, for one did Hedvige the greatest honor by eating in front of her.

And then a child—a mere halfling child—threw herself at the skirts of the statue to give Hedvige Hootleboop a hug. And this simple act toppled the statue in our direction! It should have been impossible, you see? It was criminal negligence by the gnomes. The statue was said to be untoppleable. Remy and I were both eating and didn't see it coming until it was too late. Remy was crushed to death by Hedvige's heavy bronze bosom—all because the gnomes had ignored the law. It was ruled an accident. But I held those gnomes responsible, in Remy's memory. I hunted the architects down and fed them to the boars in the Pruneshute Forest. And I continue to hold lawbreakers responsible whenever the system fails." Faucon sniffled and wiped away tears with the heel of his hand. "That is why I have been pursuing you, Agape: I was convinced your automaton was another gnomeric abomination of law like the one that killed Remy."

Agape's chin wagged and her ears twitched with sheepish surprise, but she shook her head and refocused. "Oh, no, the automaatti is harmless. And if I may say so, I'm very sorry to hear what haaappened to Remy."

Faucon relaxed just a little, as if a storm had passed. "Thank you. For the sympathy, and for your patience with this interrogation. It would seem the drubs want to eliminate all gnomeric constructs and are not above lying and even manipulating the law to make sure it happens. I was told that all such automatons posed an imminent danger to halflings. I do not doubt a word of what you've told me, and of course Gerd's word is impeccable, but I have much cause to doubt the word of Marquant Dique. That does present me with a problem, however."

"Which is?"

Faucon spun around at the approach of malevolent footsteps.

"What is it, Bernaud?"

The drub's body language contained no hint of deference, Faucon noted. It was aggressive, ready to attack. And his chest hair was full of onion skin.

"Thought I heard you say you doubt Marquant Dique."

"And if I *did* say that?"

"Well, then, we'd have something to say about that. Wouldn't we, lads?" Behind Bernaud, eleven halflings with soiled toenails and dirty gold medallions entered the tent and fanned out. Faucon noted that none of them had brought their bags of ordnance with them. It would be fists and hand weapons only, but twelve against one. They were not good odds, and the law would not provide any aid.

"What is this?" Faucon asked, moving around the table and behind Agape.

"You been listening to that stupid chicken and this dumb sheep," Bernaud sneered.

"Gryphons are not in the habit of lying, Bernaud. Drubs, on the other hand—"

"You told Marquant you would destroy the automaton, and you didn't do it. So who's the liar here?"

Faucon slipped a hand into his pocket, grasping his pocketknife. "It cannot be done."

"What do you mean? Make the mutton take us to it!"

Moving his hand to Agape's wrists, Faucon used his pocketknife to slice the ropes there, hoping the ovitaur had the good sense not to show her hand.

"She is free to go."

"She's heckin' not!" Bernaud waved his hand. "Get her, boys. Get 'em all!"

As two of the halflings moved to obey, Faucon whipped five-pointed throwing stars out of his waistcoat and tossed them at the drubs. It was so unexpected—the thought of him physically attacking them so unthinkable—that they didn't even duck. The stars thunked into their foreheads and the two fell over in a mortal chorus of surprise.

"As I said, she is free to go," Faucon repeated. "But you are not. You have all mutinied, the sentence for which is death, and as the captain in the field, I must administer justice by myself. Such is the law."

Ten against one now, but Faucon didn't care if he died just so long as that sneering, mutinous, and profoundly unhygienic Bernaud Cobbleshod died first. He drew the daggers strapped inside his blazer sleeves, leapt over the table, and charged the leader of the drubs.

Cobbleshod slapped away Faucon's first knife, but the other one plunged into the ample belly fat on his right side. Cobbleshod howled and backed up, and Faucon helped him with a swift kick to the chest. The drub fought to keep his feet but then tumbled on his back. The hunter leapt after him and stomped on Cobbleshod's throat, crushing it with his recently exfoliated and moisturized foot.

But Faucon was only able to enjoy the victory for a mere fraction of a second.

Two drubs hooked him under either arm and pulled him off their leader, driving him to the ground and pounding the breath out of his lungs. A third and fourth dove for his hands and methodically broke his fingers until he surrendered his knives.

"My hands!" he muttered. "My beautiful, hairy fingers—"

A savage kick to his ribs from the side robbed him of breath, and his eyes filled since his lungs couldn't. He saw another drub raise his foot to stomp down on his privates, and he bid his precious stones a private farewell even as he wished the drubs would be as quick about dispatching him as he had been with Cobbleshod. Such politesse was not in the nature of Dastardly Rogues, however.

A blurred shape landed a flying kick to the mid-stomp drub. He squealed and fell across Faucon's legs as the blur resolved into Agape, who stuck the landing. She planted her hoof and lashed out with another kick to the forehead of the drub who'd broken Faucon's left hand and taken his knife. The halfling's noggin squelched like a melon, and Faucon looked up at the ovitaur with a new respect.

"How's thaaat for mutton legs?" she spat.

The other drubs could have simply backed away at that point and escaped, but instead they made the fatal error of trying to attack Agape.

Do not touch the Vartija! a voice shouted in his brain, and then Faucon saw halflings halved by a swipe of talons or their heads neatly snapped off their bodies like dead marigolds by a quick and darting beak. Gryphons were efficient killers when they wished to be, and Gerd was no exception. The gryphon made quick work of the remaining drubs as Faucon coughed and wheezed, trying to catch his breath.

"Aaare you all right?" Agape asked.

"No. Fingers broken," he managed. "But alive. You performed admirably, and I thank you."

"I would glaaadly throw in with aaanyone who's fighting drubs," she said. "But now I need to know ..." He looked up and she had raised a leg, her blood-splashed hoof hovering threateningly over his face. "Are you truly finished hunting my faaamily?"

With a dead drub over his legs and his fingers broken, Faucon couldn't even defend himself, and Gerd had made it clear she wouldn't hurt the ovitaur—even if said ovitaur was threatening Faucon. So he spoke honestly, because that was his way.

"I meant what I said. I renounce this task. You are free to go."

"Oh. Well, then. Uh."

The hoof returned to the ground, and the sheep girl looked sheepish. Faucon almost smiled, because she was so clearly grasping for something polite to say in such a situation but could not think of anything.

"May I ask if there might be a healer wherever you are heading? I think I require one."

Agape squatted, and their eyes met. "Are you sure I can trust you?"

I trust him with my life, Gerd said. *As I trust you. And I am pledged to protect you both. Which presents a conundrum.*

With a sigh, Agape stood. She looked to Gerd, then Faucon, then back to Gerd. Ever so slowly, she picked up the rest of the omelet she'd been denied, tossed half of it to Gerd, and took her time eating her portion with her hands. Finally she said, "Well, I was going to head to Bruding in Borix. That's where my faaamily was supposed to meet up if we were separated." At Faucon's flash of annoyance, she snorted. "I didn't lie, though—I don't know *exaaactly* where they are.

Just that we're meeting there eventually. I'm sure Bruding has maaany healers."

"In that case, may I accompany you?"

Agape shrugged and turned to Gerd. "What do you think?"

I will happily fly you both to Bruding, the gryphon said, *for thirty ladybugge omlets.*

14.

UNDER THE SALUBRIOUS INFLUENCE OF A MOST POTENT BONING TEA

"A skilled and well-supplied dwarvelish herbalist can whip up potions of near-miraculous powers. Unfortunately, they're not often abroad in the world, but you can find them in either Grundelbård or Sküterländ in the winters, when their high-elevation herb and flower fields are covered in snow. For that reason, the absolute best time and place to become deathly ill is in the winter on the west side of the Korpås Range."

—MÜDDI BLÜS, in *Competitive Aging: How to Outlive All Your Classmates*

Kirsi had never been particularly interested in machines, but she honestly didn't have much else to do in the refugee center, so she watched Offi inspect the automaton.

"What's his name?" he asked.

"According to the information on his back, he's called Piini Automaatti. Now, let's see what he has to say for himself."

Offi pressed something on the construct's ankle, and the gem in Piini's face flared green and then gold, and he appeared to peer down at the gnomes.

"Hello, my metal friend!" Båggi boomed, but the automaton did not react. "He must have crust in his ears," the dwarf finished weakly, fidgeting at being ignored.

In a commanding voice, Offi said, "Piini Automaatti, reveal your secrets."

For a long moment, Kirsi thought something might happen. And then she spent another long moment wishing she had blessing magic instead of cursing magic, as she could've blessed Offi to succeed but definitely couldn't curse him to do so. It was a shame he didn't need his chest hair set on fire—she was quite good at that. But even she had to admit that nothing was happening.

"Well, at least he isn't chasing after those stuck-up sheep people," Kirsi said, struggling, as always, to remain positive. "Perhaps he would make a nice coat rack?"

Just then there was a mighty din down the hall, replete with human cursing and inhuman shrieking, and Kirsi hurried to look toward whatever was clattering through the front door of the refugee center.

"That thing ain't allowed in here!" a human hollered. "Take it to the hostler or the knacker—"

"How daaare you? She'll take *you* to the knaaacker!" someone shouted. "This is a refugee center, so why don't you offer a refuge instead of threats?"

The first one through the door was a distrustful-looking young sheep person in a camouflage-print tunic, still shouting at the human guard. Then came the most terrifying of creatures, a halfling. Last came a slightly less terrifying beast Kirsi knew only from her *Gnome-Eating Monsters* book: a gryphon.

"Is there a designated area for foot sanitation?" the halfling asked the human, frowning at the drab gray walls. He was sweating and something was clearly wrong with his hands.

But the human, of course, merely slammed the door, nearly catching the gryphon's tail.

These tall, hairless creatures are quite rüde, someone said, almost as if in Kirsi's head. She shook herself, wondering if perhaps Piini's ear crust was somehow catching. As if sensing someone was in pain, Bāggi bustled out into the hallway and hurried, much to Kirsi's dis-

may and without any proper introductions, toward the injured halfling, who probably deserved any ouchies he was suffering.

"Oh, my crumbled cookies," Båggi said. "Would you like a handkerchief? I do think it's a proper time for a handkerchief, and you'll
definitely need one embroidered with something cheerful." The
dwarf laid down his burdens, dug around in one of his pockets, and
came out with an array of colorful squares. "Here. A bluebird suitable
for, er, bleeding."

He handed over the handkerchief, his dark-brown eyes shining
with concern, and the halfling tried to take it and failed. It fluttered
to the ground, and he looked away, pained.

"Thank you for that kindness, but I am afraid that what I really
require is a healer. The last one, well . . . they were not quite this bad
before. My knuckles. And I would greatly appreciate it if someone
might protect my velvet-lined toe-ring case from varlets. They are
always . . . trying to steal . . . my lucky charms . . ."

And with that, the halfling fainted.

Oh, no! As the gryphon fluttered worriedly around the halfling,
Kirsi realized it had to be the monster's voice echoing in her mind.
*Faucon has abandoned us for the realm of dreams! Quickly, smöl people!
Douse him with Salubrious Juice at once!*

"We don't have that," Kirsi said, a bit sniffy. "Although I might
have an Aide of Band."

"Oh, great gibbering gumdrop trees," Båggi murmured. "An Aide
of Band will never do! Perhaps I can be of service? I do have some
training in the healing arts. Although I've never heard of Salubrious
Juice, and I'd be most interested in the recipe, I do have several calming salves and a collection of loose-leaf teas."

"His fingers are broken," the young sheep person said, angrily
frowning over the fallen halfling. "I don't think tea caaan help thaaat."

Båggi awarded her the full shine of a dwarvelish grin. "Oh, my
dear durian dumplings, but the right tea can cure most anything!"

Kirsi had only known Båggi for an hour or so, but the dwarf's
transformation was impressive. As soon as he had a job to do, he

went from shy and clumsy to determined and cheerful—well, *more* cheerful. Bäggi's eyes sparkled as he carefully picked up the fainted halfling, carried him back into the room where Offi was still working on his beloved automaton, and placed Faucon on one of the many human-sized beds.

"Piini Automaatti?" the sheep person cried, running to the machine and throwing her arms gently around him to avoid bruising herself.

Offi, who had nearly gotten trampled by her wayward hooves, frowned. "Wait, you know this guy? Oh, I get it. You must be Agape. Your parents are—"

The ovitaur looked down and sniffled resentfully. "A piece of work, yeah. I guess they went to buy new pillows and throw themselves a housewarming paaarty, right?"

"They left Piini with us," Offi said, and Kirsi could tell he was terrified that Agape would take the metal man with her and leave forever. "I just reset him."

Agape looked up with interest. "Wait, he caaan be reset?"

"My best of bosom buddies," Bäggi said nervously, "I don't wish to interrupt your rousing discussion of metal men and throw pillows, ha ha! But this halfling is in dire need of our most very immediate help."

The focus returned to the halfling on the bed, and Kirsi bit her tongue to avoid saying anything rude before she heard the full story—although she had many rude things primed and ready for when it was the correct time.

"What happened to him?" Bäggi asked as they all stood around the bed, whether on the stone floor or, in the case of the gnomes, on a wooden chair, looking down on a halfling that Kirsi found both fascinating and disturbing.

"Drubs," Agape said, and everyone nodded in understanding.

Agape told them the tale of their fight with Marquant Dique's unwashed rogues, and as Gerd added her own perspective with an abundance of umlauts, Kirsi was forced to admit that perhaps Faucon was not as terrible as the halflings she'd grown up fearing. Perhaps the creature on the cot was not a monstrous enemy and a danger, especially as he was gnomerically fastidious and had placed his own body in peril fighting the rogues. Everything she heard suggested Faucon was righteous, reasonable, generous, driven by heartbreak and nobility. It happened that suddenly, as she listened to the tale: She now saw this halfling, of all halflings, as a person.

As for Bâggi, he had his picnic basket laid out before him, which was unlike any basket Kirsi had ever seen. The top opened up into a collection of tiny cupboards, while the bottom was likewise filled with cleverly interlocking boxes, each beautifully labeled in dwarvelish script. Bâggi murmured to himself as he selected bits of dried herbs and flowers, added them to a collapsible cup, and stirred in a crystalline liquid.

"Bunions and butter beans, where did I put that bonewort? Can't make a proper boning tea without that! Going to need some more powdered moth ear, that's ever so certain. And, finally, a dash of honey mead to sweeten the healing."

"Are you sure this is going to work?" Agape asked. Kirsi guessed from the wrinkles already forming on her forehead that the sheep girl spent a lot of time being skeptical and distrusting.

The dwarf didn't look up as he mixed his powders. "Of course! And why wouldn't it?"

"Perhaaaps it's poison."

At that, Bâggi gave the distrustful ovitaur a look of horror and no small amount of hurt pride. "And why would I, a born and trained healer, attempt to hurt my patient? My healing basket contains no poisons, only healthful teas and tonics. Do you know nothing of dwarves? Or healing? Or, goodness help me, honey mead?"

"It's not the honey mead thaaat's the problem." Agape had the grace to look ashamed. "My paaarents told me not to trust anyone. They said dwarves were crude muscle armed with cudgels, which I see you haaave. Anytime we saw a dwarf on the road, we raaan the other way so we couldn't get turned in."

"Turned into what? A frog?" Kirsi asked, her curiosity piqued.

"No. Turned in, aaas in, given up to the authorities. Jailed. Our whereabouts sold to someone hunting Vartijas." Agape sighed. "We've always been hunted. For the past year, it waaas by that haaalfling right there."

Kirsi put a hand on Båggi's knee, since that was all she could reach. "Well, I trust you, Båggi. I'm sure he'll be all better in no time."

The dwarf smiled at her, and a bit of cherry pink returned to his cheeks. "Bust my bright-blue boutonniere, that's kind of you," he said. "Now, Agape, if you'll help the halfling sit up, I'll help him drink. But beware." He looked around the curious circle, his face advising them to be cautious. "This boning tea is extraordinarily potent. There could be . . . spluttering."

Everyone stood back and watched as the dwarf funneled tea into the unconscious halfling. At first, there was indeed spluttering, but then Faucon began to stir, and soon he locked his lips on the rim, gulping thirstily. As she watched, Kirsi realized that the purple bruises on his hands were fading back to a normal warm brown, and his crooked fingers were straightening like a spider stretching amid the morning dewdrops.

"Zat's verr fine," Faucon said. "Dersn't hurt atall, rilly. Smuch better."

"What's wrong with him?" Kirsi whispered.

"Nothing!" Båggi was aghast at the suggestion.

He would appear to be drünke, Gerd said helpfully.

"Oh, yes, well, dwarvelish honey mead is just the thing to soften the pain of a rough boning," Båggi explained. "Just a few drops, really. And it's not my strongest brew." He pointed to a locked compartment of his large basket. "I keep that tucked away for true emergencies."

"S'good fingies." Faucon sat up, swinging his legs around to dangle over the cot as he waggled his fingers in front of his face with a sense of wonder. "See, some halfelbings use their fingies for stealing, but zas wrong. S'agains the law. Not just little law, but with a big L. *Law.* I use m'nice fingies for paperwork. Crossin' *I*s and dottin' *T*s and sometimes a nice lowercase *j,* y'know, on a Thursday. If only . . . if only . . . I had . . . my . . ." He doubled over, face in his hands, before wailing, "Remy!" at the top of his lungs.

Kirsi put a hand over her mouth and whispered to Båggi, "Can you fix this?"

"I can't fix heartbreak. But I can whip up a quick sleeping brew."

As Båggi eagerly returned to his basket and Agape watched him with ill-concealed suspicion, Kirsi turned her attention to Offi. With the halfling out of commission, or at least too drunk to be violent, Offi was again examining Piini Automaatti. He'd dragged over a larger cot and was focusing on the metal man's back, running his fingers over one place in particular.

"What do you see?" Kirsi asked him, wishing he were his brother instead. For although the boys were twins, she'd only ever felt the squishy warmth of a smoosh on Onni.

Offi had his glasses pushed down on his nose, and she could see the black makeup under his eyes starting to smudge like a raccoon's mask. "It says right here, 'If you have questions, ask.' But it doesn't say *whom* to ask. Agape, do you know?"

The ovitaur clopped over and gave Piini a fond pat.

"My parents and their parents and their parents have roamed the entire globe for years looking for aaanswers, and we've never found aaany. No gearhaaand, nor anyone who's heard of a gearhaaand. No model number, no creator's staaamp. We've aaasked everyone we've met, but so far, no one knows."

Offi hopped down from the cot and walked around to face Piini's front. He looked up and settled his glasses.

"But have you asked Piini himself?"

Agape's mouth fell open.

"No. When I was very small and full of questions, I seem to re-member my faaather giving Piini a commaaand not to answer them anymore. So perhaps he simply . . . caaan't."

Offi grinned. "Well, as he's just had a reset and reboot, all former commands should be rendered void." He cleared his throat. "Piini Automaatti, what is your purpose?"

The metal man's head craned down, his neck creaking abominably.

"I am Piini Automaatti, created by Elder Wåkka Woorlingham-men of Okesvaa. My purpose is to provide knowledge. A purpose I haven't fulfilled in many seasons."

Piini's voice was tinny and faraway, but it reminded Kirsi of her grandfather's. He also always sounded kind and aloof and slightly surprised to be addressed.

"What kind of knowledge?" Agape asked.

There was no response, so she tried again, also beginning with his name.

"I mean, Piini Automaatti, what kind of knowledge caaan you provide?"

Piini's face swiveled toward her. "All available knowledge as collected by the Elders and stored in the Great Library in the City of Underthings beneath Okesvaa, wherein are kept all the great works, creative and judicial, of both gnomeric and halfling civilizations, including the original copies of the Elder Annals, the Tome of Togethering, and the Stern Reminder of the Looming Peril of Giants. The lending library also includes miscellaneous collected tracts on dwarves, humans, gryphons, and the world's largest collection of pudding recipes."

Offi turned to Kirsi, his eyes wide. "Do you know what this means?" he asked her.

"Really fantastic pudding might be in the offing?" Båggi interjected.

Kirsi ignored that and grabbed Offi's hands and jumped up and down. "It means that the Great Library is real. And if we can go there, we can examine the Elder Annals and the Tome of Togethering and sort out the union of gnomes and halflings! We can find the original agreement and confirm that these drubs are breaking Elder Laws. And we can take it to King Gustave and he'll fix things."

Offi shook his head at her and laughed. "Yeah, okay, I was going to say it meant I had fixed Piini, but yours is probably better."

This is good, Gerd said, rising up and prancing in excitement and whipping her tail into the face of the unconscious Faucon, which the gnomes politely ignored. *Long have I wished to look upon the Elders and read the Elder Annals. Many questions have I involving the origins of taboos among my people at the Coxcomb. Perhaps this Great Library city will fix many wronges.*

"So he wasn't broken aaat all?" Agape asked, looking on Piini with a new sort of reverence. "All my life, he's haaad that knowledge, and yet he was ordered not to speak." Then, with more command, "Piini Automaatti, is that why I was supposed to protect you? So you could get home to the Great Library?"

Piini looked at Agape, and Kirsi watched the gem in his forehead glow warmly, which appeared to make his fixed mouth smile. "I am one of the few keys that can open the Great Library. And you are a guardian of that key."

Tears welled up in Agape's eyes. "It finally makes sense. It really did maaatter, keeping you safe. All that running, all thaaat fear. I wonder when it was that we forgot what you were? Was it my parents, or theirs, or my great-grandparents? I suppose it doesn't maaatter. Piini Automaatti, what do you waaant to do now?"

Piini cocked his head. "I wish to serve you however I may. But repair would be welcome."

"Piini Automaatti, can you take us to the Great Library so we may find a Certified Gnomeric Gearhand?" Kirsi asked.

The gold man nodded. "Yes."

Let us go, then, Gerd said, *if you do not have pressing plans, such as the need to bake crepes.*

"I want to go," said Offi.

"And your brother too," Kirsi added, although she felt a little bad when he frowned.

"Oh, happily hopping hares!" Båggi gushed, joining their loose circle, his hands clasped. "A real quest! I've been searching for just such a thing, that I might purge myself of violence and return to dwarvelish society a tranquil citizen."

"But I thought all dwarves were solitary loners or loose-knit groups of brawlers?" Agape asked. "All the ones we met on our traaavels were."

Båggi frowned and shook his head in protest. "Gosh, no! Those are the lost, the ones who left on their Meadschpringå and were unable to purge their violence. We proper dwarves of society wish only a life of serenity, healing, cheerful work, and pleasant artistry. And a great many beehives. But I can't return to the High Mountain Home until I cleanse myself of violence, and this quest will surely provide the opportunity."

"Violence?" Kirsi asked, taken aback. "Why would there be violence? We're just a motley group of beings making a long journey to a hidden and legendary place in the company of a mysterious golden machine that several people are already hunting. Surely we won't encounter violence?"

"There's alwaysh violence."

They all looked over to Faucon, who had been awakened by a face full of gryphon butt and was snuggled up on his tummy with his bum in the air. "S'just how things are done," he continued, drooling onto his hairy hands. "Juss gotta keep going. Whassa few sword fights between friends?"

When the halfling began snoring, Kirsi shook her head and turned back to Piini.

"That's it, then," she said. "It's time to leave the refugee center and complete a noble quest and save our people." She looked at each friend in turn. "All our people. In fact, Offi, why don't you go get your brother?"

All they needed was the braver, stronger Numminen twin, and they'd be ready to go. And that bit about violence? Surely not. Much like her trip here, it would be a piece of cake.

15.

FLUSHED AS RED AS LINGONBERRIES
AND LONGING FOR A REDO

"There ain't no tellin' when a dwarf is actually gonna use their Telling Cudgel. Even if it grows all kinder spikes 'n' speaks to ya in the voice of yer own pawpaw, the dwarf might decide not to swing it at ya in the end. But I can tell ya that ya never wanner be on the receiving end of a swing, because that will be the end of the good day you was havin', and maybe your life besides. Are we done thinkin' aloud yet? Ya promised to buy me a beer."

—Bertie McSpinecracker, quoted in Horton Fuddy's *Condensed Book of Collected Troll Wisdom, New Revised Expanded Edition*

Deciding to take action and actually taking action, Båggi observed, were apparently two very different things.

"What now?" Agape asked, half bored and half antagonistic, almost like it was a dare that would get someone killed. For all that she was the tallest in the group, she seemed out of place and more confused than anyone else. Having met her parents recently, Båggi had some ideas why she might feel that way.

"We get ready," Kirsi said, taking control again. "We'll need to round up supplies—food, yarn, healing potions, that sort of thing. Do we have any money? We should definitely check that."

I can hunt for fresh meat, Gerd volunteered. *But we will need ingredients for sauces.*

"Thank you, Gerd." Kirsi took a cleansing breath and pointed at Offi. "You were going to go get your brother, right?"

"Uh, sure," he said. "I guess I'll go get him." The gnome boy hurried out the door and down the hall, looking, Bäggi noticed, deeply embarrassed.

"And anyone else who has people to say goodbye to should say goodbye." Kirsi looked at each of them, but no one made a move to go. Bäggi shuffled his feet, for dwarves, like gnomes, were social creatures. "Huh. Guess that's just Offi, then. The rest of us are alone, aren't we?"

And we must be gentle with Faucon. Gerd took a few steps toward the halfling's bed. *Although I think I hear something peculiar and unwelcome marching down the hall . . .*

Sure enough, the clank of chain mail and the stomp of boots rose to a clamor, followed by the heavy thud of doors kicked open up and down the hall and the terrified cries of gnomeric surprise. The door to their room was open and thus unavailable for kicking, but soon a human in full armor stood there, sword in hand, wearing a twisted grimace that even the kindest and most pacifistic dwarf would read as cruel.

"We're here for taxes," the man growled.

"This is a refugee center," Kirsi said, bravely planting herself in front of the much larger human. "We aren't citizens, so we can't be taxed."

"Tell that to Lord Ergot's dungeon. Sass-talking the constabulary is a crime. Go on, boys. Find what you can."

Two more men lunged into the room, their faces glowing with malicious intent. One went over to Faucon and attempted to slip a hand into the halfling's waistcoat.

The shriek that followed assailed not only Bäggi's ears but also the inside of his head and most of his chest cavity.

You will unhand the halfling! Gerd screamed as her beak screeched wordlessly.

Båggi's Telling Cudgel was somehow already in his hand and raised as if to strike. He watched, frozen in place, as the human guards hunched over the sleeping Faucon, one struggling to pull a velvet box from the halfling's waistcoat pocket and the other one drawing a poorly kept sword from its sheath at his waist. Such was the dwarvelish mind for smithing that Båggi paid more attention to the make and care of the human's sword than he did for the being wielding it. The man had no such attention to detail, clearly, and began waving his sword at Gerd, stabbing ineffectively to parry the strikes of the gryphon's sharp beak, which nipped red little Vs all over his arms.

Agape threw a wooden chair at the first human, who had thought he could just say "taxes" and they'd meekly let his men rob them, while Kirsi plucked out a hair and began muttering as she knotted it between her fingers, muttering something about the Noxious Ingrown Nails of Nurse Ninnian. But Båggi just stood there, cudgel half raised, unsure how to proceed. For all that he'd been instructed to purge the violence in his heart, and for all that he felt it rising like sap in a tree on a fine autumn day and recognized that the moment was quite ripe for violence, he had no idea how to fight. Dwarves, as a rule, didn't practice any acts of aggression while among society; even yoga was considered too combative. He'd never raised his hand to swat at a mosquito, preferring instead to dodge them and ruefully scratching the bites he earned as a result. His entire life, up until now, had involved peace and kindness and hugs.

Now he wanted to hug these thieves in the teeth with his knuckles.

But he couldn't.

He was frozen.

As Båggi watched, Agape picked up another chair and managed to bash the tax man's head with it, spinning him to the ground, unconscious. It was bedlam. Gerd disarmed the swordsman and knocked him over before standing on his chest, her talons sunk into his shirt as he gibbered. By Faucon's bed, the would-be thief dropped the ring box and fell to his back, screaming and clawing at his boots in horror. Båggi focused and saw that when the man got the boots—as well as a pair of socks that smelled like a peat bog—off, all his nail beds were viciously ingrown and red. They appeared to be throbbing painfully, which suggested that Kirsi's curse had worked. Trotting past Båggi, Agape, obviously much stronger than she looked, lifted Faucon from the bed and carried him like a sleeping baby. All three humans were out of commission, unconscious or dearly wishing they were.

"Let's go," Kirsi said, disgusted. "Before someone else wants their taxes."

Dusting her hands off, she proudly strode out the door. Agape followed her, carrying Faucon, and Gerd stuck her beak in the air and followed her past Båggi. The whole time, he'd just stood in one place like a butter sculpture, feeling silly and helpless and entirely out of touch with both sides of his dwarvelish person.

His violence was in there, but it wouldn't quite surface.

His usual calm was surprised and offended by the violence.

It was like being torn in half, but nonviolently.

Båggi felt something new rise up: shame.

He'd just made new friends, and he'd already failed them.

In that moment, he was no better than butter, and it made him bitter indeed.

16.

Concerned About Hairy Palms and Sadly Lacking Eyeliner

"Cardigans conceal all manner of secrets. Some of them, like belly buttons, are horrors that should properly be hidden from public view. But sometimes they hide unexpected beauty as well, honor and charity and genius too. Do not be fooled by a mere cardigan: It never tells you the full story of the gnome wearing it."

—Gnomer the Gnomerian, in the First Gnomeric Cycle, ♪♪♪♩-♩♪

Offi felt a Sulk start up in his shoulders, which hunched around his ears as soon as he was out of sight of Kirsi and the others. Of course Kirsi would want Onni along. What was an Offi when you could have an Onni instead? Although Offi felt quite comfortable with his own contributions and never begrudged his brother the popularity that seemed to follow him—and not just in the polite, ungrudging gnomeric way but in the actual, feel-it-in-your-heart way—it would've been nice if Kirsi had seen him as more than an errand boy, a stepping-stone for the Numminen brother with real leadership skills and an extremely tidy cardigan with smiling sunshines on it.

By now the original, human-sized door to the Numminens' room included a gnome-sized door painted in a pineapple motif with a gnome-sized welcome mat and a small sign reminding everyone, WELL-WIPED FEET KEEP THE REFUGEE ROOM NEAT!

Offi dutifully wiped his feet off, feeling his Sulk slide into a sort of Rage, which wasn't a very gnomeric thing at all. His shoulders un-hunched, his hands went to fists, and his chin stuck out pugnaciously. He wasn't going to go the way of his father, Old Seppo, and give up. The fight was out of the older gnome, but this younger gnome had plenty of fight left inside. Offi wanted to go on the quest and see the Great Library in the City of Underthings. He wanted more chances to inspect the golden automaton, maybe clean and oil Piini and see what other wonders he held. He was fiercely proud of unlocking the robot man's potential, even if he hadn't received any recognition for it. Onni couldn't have done that. Onni was terrible with machinery. Only Offi could do what Offi had done.

And for once, Offi wanted to take the lead.

Through the tightly fitted wooden door, he could hear the sounds of a happy gnomeric citizenry: saws sawing, hand-crank drills spin-ning, cardigans being washed, pudding bubbling over the fire, polite conversation about dandelions.

"Excellent," Onni's voice rang out, a warm tenor that made one's bones feel extra cozy and safe, as if a bathroom sink had just been scrubbed to shining. "Everything is looking great. And that pudding smells delicious."

Offi stopped in place and considered his choices.

He could return to the room assigned to his family and their gnomegrüp, explain his new quest, and listen to his father's wails about how Offi should stay home and quietly sink into a well-ordered depression like everyone else with good sense.

Or Offi could draw his twin away to explain the situation, and of course his brother would understand what had to be done, and they would join Kirsi for an adventure—where Onni, naturally, would be the leader and the star and Offi would go back to being the quiet, black-clad brother in the glasses who could sew a mean button or rig up an effective catapult for pummeling raccoons with acorns. In that scenario, his parents would be left to fend for themselves here, at the refugee center, surrounded by the terrifying humans and their horrendously beardless chins. And Offi would worry about them, knowing that Seppo was sapped. Young gnomes, after all, often stayed with their parents for years before starting a hatch of their own. It was very gnomeric, caring for one's old gnomes.

And yet.

Offi felt this strange new feeling. An Urge.

The kind of Urge they'd warned him about in school.

But when Offi looked at his palms, they weren't hairy at all, so maybe this was a different Urge.

He wanted to see the world.

But not in a book, and not out the window of a refugee center.

He wanted to see Pell on his own terms, to taste new foods instead of downing the fine puddings of home from a spoon shaped to fit his hand.

Slowly, not quite sure what he was doing or why, Offi took off his glasses. He stared at them, considering. He could see fine up close and not too terribly when looking far away, provided he squinted a bit, and not like his brother did when he wanted to look more heroic. In fact, if Offi was honest with himself, the glasses were in large part an affectation, and he had chosen the clunkiest, heaviest black ones he could find, as they made his kohl-lined eyes pop.

Bending at the waist, he put the glasses on the ground and lifted his foot. But he couldn't quite bring himself to smash them; such was not the gnomeric way, and for all his Urge and his recent Descent into Personal Psychic Darkness, he was still a gnome. He didn't even have a broom and dustpan. Instead, he tucked the glasses into his pocket and hurried down the hall to a human-sized restroom he'd passed earlier, in which some thoughtful gnomes had built a smaller, more gnome-sized facility under a cabinet, together with a smaller door built into the large one. Slipping within, he firmly locked the door and spent a moment in the darkness, contemplating the enormity of what he was about to do. Somewhere down the hall, he heard a Proper Hubbub, the clink of metal and shouting and bumping about, but he could only assume it was the humans fighting among themselves or doing something protective, as the refugee center was, all agreed, a Very Safe Place.

Turning on the lights and gazing into a gnomeric mirror that was almost ludicrously clean compared to the human one above the cupboard, Offi turned his face this way and that, trying to look more Onni-ish. He scrubbed off the eyeliner with the provided beard oil and towel and coaxed a curl onto his forehead and forced his mouth into an easygoing smile. His cardigan, at least, was already horrifically cheerful, if a bit old. Without his glasses and his black cardigans, he and Onni were truly identical. The only difference was that now Onni would be staying here at the refugee center to keep his people safe and jolly while Offi would be going on an adventure.

Because Offi was going to pretend to be Onni.

Was it cruel to leave without explanation? Would his family worry? Perhaps a little. No, he had to be honest: They would worry, and they would Sulk, and they would Sigh Dramatically and sniffle a bit. But if he tried to explain it to them, they would never understand. Gnomes did not yearn for adventure. Gnomes chose a hole, tricked it out, and died in it, surrounded by nicely folded cardigans.

Offi dried out the bathroom sink, turned off the light, and walked back toward his friends—but were they actually his friends? Gnomes rarely spoke to the taller folk, and even then it was usually business; taller folk used shocking curse words and sometimes went days without washing their bums. It was uncivilized—*they* were uncivilized. But, outside of Kirsi, from here until their quest was complete he would be in the company of people who were distinctly ungnomeric, from their variously shaped uncovered heads to their hooved, or hairy and beringed, feet. Was it even possible for such different beings to become friends? He supposed it must be, since they were certainly not enemies. They had the beginnings of a fellowship, at least, and was that not a foundation for friendship?

As he resumed walking toward them, he puffed out his chest like he thought Onni would and pasted on a confident smile. And it was truly strange how with each step he felt a little more firm, a little more sure, a little more swaggery, of all things. A little more Onni-ish.

So this is what it's like, he thought, *to be a Gnome of Great Certainty.*

In fact, he was thinking so hard about how pleasant it felt, pretending to be Onni, that he wasn't quite prepared for the part where he actually had to be Onni—right down to fooling Kirsi, who'd known both brothers since the cradle.

The first thing that happened was that Kirsi barreled into him with a squeal, squishing up against him and lightly brushing her nose against his before pulling away and tugging her cardigan back into place.

"Oh, Onni! I'm so glad you're here." Kirsi looked down and blushed. "I mean, *the more the merrier, happy as a terrier,* right? Did Offi tell you the plan? Did the humans rough you up?"

Offi noted that she didn't actually ask where Offi was, but he chose to forget it because of the way she was looking at him. Or Onni. Or him.

Because from here on out, for all intents and purposes, he was going to be Onni.

He smiled as his brother would. "Offi told me what was happening. But he chose to stay behind and help our father. Never was much for bravery, was he?"

Kirsi giggled. "No, I suppose not. Remember that time you and I climbed that tree near the school hatch when we were wee, but he stayed on the ground and pulled out a measuring tape to determine the trunk's diameter?"

Offi had to laugh along like this was great fun, but he did indeed remember that day, and he had been most pleased to record several notable measurements of the tree in question in his journal that night.

"Silly Offi," he said instead, forcing his mouth into a smile. "But enough about my brother. Are we ready to leave? And why . . . is the room full of unconscious people?"

"Oh, they attacked us, but we won. No big deal." Kirsi took a step back and a tiny frown of worry formed on her face as she scanned him. "But did you not bring a pack? And wasn't Offi wearing the same color cardigan?"

Every muscle in Offi's face wanted to react with a terrified grimace, but he fought the urge and shrugged. "We're twins, and we were only able to pack ten cardigans each for the trip. When I put on this one this morning, Offi chose the same color. You know. To be like me. And I chose to leave my pack behind in case an orphan needed it."

Kirsi held her clasped hands to her cheek and sighed in a dreamy sort of way.

"Oh, Onni. That's just the sort of thing you'd do, helping orphans."

Offi almost felt bad for lying to her, but he realized that when he didn't return, having left no note for his family, he would be presumed dead and the cardigans in his pack would eventually be given to orphans anyway. He felt a stab of guilt, but the choice was made. The trip was happening, cardigans or not. He would return a hero, and his parents and brother would be proud and happy—unless they chose to never forgive him. He supposed that was an option too, and the risk he was taking.

If you leave your family and home, you're not such a gnomeric gnome, Onni would've quoted just then.

The others gathered around, and Kirsi introduced them, and Offi pretended he'd never met any of them before and remembered to feign slight terror as Gerd looked him over, since gnomes were smöl people and generally concerned about large, hungry monsters. He noted that Bǻggi in particular seemed troubled, but he didn't see any signs of physical damage despite the fight that had torn the room apart. It wouldn't do to ask about it; Onni had never met the dwarf—any dwarf—before and would therefore not know that anything was wrong.

"Well," Kirsi said, hands on her hips in that familiar way. She had always been the one organizing playground games at school, and Offi was not surprised that she would be organizing their expedition. He was, however, surprised to find her looking at him with bright eyes.

"What now, Onni?"

"Ah." He cleared his throat and smoothed down his cardigan, as Onni often did when thinking. "We ask Piini to take us to the Great Library, I guess."

Agape's dark eyes narrowed as she cocked her head at him. "Wait. You just showed up. How'd you know thaaat?"

Offi tapped his forehead. "Twin knowledge."

"Of course." Agape nodded along like this made any kind of sense. "Yeah, I've heard about thaaat before. I met these twins down in Taynt who did thaaat."

"Taynt?"

"It's near Limpf."

"Where's that?"

Her eyes shifted in a cagey sort of way. "I don't know, exactly. We didn't use maaaps or follow established roads and paaaths very often, because we feared people would search for us on them and maybe pick up our trail. We just moved every couple of days. So I know all the place names and I caaan tell you that Taynt is kind of dirty with an unpleasant odor to it, but I'm not sure precisely which earldom it's in. One of the southernmost ones." She transferred the sleeping halfling to a cradle hold in one arm and patted her bulging pack with the other hand, in a way that seemed compulsive and unconscious, before turning to face Piini. The golden man always seemed a step away from her, completely still but ticking softly in a way that Offi found deeply comforting. "Piini Automaatti," she said, "will you take us to the Great Library?"

"Yes," he replied, but remained still.

Agape rolled her eyes. "Okay, so thaaat was probably the wrong way to phrase it.

"Piini Automaatti, lead us to the Great Library now." As an afterthought, she added, "Please?"

Piini turned to walk down the hall, but something occurred to Offi. After watching Agape ask the wrong question, and considering how much they didn't know about their quest, it seemed foolish to just bust out the door following an old machine. What if Piini wasn't programmed to follow roads and walked them off a cliff or into a dragon's nest?

"Piini, wait," he called, but the machine didn't even pause. "Agape, please ask him to wait."

"Piini Automaatti, wait."

The machine stopped, and Offi hurried around to face him. The flat face angled down, and Offi's fingers twitched for a dainty brush-and-pick set that would allow him to tidy up every grimy crevice.

"Piini Automaatti, is there anything special required to enter the Great Library?"

"You will need the Vartija."

Offi's eyes flicked to Agape, who blinked in surprise. "Piini, why do we need the Vartija to get into the Great Library?"

"The entrance to the City of Underthings is hidden well. Only the aura of the Vartija will reveal the entrance, and only her willing, unforced request will deactivate the automaatti defenses there."

The ovitaur's eyes rounded in shock.

"Oh, galloping grapes, Agape, you're the key!" Bäggi exclaimed. "And you asked the right question, my good gnome!" He looked as if he wanted to hug Offi but also recognized that it would present many physiological challenges and probably prove deeply uncomfortable for all involved. Beard entanglement was a real possibility.

The ovitaur seemed very uncomfortable to be the center of attention, and she muttered, "Great. I'm the key. Piini, let's get out of here."

The metal man walked toward the main door, and the group followed him. Agape went first, carrying Faucon, and Gerd followed just a little too close behind, as if she suspected the ovitaur of foul play, and not of the eggish kind. Båggi went next, humming a jolly little song to himself. Offi had always heard that dwarves were violent, untrustworthy creatures, so he was deeply confused to find Båggi dancing along and looking pleased as plum pudding to be included. He and Kirsi came last, and he found himself almost jogging to keep up with the much longer strides of the others.

At the door, a human guard leaned back on a poorly constructed chair tipped against the wall, drooling down his bare chin. Piini stopped before the man as if waiting for the door to open. Agape reached for the lock, but the second the rusty metal began to slide, the human's chair crashed down and his bulging eyes took in their crew with suspicion.

"Whassall this?" he asked, slurring. Offi smelled his stomach-churning yeasty breath and connected this smell to the stains down the man's shirt and a large mug on the ground by his scandalously unpolished boots.

Båggi chortled and threw his hands wide in excitement, beaming a winsome smile. "We're a group of friends going on an exciting quest!"

The human raised a bushy eyebrow, then looked from one to the other of the group, as if trying to find the right person to talk to and failing completely due to a lack of humans.

"Buncha weirdos, going on a quest?" he muttered. "Is this one of them *Incredible Journey* things? Or is it that bloody grail again? Are you playing Fellowships of the String? Do your parents know? Look, just go back to your room, kids. Ping-Pong contest tomorrow after lunch."

"We will not play Ping-Pong," Kirsi said, stepping up, her hands in fists. "We are free citizens of Pell, and we can come and go as we please, and we're going."

The guard's eyebrows drew down, and he put a hand on his crossbow. "And who are you? The queen of the Itty Bitty Snitty Committee? You don't go unless I say you can go, tadpole."

Let me pluck his head from his neck like a ripe peach, Gerd said. *That will teach him to suggest Ping-Pong to a mighty gryphone!*

The guard pointed the crossbow at Gerd. "I hate cats," he said. "And birds. And freaks of nature. Get that thing out of here. Take it to the hostler. The gnomes have to stay here, but the rest of you can go."

"Why do the gnomes haaave to stay?" Agape asked.

"For their own safety. Lots of halfling violence right now. Lord Ergot is trying to restore order."

Hearing a slight murmur, Offi looked over to find Kirsi focusing on the man's crossbow as she whispered under her breath, balled up a hair, and ate it.

"The gnomes will go with us," Agape said, and her hoof scraped the stone like she was preparing to charge.

"Nope, they'll stay here," the guard insisted. "So are you going on your quest or not?"

"Oh, we're going," Agape said.

Kirsi gave Offi a look that clearly said, *Things are about to get heckin' Rebellious.* "I guess we'll stay, then," she said, turning away from the door. Offi turned with her, and she reached out and squeezed his hand, which was about the same as squeezing his heart.

"Right," the human said, sniffing in satisfaction. "The rest of you have fun getting killed on the streets."

As soon as the door was open, Kirsi shouted, "Everybody, run!"

Agape commanded Piini to run and broke into a very sheepish sort of zigzaggy, bulgy-eyed, baa-filled trot. Faucon bounced bonelessly, draped over her arm like a sack of discount cornmeal. Instead of using his cudgel on the guard while he had the chance, Bäggi was jogging after Agape, shouting, "Whee!" Gerd stepped out and took to the air as soon as she could. Kirsi grabbed Offi's sleeve and yanked, and then they were running together.

"But the crossbow!" he shouted, as the human grunted and

squeezed the trigger. He must have had the safety on, since nothing happened.

"Don't worry about that. Follow Piini."

Offi kept running and heard the human cursing behind them, but no bolt pierced his cardigan. He looked back and saw the guard manically squeezing the trigger, trying to shoot one of them down, but to no avail, thanks to Kirsi's bristlewitchery.

The golden man led them down a dirty alley, around some rain barrels filled with bathing fairies, and down several more streets. It took everything Offi had just to keep Agape and Båggi in his sights. He was out of breath, and his leg warmers slipped down around his ankles, and his cardigan went askew.

"Oof!"

He looked back to see Kirsi sprawled on the filthy cobbles, struggling to stand without stepping on her ankle-length skirts. A shadow from overhead settled over Kirsi, and every gnomeric instinct told Offi to freeze in place, as a raptor was about to claim an unlucky gnome for dinner.

Can't be helped, can't be stopped, put less pudding in the pot. The old rhyme gnomelets sang when playing double Dutch jangled through his head, making him ill.

"No," he muttered. He ran for Kirsi, grasped her hand, and pulled her to standing, where she clung to him.

"Oh no! There's mud on my cardigan!" Kirsi shouted.

But Offi didn't have time to say anything before he felt the sudden smack of claws around his waist, tightening painfully, and then the swoop of his feet leaving the ground along with the disconcerting feeling he might have left his stomach behind. Kirsi still clutched at him, filthy cardigan or not, and he felt it was more than appropriate to clutch at her, and the world went strange as they soared out of the alley and into the sky.

I will be as careful as if you were sweet, tender egges, poached and ready to be placed on toast, Gerd promised, and Offi looked up to see the underside of her beak, her tongue sticking out just a little to flap in the breeze. *Delicious poached egges . . .*

"We are not eggs!" Kirsi shouted into the wind.

Gerd squawked a laugh. *You are funny, smöl one. Of course you are not an egge! You have intestines, and egges do not; that is an easy way to tell the difference. If you do not wriggle too much, I will keep your intestines safe.*

Offi couldn't relax, but he did his best not to wriggle. He even found the courage to open his eyes briefly, but the view of Bruding was far from idyllic. Thatched roofs filled with holes and tortoises, gloomy little tufts of smoke, alleys hosting all manner of trolls and humans doing unsavory things. From overhead, Offi saw few, if any, halflings in the city, so there seemed to be no reason for Lord Ergot to order the gnomes to remain in the Ping-Pong Palace. He glanced at Kirsi to find her focusing up ahead, her arms spread wide as if she, too, were flying. She wasn't looking down, though—she was watching the horizon, where the grand swells of the Honeymelon Hills framed a ribbon of green.

We must wait while the sheep person and the dwarf exit the foule town at the proper gate with Faucon and the robotte, Gerd explained, and Offi realized he was getting comfortable with a gryphon speaking in his head. *I will sing you the sägga of my people as you enjoy the foine sights of the blü sky.*

She cleared her throat and let loose with a series of noises that sounded like a dying mule murdering a violin. Offi's eyes met Kirsi's, and she gave an exaggerated smile, which he tried to mirror. The gryphon was probably not interested in constructive criticism. And perhaps, where she came from, it was a very beautiful thing to murder a violin.

After such a long time that Offi contemplated wriggling and falling to his death to end the aural onslaught, Gerd gave a final gurgle and briefly purred.

Perhaps now you will understand me better, she said.

"Thank you, I think I definitely do," Kirsi said brightly. "Hey, isn't that them?"

Far down below—farther than Offi really cared to think about—the ovitaur and the dwarf sat on a log; Faucon paced around Piini in annoyance while glancing up at Gerd and motioning for her to land. Whenever Offi saw the halfling, he felt a rush of deep-seated hatred. It was strange to have one's head understand something completely and one's heart stubbornly continue to protest it. As Gerd gently circled down to the ground, Offi couldn't help it. He had to ask Kirsi.

"The halfling. Do you trust him?" he whispered.

Before Kirsi could answer, Gerd broke in.

I have made it clear: Faucon Pooternoob is above reproach. It is not wise to challenge gryphones. We do not lie, but we do take offense at any suggestion that we do.

Talons briefly squeezed his middle in warning, making his intestines scream.

"Sounds like we have no choice but to trust him," Kirsi said, to which Offi merely grunted in pain.

But as the gryphon delicately placed him on the ground and Offi straightened his cardigan, he glared at the halfling. The halfling, in turn, glared at him. Faucon didn't appear to be entirely back to normal and his eyes were still bloodshot, but he seemed to share the same deep-seated antipathy that Offi felt.

"So we're all back together!" Båggi enthused, completely missing the tension. "Plus one! Look! I found a bumblebee! Her name is Queen Buzzabeth!"

True enough, the dwarf had a red string tied around his finger, and at the other end of the string was a fat striped bumblebee, lazily flying in circles, the string tenderly tied in a nice bow around her abdomen. The bee, Offi noted, seemed pretty happy about the whole thing, and he wondered how Båggi had gotten the bee to submit to being leashed like that. Gerd wandered off into a nearby stand of trees to investigate some chittering noises and loudly urinate on something while purring.

"So what now?"

Offi asked the question, but everybody looked at Kirsi.

"Nothing's changed. We go to the Great Library."

Agape was digging a hole in the turf with a hoof and failed to meet anyone's eyes. "So you all waaant to go with me? Still? After all that? Threatened by a human, caaarried into the sky, running through the streets like criminals? We've only been at this quest for an hour, and it's a mess."

"A mess?" Bäggi laughed. "It's been very merry indeed! And I found a bee!"

Gerd trotted out from the trees with blood and viscera dripping from her beak. *Very merry,* she agreed. *The squirrels here are tastee and plentiful.*

"Just . . . just don't come along if you're going to give up later on," Agape said, her voice a raspy whisper. "If aaanyone's going to drop off, do it now."

"But why would we drop off?" Kirsi asked. "We want to see the Great Library as much as you do. It could save our people. Our entire species."

"And the laws—the laws written down," Faucon said, reverence in his voice. "Think of them! Why, there could be accords. Amendments." His eyes closed, and he gave a little shiver of ecstasy. "There could be *codifying.*"

"I was told to find a quest, and this looks like the quest for me." Bäggi beamed, and Queen Buzzabeth executed a dizzying spiral of glee, seemingly in agreement.

"Yeah!" Offi added, punching the air with one fist in a jaunty manner and feeling sure that Onni would have said something similar at that particular moment.

Agape sighed, and she looked so sad that Bäggi offered her an embroidered handkerchief, this one sporting a smiling pine tree.

"I don't know, you guys. Maybe we should forget it aaand Piini and I will just keep doing what we've always done. Moving around, all that. You guys might get hurt, or bored, or . . . I don't know. I just have a baaad feeling about this."

"No."

Everyone looked to Faucon as he stepped forward and solemnly knelt before Agape.

"I will protect you as we journey to the Great Library. You have my sword."

Kirsi stepped forward to kneel, plucking a hair and tying it into an intricate design. "And my cursed bows."

Båggi trotted up and knelt, offering his picnic basket. "And my snacks!"

Gerd gave an elegant bow, and Offi was the only one still standing. He quickly took a knee, feeling rather overwhelmed.

"Yeah. I would . . ." Offi grasped for something significant to offer, to prove his commitment to the quest. ". . . shave my beard if it would help."

For a long moment, it felt as if the clearing was bathed in sunlight and magic, as if something very grand and important was happening. Then Gerd jumped on a wild ferret, crunched its spine, and swallowed it before burping, and the moment was over.

"So let's just go now," Agape said.

A magnificent quest has begun, Gerd agreed. The gryphon took a single step before the sound of extraordinary flatus emanated from her noble flanks. *That wasn't me,* Gerd said, her eyes darting among them. *That was the squirrels. In the trees.*

No one argued with her, but Offi privately noted that Gerd lied about at least one thing, and she certainly put the *ick* in *majestic.*

17.

IN A VERY PRETTY PLACE WHERE FORESHADOWING INTIMATES TROUBLE

"Look, I'm not saying *all* trees, okay, but, yeah, *most* trees, if you give them opposable thumbs and a hatchet, they're going to be out there cutting lumberjacks down *first,* know what I mean? Get a load of those Perilous Poplars outside of Songlen. They just *eat* people, am I right?"

—PERRY WYNKKEL, owner of the Grakkel lumber mill, shortly before a tragic hatchet accident

So they weren't leaving, Agape thought.

They were staying.

They were actually *choosing* to stay with her.

Despite the danger, the uncertainty, and yet more danger, these complete strangers claimed they were going to go with her on her life's quest—even more, they had pledged to do so. Agape had spent her entire childhood believing that the destiny of a Vartija could only be solitary and lonely—unless, perhaps, she managed to stumble upon another ovitaur who didn't mind an anxiety-filled life on the run that could only end in the horrors of childbirth and perhaps a singed caftan, if she were lucky. Her parents had drilled into her the truth of her future: *Trust no one. Stay nowhere more than three nights. Set up traps. Don't light campfires. Remain miserable. It's your duty.*

But now she wasn't solitary. She wasn't lonely. She almost felt as if she could trust . . .

Almost.

And she was, for once, following Piini Automaatti instead of trudging ahead of him, and it was the strangest thing: Normally she expected that his aged gears and crusted cogs would grow so decrepit that he would just stop in place at any moment, one foot forward and one foot back, frozen in time. But now, leading the way to the Great Library, the machine had begun loosening up, his arms swinging with purpose and his stride so long that the gnomes were going to have trouble keeping pace. Agape would've bet good money that the gryphon was going to eat those gnomes, who looked a little like cupcakes brought to life and plunked into cardigans. But yet again, she'd been wrong.

They set off immediately, as time suddenly meant something. Every moment they weren't traveling was a moment that the half-lings' depredations against the gnomes would continue, a moment that the law was letting the people down. The way Onni and Kirsi looked at Faucon reflected how Agape felt inside when she thought about trusting anyone: fearful and angry yet foolishly hopeful at the same time, as if her guts were made of irascible hummingbirds. And yet no one complained or argued. The poor gnomes jogged to keep up, and Båggi bounced along, singing to Queen Buzzabeth, and the gryphon alternated soaring gracefully with messily disemboweling adorable forest creatures and choking them down. Agape had always longed to see a magical gryphon, but she'd never imagined they were quite so gross.

Not that she was going to ever let Gerd know she was gross, which is why it was a good thing the gryphon's ability to project thoughts only went one way.

The terrain here was familiar, and Agape remembered touring this area outside the border of Borix when she'd been around nine. The humans built dreary cities surrounded by walls that seemed to keep them in more than keeping anyone out, as everyone else generally had better places to be. But near the borders of the Skyr, she recalled, the gnomes had taken precautions against the lack of foodstuffs caused by the humans' poor farming practices and tendency to over-hunt the wilderness. They had hidden gnomeholes all across the land with caches of supplies and emergency cardigans. Along well-traveled roads, these wee burrows of safety were marked with flag-poles covered in Alphagnomeric script, which provided instructions on how to find the refuge nearby. Most of the "tall folk" could not read them, but Agape's family could, and she had fond memories of a cheese-stuffed belly. She spotted one such pole on the road leading north to Pavaasik and pointed it out to the others.

"We caaan stock up for our journey nearby."

Onni blinked. "You can read that?"

She raised a challenging eyebrow. "Sure."

"Okay, we'll let you find the gnomehole, then," he said with a shrug, clearly daring her to prove it. She shrugged back but said nothing as she read the instructions and found the hole fifty gno-meric paces off the road to the northeast by tugging on a particularly cheerful daisy until a section of turf pulled up, revealing a hatch.

"I didn't know sheeple could read Alphagnomeric script," Kirsi said.

Agape bristled. "Some can. And I prefer *shaetyr* or *ovitaur*, if you don't mind."

Kirsi looked abashed. "Oh, I do beg your pardon. Thank you for telling me. I'll remember."

"Someone called me a doof last week," Båggi said, cheerfully try-ing to dispel the awkwardness. "An old lady I met on the road. And I told her, *It's pronounced as dwarf, my lady,* and she smacked me with a cane and told me the wharf was in the other direction, ha ha!"

But Agape wanted food more than fellow feeling. The cache con-tained water, wine, crackers, honey, dried cured meats, dried fruits, and wheels of hard cheese, which Onni and Kirsi handed up to the others. Faucon was overjoyed to find a package of yogurt-covered cranberries, and all agreed he needed them to build up his strength and prevent bladder issues. There was a ledger inside, and Kirsi signed it so that her family would be billed for the goods—a practice that Agape's family had never followed. She imagined they owed the gnomes quite a bit by now, and it occurred to her that their life on the run had been a rather selfish one. All taking. No giving. She put a protective and guilty hand on her pack, just thinking about it.

Although Agape's parents had mostly kept to rural areas—farms were easy to plunder or beg at and enjoyed fewer predators than actual wilderness—they did occasionally have reason to go into a city and have a real bath or a meal or pick up some supplies. Agape's mother was usually able to bring in some money with her carved-wood jewelry, and the entire family would whittle around the unlit campfire every afternoon, creating things they could sell in the cities. Her father crafted fancy wooden salad tongs out of soft woods that he polished and oiled, but Agape enjoyed making tiny animals and people that she saw during her travels, endowing each with a little tuft of her own wool and carving a title and her initials onto their bellies. She was currently working on a round little gnome and was planning on giving it a wild and literally woolly beard.

When they came upon a small river, the sun was mid-sink, turning the frothing green water into an array of beautiful colors. Piini assured Agape that he could cross it easily and she was all ready to go, but as soon as the gnomes caught up with the group, they fell down on the ground, panting.

"I've never been this tired in my entire life," Kirsi moaned.

"My blisters have blisters," Onni added. "My calves are screaming. My knees are swollen. Everything hurts!"

"Well, let's just cross the river, and—"

"No!" the gnomes shouted in unison.

The halfling and the dwarf, both of around the same height, stared at them in surprise.

"I have never heard a gnome yell before," Faucon said.

"Yeah, well, you've probably not ever met a gnome who walked this far before," Kirsi spat. "We are a smöl people of dainty legs and we're not known for cross-country expeditions. You do understand that for every step you take, I have to take three steps just to keep up?"

Faucon raised a tufty eyebrow at Kirsi. Everyone was silent, waiting to see what kind of ancient battle between their two species would rage.

But the halfling merely bowed his head. "You make an excellent point. I had not considered that, and I feel like an oblivious dodunk for not thinking of it. An unobservant mumchance. My apologies. As it happens, my feet are also in need of rest. I will admit that a nice foot bath, followed by a communal foot rub with penetrating unguents, would not be unwelcome."

Kirsi sighed in relief. "Yeah. A nice soak would be terrific."

"Did he just suggest we all rub each other's feet?" Agape muttered to Bäggi. "Because no thanks. I don't want to lace my fingers betwixt any of your toes, nor do I want you exploring the crevaaasses of my underhooves."

But that was apparently not what Faucon had suggested at all. He reached into his portmanteau, and the gnomes flinched, expecting firebombs. Instead, he pulled out a flat rectangle he called an Amazing Basin. After a few adjustments, it had become a box, which he filled with river water. The halfling worked with concentration and delicacy, adding a variety of soaps and oils from his bag to the water. Then he sat on the log, carefully removed his toe ring, and dipped his large, hairy feet into the basin, wriggling his broad toes. His grin, when it appeared, was wider and more genuine than Agape could ever have guessed. The halfling was such a serious sort, not at all like the halflings her family had encountered on their perambulations. No, those halflings had been dirty and talked out the sides of their mouths, smiling and laying on the charm, offering outrageous deals if someone would just follow them into lightless alleys to complete the transaction.

Everyone else but Gerd was waiting for their turn to enjoy the basin, but Agape had the hardy hooves of a sheep and had spent her

entire life walking, often from dawn until dusk, stopping only to for-
age for edibles along the path. No one else had even begun the work
of making camp. Twigs and stones were everywhere, and Båggi had
carelessly deposited his picnic basket and mead cask rather close to
an anthill. No one was collecting wood for the campfire, lit or unlit:
Perhaps, just this once, with the protection afforded by the group, she
could enjoy actual flames. Giving a deep and sheepish snort, Agape
set to making a camp, finding satisfaction in the repetitive and familiar motions. Piini followed behind her at a well-programmed distance, his nearness a pleasant comfort.

As she was dragging logs around the prospective fire, Båggi was
listening to his bee buzz in a rather urgent manner.

"Oh, this is a good spot, here by the river? Very well, then. Please
land on that fallen log and I'll untie the string." The bee obliged and
Agape watched, slack-jawed, as Båggi untied it and waved goodbye
when the fuzzy body buzzed off. "Farewell, Queen Buzzabeth! I
hope your new hive is prosperous and healthy."

"You can really talk to bees?"

Båggi nodded, making his chin jiggle enthusiastically. "Oh, my,
yes! Anybody can talk to bees. It's making yourself understood that's
the real trick, and most dwarves know all about that."

"How?"

"Well, we all get the talk from our parents when we're young."
Båggi looked at her expectantly and continued when she merely
raised her eyebrows. "You know. The one about the bees and the
bees?"

"You mean the birds aaand the bees?"

"No, the bees and the bees." Båggi wrinkled his nose in confusion.
"Birds and bees? Who ever heard of such nonsense? They're all the
wrong sizes for that sort of thing." His eyes abruptly widened, and he
hurried to assure her. "Not that never having heard of something is
bad. There's nothing wrong with not knowing something, and there
is always the chance to know it, ha ha! You have such differing tal-

ents and skills. I'm so impressed that you can read Alphagnomeric. What else can you do?"

She considered the question, not sure how much to share. "I can whittle a piece of wood into most anything. We haaad to do something with all the kindling we never lit up."

"If you never lit your fires, what did you do for light?"

"We used fairy laaanterns with consenting fairies. Usually it's easy to trade them a night of light in a laaantern for a bit of milk and honey."

"Milk? Do you . . . make milk?"

Agape bleated in surprise and crossed her arms over her chest. "No! I meant cow's milk or goat's milk from local farms!"

Bågg's eyes squeezed shut, and his cheeks went red as strawberries, and he bonked himself a couple of times on the head with his cudgel. "I'm sorry! There is so much I don't know. I can recite for you the epics of my people and prepare a salve for your wounds or a tonic for your ailments; I can talk to bees and brew delicious mead; but I know so little about other peoples that I constantly give offense. Please forgive me, Agape. You are the only shaetyr I have ever met, and I hope I am not giving you a poor opinion of dwarves."

"My opinion is that you should aaall get out more. Every dwarf on Meadschpringå makes boneheaded comments like thaaat to someone and ends up in a fight."

"Oh, I know, I know! The isolation is not good. It's one of the reasons we must all come down from the mountains. It is a time of much-needed growth. But growing is often uncomfortable. Painful, even."

His lower lip was trembling, and Agape was terrified he was going to cry and that she might be required to comfort him, which would involve all sorts of awkward things like hugging or patting or saying horrific phrases like *there, there.* Up until this week, she had barely touched anyone outside of her parents, and her mother had constantly warned her about terrible diseases carried by strangers, so she was rather concerned about catching some bug or another that might be living in Båggi's beard.

"Don't feel baaad," she managed. "Everything will look up tomorrow morning."

"It will?" Båggi asked, daring to hope.

No, Gerd said from somewhere nearby, accompanied by the death squeaks of a pine marten. *There will be a rainstorm tomorrow. I can smell the aether churning. The lightning will be most violent; the clouds will be most glümee; the air will be most moïste.*

Båggi sighed, dejected. "Oh, crumbs. Can't even rent an umbrella. I was not prepared for this."

Hunching his head in between his shoulders, he stumped off toward a twisted old willow rooted in a crook of the river. With the sun's rays painting everything pink and purple and the willow's whips whispering in the wind, it was a very beautiful place for a dwarf to have a nice sulk. But as soon as Båggi walked under the grand green canopy, the tree shivered, and the leaf-lined branches bent down and shot into the ground around him, going ramrod straight and effectively caging him.

"Båååååååggi!" Agape cried, galloping two steps away from him in sheep-like fear before forcing her legs to turn and take her in the other direction. "Somebody, help!"

She ran to where Båggi was struggling to escape, wrapped her fingers around the branches, now effectively bars, and tugged as hard as she could. They didn't budge, bend, or break, but a few of the tree's furry catkins did flutter to the ground in annoyance.

"I didn't know trees could do this!" Båggi exclaimed. "Maybe it's nice, though. Does it want to be friends? Should I . . . hug it?" But Agape could hear the tone of terror in his voice and see his knuckles gone white. She could also see, at the base of the trunk, a rather ominous hole. It was large enough to fit a dwarf in.

"This is not normal," she said, reaching for the whittling knife at her belt. Gritting her teeth, she sawed at one of the willow branches, but it merely bled sap and utterly resisted weakening. "Faucon, your sword!" she cried.

The rest of the group galloped into view, led by Gerd and Faucon, with the gnomes trotting breathlessly in their wake and wincing with each step. Faucon had his sword drawn.

"Stand back," he muttered darkly.

Agape got out of his way, and Båggi scrunched down into the corner of his willow cage. Faucon took up a dancer-like position, one hand behind his back and the other brandishing his sword, but as he leapt forward to strike, the willow branches shot out with equal speed, wrapping around his wrist and, to Agape's horror, his neck. She lunged forward to try to slice the branches holding him, but they caught her too. Bleating in fear, she struggled to get loose and run away, but her hooves merely carved a groove into the soft turf as the tree pulled her closer to its gnarled, pitted trunk and the hole that looked ever more like a hungry mouth. With the implacable tenderness of an angry parent, the slender, vine-like branches pulled Agape and Faucon more firmly under the tree's canopy and rooted new branch-bars to trap them in cages just like Båggi's.

A loud and insulted beeping off to Agape's right suggested that Piini was moving to protect her, but the aged machine wasn't fast or strong enough. The branches caught him too, curling into the crevices between his limbs and body and holding him fast to the ground.

"What is happening?" Kirsi shouted. "Is it a person or a thing? Is it evil or hungry? Did anyone remember to use manners?" Trotting up to the edge of the tree's periphery, she gave one of her signature curtsies and said, "Hello, beautiful willow. Would you please, pretty please with pudding on top, let go of my friends?"

In response, the tree's vines shot out to grab her. She was saved at the last minute by Onni, who grabbed the back of her sweater and tugged her onto her rump.

"Sorry for rumpling your cardigan," he said.

"I forgive you," Kirsi replied, with what Agape considered a strange amount of formal frostiness as the gnome girl brushed the wrinkles from her blue sweater.

"I'm afraid it doesn't want to be friends after all," Båggi moaned from Agape's other side. "I hugged it, and it gave me a splinter! The under-the-nail kind!"

This tree defies nature! Gerd called. She dashed back and forth in front of Faucon's cage, tail lashing as she hissed and spit. *I wish to fight it! Fight me, tree!*

But the tree ignored her, possibly because it couldn't hear thoughts and possibly because it seemed to ignore everything that wasn't close enough to grab. Plus, it was hungry. The branches of each cage moved one bar at a time on the outer edges, lifting from the earth and then replanting a bit closer to the center, where the hole at the base of the trunk definitely looked more mouthy. They would be swallowed up soon if the gnomes didn't act.

"What can we do?" Onni asked.

"I kind of thought you would just . . . know," Kirsi said, scrunching her eyebrows at Onni.

"I didn't really battle willow trees back home in Pavaasik," he said, a little sniffy, and rubbed the place between his eyes. "We should ask Piini. Piini Automaatti, what kind of tree is that?"

"It is known as a willowmaw. It will eat any kind of meat."

"Piini Automaatti, how do we fight it?"

"Stand back and fire flaming arrows into it."

That wouldn't help. If they set the tree on fire, they'd set their trapped friends on fire too. And they didn't have bows and arrows anyway.

Gerd took to the sky, circling overhead, and she let out a mighty squawk. *Something is coming!* she shouted. *I see it moving through the forest, shaking the branches.*

Båggi had his hands on the bars of his wooden cage, staring at them forlornly, his cudgel slung dormant and useless at his side.

"Now would be a good time for thaaat cudgel!" Agape shouted to

Båggi, but he just held up a red swollen finger and muttered, "Splinters make me sad."

For her part, Agape was still trying to break or slice the branches, but Faucon stood calmly in the center of his cell, rubbing his chin as he considered the maw of the tree toward which they were being drawn. It was unnerving, for Agape, how calm the halfling seemed upon the cusp of becoming fertilizer.

It approacheth! Gerd called, and Agape's head snapped around toward the strange sound coming from the wood.

Everything went silent, and then a man's voice rang out, deep and booming, saying the last thing anyone expected.

18.

Wrapped Warmly and Perhaps Too Tightly in the Arms of Unwanted Hospitality

"The first rule of demigods is that you don't talk about demigods. The second rule of demigods is that—ghrktff!"

—Töiler Dordin, in *Secrets They Don't Want You to Kno—ghrktff* (unfinished)

Kirsi wobbled on feet that were mostly blister, disappointed that Onni hadn't already heroically saved the day and anxious to see who this new possible hero might be. His voice was jolly and as welcoming as a bowl of roasted chestnuts as he sang:

> *"I'm Tommy Bombastic and I'm here to say*
> *That it looks like you might get eaten today!"*

A man emerged from the woods, snapping his fingers and doing a little dance that suggested he was entirely lacking sympathy for the plight of those caught by the willow and close to being dragged into its dirty hole. His features possessed a mixture of traits from gnomes, dwarves, halflings, and humans, all without really representing one species completely; he was like a person milkshake. His beard was bushy and long, his cap hung at a rakish angle, his cardigan was well kept and embroidered with shooting stars, and the belt buckle struggling to hold in his round belly featured a hedgehog and instantly reminded Kirsi of the one Båggi wore. The man's feet were bare, and although not nearly as hirsute as those of Faucon, he was wearing a rather fetching gold toe ring with a cut ruby nestled in the center on his second toe.

"Help?" Båggi said in an experimental sort of way, as if he wasn't quite sure of the protocol for talking to strange dancing men with nice belt buckles in the middle of a life-or-death situation.

"Hey, ho, here we go. You messed with the Willow of Death, you know."

As the man finished this last bit, he did a handstand and waggled his legs, ending in a sort of spin on his shoulder that made Kirsi and Onni both grimace at the grass stains that should've appeared on his cardigan. But his cardigan remained perfectly perfect, and Kirsi began to suspect that magic was afoot.

What is this? Gerd asked, landing between the man and the captives and going into a protective crouch.

> *"I told you once but I'll tell you twice:*
> *I'm Tommy Bombastic, so you'd better be nice!*
> *I'm older than Pell and you'd better step back;*
> *Let me save your friends from this Willowmuck attack."*

Tommy, if that was his name, ended on his side, one arm supporting his head and his leg kicked up in a saucy manner.

"Are we . . . supposed to clap?" Kirsi asked, giving a brief curtsy.

Leaping to his feet, Tommy swaggered over to the willowmaw—named Willowmuck, apparently—with the whole party watching him. He ducked under the canopy, but the vines and branches didn't touch him—they actively moved out of his way. With a wink, he casually approached the ragged maw and whispered something into the tree's bark. The tree shivered as if in surprise, and the branches forming the cage went noodly and withdrew into the canopy so suddenly that Båggi, who was clutching them, got burns on his hands.

Slender withes swooped down to pat them all gently on the shoulders, as if in apology.

"What the Pell?" Agape asked, rubbing the places on her wrists where branches had held her.

Tommy raised his eyebrows at her and swept his hands in a *get away from the murdertree* sort of way, so Agape helped Båggi stagger out into darkening dusk, where the logs were laid out around the not-yet-and-possibly-never-to-be lit campfire. The ovitaur and the dwarf sat together, huddled almost shoulder to shoulder, Kirsi noted; it was as if Båggi longed to snuggle closer in an unromantic way, while Agape was terrified of being touched. Accustomed to the general cuddliness of gnomes, Kirsi felt bad for them both. Piini glumped along and took his place behind the ovitaur. Onni sat back against another log, and Kirsi joined him, their dainty legs splayed in front of them and quivering with exhaustion, and Faucon casually strolled away from the tree, sword in place, as if he hadn't been held captive by branches just a few short moments before. As for Gerd, she kept her distance from Tommy, pacing back and forth with her neck feathers up and her ear feathers down in a mixture of fear and distrust.

Once everyone was seated, Tommy did seven handsprings, landed facing the pile of branches, tossed something among them, and held up his arms as flames roared against the first shy twinkling of evening stars.

"Oh, my snuff and other stuff, that was impressive!" Båggi shouted, although Tommy did hold a finger to his lips to quiet the overexcited dwarf back down. When everyone was silent and focused, the man gave a bow and began singing in a sort of angry, poetic way that reminded Kirsi of a fist rapping at a door.

> *"Hey, yo, fiddle, o. I already told you my name.*
> *I'm Tommy B. and living long and well is my game.*
> *I'm older than your grandma's socks and wiser than her noodle,*
> *I'm dancier than a frying frog and fancier than a poodle.*

I saved your butts from the willowmaw
But it looks like you're still in trouble,
So follow me home for some ale with foam
And if you're pretty, I'll make it a double."

When he bowed, there was an odd silence, followed by polite but unenthusiastic clapping. Kirsi clapped for the part where Tommy had saved her friends from a hungry tree but not so much for the part where her allotted ale depended on a physical exam and arbitrary judgment of physical beauty. Her eyes met Agape's, and Agape gave her a look that said, *Oh, great. Another one of these guys.*

"Ale! Oh, I do so love a mug of frothy ale!" Bāggi enthused. "And his hat is oh so dapper," he stage-whispered to Agape. The dwarf bounded over to his worldly goods and began to rummage gingerly around in his picnic basket. "I, for one, am ready to enjoy your hospitality, friend! But I confess I need to quickly apply some of Thurgood Thane's Pain Nixer Elixir, and maybe a squirt of No-Hurt Burt's Ouchie Soother and Skin Smoother as well, for that Willowmuck sure made a mess of my hands."

As the dwarf rubbed flowery-smelling goop on his hands and moaned in relief, Agape stood and shouldered her pack. The look she gave Tommy Bombastic suggested she wasn't so sure about their current situation.

Considering their run-in with the willowmaw—whatever that was—Kirsi had to assume this particular area was more dangerous than most, with or without a campfire, so she, for one, was willing to follow their savior. She, too, stood and shouldered her pack, and Onni followed suit. Faucon stood as well, and they all gave one another grim nods as if to say, *Well, here we go, possibly following a lunatic to our doom.*

Tommy skipped along, fairy lanterns appearing in each hand. Bāggi followed him, imitating his dance, with Agape and Piini following close. Kirsi and Onni went along in the gnomeric way, but Kirsi could hear Faucon and Gerd whispering in their wake. Eventually the gryphone capitulated and paced along in back, though she kept making some noises deep in her throat that curiously sounded somewhere between a trill and a growl.

"What about the fire?" Agape asked, turning to watch the flames leap high.

Tommy gave her a head nod by lantern light. The trapped fairy within the pierced metal could be heard screaming faintly.

> *"Forget about the fire, babe, and come to see my tree.*
> *Those flames will simmer down but you'll get hot when you're*
> *with me."*

"Ooookay," Agape said. She dropped back, just a little, as if fearing Tommy might try to put a proprietary arm around her shoulder.

Kirsi did her best to remain cheerful, but her feet and legs felt like mincemeat. When she stumbled and squeaked for the third time, she felt hands gently grasp her middle and swing her through the air. Too tired to protest, she hoped whatever was going to eat her did so quickly and without too much smacking of the lips. But then she landed on Gerd's back, and Faucon swung Onni up behind her. The gryphon's fur was soft and clean, her stride easy and languid.

Faucon thought you would be more comfortable traveling this way, Gerd explained, almost a whisper. *I hope you will find some succor as your smöl feet suppurate. I will clean my fur later.*

"Many thanks," Kirsi said with great feeling, echoed by Onni. She risked a glance at Faucon. To think: a halfling considering her feelings!

For a while, Kirsi slept, splayed over Gerd's wide back. After what felt like hours, they came upon a huge, sprawling tree that had to be centuries old, its long branches supported here and there by bars and props as they swooped toward the ground and angled back upward. Various rooms and bridges and twisted sets of stairs were strung together in what would've been a very classy home had there not been a giant fairy-lit sign reading TOMMYWOOD plastered across the front.

Fireflies blinked along with a dance tune floating on the breeze, and drunken pixies sat on a branch, hefting tiny mugs and hollering things like, "Yeah, sweet cheeks! I like that mutton!" and "Flash me some ankle, dainty legs!" and "I'll put the fun in gryphon, girly!"

"Um," Agape said.

"I second that um," Kirsi added.

I wish to eat those pixies, Gerd confirmed. *With or without sauce. For once, I do not feel picky.*

But Tommy was throwing open the main door, ushering them into a warmly lit kitchen. The air was perfumed with a cologne that made Kirsi pinch her nose to keep from sneezing. Although she instinctively distrusted Tommy Bombastic, she also understood that he was a being of great power and she should avoid rousing his anger, especially over his choice of eau de toilette.

As she stepped into the kitchen, she realized something was amiss with Agape: Piini still stood outside at the bottom stair, focusing on it. Most likely, the machine had run the calculations of his mass compared to the stair's delicate carvings and determined it wouldn't hold his weight. Poor Agape looked as if she felt quite vulnerable without her metal friend.

"Piini Automaatti, wait there. I'll be aaalright," the ovitaur said.

He looked up, and his eyes gave an interrogative flare.

"It'll be fine."

The machine's head hung, and Kirsi felt sorry for them both. She missed her family every day, and now Agape had lost her parents and was finding places in the world where Piini could neither follow her nor protect her.

Tommy directed them to sit around his table, which somehow had exactly the required number of chairs and in the correct proportions for his guests. The place settings were fine crystal, the silverware slender as twigs and glimmering with polish. It did not escape Kirsi that she and Agape were seated to either side of Tommy, their chairs snuggled up close to his, even though Kirsi had done her best to select the farthest chair from their host. As the table magically pulled up to her lap, a foamy mug appeared by her fist, placed there by a sad-looking tree girl with long, curling green hair and smooth brown skin. There were three of these girls, bringing trays of sweet breads, rashers of bacon, fluffy mounds of eggs, and veritable log houses of hot buttered toast. They were dryads, if Kirsi remembered their species correctly from her *Monsters of the Not-Gnome-Eating Variety* textbook—each willowy and beautiful yet slumped and defeated. When Kirsi saw Tommy slap one girl's bum as she hurried past, it was clear that the girls were not here by choice or happy about their tenure.

Agape must've been thinking the same thing. Neither she nor Kirsi had touched the food, although Båggi and Onni were shoveling cinnamon rolls into their mouths and Faucon had somehow managed to devour half the toast and was daintily patting at his lips with a napkin. Gerd wasn't eating at all, and considering the gryphon's appetite, Kirsi knew what a big deal that was. Smelling the bacon, Kirsi picked up a piece . . . but then she saw the sad eyes of the dryad girl hovering nearby with another platter and put it back down.

"Tommy, we'd love to meet your friends," Kirsi said, smiling hopefully at the nearest dryad.

Tommy just waved that away before saying,

> *"Forget the help. It's plain to see*
> *I'm Tommy Bombastic, so it's all about me."*

The dryad gave Kirsi a thankful if apologetic look and hurried away.

Båggi, who had already finished one mug of ale, grinned at the girl pouring a new helping from a pitcher, his cheeks rosy and the tip of his nose going flat-out red.

"My goodness, friend! What a fine host you are! This ale is magnificent!" he boomed.

Their host tipped his hat and leaned back in his chair, sipping his own ale.

"When you're Tommy B., only the best will do.
Both for me and my bros. But let's talk about you.
You're a strange little group going on a quest.
What is it you seek? Get it off your chest."

Agape looked to Kirsi, and Kirsi looked to Onni, but Onni opened his mouth and said nothing. Faucon remained tight-lipped, arms crossed over his round belly and ale untouched, and Gerd sat at attention, eyes ablaze.

Båggi lapped up his ale from a spill on the table and said, "Oh, and what a quest! Our metal man knows where—"

"To find the nicest cardigans," Kirsi interrupted.

"We gnomes are really into cardigans," Onni offered weakly.

Tommy's grin briefly slipped into frustration.

"I'd like a cardigaaan too," Agape said, trying to bolster the lie as she fiddled with a crystal saltshaker. "Wool on top to match the bottom, you know?"

"No, no. The hale has gone to your eds," Båggi said, a little too loud. "For what we sheek is far grander, a very legend, the famed Li—"

"Lice repellent," Agape smoothly interjected. "It's a really big problem." She gave her head an exaggerated scratch. "Not the sort of thing one generally discusses at the table, though. Right, Kirsi?"

Kirsi's eyes flew wide before she, too, began vigorously scratching at her fine russet beard. "Oh, yes. Many a time have I been befouled by pestilence, but this is by far the worst case of lice I've ever had. Why, even my lice have lice!"

"Lice?" Onni asked, terror written plainly on his face and one hand to his scraggly beard. Kirsi elbowed him in the side.

"You don't have to pretend," she said through gritted teeth. "We're among friends. And what are a few vermin among friends?"

Very slowly, Faucon brought his large, freshly cleaned foot onto the table and scratched like the dickens at the hair there. "Terrible things, toe lice," he said, his mouth turned down almost comically.

"They exacerbate my foot fungus. And when they interbreed with the bedbugs, well. You know."

Tommy put his ale down, his smile turned upside down. He stood, gesturing to the door.

> *"Well, it's been nice meeting you and hearing of your quest*
> *But it's getting pretty late and Tommy B. requires rest.*
> *I'd invite you all to stay but I'm afraid that space is dear*
> *So I'll wish you all the best and send you far away from here."*

Tommy stood and snapped his fingers, and the table jumped away from the guests, their chairs scooting back. Kirsi's choices were to get dumped on the floor or stand, so she caught herself and hopped down from her seat. Tommy bowed them out the door and down the stairs, where Piini waited.

"I'd just thike to lank you for your foine hospitality—" Båggi began, but Tommy Bombastic had disappeared. "Where'd he go?"

Just then the three dryad girls hurried out from the kitchen and down the stairs, each carrying a basket filled with what appeared to be the remaining food, which had all been whisked off the table, somehow, while Kirsi wasn't looking.

"For your journey," one of the girls said, head bowed as she handed Agape a basket.

Kirsi heard Agape whisper, "Do you need help?"

"Our father is Willowmuck, that willowmaw you met, and . . . it's complicated," the girl said, drawing back. "But thank you for asking."

"Is this a legal issue?" Faucon asked, and for all that he was always very formal, Kirsi saw real concern in his eyes.

"It is. There was a transaction, and favors are owed, and . . . well, like I said, it's very complicated."

"Is there a contract of any kind? Something I might be able to review?"

"Oh, yes," another dryad said. "We all have a copy. It's . . . binding." She withdrew a scroll from her apron pocket and held it out, unfurling it in front of him but not letting it go. "You can read it, but it can't leave my hand."

"I understand." Faucon took the edges in his fingers with great dignity and read it so swiftly that Agape wondered how he could be processing it all. The scroll continued to spool in front of him, forming ribbons on the ground, surrounding Faucon like paper snow, and finally the halfling smiled, waggling a finger at the scroll. "Ah. Here. Clause Seventy-nine, Paragraph Six. This is an illegal provision. Your indentured servitude cannot be coerced or compelled in debt of another or else you are chattel; it violates your basic right of body autonomy, guaranteed throughout Pell." He went on to spout jargon that was indeed very complicated and ended with "and therefore the entire contract is null and void."

The dryads grinned and hugged one another.

"So he can't legally keep us here?" one asked.

"No. As your attorney, I hereby contest this contract."

"Our attorney? Wait—how much will that cost?"

"You served me food earlier and I will consider that payment enough. That and the distinct pleasure of showing this trumped-up scofflaw that he cannot simply make up his own rules outside the law." Faucon withdrew a tooled-leather pen case from his portmanteau. With the quill and ink within, he scratched on the scroll. Within seconds of his final flourish, the scroll took on a golden glow, floated in midair, and exploded in flame, leaving a pile of ashes at the dryads' feet and demonstrating the true power of attorney. He repeated the process with the contracts of the other two dryads.

"We're . . . free?" one of them asked. She took a few careful steps away from Tommy's house, then began skipping around. Her sisters joined her. "It's been centuries since we could leave Tommywood!"

"What will you do?" Kirsi asked. "Do you need anything?"

The dryad smiled. "Freedom was all we wanted. Thank you so much." She held out a smooth brown hand to Faucon, a tiny acorn cupped in her palm. "It's a small gift, freely given, but perhaps it will help you on your quest."

"Your quest to get rid of lice," one of her sisters added with a smirk.

The door to Tommy's house burst open, and he stood there in a bathrobe, clutching a flaming scroll, so furious that smoke was coming out of his ears.

"Tommy B. is no one to mess with!" he howled, his eyes lighting on the dryads. "You owe me!"

"Willowmuck may owe you something, sir," Faucon said, "but these dryads do not. You cannot compel their service."

The first dryad whispered, "Good luck!" and she and her sisters fled into the night.

Kirsi wanted to follow them, to get far away from whatever Tommy Bombastic might actually be, but Faucon's peculiar behavior was too interesting. The halfling didn't move, didn't run, didn't panic. He merely replaced his quill in his pen case and put his pen case in his portmanteau before calmly standing, back straight, to face Tommy.

"I'll be reporting you to the Fae Council," he said stiffly. "For all that your bacon is deliciously peppery, your legal arguments are unmitigated garbage. And don't even think of harming us. Amendment Three-twelve, Paragraph Seventeen, Clause Eight. Good evening, sir."

With his nose in the air, Faucon turned and walked away with great dignity. Gerd knelt by Kirsi's side, and Agape boosted the gnomes up onto the gryphon's back before following Faucon down a path that had appeared as if out of nowhere. Piini trailed behind and Bäggi staggered after them in confusion, perhaps trusting that what had happened would be explained later. Gerd soon caught up to Faucon, but Kirsi couldn't resist looking back over her shoulder to watch Tommy argue with one of the drunk pixies, who was wearing a poorly tied tie and carrying a booger-spackled briefcase.

For some time, they paced along in silence, and Onni fell asleep behind her, his arms wrapped around her waist in a way that made

Kirsi too excited and smooshy to sleep. She buried her face in Gerd's neck to hide her rosy cheeks.

"What's Amendment Three-twelve?" she heard Agape ask the halfling a while later.

He didn't turn around as he answered.

"To put it in layman's terms, demigods are forbidden from being jerks," he said. "No matter how delicious their bacon is. Tommy B. has gone by many names throughout history, and much of his braggadocio is actually based in fact. He was originally one of the good guys, but if history teaches us anything, it's that power and privilege corrupt. These old gods get to a point where they think no one can tell them no, but that's only because they haven't met the right lawyer." Leaning in, he whispered so that Kirsi barely heard, "And speaking of which, just a word to the wise: I saw what you did. Stealing from demigods—or anyone, really—is not a good idea."

It was Agape's turn to put her nose in the air. "I don't know whaaat you mean," she said.

But Kirsi could tell that was a lie.

When the halfling wasn't looking, Agape slipped a crystal saltshaker out of her tunic and into her pack, where it landed with a clunk and rattle. The ovitaur looked terribly guilty, and when her eyes landed on Kirsi, Kirsi was very glad she was accomplished at feigning sleep.

"It's not stealing if you leave payment," Agape said to herself, almost as if reciting her own gnomeism. "No laaaws have been broken."

Kirsi didn't believe it, and she didn't think Agape did either. This secret, Kirsi thought, would eventually bite someone on the rump.

19.

Athwart a Company of Tendentious Trolls and Halflings

"Sometimes it takes horrific atrocities to turn a peaceful soul to anger, and sometimes blood will be shed over something as simple as the loud enjoyment of dairy products. Kolon and Teabring went to war for three years because a man from Liaoxing slurped his yogurt and moaned indiscreetly. Granted, the moan was wanton and delivered in a wildly inappropriate moment, but still."

—Zheng Jin, in *Why Can't We Just All Slurp Along? A History of the Yogurt War*

It washed over Båggi slowly, but once the flood of revelation engulfed him it was all he could do to keep his head above metaphorical water. Tommy Bombastic wasn't actually that swell a guy, and the increasingly sober dwarf had not seen any of the signals since he'd been so giddy with his escape from the Willowmuck followed by the offering of free food and drink. Only after Faucon had released the dryads from their servitude did Båggi's liquor-fogged brain see that he'd missed something crucial. There had been people in need of help in plain view, and he hadn't seen them. He had missed an opportunity to serve others, and there was no one to blame but himself. He had been complicit. He glanced at his cudgel, but even it looked embarrassed.

He thought he understood now why so many dwarves went to pick a fight with the centaurs or the elves to end their Mead-schpringå as soon as possible. A quick kill and a lifetime of guilt sure seemed easier than this festival of embarrassment and shame he was feeling. So far all he'd accomplished in the lowlands was escorting a queen bee to a new home. He had, he supposed, learned quite a bit, and that shouldn't be discounted, but mostly what he had learned was how staggeringly much he did not know. He wondered if he would ever be able to catch up. Regardless, he knew it was his duty to try.

The party did not bother returning to their campsite, since that would be backtracking, and also since it appeared to be the hunting ground of a predatory tree covered in seemingly innocuous pussy willows. Instead, they plodded north toward Pavaasik to put some distance between themselves and Tommywood. Once they found a small meadow and Gerd had scouted it to make sure it was safe, they built a new fire, and Faucon gave the gnomes some time with his Amazing Basin, as their tiny feet looked like shredded meat. They were worn out, poor things, and Båggi pillaged his stores to whip up a homemade version of Buff Billi Bruce's Spruce Goose Vamoose Juice and set it to chill and ferment overnight. That would get them going in the morning. In the meantime, he offered them a dab of Fifi Fipper's Foot Fixer Elixir and a heartfelt apology.

"My friends—I hope I may still call you that—I am so sorry for my verbal incontinence earlier and for plunging us into danger in the first place. I will try to make amends and be more circumspect in the future."

They all reassured him that no harm had been done, and he left them to relax and selected a sleeping place just a little ways away but nowhere near sentient foliage. He rather needed some time to rest as well; it had been an exhausting day, both physically and emotionally. Curled up with his back to the fire, he hugged his bunny-shaped hot-water bottle and longed for the days when his biggest problem had been a tangle in his beard.

Båggi woke up in the rain that Gerd had promised was coming. The fire was beginning to hiss at the droplets pattering down, but it was mostly coals at this point; no fresh log had been placed on it for some while. He quaffed a vial of the Vamoose Juice he'd prepared last night to test its vamoositude and set about packing up with a newfound energy. Others were rising too, and he offered them their own vials of Vamoose Juice, which they accepted with thanks. As the old dwarvelish saying went, it was better to tramp through the rain with a smile than to lie down in the mud for a while and get piles.

They kept the Honeymelon Hills on their right as they walked, and Faucon suggested that they pass the time by hearing the Tome of Togethering, since Piini had the whole thing in his memory and none of them had ever read it.

Båggi wondered why. "Are you not taught its contents in your schooling, if it is the foundation of your country's origin?"

"It's summarized," Kirsi said. "Or more referenced than anything else. The office of the kanssa-jaarli came from the tome, basically, and the King of Pell has always accepted that. I was never taught much else."

"Nor I," Faucon said. "My law professors told us that few if any copies remained, and that we were supposedly following the spirit of the tome if not the actual letter of it."

The automaton obliged their request and began speaking in a tinny monotone, and it was extraordinarily dull language to Båggi's ears. The text of the tome often surprised the gnomes and the halfling, for the system of government it described had little to do with their current method of rule, beyond the dual earldom of the kanssa-jaarli. There were many grunts of surprise and mild oaths from the Skyrlings, followed by little comments: "That's different," or "Why don't we still have that?" or "Wow, so *that's* what the Second Amendment actually means?" or some variation on those themes. And when it was over, past lunchtime and into the afternoon, they decided to make camp a bit early by a winsome stream winding through cottonwoods in a meadow.

Faucon plopped down in the grass, stunned, and began chucking ingredients into his Amazing Basin. "I am dumbfounded," he said. "Most of all because it would appear that we have deviated so far from the laws outlined in the Tome of Togethering, and yet . . . no one cares."

"Our people care," Onni said darkly. "But we tend to get blown up before we can do anything about it. Wasn't Bootsy Blütendoomp going to go petition the kanssa-jaarli before her hatch exploded?"

"I do believe she was," Kirsi said, her nose wrinkled pugnaciously. "In fact, now that I think about it, no one from our town has successfully contacted the kanssa-jaarli in months. We don't even get the biweekly letter and crossword from the Toot Towers anymore."

"When laws are forgotten, someone dishonest is benefiting," Faucon said gravely.

"What do you think we should do?" Kirsi asked. "You seem very law-ish."

"That . . . I do not know. It is one thing to know the law and another thing entirely to have to prove the law exists. To find a way to make oneself heard, and to make it matter, is rarely an easy thing, even when the courts are on one's side and one's toe hair is perfectly combed."

Båggi thought it was a marvelously confusing time to learn about life in the lowlands, when the inhabitants who'd lived there all their lives were so befuddled. But he would learn little by talking, so he kept quiet for most of the journey to the gnomeric city of Pavaasik.

Once on the outskirts, there was some argument about whether to venture into the actual city limits. Agape and Kirsi were adamant about staying away from the rising trails of black smoke they saw and keeping Piini out of the clutches of the drubs. Faucon thought he would present a target for gnomes and halflings alike. Onni wished to see if he might not return to the Numminen farm to cobble together what he could of the remaining weapons and gadgets in the workshop, if the halflings hadn't ruined it. Gerd wanted to see whether some farmer might be willing to sell her some swamp radishes—a vegetable she claimed was vital for gryphon beak and talon health—in exchange for eliminating any vermin they had. Bäggi didn't care as long as he got to come along and help and possibly pet a friendly alpaca.

They compromised. There was an engineer friend of Old Seppo's who lived on the northern outskirts of the city; Onni thought that his hatch might be burned out, but it was doubtful that the halflings would have destroyed or even found his secret workshop. "His name is Eino Partanen. Oldest gnome I know and the most stubborn. He's probably still living in his workshop and the drubs have no clue," he said, and Kirsi nodded.

"I know Eino. He's tough and thin, like a piece of steak, you know, that gets wedged in between your teeth and you can't get it out for days no matter how much you try."

"He's a bit of a living legend among the gnomes," Onni explained to the others. "Back when he was a gnomelet, he designed a bunch of new weapons to strengthen the defenses along the Kivi-Grumpuddle Crevasse, to make sure the giants never dared to invade the Skyr again. He invented the Doompunch Crossbow, the Triple Saw Blade Launcher, and the Gelatin Catapult."

"I beg your pardon. How does a lump of gelatin stop a giant, rather than simply strengthening his or her bones and improving the luster of skin and hair?" Faucon asked.

"It's definitely not dessert. The payload is a sphere of gelatin with a chamber in the middle that mixes up a caustic acid in mid-flight. It explodes on contact and the target basically melts—leaving behind a puddle of yet more gelatin."

"Zounds. I suppose we should approach his place of residence with an excess of caution."

"We'll be fine with Eino. Can't say what we'll meet on the way there, though."

"Our doom, most likely," Agape muttered.

They agreed to investigate, at least, and Båggi frowned and kept his cudgel in hand as they circled the city clockwise, occasional shouts and screams reaching their ears, faint and tinny in the distance. The dwarf was ready to get angry again, anxious to help the helpable and stop the needs-stoppingers. All he needed was a clear case of good versus evil, bullied versus bully. Some signs or labels would not have gone amiss.

The rural landscape that supported Pavaasik was largely quilted fields of crops separated by stands of trees that acted as windbreaks and property borders. Raptors raptly watched from the trees for something delicious to walk by. Snakes snaked through the tidy rows while trying to eat the same creatures as the raptors. Båggi and his companions saw no one, just a few lonely alpacas and donkeys here and there, raising the question of whether the farmers were keeping their main herds elsewhere or if they had already been rustled by halflings. Not knowing much of livestock, Båggi briefly considered whether these lone creatures might be spies or otherwise harborers of ill will, but the alpacas burbled when he patted them and were simply too cute to doubt in their cardigans and striped scarves.

"Okay, this is the border of Eino's land," Onni said, gesturing to the patch of timber they'd just entered. "Stop here until we get his permission."

Båggi was curious how they'd secure that permission, since he saw no other gnomes nearby apart from Onni and Kirsi.

Onni pressed an odd knot at the bottom of a birch trunk and stepped back a few paces, staring at a branch stump a bit higher on the trunk. Båggi stared at it too, thinking perhaps there was another button hidden there and Onni was trying to find it. But, instead, a circular slice of the bark slid to one side, revealing a glass lens. A voice like creaky old leather came from the tree.

"Onni? Heard your hatch got firebombed. Are you a ghost?"

"No. We escaped. Family's safe in Bruding."

"Good. Now what the hork do you want?"

"Long story, but I'm traveling with some people to Okesvaa to do something important. May we come in?"

"That depends. Who's with you?" Båggi and the others got dragged in front of the lens, and there was significant surprise at seeing Gerd and Piini Automaatti but no trouble until the end, when Onni pulled Faucon into view.

"Whoa, there! Are you out of your mind, Onni?"

Several clicking sounds within the tree suggested weapons were being aimed at the halfling, but Faucon didn't budge. Båggi was most impressed with his sangfroid.

"No, Eino. Listen," Onni said. "Faucon is not a drub. He's traveling with us because he's dedicated to taking down the Dastardly Rogues."

Eino snorted. "A halfling, acting against Marquant Dique? Balderdoosh! You know what I think, Onni? I think you're a prisoner of that halfling, and he works for the Department of Gnomeland Security, and they've got your family hostage, and you've been sent here to talk your way into my home. Ha! Nice try! They haven't been able to get me out and they're not gonna."

"What? That's . . . well, that's actually something the drubs would do, isn't it?"

"You're not helping, Onni," Kirsi said, whispering.

"I know, but I understand where he's coming from. I'm not sure how to convince him."

"Hold on a minute," the voice said. "Bring back the dwarf."

"Me?" Båggi was surprised. He stepped in front of the lens again and waved uncertainly, wishing he had balls of steel like Faucon, or at least nuts of hickory or orbs of roughly tumbled topaz—anything to hide the shaking in his hands and help the cramping in his toes.

"If you're on your Meadschpringå, then you'd have a Telling Cudgel, right?"

"Correct, sir. It's right here." Båggi held it up in front of the lens.

"A bit closer, please, and turn it all around so I can see it."

Puzzled but happy to comply, Bäggi inched forward and rotated the cudgel around so that this mysterious gnome could inspect it. The grain of the Korpåswood was really lovely, he thought, streaks of rich dark brown among the honeyed tan. If he couldn't have balls of steel, at least he had a polished wand of rock-hard wood.

"Interesting!" Eino barked, because all he seemed to do was bark. "What that tells me is you haven't gotten truly angry yet."

"No, sir, not yet."

"Good enough. The halfling can't be all that bad, then. Tell you what. You're all welcome to come inside the workshop, but I'll thank you to leave your weapons at the door. Can't really have you anywhere else; workshop's the only place the gryphon can fit. But if the halfling tries anything funny, you'll be carrying him out in pieces. Without his toes."

Bäggi was surprised to hear Faucon gulp audibly, but the stoic halfling said nothing.

Onni grinned. "Thanks, Eino."

There was no reply except the click of the lens disappearing into the bark again, and then a treeless portion of the lightly timbered area shuddered and the leaves shifted. An expanse of turf and bushes lifted up entirely from the ground, revealing a wide ramp leading underground, with plenty of room for Gerd to walk down without crouching.

Agape blinked. "Impressive. But why does he need an entraaance like this?"

"He builds some pretty big stuff sometimes. You'll see." Onni led the way down the ramp, Kirsi at his side, and the rest of them followed.

A wizened gnome with tufty white hair, weathered reddish-brown skin, and an oil-stained blue cardigan embroidered with cogs waited for them at the bottom of the ramp, one outrageous white eyebrow raised in suspicion. They could see the stains clearly because he had split his snowy beard into two braids and wrapped them around the back of his neck, keeping it out of the way while he was working. He pointed with a begrimed finger to a workbench off to his right, one of many, which had some space cleared on it. "Weapons there, please. I don't want to lock them up, but I don't want them in easy reach either." He backed away, still wary of his visitors, and watched to see if they complied.

Bâggi assumed the lump in the old gnome's pocket was some kind of weapon, but he also rather hoped it was cheese. As for his own weapon, he grinned and put his Telling Cudgel down next to the various gadgets and things the others were unloading. Faucon removed his weapons deliberately so that Eino could see how thorough he was being, and Bâggi was impressed at how many weapons the halfling had stashed in his waistcoat and trousers, not to mention some tiny blow darts nestled in his toe hair.

Stepping forward a little bit to give the others—especially Gerd— room to crowd in, Bâggi craned his neck around and let his jaw drop in astonishment.

"Great galloping goosemeat, my good gnome! This is a most impressive workshop!" Bâggi had never seen the like.

Had it merely been the width of the ramp and then extended some distance underground, that would have been remarkable enough. But it just kept on going, far to either side, full of low, gnome-sized tables and taller ones for larger projects, which Eino could access via scaffolds or ladders. There were some very large objects—vehicles and the like—that Eino could not possibly work on alone. He had automatons lined up against the far wall as well as a tracked crane system in the ceiling, which would move large pieces of metal about. There was a welding station and a smithing bellows and parts everywhere along the perimeter, with the assembly and storage area taking up the majority of the floor.

Bâggi didn't know what he was looking at, mostly—there were shiny clockwork gadgets and thingies and doodads galore—but he knew he was looking at the output of a brilliant mind. He didn't wish to pester the gnome with all the questions he had, but Faucon apparently had no such misgivings.

"What is this device that looks similar to an arachnid?" Faucon asked. It was extraordinarily shiny and had eight legs and some rather unusual-looking chelicerae, but it had no eyes.

"Oh, that's just a spider shaver," Eino said.

"I beg your pardon? Why would you wish to shave a spider?"

"I wouldn't. You lie down on your tummy and it will crawl on your back and methodically shave your back hair with those little mouthparts. They have razors on them."

Faucon was delighted. "What a novel solution to an ancient problem. And the hair goes where?"

"Into its belly. You set it loose in the garden when you're done and it adds your back hair to the compost. I grow prizewinning tomatoes with that compost."

"You are a genius indeed, sir!" Faucon gushed.

He began to ask how it was powered, but Kirsi gave a fussy sigh and changed the subject. "Might we use your kitchen, Eino? We won't raid your pantry, because we have some food we can cook up, but a proper kitchen instead of a campfire would be lovely."

"Of course, of course! Kitchen's in back on the east side of the shop. There's plenty of food and I don't mind sharing, so fix what you like."

"Do you have fresh eggs?" Faucon inquired.

"Absolutely. More than I can eat. We should whip up a mess of them using my Massive Mess Egg Whipper. Follow me."

Gerd trilled her excitement deep in her throat, and soon Faucon and Eino were trading their tips for making fluffy omelets (which Gerd corrected to *fluffee omlets*) and there was much gustatory delight around one of Eino's workshop tables, as well as discussion of what had been happening in town.

"Most everyone's fled to Koloka or Okesvaa," Eino informed them. "Some headed for Soperki, others for Bruding. I don't know why the halflings are doing this." He cocked an eyebrow at Faucon. "Do you?"

"I do not. I was not involved in the decision to sack gnomeric cities, and whatever reasons are on offer, I reject them. It is a clear breach of law and I think the Dastardly Rogues Under Bigly-Wicke should be wiped out. The Department of Gnomeland Security is a cruel farce, as it only serves to expel gnomes from their proper homes."

Kirsi said, "I think we should ask ourselves why Lord Ergot wanted to keep the gnomes in the refugee center. I wonder if he's not working with the drubs somehow."

No one had an answer to that, though they all admitted it was plausible.

"So where are you all headed, then?" Eino asked.

"The Great Library, underneath Okesvaa," Onni said without hesitation. "We know how to find it."

Eino's silverware clattered onto his plate, his fingers suddenly boneless.

"The Great Library is real? Not a tall tale?"

"It's real."

Eino's expression darkened and he waggled a gnarled finger at Onni. "Don't mess with me, now, boy. Your father and I go way back, and if you're joking around, then I'll feed you to a solar-powered wood whittler and have done with it."

Båggi wanted to invite the useful old inventor along instantly, but after his indiscretion with Tommy Bombastic he was reluctant to say anything.

Onni replied, "It's all true, Eino. Piini Automaatti here was made in the Great Library by real gnomeric gearhands. And Agape is a Vartija. She can find the entrance and get us in."

Eino blinked at the metal man and then at the ovitaur. "It's really true?" he whispered. Then, louder, he said, "Let me go with you." He gulped audibly. "Please. It's all I've ever wanted since I was a wee gnomelet. I've always longed to be a gearhand. Didn't even know if they were a myth or not. And I may be old, but I think there's still time. My mind is still sharp. My hands are still nimble."

"I think you qualify, Eino, no worries on that score," Kirsi said.

Bäggi noticed that Onni looked a little nervous for some reason, but perhaps the gnome just needed to use the restroom.

"I invite you to join us, provided everyone is in aaagreement," Agape said, and with the Vartija's consent, Bäggi felt he could offer his enthusiastic support to the idea, nodding *so* enthusiastically that his beard went all fluffy, the highest unspoken praise among dwarves. Perhaps he wasn't sure when to show anger, but he knew quite well when to express joy at seeing a good person's destiny come to pass.

"It will take us several days to get there from here," Kirsi said, "but at least your dream is only days away."

"Well, I might be able to help with that. I have a half centipod, you see. It could use a little work, but we should be able to get it in shape."

"Forgive me for asking," Bäggi said, "but what is a half centipod?"

Eino shrugged. "It's the same thing as a quinquagintipod but much easier to say."

Onni offered an explanation Bäggi could understand. "It's a transport with fifty legs."

"A transport?"

"And a fine one too," Eino assured him. "Buried in the workshop, but we can excavate it, put some oil in the joints, give it a fuel bulb. It's big enough to let all of us ride on it, but it doesn't really have an air freshener, I'm sorry to say. I've heard halflings smell like cabbage."

"How peculiar," Faucon said with the slightest smile. "I was taught that gnomes smell of fried liver."

That is not how either of those people tastes to a discerning palate, Gerd offered.

"Isn't prejudice ridiculous?" Bäggi broke in. "Now, back to this machine. What sort of fuel does it run on?"

"A volatile mixture of death screams and winterborne angst."

"Ha ha," Bäggi said, and smiled broadly. He wasn't sure if it was a joke, but he'd rather laugh and be told it was serious than take it seriously and not get the joke. "Death screams. Ha!"

Nobody contradicted Eino, however, so Bäggi's smile faded. He couldn't imagine how death screams and angst could be converted into fuel, but he felt sure he didn't want to find out. He waited for someone else to ask about the source of the fuel—whose screams and angst, for example, were used for this? And what happened if there were leftovers? Could they be stored in bottles or used to power can openers?—but no one brought it up, so he supposed it must be common knowledge in the lowlands.

"If I can ask you to help me get the half centipod ready to go, I'll round up some things for the journey and put the place in order, make sure the farm and all the traps around my hatch are on automatic."

"Sure, Eino," Onni said, looking excited at the prospect, and the old gnome led them to the opposite side of the workshop, where the half centipod was half buried in scrap metal, torn cardigans turned to dust rags, and tools of unknown utility.

"The lube is over there," Eino said, pointing to a fifty-five-gallon drum of it. "And there are plenty of shop rags lying around on the tables. You get to lubing, and I'll bring back a fuel cell."

He left them in front of an impressive vehicle that was easily the length of a giant stretched out for a nap. It had a flat deck with benches that doubled as storage and a raised dais with a captain's chair, steering wheel, and various gauges and gearshifts. A few posts around the perimeter held up a rudimentary roof to keep off the rain, and blinds could be unrolled to shield riders from the sun, but considering the decorative elements—including daisies and ducklings—it was clearly meant for sightseeing rather than any sort of military vehicle. All of this rested on fifty sectioned brass legs that rose from underneath like an insect's.

Båggi stowed his own gear inside one of the benches, then helped to clean and lubricate the joints of the legs. Agape ignored the transport at first and tested some of the cleaning solution and lubricant on Piini Automaatti, who agreed that both substances were salubrious for his mechanical well-being. Gerd found a corner in which to sit and groom her wings, softly trilling as she did so.

As they were finishing up, a crane whirred into action above them and a hook laden with several packs traveled in their direction. It purred to a stop above the half centipod, and three automatons with long arms clomped over and unhooked the packs.

"Right, ready to go, then?" Eino's voice called. He was burdened with two red glowing bulbs the size of grapefruits, which he held clutched against his chest. "Hop in. There should be room for everybody but the gryphon."

There certainly was. Båggi chose a bench opposite Agape and Piini Automaatti as Eino performed his gnomeric magic and brought the machine to life. A loud thrumming noise purred underneath the vehicle, and the legs lifted in clacking sequence and came down again, confirming that they were functional.

"Excellent," Eino declared, his eyes alight with excitement, and it seemed to Båggi that years had dropped away from his face with the prospect of the journey ahead. "I don't have enough fuel to get us all the way to Okesvaa, unless anyone is into either screaming or torturing anyone else into screaming. No? Fair enough, but this should shave a day or two off the journey and save our legs." With a loud clunk and a lurch, the half centipod moved forward as Eino settled into the captain's chair and steered the vehicle up the ramp.

Once outside, they headed north across farmland. The ride wasn't terribly smooth, but it wasn't jarring either: Båggi enjoyed it tremendously, although the bones of his spine seemed looser than usual, and smiles were easy to find.

Unfortunately, their transport was also easy to hear and spot from some distance. They were pursued on two occasions by pairs of patrolling halflings mounted on alpacas—albeit the sort wearing armor instead of cozy sweaters—but Gerd swooped at them in both cases and the pursuers abruptly lost interest.

The speed wasn't miraculous—more like a brisk jog than anything else—but they could take their ease and didn't have to carry their burdens or suffer their blisters in the meantime. It was quite restful, Båggi thought, and he privately told Onni that going to see Eino had been a smashing good idea.

They crossed the river that eventually emptied into the Dämköld Sea at Soperki and made camp on the eastern bank. Their fire was hailed shortly after dark, and it turned out to be a family of gnomes who'd been hiding only a short distance away. A frazzled matriarch approached, and once she determined they were safe, she called her husband and little boy to join them. They looked tired and their cardigans were torn and frayed. They had very little food with them and almost nothing in terms of belongings. They clearly had left Pavaasik in a hurry, and they regarded Faucon with much suspicion.

But they knew Eino, and he knew them.

"The Savelas!" he cried. "I'm so glad you're alive!"

Onni and Kirsi had heard their name around town but had never met them before. They were light-skinned, rosy-cheeked folks with a wee gnomelet named Toivo, who was only six. He had a little stuffy replica of a Beauner whale clutched in one arm, and Båggi thought he might be the cutest thing ever. He rummaged around in his pack while introductions were being made, and when it was his turn he beamed at the Savelas.

"Hello! I'm Båggi Biins, dwarvelish herbalist. You look like you could use a draught of Black Jack Proudsack's Lilac Slurp Snack! It's an exhilarative restorative and safe for gnomes."

They accepted the tiny shots he'd poured into wee travel glasses and downed them, thanking him afterward and claiming to feel better already. Shortly thereafter they were invited to dinner and to travel along in the half centipod the next day, for there was plenty of room when one was of gnomish size. They swapped tales and sang songs around the campfire, and Båggi recited an episode from one of the dwarvelish epics about the hero Smeggi Spheers.

The Savelas shared that the Dastardly Rogues had driven them from their home, along with their entire neighborhood, and they had heard that roads in and out of most gnomeric cities were now patrolled by halflings on alpacas. They had only escaped one such patrol by sending their trained dachshunds to harry the alpacas, but the dachshunds had never returned from their valiant effort. Poor wee

Toivo began crying as soon as he heard the word *doggy,* and although she'd been quiet and held herself stiffly around the newcomers, Agape hastened to carve a tiny wiener dog from a chunk of wood to make him smile again.

Knowing of the many dangers lurking along the roads made the trip far less relaxing. But they took to the fields, where there were deer and antelope for Gerd to hunt. At least they had plenty of supplies for the rest of them, thanks to Eino.

The miles crawled past—or, rather, they crawled past the miles—and it was all very merry, outside of the existential dread and continuing lack of dachshunds. Outside of Okesvaa, however, the half centipod wheezed and coughed and ground to a stop.

"Out of fuel, I'm afraid, but we're almost there," Eino said. They were on the northern wooded foothills of the Honeymelons, and the old gnome pointed at the eastern horizon. "See that line of trees in the distance, heading north from the hills? That's the river that flows all the way to Cheapmeat feeding those trees. Okesvaa is located near the headwaters of that river. We can make it there in an hour or so on foot, I bet."

"So you're just going to leave the transport here?" Kirsi asked. Eino shrugged.

"Sure. It wasn't doing anything in my workshop except collecting dust. Got more use out of it than I ever thought I would again! Can't get more fuel anyway. Those were my last two bulbs, and the Screaming Grotto is pretty much tapped out."

"Is that grotto somewhere in the Skyr?" Båggi ventured.

"No, no. It's in the Siren Sn'archipelago."

Båggi decided he didn't ever need to go there. He joined the others in groaning and cracking their backs as they unpacked the benches and shouldered their burdens. The Savelas didn't have much to carry and wee Toivo was anxious for a walk, so they disembarked first to let him run around.

Gerd had been walking next to them but took to the air to scout the road from above, since they were leaving the vehicle and its relative safety behind. Båggi strapped his picnic basket to his back, hoisted his mead cask onto his left shoulder, and held his Telling Cudgel in his right hand. In truth, he welcomed the familiar weights. He flashed a grin at Agape and she shook her head at him.

"Always haaappy, aren't you?"

"I was rueful once. Once! Ha ha!"

"Ha ha!" A strange voice called from the trees at the base of the hills, the tone mocking. "Time to be rueful twice. You'd rue the day, in fact, if you were going to live through it."

Agape's head whipped around. "Whaaat?"

Beware! Gerd's voice shouted, though Båggi saw that she had climbed quite high above them and was banking around in their direction. *A motley crü of halflings approaches!*

The halflings that emerged from the trees were indeed motley, but they all wore the medallions of the Dastardly Rogues Under Bigly-Wicke. Their predatory grins did not bode well, but Båggi thought they would vanish once they saw Gerd.

"Road to Okesvaa is closed," one of them said. "No one in or out. Everybody dies. That's the deal and you have to take it."

Wee Toivo began crying, and the Savelas started to scurry back to the half centipod.

"No, no, stay still now," the halfling said. "McDeathbreath, you're up."

A tall, thick, pear-shaped troll charged out of the trees and swept an enormous club at the Savelas. Their cries abruptly ended with a crunch before their bodies flew through the air to fall bonelessly some distance away.

The halflings laughed and applauded as if death were some entertaining sport, even as Agape, Faucon, Eino, Kirsi, and Onni gasped in horror.

Båggi's muscles tensed as his blood rushed to his brain and back to his extremities again, his skin radiating a furious heat. He carefully put down his mead cask and picnic basket, but his fingers tightened on the Telling Cudgel and he could feel it changing. It was the most natural thing in the world for it to transform now, for he had something he wished to tell that troll. Never mind that it must be five times his size and probably responded to criticism by administering blunt-force trauma.

"Let me tell you about right and wrong," Båggi seethed, pointing at the troll as he stalked forward. Agape told him to wait, but he ignored her as the troll pivoted to focus on him. "Let me tell you about justice. About what happens when you step across the line of decency and tread on evil ground."

"That's right, McDeathbreath, shut 'im up," one of the drubs said, a leering grin plastered on his face. He clapped a couple of times in encouragement. "Dwarves are high in vitamin D!"

With a gurgling roar, the troll raised its club and lurched in Båggi's direction. Feeling his energy surge, Båggi raised his own cudgel, sprinted forward, and rolled underneath the strike as it pummeled the earth where he'd been a split second earlier. He bloomed from the ground like a fried squash blossom and gripped the Telling Cudgel in both hands, noting that it was no longer a friendly walking stick or even the threatening weapon that had briefly showed itself to the cabbage pastor. Now it was a horror of spiked hardwood glowing with coruscating red and orange lights, which he did not expect but which he hoped would mean a bonus payload of pain for the troll. He swung his cudgel with everything he had at the troll's armored knee, the very first act of premeditated violence in his life, and hoped that one of his spikes might find a gap in the armor and bring the troll down, even if it was on top of him.

What happened instead startled everyone, including Båggi.

The troll's knee exploded.

The sound of the cudgel hitting the knee was not a smack or thud but more of a detonation, and not only did the troll's leg come off at the knee, the rest of his body fairly launched backward in a low trajectory that wound up instantly crushing a couple of the drubs in his party. His entire body smoked and sizzled inside the armor. He twitched and screamed, and then expired. Båggi blinked, recalling that Brother Bo Boffing had predicted he would slay two halflings and a troll. But the Cabbage Pastor had neglected to mention that they would be murderers who dearly deserved to be slain.

Båggi regarded his Telling Cudgel with wonder and perhaps a twinge of worry. The red lights were gone and some of the spikes looked less sharp now that the troll was dead, but it was still a fearsome weapon.

"Gadzooks," a voice said, and Båggi turned and saw that it was Faucon, his eyes large and his mouth half open in surprise. The rest of his party was likewise gobsmacked, blinking at the smoking corpse of the troll and then at him.

But Båggi wasn't satisfied. He turned and saw that the bodies of the Savelas were still sprawled in the dirt, and the drubs who'd ordered the troll to slay them were standing there as if they deserved to live after ordering the deaths of innocents. A growling noise rose in Båggi's throat, and the halflings realized they were in mortal peril. They tried to deliver some to Båggi first, tossing throwing stars and knives at him. But he squared up behind his cudgel, the spikes lengthening like the feathers of a most deadly fan and slapping the stars and knives out of the air. That danger past, he closed the distance, holding his weapon in front of him until it was time to bring it down upon their heads. The spikes shortened, thickened, and dealt unto them the death that they had dealt to the Savelas, and probably to many more besides. The last one ran, and when Båggi gave chase, the drub looked back over his shoulder and cried out in despair, "Mercy!"

The plea only served to enrage Båggi anew.

"Where was the mercy for the family you killed? Where was your voice, standing up for the innocent? That little gnome boy your troll batted through the air—where was the mercy for him?" The halfling sniveled and let loose a final cry of despair before the Telling Cudgel ended him in a hairy meatsplosion.

In the silence that followed, Båggi took deep gulping breaths and said, "It's done. It's done." His muscles quivered, but he did not let go of the cudgel, for he wanted to see it return to its peaceful shape, to see it signal with a bee-shaped pattern in the grain at the top that he was at peace and could return to his mountains. "It's over now," he added, a cautious smile of hope tugging at the corners of his mouth. "The violence, you know? Ha ha! It happened, so it's gone, it's all out of me."

The Telling Cudgel finally scraped and shifted and smoothed out from its fearsome configuration to something a bit less threatening, but it stopped far short of a peaceful walking stick. The exterior retained wee knobs of hardwood where there used to be spikes, and there was no friendly bee figure carved into the grain. Instead, there was a gryphon.

"Why is there—" Båggi began, but he was interrupted.

You did a good thing, Gerd's voice said in his mind as she landed next to him. *I would have done the same had I not been so far away. I am glad you acted quickly.*

"But . . . it's done now, isn't it? Why hasn't my cudgel transformed to peace?"

This smöl part of your task is done. But not all of it.

"All of what?"

The gnomes. The halflings. Their brouhähä. There is much wronge here. It is in the air, the very wind. As a dwarf who has sung to the winds in the mountains, you should be able to sense this. The rain will not wash it clean. We must help.

"We must? Why do we have to do it?"

Because we cannot sleep while evil wakes.

"Evil is always awake."

Then we must always fight.

"*Always* fight?" Båggi said, his voice tiny. Perhaps this is what happened to other dwarves who never came home. They realized they must always fight and could not in good conscience remove themselves from the fray, even if they wanted nothing more than to return to their snug mountain aerie and content themselves with a wee bit of wisdom and a great deal of mead.

But looking around at the dead halflings and the troll, and realizing that he had done all that violence, Båggi felt ill. He didn't think he had the temperament to always fight. And why would his limbs not stop shaking? It wasn't cold outside.

The others came over and they said things to him, but it was all noise; he couldn't process any of it.

"Forgive me, friends," he said. "I think I need to be alone for a little while."

He wobbled on shaky legs to the side of the road and fell to his knees, leaning on his cudgel with both hands, head down in front of it. He tried to get control of his breathing and find some smöl spot of peace in the tempest of emotions he felt. He didn't *like* being angry or violent. It had done nothing to save the Savela family. He wasn't sure avenging them made a difference either or whether it was truly justice to execute the troll and the Dastardly Rogues. The only good that could possibly come from this experience was preventing the same fate befalling others, but imprisoning them would have accomplished the same goal. Not that there were any prisons nearby capable of housing trolls.

What worried Båggi most, and what lit a burning coal of doubt in his chest, was the source of that red eldritch energy that had blown up the troll. He had never heard of a Telling Cudgel behaving that way, although most dwarves were quite shy about recounting their Meadschpringå tales. Was *that* how hot his anger burned? If so, how would he ever be able to quench that and live in his mountain home again?

The wind moaned and wailed and he opened his senses, taking it all in. It stank of death and lonely onions.

Gerd was right: There was much wrong in the Skyr and much work to be done.

And Båggi, it seemed, was destined to do some of it.

"Ha ha," he thought sadly.

20.

UNDER THE BOASTFUL AND BESTIAL EYE
OF A DIGNIFIED SYLVER UNGULATE

"The first creation in the famed Affirmation line of the Gear-hand Handiworks was the Pompuss, a megalomaniacal metal cat that everyone uniformly hated. The Cocky Cock was likewise an immediate flop, outside of a few sales to collegiate fraternities. The line only devolved from there until someone had the bright idea that maybe it wasn't the construct that should be so confident but rather the owners—for who couldn't use an extra shot of self-esteem? The Affirmation Gecko was thus invented and to this day is the bestselling PickaPet in history."

—TED ANTIKK, in *Nice Purchase, Pal! Way to Select the Perfect Book About Affirmation Geckos and Other Gnomeric Constructs!*

It was a most troublesome feeling, Gerd thought, to be surrounded by people yet know yourself to be alöne; it was quite different from being by oneself. She had felt that in the past and she often felt it still, but right now the young dwarf, Båggi Biins, was feeling it sööper badde. She could not help except to tell him he had done well, for he had. But he must struggle and win the fight within his own mind, and she could already tell it was a tougher fight for him than defeating the troll.

He rose from his knees after a while and helped bury the Savela family. They left the troll and halflings where they lay, and Gerd scouted for more such ambush parties ahead of them as they walked the rest of the way to Okesvaa. She found two patrols of halflings mounted on alpacas and dealt with them by flying overhead and screeching at the alpacas, which terrified them, and then speaking to the halflings.

These are my hunting grounds. You can ride far to the north right now and never come back here, she said, *or I will eat you. Choose now.*

Those halflings turned north, leaving rivers of alpaca plops and forgotten scarves behind. Gerd rejoined her party on the ground as they neared the town; they saw several other families of gnomes lying dead near the road, victims of the halflings, and they buried them all. The aged gnome and the young gnome had crafted mechanical shovels from the broken conveyance, but many blisters were made that day, nonetheless.

When they reached Okesvaa, they were confronted by shining automaatti that looked quite different from Piini. These sylver men had crossbows and swords and other things that looked like weapons. Gerd suspected they would be able to kill her easily and she would be unable to defeat them; she remembered well how she had been unable to move Piini at all. The sylver men were fine with letting the gnomes and the dwarf enter the city, but they were not going to let Faucon or Gerd pass until Agape told them she was a Vartija and the halfling and gryphon were her guests. There was some spirited communication after that; the sylver machines glowed and beeped and booped and told them to wait. A gnome in a severe khäki cardigan soon appeared with a birdlike construct perched on his shoulder. His skin was warm browne, and his beard had many beads and medals in it. He said his name was Captain Pekka Fassinen.

"Right, who's supposed to be the Vartija, then?"

Agape raised her hand. "Me, sir."

"Going to have to check on that. Just stand still while this lookit has a look at you."

The lookit, Gerd discovered, was the construct on Captain Fassinen's shoulder. It had the body of a bird, and its wings fluttered so fast that they blurred, but it had no beak. It had only a golden globe for a head, and once it hovered in front of Agape, this irised open, revealing a shiny whyte bulb of light. This whyte light played over Agape's face and head and then, after several seconds of this, turned greene. Captain Fassinen had evidently expected some other color, for his hooded eyes flew wide open and he gasped.

"You really are the Vartija!" he said.

"Well, yeah," Agape said, tucking into herself as everyone stared. "One of them, aaanyway."

"No, no, you don't understand. You're the only one left."

Everyone blinked a couple of times and then said, "What?" in unison.

"The halflings have wiped them all out. Even the one guarding the recipe archive."

Gerd hootled in mourning. *All those varmint casseroles. The squirrel dipping sauces. Gone forever!*

"Everyone should know!" the captain said, his excitement plain. "Would you mind if the lookit perched on your shoulder with its green light glowing?"

"I think I'd raaather not," Agape said. "We need to get to the City of Underthings."

"Of course, of course! I can't help you find the Vartija entrance—nobody knows where it is, you see. We haven't had a Vartija come back in my lifetime. I don't suppose you know where it is?"

"No. How could I? I've never been here. My paaarents told me it's the one city I was never supposed to visit, due to a sheep-eating cult."

"Then why have you come?" Gerd noticed that he did not deny the existence of such a cult.

"Because I need aaanswers, and because Piini Automaatti needs repair."

The captain's beard made clacking and tinkling noises as he leaned to one side to take in Piini over Agape's shoulder. "Golden gears and goose oil, that's an old model! They seriously do not make them like that anymore."

"Yes, well. Aaall the more reason to hurry." Gerd watched Agape cross her arms and figured it must mean she was growing impatient. The captain came to the same conclusion.

"Oh! Yes, you'll be wanting to be about your day. But I must ask you a couple of questions first. Did you meet any resistance on your way here?"

"Yes. Halflings and a troll were killing gnomes coming and going from Okesvaa to Pavaasik."

"They *were?*"

Kirsi bustled forward to stand in front of Agape. "The dwarf and gryphon traveling with us avenged all their victims, and we buried all those we found, with their cardigans freshly brushed. But the half-lings said they aren't letting anyone in or out of the city. So you may expect more such parties to be lurking outside the city to the north and east; I suspect you have been placed under a secret siege. I would advise your people not to leave without significant protection—maybe escort them with some of these automaatti you have."

"Hmm. That would explain why no one has arrived in recent days. I will let the kaupunginjohtaja know."

"Yeah . . ." Agape said, and her eyes shifted to Kirsi with a clear plea for help. "Let thaaat thing know . . . stuff."

"He means the mayor," Kirsi whispered, but Gerd heard. The lon-ger word was comforting to her, quite similar to the gryphon word for "the feeling of choking on half a mouse because tails are tricky, so just double down and don't give up."

"And who is this halfling?" Captain Fassinen asked, pointing at Faucon. "A prisoner?"

"No! His name is Faucon Pooternoob."

"Of the Toodleoo Pooternoobs," Faucon added helpfully, as if it would shed light on Pooternoobery.

"He's not with the Dastardly Rogues. He's been quite helpful since he stopped hunting me."

The captain did a double take. "I beg your pardon?"

Agape shook her head, her ears flopping in front of her face. "It's in the paaast. We worked things out."

"All right. Do you trust him to accompany you to the City of Underthings?"

Agape's gaze swung to Faucon and then to Gerd. Gerd nodded at Agape. *I vouch for him and will answer for his behavior,* she said.

The shaetyr nodded and said, "I've aaaccepted that without question up to this point, but now that it's clear there's war going on and we're talking about the safety of an entire population, I think I need to know why, Gerd. Faucon, please excuse me. There's just too much aaat stake."

The halfling bowed and stepped back. "You are excused. Were we about to enter a halfling city, similar questions would be raised about the gnomes. By all means, please discuss it. I shall withdraw some distance so that you may do so in private."

"Thank you."

They waited until Faucon had walked a good distance away and begun to braid his toe hair with great focus; then Gerd lay down so that her belly was in the dirt and she addressed them, including Captain Fassinen with the shiny beard.

A couple of months ago, I was hunting far from the Coxcomb, Gerd began, *and was in the territory of the Skyr, just to the east of the Figgish Fen. I wanted an antelope, and the ones east of the fen are quite tastee. But while flying over the plains I saw a group of halflings and then one odd shape some distance away, on the ground and in obvious pain. I assumed it was some sort of prey and flew down to see if it might be edible, and it was Faucon. He had a large barbed thorn in his foot. He could not pull it out; he could not walk upon it. I could also do neither of these things for him. But I took him to his camp in my talons, and his companions pulled the thorn out of his foot and bandaged it. In return, he made me my very first omlet.*

Gerd trilled at the memory, and her feathers fluffed up around the crest of her skull. *It was so tastee. He made me seven fluffee omlets so I wasn't hungry anymore. And then I flew back to the Coxcomb.*

Her feathers flattened. *I was told almost immediately that I smelled of egges.* Why do you smell like that, Gerd? What have you done, Gerd? Have you eaten egges? *they asked me. And I said no, I'd eaten omlets. Those are made of egges, they said. And then I was cast out of nest and keep—thrown out the gryphone door!—for violating one of our oldest laws. I did not even know of this law before I broke it! We never had egges or chickens at the Coxcomb, so the subject had never come up. My family was shamed for raising an egge eater. No one wanted to speak to me.*

Gerd hootled sadly. *I did not know where to go, so I flew back to Faucon. He told me that there was a difference between laws and justice, and sometimes laws created injustices when they were meant to correct them. But mostly laws are intended to create a just society, so we must follow laws or else there will be corruption and anarchee. It is interpreting and applying the law that is often difficult. We have spoken for many hours on the topic, and he is not like those halflings who wear medallions. He is for law and justice—for everyone. Now that he knows the Dastardly Rogues lied to him, that these actions against the gnomes are unlawful, he is dedicated to bringing them to justice, both for himself and his lost love and for the greater goode.*

The gryphon reared her head back and made some noises that might have been laughter. *Besides, I can see his aura like I can see yours. He is speaking the trüthe about wanting to destroy the Dastardly Rogues. He is on our side. You need not worry about him.*

Agape nodded. "That is consistent with what I've seen and heard from him so far. I aaam satisfied. To answer your question, Captain Fassinen, I trust the haaalfling and the gryphon as well."

The decorated gnome muttered an order to the automaatti, made a flourish with his hand, and stepped aside. "Then I welcome you all to Okesvaa."

There were no fires in the gnomeric capital, no skülking halflings throwing bombs. Just happy smöl people in cardigans and hats of blü, yellö, redde, and greene, selling fishes and früts and vegetables in the marketplace and more egges than Gerd could ever eat. There was a section of the market purveying automaatti designed to perform all sorts of tasks, from shiny goldenne men who wouldn't shut up, to rolling ballish bots who chirruped pleasantly, to a thing much like a garbage pail on wheels that seemed smarter than it had any right to be. As Gerd listened to the gnomeric salesmen haggle, she learned that one automaatti was capable of making almost any kind of cold sandwich and could be programmed to avoid allergens. Hot-sandwich models were a significant upgrade. One automaatti was a remarkable device that would scoop up cat waste, fumigate the area, and then ruthlessly, mercilessly, launch said waste into a suborbital flight ending somewhere in the Dämköld Sea. It came as a matched set with another automaatti, which cleaned up cat bärffe and hair-balls.

Half of the city was underground, and what was visible above were often simply entrances to subterranean businesses or homes. Luckily, the wagon entrances were big enough to host Gerd's bulk, and she was soon enjoying the sights of a colorful underground bazaar while Agape searched for some hidden döör. She was sitting for a sketch beside Okesvaa's mayor, who wore a blü cardigan with finely stitched gryphons for the honor, when Båggi came running up, all out of breath.

"We found it!" he enthused in that enthusiastic way he had. "It's like Agape knew exactly what to do!" His eyes went faraway for a moment. "How happy that must be, to know. Ha ha!"

I will follow you, Gerd told him. His Telling Cudgel was still in a semi-warlike state, with chubby nubs along its length, but his excitement was real, merely overlaid with a sort of melancholee. His beard had been expertly braided and bedecked with jolly redde berries.

"Agape reasoned that it must be in a somewhat largeish area," Båggi said, "since some Vartijas were humans. You'll never guess where she found it! But guess anyway."

They were deep in the subterranean bazaar, and the walls and ceiling had been tiled in glorious blüs and indigös with sparkling stars of lemon yellö.

Next to a cheesemonger? Gerd ventured.

"No, but a particularly excellent guess! The entrance is in fact next door to a meadery in the Happi Hatte Hutt!"

Are the hattes happi or is it the hutt that is happi?

"Both, I think. Here it is."

Gerd ducked through the entrance and followed the dwarf back to the stock room, which was quite a squeeze for her. All the smöl people were flushed with excitement and smiling wide smiles. Many hatboxes had been moved and piled on one side, for in one corner the shining outline of a large door waited.

"I found it, Gerd!" Agape said. "This door became visible aaafter I walked in the room!"

I can see. But how does it operate? I do not see a convenient knob or handle.

"Well, there's always knocking." With great authoritee, the ovitaur rapped on the metal.

A smöl window slid open, and two whyte lights shone out.

"Who dares approach the grand frilliness of the City of Underthings?" a bass voice boomed.

"I am Agape Fallopia, the laaast of the Vartijas."

Focused beams washed up and down Agape before the two whyte lights turned greene.

"That"—the voice boomed—"checks out."

The door slid open with a Grand Squeake, revealing that the two lights were actually eyes that belonged to a very strange creature that Gerd would've enjoyed challenging to a wrestling match, had it not been crafted of metal and thus even heavier than Piini Automaatii.

"Is that a . . . a wildebeest?" the smöl elderly man named Eino asked, squinting.

The venerable head inclined in a bow. "I am Wilbore the Wildeboast, my good sir, and obviously the finest example of my kind. I was created by the Gearhands of Old and assigned my task by the Elders: to greet and guide Vartijas, of which you are apparently one."

The thing was much like a Noble Goat or Droopy Stagge, to Gerd's eyes, with a distinguished ungulate face dominated by a long nose, four hooves, and curving horns of shining sylver. Its body was finely chased to appear hairy, the metal a dignified graye.

"Do come in, and please show proper wonder for the finest city ever erected."

The wildeboast stepped back to allow them passage, and the door closed behind them, leaving the employees of the Happi Hatte Hutt behind. Gerd wondered if the hutt was less happi now that they had to rehang their hattes on hundreds of hooks.

They were in total darkness for a brief time, but then lights flickered on to reveal a featureless hallway.

"You will note the featureless nature of the hallway," Wilbore said. "It was designed to heighten your excitement upon seeing the true splendor of what lies beyond. Why, no plainer, more boring, more anticlimactic hallway has ever been seen!"

The wildeboast led them forward until they reached a large platform elevator filled with gears and levers and buttons.

"If I might call your attention to the splendid way I correctly and confidently work this machinery," the automattii said quietly. "You will notice that even though it was not crafted for my anatomy, I remain utterly in control."

Wilbore grasped a lever in his metal teeth and pulled it while waggling his expressive eyebrows for emphasis, and the floor vibrated for a second as they began to descend.

"Why have you come to pay your respects to the City of Underthings?" the wildeboast asked.

"We seek a Certified Gnomeric Gearhaaand in the Great Library," Agape responded. "My automattii requires repair and cleaning."

Wilbore's visual sensors traveled up and down Piini's form. "Yes," he said, with a shiver of distaste. Piini's head drooped. "This bot is indeed a hotte mess. The hottest mess I have ever beheld. Now, please prepare yourselves for your first breathtaking view of the most wondrous place in the entire universe, the City of Underthings!"

21.

SURROUNDED BY CLANDESTINE WONDERS AND EMBROIDERED COVERALLS

"The Skyr is home to two sub-subterranean cities. From the city underneath Okesvaa we get wondrous inventions. From the city underneath Bigly-Wicke we get nothing but corruption, orders for takeout food, and backed-up sewers."

—HELMI PIIPPOLA, in *Navigating the Perils of Public Plumbing*

When the elevator stopped and the doors opened, the smöl people all gasped and said, "Ooooh" and "Wow," and the wildeboast said, "I told you so," and Gerd trilled in pleasure. Faucon carefully schooled his expression, but even he was impressed. The City of Underthings was a legend halflings either disdained or ridiculed, but its reality was even more wondrous than the wildeboast had promised.

The ceiling was much higher than he'd expected, higher even than the one in Eino's workshop, and he was glad Gerd would not have to duck her head to walk around. She might even be able to fly, but only at risk of colliding with other flying things and crane hooks and whatnot. It was a very busy place, but a series of color-coordinated lights, well-placed signage, and traffic-conducting automatons promised an orderly sort of rule.

The wildeboast led them along, pointing out this or that architectural wonder and appearing to gain great pleasure from their expostulations. Faucon did his best to remain unintrusive, keeping his body between Gerd's bulk and the grouping of the ovitaur and her automaton. Eventually a party of gnomes greeted them with great pomp, and Wilbore turned to face Agape.

"I will leave you now, fair Vartija and friends, but please know that you are without a doubt the finest Vartija I have ever met, being the first one, and that I shall record you in my memory banks with the same fondness with which you shall forever recall me, Wilbore, the most amazing—"

An older gnome with fantastic posture stepped forward, smiling. "That will be all, Wilbore. Thank you for your most exemplary service. Please return to your post." The wildeboast bowed and returned the way they'd come, softly boasting to himself about what a phenomenal job he'd done at walking away.

These gnomes did not wear cardigans, it seemed, instead favoring red overalls garnished with tool belts; they also sported helmets and goggles. They appeared clean, outside of oil smudges that suggested an appropriate level of crafting, which Faucon appreciated.

"I am Hellä Traktiv, kaupunginjohtaja of the City of Underthings for the second quarter. It is such an honor to have you visit us, Agape Fallopia. But wait." Hellä craned her head this way and that to see around Gerd, and Faucon put his shoulders back and stepped forward, prepared for the moment he'd grown to hate. "Why have you brought a halfling into our orderly city?" she shouted. Faucon refused to flinch, even as gnomeric weapons and bung wrenches appeared in every hand, all pointed directly at him.

Agape rubbed a place on her forehead. "His name is Faucon. He's a good guy. He's not a drub. He's helping us. How faaar do I have to get on this quest before people stop letting their prejudice gum up the works? You're wasting valuable time."

Yes, Gerd quickly agreed, and Faucon's heart thumped with gladness for her friendship. *His aura is as clear as that of the Vartija. Perhaps someone could give us a Certificate of Authenticitee so that we might skip this step the next tyme we meet someone?*

Faucon held out his hairy wrists. "Manacle me if it makes you feel better. I wish to see Agape complete her quest and am willing to sacrifice my freedom temporarily if it will soothe your mind."

Hellä considered them all, hands on her hips. "There is no precedent for a halfling in the City of Underthings. I'll allow you to remain with your party, Faucon, but know that you will be closely watched. And that a Charm of No Telling will be placed on you before you leave this place."

Faucon nodded once and stuck his hands in his pockets. They were chock full of throwing stars, but the gnomes didn't know that.

Hellä reschooled her face into something more welcoming and warm. "Now. Vartija. We are so glad you found us. You seek a Certified Gnomeric Gearhand?"

"Thank you. I do. This is Piini Automaatti."

Hellä gestured to a gnome on her right, a pale-skinned woman with a graying beard. "This is Inka Nurmi. She will happily repair and clean Piini Automaatti for you, after which you may decide what to do with him, though we hope you'll leave him with us."

Agape blinked. "I'm sorry, what? I don't understaaand."

"If you'll just instruct Piini to let us service him, Inka will get to work, and we can get you back topside and on your way."

"That's not the only reason we're here. The gnomes aboveground are in trouble. The halflings are taking over, doing horrible things. Did you know?"

Hellä raised an eyebrow. "We have heard rumors."

Agape shook her head. "It is almost certainly far worse than you haaave heard. We need to get copies of some documents in the Great Library and bring them to the King of Pell."

"We'll get to the library, then, if that's what you need. But, first, Inka needs permission to service your automaatti. He is long overdue, you see."

"Okay, sure. Piini Automaatti, go with Inka and let her restore you to good working order."

The automaton clomped after Inka, who led him to the left. Hellä Traktiv gestured to their right. "This way to the Great Library, then."

Everyone followed Hellä in a bit of a daze, disoriented at the sudden and unceremonious departure of Piini. Faucon noticed that a particularly beefy gnome paced beside him as they walked, something between an honor guard and a . . . prison guard.

You know, Faucon, Gerd said in only his head, a skill they'd honed in their time together. *It is interesting, this sense that something always there but unnoticed is suddenly gone, leaving a hole in its place. A Distynct Lacking, perhaps. Our original goal was to destroy the yellö man, but now his leaving makes me blü.*

She was right, of course. Much had changed.

As they passed through the City of Underthings, Faucon was amazed at what the gnomes had accomplished. For all that he'd grown to think of gnomes as shoddy busybodies, the city stood testament to law, order, and excellent building codes. Automatons stood like soldiers at the ready, while whistling birds flew to and fro overhead and lizards scurried up and down the columns. Each statue included a plaque naming its creators and the filing number of its official paperwork. As they oiled their machines and ate their food and trundled around in their vehicles, the populace seemed happy, healthy, and, most important, clean.

Faucon, Gerd said in his head, *I notice that these smöl people seem to serve the machines they've created to perform their work. It is moste strange. What if the machines should gain sentience and rise up against their creators?*

"That would be their business, Gerd," he said quietly. "They would not welcome a halfling's intervention."

If the machines do rise, she said, more to herself than to him, *I'll be back.*

Finally, Hellä bid them pause at a food establishment just outside a grand edifice that had to be the Great Library. Agape seemed jittery and anxious to enter, but the mayor had that sort of quiet iron strength that suggested no one would move farther until they'd endured gnomeric hospitality. As he'd missed third breakfast, Faucon did not protest. As soon as everyone was seated at a wide table made of hard polished planks from the Morningwood, automattii crafted to look like otters brought them hot chocolate with marshmallows, on silver trays. They brought Gerd a nice blended meat smoothie, at which she gurgled outwardly while her inner monologue purred along.

Mostly squirrel and chipmunk, but with a little groundhog thrown in for spice!

At the gryphon's squawk of surprise, the mayor mentioned that the undergnomes fished upward, using hunting chimneys and telescoping squirrel-fishing poles.

Hellä Traktiv toasted their health and stared at them firmly as they drank their cocoa and ate tiny sandwiches. When even Kirsi had given a polite burp, Hellä led them to the high, grand doors of the library, which opened inward to show a magnificent gold chandelier and the most orderly, beautiful, squeaky-clean floor-to-ceiling bookshelves Faucon had ever beheld.

As one, the party intoned, "The Great Library!"

"Hey, that was the best tone of awe I've ever heard!" a nearby metal lizard enthused before scurrying off.

Hellä allowed them adequate time to gape, then directed them to sit at a round polished table. There was a general air of readiness that Faucon found invigorating.

Hellä turned to Agape. "Now that we are in the Great Library, I must ask you a question: Did you ever ask Piini to recite the Elder Annals for you?"

"No. We listened to the Tome of Togethering."

"Ah! No doubt you noticed that many of those old laws are no longer in effect."

"We did."

"But all is not lost."

Hellä rapped the table with a fist, and silver automatons delivered three ancient books to the table: the Tome of Togethering, the Stern Reminder of the Looming Peril of Giants, and the Elder Annals! Even Faucon was dumbfounded. To think: The original works that had shaped his people! The ultimate bottom line of law!

"If you attempt to touch these tomes," Hellä warned, "your knuckles will be rapped, and you'll be removed from the Great Library permanently. Now, the Elder Annals were written—and, indeed, this protected city was built—with the assumption that those laws would eventually erode and cease to exist. The Elders knew that one day either the gnomes or the halflings would try to centralize and consolidate power over the other. That's why we built this city—because to consolidate power, one must control information. We protect that information. The Elder Annals explain why the Vartijas were created."

"And someone made them both disappear," Agape said.

"The gnomes among the Elders believed that anyone interested in power would eventually come after the Vartijas. And they were right. What we don't know is who."

The halflings are responsible for hunting Vartijas. They hired Faucon to hunt Agape, Gerd said.

"The Dastardly Rogues Under Bigly-Wicke under Marquant Dique, to be exact," Faucon volunteered. Hellä's eyes swung to Faucon.

"I am no longer in their employ," he explained. "But that is how I know they are responsible. I was hired by Marquant Dique under false pretenses to destroy Piini Automaatti."

"Then we can no longer stay hidden here and hope for the best aboveground. We must create enough automaatti fighters to beat back a halfling invasion. There is much for me to do. Now: What will you do? What do you need from us, besides copies of the great tomes?"

"I ain't part of this dinkum quest," Eino said. "I came here to become a Certified Gnomeric Gearhand, maybe help produce those automaatti you were talking about."

"We can give you the gearhand exam, certainly," Hellä replied. "And if you don't pass, there's always Gnome Unity College to help you get up to speed." The old gnome dipped his hat, delighted.

"And how about you, sir?" Hellä asked Faucon. "What will you do?"

"I wish to destroy the Dastardly Rogues Under Bigly-Wicke and live under a government that respects the rule of law," Faucon replied. "Preferably a return to the equitable system our people enjoyed under the Tome of Togethering." His eyes alighted on the ancient book, crawling hungrily over the golden binding.

I wish this also, Gerd said. *I would like a nest and keep in the Skyr. With laws. And maybe one of your machines that make meat waffles.*

"We may be able to help with that," Hellä said, smiling at Gerd. She turned to Båggi Biins. "And you?"

"I wish to complete my Meadschpringå," Båggi said, "and I believe that means I should help my friends restore order in the Skyr."

"I want the same thing," Kirsi added. "I want to bring peace back to the Skyr so we can enjoy our land and Båggi can return to his mountain home."

Onni nodded and twirled his finger around to indicate the others. "What they all said."

"A unity of purpose. Good." Hellä nodded at them and turned to Agape. "And you?"

"I . . . don't know. Don't I need to protect Piini?"

"Not anymore. You've fulfilled your function. You need not be a Vartija any longer. In fact, now that he is returned, it would be in your best interest to divest yourself of the aura, as it will draw those who wish to hunt you. It's like wearing a pork chop around your neck in the Figgish Fen, honestly. We would like to keep Piini, if you don't mind, for there is much for us to learn from an automaatti made many generations ago. But you are welcome to do whatever you wish.

You may stay here with us and pursue any vocation you like, or not work at all, in recognition of your service. Or you may go into the world again, with or without Piini. Your call. As we gnomes always say, *Do the thing that makes you sing!*"

Agape sat back in her chair, stunned. "I . . ." Her voice died out, and she swallowed. "I don't sing. And I'm not a Vartija aaanymore?"

"You've protected your charge, frustrated the plans of the halflings, and brought news that will mobilize our fight in accordance with the Elder Annals. Your responsibility is fulfilled. So: What would you like to do?"

Agape looked around at her companions.

Her desperation smells somewhat like chipotle mayonnaise, Gerd privately noted to Faucon.

The ovitaur's mouth was open, but no sound came out.

It is good that you would try gryphon speech, Gerd said, *but you are doing it wronge.*

Kirsi gave her fierce grin and stepped forward. "Come with us, Agape."

"Yes!" Båggi enthused. "We need someone of your wit and strength!"

I, too, once found myself without a home. But you have boon companions and are both wanted and needed, sheep person. You would honor us with your company, Gerd said with an enthusiastic hootle.

Faucon remained silent; either Agape would heed the call to action or she would ignore it.

"I . . . would like to see the Skyr at peace again," Agape said. "So I guess I'll come aaalong."

Gerd trilled, and Faucon smiled to himself, and the others cheered, and the hunter let that die down before he spoke.

"It seems to me," Faucon finally said, recognizing that what this group needed wasn't purpose and cheering but an orderly plan, "that someone must approach the kanssa-jaarli with proper copies of the Elder Annals. What has happened to the gnomeric half of the two earls that would allow the halflings such freedom to spread disorder? The Toot Towers are open to the public, and as citizens, we have the right to ask questions. That might be more sensible than approaching the king, who has thus far remained ambivalent to the plight of the Skyr."

"But what of the Dastardly Rogues?" Kirsi asked.

"I wish to expunge the remaining reservoir of my violence upon them!" Bäggi said, but when he hefted his Telling Cudgel, it had a book carved into it and looked more like an umbrella than a weapon.

"Even in our full power, our small party cannot fight them." Faucon looked to Hellä. "But an army of automaatti could."

The steely-eyed mayor nodded. "True enough, and canny. We can assault them with automaatti and would welcome a chance to try some aggressive prototype devices."

"So you're the brawn, and we're the brains?" Kirsi asked.

Hellä grinned a vicious grin. "I'd like to think we also have brains, and you also have brawn, or at least a gryphon. We can provide you with supplies and weapons, as well as a cadre of lookits to send us regular updates. In case you have difficulty speaking directly with Jarmo Porkkala, the gnomeric jaarl, I will give you a letter with my official mayoral stamps and curlicues on it that will grant you an immediate audience. You must deliver the Elder Annals to the jaarl, and I will send a copy to the king."

Gerd had grown bored with the proceedings and left her place at the round table to pace in a way that appeared menacing to anyone smöl enough to be swallowed in one gulp. Hellä absentmindedly waved a hand, and a dapper automaton librarian hurried over and bowed to the gryphon, asking, "How can we help you, fair gryphon?"

Do you have any volumes of gryphone poetry? Gerd asked.

"Of course! The Great Library has most everything. Any particular poet?"

I wonder if you have any of the lesser-known works by Hurp Blep.

"Ah, yes, the master of screech sonnets! We have three volumes of what are generally considered his lesser works. Shall I bring them all?"

Do you have Death Screams of Squirrels I Snacked Upon This Fortnight?

"Yes."

What about An Embarrassing Berry Snarled in the Hair of My Hindquarters? *You have that too?*

"We do! I will have them brought to you here, along with a refreshing snack."

Soon enough, the gnomes were able to return to their plans, as the gryphon had a fish milkshake and several books of poetry in front of her.

"I would be honored to turn the pages for you," the librarian said. "Shall I begin at the beginning, or were you interested in something specific?"

"Sonnet Number 42" in the Squirrels volume, if you please, she said.

Much to Faucon's surprise, Gerd read aloud just for him, the voice in his head taking on a melodramatic tone he'd never heard from the gryphon before:

In midnight moon-tyme, in sylent darkness
I fly, owl-quiet, in silken air dreams
Of meaty updrafts in cöbält starkness,
And hear in both earholes the fryghtsick screams
Of springtyme squirrels as I crunch their spines—
Sweet music of the hunt a heartbeat's drum
Suddenly stopt, tailbrushes twitch once, signs
Of life extinguish, and their flesh is yum.
But O! My fyne feathered lüv, if I live
For aught else, 'tis to provide for thy lack,
And gladly would I starve, gladly would I give
The death screams of the squirrels on which I snack.
For thy joy is my food, thy rest my sleep;
'Tis thou, my lüv, who art my nest and keep.

The last two lines were delivered in a strangled hootle that caused Faucon some alarm.

"Gerd, are you well?" he asked. "Were there bones in the shake?"

Gryphones cannot cry, but these words make my gizzard ache. I do not have a fyne feathered lüv, nor will I ever . . . now. But I must content myself with fyne friends, even if they are not feathered. You are a fyne friend, Faucon, one who appreciates me as Gerd and not some idealized gryphone who had never supped upon the forbidden egges.

Faucon was quite moved, and he put a hand upon Gerd's furred shoulder. "Groogle," he said, his first attempt to speak in her language.

I think you meant to say friend, but you said biscuit, she told him. *Still, it is enough.*

Their moment was interrupted by Kirsi, who called, "We'd best get on the road. Are you ready?"

I was not finished reading, Gerd said, *but I suppose I can go now.*

"Would you like a to-go cup?" the librarian asked.

What is that thing you said?

"We can load all of Hurp Blep's poetry into an automaatti in the shape of a bird—a Carrier of Underthing Poetry, in this case. It will follow you and require no maintenance, and it will recite any of Hurp Blep's works for you on command in the original gryphon language or translated into any Pellican language you wish."

Is this magick?

"It is gnomeric technology. We have made some improvements since the time of the Piini Automaatti you brought in. He was essentially an early reader model with some added functionality."

I would like that very much. But what do I do when I am finished with the bird reader?

"Tell it to return here and request some other work, if you wish. The bird will eventually find you again and recite any new work you have requested upon command."

This . . . this is an extraordinary library. I begin to see the valü of smöl people.

"Thank you. We do try our best. We'll send the bird to find you when it is ready."

"It really is something, is it not?" Faucon asked as they followed the others out of the Great Library and into the city again.

It was a pleasant place to be. For all that Faucon had grown up in halfling restaurants and artisan workshops, he felt most at home among precision and cleanliness, and the City of Underthings had both in great quantities. The people had a quiet and orderly but bouncy way about them—except for some sort of strange brouhaha happening up the street. Faucon went up on his tiptoes to look ahead and see what kind of miscreants such a society could produce.

The din seemed to be coming from a knot of gnomes in red coveralls who were shouting and waving their tiny arms, but Faucon couldn't quite pick out their words among the overall hum and mechanical drone of the city. Soon, gnomes were screeching and grabbing their hats as they dove out of the way of a golden automaatti that was moving fast along the streets toward them. Its shape resembled . . . well, not an otter or a snake and not precisely a spider either, though it was very low to the ground and reminded Faucon a bit of Eino's half centipod, but much smaller and obviously not intended to be a transport for anything bigger than a halfling-sized jug of ale. It looked like it had somewhere to go and it was impossible to know what to do about it, so Faucon politely stepped to the side in case its mission was important. By the time he realized what was happening, it was too late to do anything about it.

The automaatti did indeed have somewhere to go: Its destination was Faucon's bare feet, and it swerved directly for him and used its many appendages to lock on to his ankles and wrap its body lengthwise along his ten toes, encasing them completely. It was somehow both cold and hot, smooth and sharp, and in the process tackled Faucon to the ground as he tried to escape and was essentially tripped. Everything happened so fast that all he could really feel was fear and an uncomfortable squeezing.

It was at that point that everyone moved to help, understanding that something was very wrong. But it was already too late: The automaatti's body convulsed, and Faucon screamed in agony.

"Augggh! My tooooes!" he cried.

The automaatti disengaged, and as if through someone else's eyes, Faucon saw that his toes—his beautiful, perfect toes!—were little more than wee limp bags of meat, the bones in them pulverized into bits and no longer resembling digits.

One of the gnomes in red who'd been waving from a distance caught up, puffing for breath, and said, "Oh, no!" as he stared down. Faucon blinked and saw two of him.

"Help?" asked the gnome, who looked up and said, "He's in shock."

"What the Pell just happened?" Hellä Traktiv said, towering over Faucon now that he was splayed on the ground in excruciating pain. He could feel his heartbeat in his ears—*thumpity-bump*—and beyond that, only the screaming nerves below his ankles.

"I'm so sorry, we didn't know there were any halflings in the city, or we never would have run the test sequence," the gnome in red said. "When we turned it on, it just took off, following its programming. That was one of the new HTS drones you recently ordered for the coming offensive."

Hellä gasped.

What does HTS stand for? Gerd said.

The gnome trembled and quaked as he looked into Faucon's eyes. "It stands for Halfling Toe Smasher, and its work cannot be undone."

22.

Suffering from a Distinct Lack of Toes on a Gurney on a Train in a Tunnel

"The number of gnomes who were accidentally stabbed in the throat by pencils stored in their beards used to be quite high, until someone invented a throat-safe pencil. Better to invent that, apparently, than to cease using beards for pencil storage."

—Herko Sokka, in *A Brief Illustrated History of Gnomeric Cleverness*

Faucon paused his screaming to yowl, "My toes! My beautiful toes!" and Kirsi hurried to hold his hand. She didn't know anything about healing, and she couldn't curse an injury away, but she was quite good at patting and squeezing hands and saying reassuring things that meant nothing. They had praised her, back in school, for her natural talent at letting her eyebrows draw together in sympathy and nodding at exactly the right time—sympathetic furrowing, the medal read. She realized, as her smöl fingers wrapped around his slightly larger, far hairier ones, that she had never touched a halfling before. Her parents had taught her from a young age that it would cause boils to break out across her nose, make her beard fall out, and irreparably wrinkle her cardigan.

None of these things happened. People taught their children awful things sometimes.

"Surely someone can help him. Don't you have surgeons here?" she asked, feeling his tension and terror as his fingers jumped and clutched at hers.

Hellä shook her head sadly. "We do have surgeons, but the problem with designing a machine to destroy halfling toes permanently is that when you do a good job, it can't be reversed. I assure you that those toes are in their death throes. The phalanges have been thoroughly pulverized to a fine and most moist meat powder."

"Oh, my saddest boyhood britches," Båggi murmured, pausing as he mixed potions to peer over his picnic basket to examine Faucon's toes. "My friends, this sort of ruination is beyond the aid of my boning tea. That only mends clean breaks and can't fix pulverized bone. But perhaps . . ."

"Perhaps?" Kirsi pressed.

"Perhaps I can help him go to sleep while we worry over how to help. All the screaming isn't very good for one's nerves, is it? Ha ha!"

Kirsi had noticed that the poor dwarf only said *ha ha* when he was panicking or terrified, and she didn't want to make him feel worse, so she just nodded and said, "Yes. If you can gift him with unconsciousness, I'm sure he'll thank you. Sometime in the future."

Faucon gave his tacit agreement by continuing to scream.

With great gravitas, Båggi went to his mead cask, turned it upside down, and popped the bottom off, revealing a thick golden-brown sort of jelly. A boozy, honey-sweet scent filled the air, and even Faucon momentarily stopped screeching to take in a deep breath.

"This is the mead seed," Båggi explained. "The most concentrated heart of dwarvelish mead. A thimbleful might make you wee ones sleep for a week, so I must carefully administer this dose." From his basket, Båggi withdrew a special spoon, hand-hammered with a honeycomb motif in the handle. He scraped up about half a spoonful of the mead seed and slipped it delicately into Faucon's yowling maw.

"Ahh! Ahh! Oh! Oh. Ohhhhh." Faucon went from frantic, red-faced, and terror-filled to sleepy and smiling. "That'll do," he murmured, and Kirsi's eyes flew wide to hear him use a contraction. The mead seed was potent indeed. His eyes fluttered closed, and his breathing grew deep. Everyone sighed in relief at the complete lack of screaming.

"I can dull pain," Båggi said quietly. "But I can't fix this."

Some things can never be fixed, Gerd said, her voice calm in Kirsi's mind.

The gryphon had first responded to Faucon's situation by attacking the machine that had hurt her friend, and once she'd torn it apart, she'd spread her wings and raised her ruff, warning off any gnomes who might come near. Now it would appear she'd come to terms with the grim finality of the situation.

But broken things are still worthwhile, she continued. Her noble head rose, her piercing eyes pinning Hellä and the gearhands. *And I do not just mean egges. Perhaps you cannot fix him, but you can help him. You are smöl people of vision, are you not? Bring me an invention that will aide this fyne halfling. If you cannot help, if you can only hurt, then you have forgotten the ways of the Elders. Which, by ancient law, means I can eat you in one bite. Because those are the rules.* She licked her beak and stared.

"Help him?" the gearhand muttered. "She told you: We can't!"

"But you can!" Onni said, looking up, his eyes alight. Kirsi hadn't noticed him kneeling by her side; he'd been oddly quiet during their deliberations of strategy. "You're inventors, so invent something. Something to aid his mobility."

"Huh," the gearhand said, scratching his beard bun. "A rolling chair wouldn't work so well for your journey, but if we amputated his toes—"

No! Gerd hooted. *He prizes his toes above all else, except the memory of Remy!*

"They'll only cause him pain from here on out." Kirsi reached out to gently stroke Gerd's talon, and the gryphon allowed it. "But if they're removed, that pain will fade. It will be a kindness." She looked up at the gearhand. "So can you do it? Can you build . . . I don't know. A boot? Some sort of contraption?"

Onni pulled a small book out of his cardigan pocket and started sketching with a pencil Kirsi hadn't noticed stashed in his beard. "Something like this, maybe?" He passed the notebook to Hellä, and she and her gearhand studied it. Kirsi got a glimpse and felt her smoosh ratchet up into nearly explosively squishy territory. She hadn't known Onni had any skill with gnomeric devices. Perhaps grouchy old Offi had taught him something, after all. But now Kirsi realized the truth of the well-known gnomeric saying *Once you go mechanical, prepare to be fanatical*. A gnomeboy with a crisp cardigan and a pencil in his beard was most attractive.

"I can do that," the gearhand said. "The design is quite clever, actually. You've a gift, boy." Onni gave a heart-melting grin that seared itself on the backs of Kirsi's eyeballs.

"Then go to your workshop and begin," Hellä said before turning to Kirsi. "I will engage our finest surgeon to operate immediately. You can all stay here for a few weeks as he recuperates—"

"We don't have that kind of time, by dinkus," Kirsi reminded her. "Gnomes are dying willy-nilly aboveground. Perhaps you're insulated from it down here, but we've seen it firsthand. Give us Onni's invention and a rolling contraption to get us going, and Faucon can recuperate on the way."

Hellä shook her head in amazement. "You're very driven."

Kirsi, for once, didn't smile. "Someone has to be. We must go to the Toot Towers to see the gnomeric jaarl, and we must have the proper documentation in hand to convince him that what's occurring is unlawful. So fix our halfling, give us the requisite travelers' gifts, provide us with the proper paperwork, and get us going as quickly as you can. I assume we'll have to stop in Muffincrumb and Caskcooper on the way."

The look Hellä gave her was almost . . . no, it *was* admiration. Onni was grinning too.

"If that's what you need to save our people," the mayor said, "then we'll do it."

A few hours later, Kirsi and her friends stood at a giant iron door fitted with a multitude of interlocking bars. Faucon lay flat on a brass gurney, his bandaged feet sticking out on one end because the gurney had clearly been crafted for gnomes. He slept, thanks to Båggi's mead seed, but it was troubling to note that the halfling's feet looked vastly truncated. Kirsi had never before appreciated how long half-ling toes were, since their absence left such a void. Gerd meeped over her friend, a heartbreaking sound.

Hellä and Inka faced them, the mayor looking dapper and impor-tant and the gearhand utterly smeared with grease, her beard a mess but her smile triumphant.

"Here is everything you should need," Hellä said. "The letter I promised, two official notarized copies of the Tome of Togethering and the Elder Annals with the important bits highlighted, and an official writ so the gnomefloat gnavigator will give you priority ac-cess to travel the Rumplescharte River."

"Why two copies?" Kirsi asked, holding out a hand to take one of the two proferred gnomesacks as Onni took the other.

"Because what kind of fool on a dangerous quest would take only one? One of you might get eaten by a murderguppy or fall into a crevasse or lose your pack to a ravenous giant wasp hungry for paper. This is a library and seat of some power; if we can't make notarized copies, we're not very good at what we do. And on a personal note, I wish you well. I haven't stood in the unfiltered sun for a decade, and I hope the overlands will be free and happy again someday."

Hellä leaned over, and Kirsi met her, rubbing noses in the ceremo-nial fashion. Kirsi realized with pride that she was being treated not as a gnomelet but as an adult and equal.

A loud, hiccupping sob interrupted the gesture, and Kirsi looked to Agape. The ovitaur was bawling, big fat tears on her cheeks—but she was trying hard to hide it.

"Agape?" she asked. "What's wrong?"

Agape sniffed and turned away. "Nothing."

Nothing doesn't generally involve so much honking, Gerd said. *There is no shame in crying. I often wish I could cry. You can tell us what ails you, sheep person. Is it indigestion?*

"No. I'm fine. Really." The ovitaur turned completely around, her shoulders shaking.

Kirsi wanted to reach out, but the size difference made it awkward and she didn't want to pat the ovitaur's fluffy butt. "I am not familiar with the ovitaurian ways, but I do not believe that's what fine looks like. Although I would normally go with the gnomeism *Keep those feelings tamped down firm to keep from making others squirm,* I really think you might need to talk about it."

Agape looked like she wanted to continue feigning okayness, albeit poorly, but she also looked like she might explode, and then she did. "I just didn't know losing people could hurt so much!" she wailed. "I've never lost aaanyone! My whole life, it's been mom and daaad and Piini. But now Piini is gone, and my paaarents left me behind, aaand aaand aaand I FEEL SO BAAAAAAAD."

Onni and Båggi looked helplessly to Kirsi, who put on her brightest smile and went in for a Grand Comforting.

"I know you thought your parents and Piini would always be with you, but sometimes we outgrow things from our youth," she said. "I had a stuffed mushroom that I loved to rags, and one day I put it on the shelf. I don't love it any less, and I don't forget it. It's always a part of me. But I carry it in my heart instead of my arms."

"I caaan't carry Piini, because he weighs a million pounds!" Agape wailed, and Kirsi realized that there was a vast difference between feelings being real and feelings being based on reality.

"It's more of a metaphor," she said, patting Agape's knee. "Piini belongs here, and it was you who brought him here. With both destinies fulfilled, you're free to seek your own happiness. Like your parents are seeking theirs. They just waited until their fifties to grow up, I guess. But you can grow up now. And you have friends. Us."

Agape ignored that kindness and shook her head, and tears flew willy-nilly. "But why caaan't Piini come with me?"

"He is happy in the library, I assure you," Inka said, stepping forward. "A machine is happiest fulfilling its purpose. Out in the world, he'll just get gunked up and bogged down. And your friend Eino will help to keep him well calibrated. They will give each other purpose."

"That's by dinkum true!" Eino enthused. "I can't wait to get him all oiled up!"

But that only made Agape cry harder.

"Wait," Kirsi said. "I have an idea. Inka, did you replace any parts on Piini? Any cogs or springs?"

Inka looked confused but dug around in her cardigan pockets. "Plenty of them." She held her hand out flat, showing many smöl cogs and bits, all grimy but with revealing glints of brass underneath. Kirsi selected the prettiest of the cogs and held it up to Inka.

"Can you shine this up a bit, perhaps?"

Understanding Kirsi's plan, Inka used her pants to wipe the gunk off the gear and hold it out to Agape.

"Carry this with you, Agape," Kirsi said. "Keep this piece of Piini with you always, and remember the good times."

Agape reached out, tentative, and held up the cog to the lanterns. "I caaan find a chain for it in Caskcooper," Agape finally said, pocketing the cog. "It's a very aaartistic city." Her sobs had fallen off, and although she still looked sad, she seemed capable of going on a journey without waking every predator in the forest with damp bleating.

"Then you're still coming with us?"

Agape's shoulders rose to brush her drooping ears. "I guess. For a little while. If we're going in the same direction and all. Aaat least until I find . . ."

"Your purpose?" Båggi asked, perking up.

"Something to do," Agape shot back. It seemed to Kirsi that Agape was hiding her fear under a Definite Grouch, but that sort of knot took a while to unsnarl. The best thing for them all would be to get on the road.

"Then let's go," Kirsi said, waving an arm at the door. "*Better to be on your feet and atrot than to stick around standing and stirring the pot.*"

"My brother loves that one," Onni said with a snort.

She gave him a sharp look. "That's because it's good advice. Come on."

Hellä gave Kirsi a key and explained how the door worked, and Kirsi was about to suggest this task be given to Onni when she suddenly realized that she had become the group's de facto leader. It was a very peculiar feeling, as her parents had raised her to be a proper follower, but she merely took the key and nodded solemnly.

"Thank you for everything, Hellä," she said, trying out her own authority by addressing the mayor by her first name. "Well, everything except for destroying and removing Faucon's toes."

A very awkward moment ensued in which no one could look at anyone else and Faucon gently snored, then Hellä recovered herself.

"Good journey," she said.

Everyone hugged Eino and wished him well, and many *by dinkums* were exchanged, and then Kirsi opened the grand door and stepped into the long, dark tunnel.

The long, dark tunnel wasn't so bad, as it contained a pleasant train that smoothly transported their entire group miles with the press of a button. And it actually wasn't that dark, as the gnomes had cleverly coaxed some sort of glowing green algae to grow along the ceilings and in decorative patterns along the walls.

"Heavens to humble pie!" Båggi enthused. "I knew you gnomes were clever, but this is a startling piece of engineering!" The dwarf was reclining in a chaise, eating off a cheese and fruit plate he'd created to serve the group.

It was true—the train was quiet, clean, and quick.

"But we owe some thanks to you dwarves," Onni told him. "These tunnels were made by your people in their quest for metals and jewels, according to this pamphlet I picked up in the Great Library. We merely adapted it."

"And the poetry painted on the walls is a halfling addition."

Everyone turned to Faucon, who was sitting up on his gurney, looking exhausted and sleepy and ever so slightly cross-eyed.

"My good friend!" Båggi shouted. "You should be asleep! Let me find my bottle of Dr. Dogoode's Dreadfully Delightful Dozy Doses."

Faucon held up a hand. "No, no. I have slept long enough. I must come to terms with my reality." He sighed, his shoulders rounded. "I . . . my . . . the toes are gone?"

Gerd padded to his side and rubbed her head against his shoulder, leaving a small puddle of eggish drool. *There was little choice, Faucon. They had been truly pulverized to Ranke Nubbins.*

"I suspected." Faucon put an arm over his eyes. "A halfling knows when he's been untoed."

"But we've created a solution," Onni said. He held up a new contraption that looked like a mousetrap battling to the death with part of a small buffalo. The brass was dull and smeared with grease, signifying it wasn't yet completed, but the fur lining was mercifully clean. "The gearhand did the tricky mechanical bits, but I'm finishing the finer details. The train's workshop is well stocked, so I should be done by the time we reach the end of the line."

"What kind of contraption," Faucon sniffed, "can replace a halfling's toes? Where will I wear my rings?"

He pulled the velvet ring box from his waistcoat pocket and flipped it open to show a dazzling array of toe rings. Onni held out a familiar iron ring stained with blood, but Faucon wouldn't take it. "Useless foppery now, I suppose," he muttered, and he let the box drop on the carpet with a muted thud, sending the rings tumbling.

No, Faucon, Gerd said, feathers up and eyes stern. *No. This smöl person is making something to help you. His aura is Moste Earneste.*

"I think I would prefer the gurney," Faucon said, suddenly frosty and seeming a good deal older. "My good dwarf, might I partake of those Dozy Doses you mentioned? I do believe I have had enough of consciousness for now."

Agape had remained silent through this exchange, but now she scrabbled about, collecting the rings and fitting them back into their specially shaped slots, including the one Onni offered. The ovitaur seemed angry and was bleating softly under her breath. Båggi administered two round pills that looked like bouncy balls made of velvet, and Faucon was soon snoring again. Agape muttered something undetectable as she tucked the box against Faucon's side and did an Anger Flop on one of the empty train benches.

So Agape was quietly fuming, Onni's shoulders were in a Grand Slump, and even Båggi seemed almost unjovial. Kirsi realized she had to bolster their spirits somehow. Now was the time when a blessing would come in handy but a curse was utterly useless. That wouldn't stop her from trying.

"Onni, you've got to finish that device before we arrive," Kirsi said. "He could use a spot of hope." With new steel in his eyes, Onni nodded once, straightened his cardigan, and took the contraption to the workshop. "And, Båggi, can you create your own custom treatments?"

The dwarf looked flustered and fiddled with his belt buckle. "Of course. Many teas and tonics and salubrious mixtures are possible when one knows the chemistry and properties of various herbs. But I've never encountered a situation quite like this."

"Faucon will need something that dulls pain while providing energy, which I realize might be contradictory. Can you whip up something like Båggi's Big Dog Grog Analogue, maybe?"

Båggi's eyes lit up with an almost religious fervor. "Yes. Oh, my butter beans, yes! A little gentian, some poppy, a large dollop of honey, a speckle of mead seed, some firedragon pollen . . . yes yes!"

Moving faster than Kirsi had ever seen him so far, Båggi yanked open his picnic basket and riffled through his medicinal supplies, seeking out the ingredients he'd just listed. She smiled to herself. This being in charge—it was quite satisfying.

"I suppose you waaant me to do something too?" Agape, the only person without a job, asked sullenly.

Kirsi thought about it and knew exactly what to say.

"Perhaps you can do some of your carvings? We could sell them in Caskcooper to pay for supplies. Our group . . ." She looked from Gerd to Faucon. "Well, we eat a lot."

Agape blushed angrily and looked at a point somewhere over

Kirsi's head. "No way," she said. "My paaarents told me my art would never be up to snuff, and I'm not about to maaarch into a store and get laughed at. I'm no aaartisan."

Kirsi went red too, but with anger.

"Yes, you are! You create art, and therefore you're an artisan. What kind of parent would tell their daughter she was bad at art?"

Agape shrugged. "The same kind that already haaad a down payment on a new house and raaan off the moment they could be free of me."

"That's as silly as a hedgehog in a hat. Your parents were wrong."

"Maybe." Agape looked out the window, watching the brightly colored halfling poetry and murals pass by as the train hurtled through the surprisingly well-lit and safe tunnel.

"Artists can't stop arting. There are some lovely bits of wood in the workshop. Think about it." With a reassuring smile, Kirsi slipped into the well-appointed washroom and plucked a nose hair. She could only make a tiny knot with it, but it would have to do. She wasn't going to waste something as special as a beard hair on this curse.

"Agape's awful parents in your retirement days: *May you realize the error of your ways . . . and may all your baaas turn to neighs.*"

She swallowed the tiny hairball and hoped both Agape and Faucon would find their calling, as she had. They were both hurting inside, but it would take more than a friendly push and a little nose-hair curse to fix the cracks in their hearts.

As for Kirsi, she looked in the mirror and saw someone new. Not the follower meant to live underground, toeing the line and keeping her mouth shut. Not the bristle witch who wasn't quite right and would never live up to Granny's blessings. Now she finally understood: She had been born to eat hairballs, kick butt, and lead this ragtag group to save the Skyr and, ultimately, understand themselves.

Eating hairballs was going to be the easy part.

23.

UNDER ASSAULT BY SALTY MERMAIDS

"There once was a little mermaid named Ariel, and she fell in love with a human prince. Or, more specifically, his duodenum, eaten raw with a side of kelp. I didn't mention that part in the fairy tale, did I? Bad for tourism, and I hate getting sued."

—HANS CHRISTIAN DANDRUFFSPOON OF THE TOODLEOO DANDRUFFSPOONS, in *All Stories Are Lies, Child: A Self-Exposé*

The train jerked, and Agape bleated and tried to cover it up with a belch.

"Bless your mess with that chirp of a burp!" Kirsi said cheerfully and gnomerically.

"If you find yourself indigested, I have some Uncle Chuck's Raspberry Reflux Rounds," Bȧggi offered.

"Uh, thaaanks but no thaaanks. I think I'm just going to go, uh, explore the train."

Agape kept many parts of herself hidden from her traveling companions, and this was one of them: her fear of things that a sheep shouldn't encounter. She found an empty car and crawled under a bench to breathe into a paper bag and softly bleat to herself. It took a lot of energy to act tough, and heartburn pills wouldn't help her heart.

Piini's loss only served to deepen her unhappiness. Kirsi had been correct—he was her main source of comfort, even more eternal in his devotion than her parents. And now they were all gone. Agape reached a tentative hand into her pack and pulled out the first thing she touched, a saltshaker with the distinctive ceramic glaze and stylized flowers of Humptulips in Grunting.

Well, maybe she still had one sort of comfort.

But then she was bleating again and aggressively tightening her sphincter as the train rolled to a smooth halt and a cheerful gnome's voice hummed, "Happy travels, everygnomey!" over a tinny speaker. Crawling out from under the bench, Agape stood and burped for real. She hadn't told anyone, but she easily got sheepsick.

"Agape?" Kirsi called.

Shoving the saltshaker back into her pack, Agape hurried up the carpeted aisle, hopped to the next car, and found the party waiting for her. They'd be near Muffincrumb now, and they could take a riverboat ride to Caskcooper and thence on to the Toot Towers. As she'd reminded them, Caskcooper was a lovely city. And she was thinking about staying there, where it was mostly safe and where she felt comfortable, instead of venturing directly toward vast amounts of danger. The only thing her parents feared more than being caught with Piini was dealing directly with the government, which was exactly what her traveling companions planned to do, the fools.

You'll always lose when you fight authority, laaambykins, her father had said. *Much safer to put your head down and graze like reasonable shaetyrs. But don't aaactually graze, because you don't haaave four stomachs aaand you'll probably die. It's a metaphor.*

And here Agape was, on the road to the giant, gaping, carnivorous maw of government. The relief she'd felt when the group had chosen to go with her to the Great Library was ebbing away as she considered this new fear: that she would put her trust in these people, grow attached to them, and they would abandon her like everyone else had. Or die, which was pretty much the same thing.

The gnomes bounded down the ramp with the bouncy enthusiasm they applied to everything besides heel blisters and headed directly for a door set in the smooth wall of the cave. UP WE GO TO MUFFIN-

CRUMB, it said. Faucon's gurney rolled down the ramp next, controlled by a metal box in Onni's hand. Behind the sleeping halfling paced his gryphon protector, and last came Bäggi, laden with his picnic basket and cask, grinning.

Up ahead, Kirsi pushed a jolly, candy-like button on the wall, and a door slid open to reveal a gnomeric elevator. When everyone else stepped or rolled in, Agape did too, shoulders hunched and head bowed. As soon as the box began to rise, Agape felt panic grip her. She was trapped! But then she reminded herself that when the door opened again, there would be reasonable things like trees and grass, no more of this slick metal with its scary smells, many of them wafting from the crouching gryphon.

The elevator door slid open on an idyllic forest tableau. Somewhere nearby, water burbled in an agreeable sort of way. There were sturdy trees, berry-laden bushes, and fat squirrels scampering about beatifically—until the gryphon bounded out of the box and tore them to meat confetti.

Agape couldn't help it; she took a few halting steps, her hooves sinking into rich loam, folded to a sheepish crouch, and rubbed her face on the ground until she couldn't smell metal anymore.

"Um, my friend, are you quite all right?" Bäggi called. "I have several ointments for rashes of the face. And posterior." The dwarf's mouth abruptly formed an *o* as he realized he had just said that aloud, then he grinned nervously. "Ha ha! Not that I've ever needed those! Just, you know. Best to be prepared! You never know when you're traveling, am I right? Ha ha!"

"Shh," she said. "I'm communing with nature."

The dwarf gasped and looked away. "Right here, in front of everyone?"

"Not thaaat kind of communing. I just . . . like it up here better. Sheep are not underground sorts of things, obviously."

"Ah, yes. I understand. Well, how are you with watercraft?" He pointed ahead.

The gnomevator had sunk back into the earth, the grassy gnoll on its roof perfectly blending into the surrounding forest. And on the other side of that gnarly gnome gnoll was a river, and on that riverbank waited a boat helmed by a metal man who looked like the younger, streamlined brother of Piini Automaatti, aside from his jaunty white cap. Her heart bonged with homesickness, even though she knew this metal man was nothing like *her* metal man. The passenger barge was big enough to fit them all, sitting low in the water with guardrails and a striped awning with jolly tassels.

"Here we are," Kirsi confirmed. She walked toward the floating barge and said in Alphagnomeric, *"You can't dispute the fruit is cute. Does that compute?"*

The automaton's head turned toward her with nary a squeak or squawk. *"It does compute and is quite astute.* Please step aboard, miss, and mind the gap."

A ramp appeared and landed softly onshore, and everyone but Agape clambered aboard. Onni used his little metal box to transform the gurney wheels into metallic kitten feet, which clanked up the ramp merrily to install Faucon down the center aisle.

"My first water adventure!" Båggi chortled. "Oh, my goodness. I am afloat! Adrift! Oh, my rosy rhubarb, what a treat!"

Gerd observed the boat and fluffed her feathers. *As you float on the hideous water ribbon, I shall float overhead, where things do not Squirt Atrociously unless I am eating them.*

The gryphon launched into the air and circled overhead, snapping a robin out of the sky and swallowing it whole with a horrible glugging noise and a resounding belch.

That left just Agape on land, and she looked into the forest—the Pruneshute Forest, if she remembered correctly—with abject longing. How easy it would be to dash under the boughs of the pines and birches and maples, find some enigmatic rock formation, and disappear.

They probably wouldn't even notice she was gone. It's not like they really cared about her.

"Agape?" Kirsi called, just like she had on the train.

Agape was frozen. Everyone was looking at her.

But not in a scary way. In a welcoming way.

"We can't leave until you come aboard." Kirsi patted the seat by her side. "Wanna sit with me?"

Never, not a single time in her life, had someone invited Agape to sit with them.

Her heart welled up out of her eyes, and she cleared her throat. "Uh, sure."

She might as well go with them. She could always stay in Cask-cooper if things got weird.

"On my waaaay," she said.

The metal floor of the barge was terrible for trotters, but Båggi leapt forward to help her. She was soon settled next to Kirsi, who pulled some knitting out of her pack and offered to show Agape some stitches.

The river journey was balmy and pleasant, at least until Gerd, fly-ing overhead, asked her pet library bird to recite some horrible gryphon poetry that sounded like a snake choking on a trombone. Kirsi and Båggi played a game called I Spy with My Wry Wittle Eye, which involved pointing out perfectly obvious things. Onni toiled away at the metal contraption he was making for Faucon, and Fau-con continued to snooze. Agape soon had the beginnings of a nice purple scarf on her needles, and the focus dissolved enough of her awkwardness that she and Kirsi were laughing together.

When she heard the first splash, Agape just assumed it was Gerd befouling the water. But the usual foul reek wasn't there, and the next splash was much bigger. Agape looked up and bleated in surprise, because what she was seeing couldn't be possible.

Human eyes were staring at her from the water. Blue ones. With eyelashes and everything. But they were stuck onto either side of a large fish's face. Its fish mouth was open and replete with human teeth, and its webbed hands clawed at the slow-moving water, churning it white. Several more such heads popped into view in the river behind the boat, the eyes blinking excitedly as the things made a horrible barking noise like a reverse throw-up.

"Kirsi—everyone—what is thaaat?" Agape shouted.

The barge shook as everyone's feet hit the floor and ran to the back.

"Oh, my grossly grumpy gravy, that does look a bit unpleasant!" Bäggi cried, tugging his beard in distress.

One of the creatures swam forward, its slimy, scaly tail slapping the water, with fat salamander legs paddling like billy-o to either side of it.

"Gnavigator, what is that thing?" Kirsi asked in her bossy voice.

"Why, that's a mermaid, miss!" the automaatti said, cheerful as a sunbeam. "A whole school of them! I do hope you brought your mermaid repellent."

"What's mermaid repellent?"

The automaatti's head turned one hundred eighty degrees to smile at them with brass teeth. "Around here, it's a very large harpoon. Pesky things, mermaids."

Onni ran over to the automaatti and scrambled up onto a stool to read the thing's back, squinting to do so.

"This one can't fight," he said. "Screwed down to the deck. Navigation, cheerful commentary, and tea service only." He sighed and reached for his nose like he was going to push up glasses but was briefly confused to find them gone. "We're going to have to take care of them ourselves."

"But I thought mermaids were beautiful!" Bäggi shouted, still distressed and not even reaching for his Telling Cudgel, for all that it had begun to gently glow, this time a bright bluish-green. "Mermaids are supposed to have a maiden dwarf's head and upper bits with a resplendent koi tail!"

"No, no," Onni disagreed. "They're gnome girls on top and salmon on the bottom, and they grant wishes."

"Where'd you hear that?" Kirsi said. "I read a book about how they were human ladies with two fish tails who lured men to spend their disposable income on burnt kuffee."

The horrors were swimming closer now, fighting the current toward the boat. One of them reached a slimy hand with bulbous salamander fingers for the ladder, and Agape instinctively kicked it with a hoof, knocking it back into the water.

"Well, you're all wrong!" she shouted. "They're ugly aaand quite possibly hungry!"

The groan of metal echoed from up front, and they turned to find one of the mermaids crawling its way onto the boat, her blue eyes rolling all around in her fat carp head as she slithered across the slick metal and her wet fingers grasped for Onni's leg. At the last moment, Gerd swooped down, pecked the mermaid's back, and flapped out of reach. The mermaid hissed but didn't retreat into the water like a reasonable monster.

"Good eating, mermaids," the boat pilot noted. "I'm programmed with many recipes for mermaid meat, if your hunt is successful." Then he whistled a tune and went back to pretending to spin a steering wheel.

"Are there any weapons?" Kirsi asked him.

"Not unless you brought 'em," he chirped in a folksy voice. "Not the usual season for mermaids or murderguppies, so the harpoon system is out for maintenance."

"I may have a solution," Faucon called, rising from his gurney to blink at the hideous monsters trying to crawl onboard while gnashing their teeth with fishy smacking noises. He fetched an acorn out of his waistcoat pocket, holding it up. "The dryads we helped in Tommywood gave me this boon and intimated that it might render us some aid."

"Yes, of course!" Kirsi sang. "The magic acorn will save us!"

"Witness," Faucon said, closing his fist around the acorn. "O daughters of Willowmuck, I call on your sacred acorn for luck."

A breathy giggle issued forth from Faucon's fist, and when he opened his hand, a gaseous green cloud formed in the air above his palm, the acorn crumbling into dust. The cloud swirled and coalesced into the svelte shape of a dryad.

"Hey there, hero," the gassy dryad cooed. "Thanks again for helping us. You're so strong and capable. Whatever you're up against, I know you can handle it. Go get 'em, you halfling hunk." She giggled once more and then dissipated in a puff of green glitter, leaving Faucon to make a small sound of outrage.

"That was, shall we say, anticlimactic," he intoned.

Agape snorted, ears flapping. "Thaaat's it? Well, I guess we're all going to die, then."

But Kirsi, she noticed, had plucked a hair from her beard and was whispering to it, and Onni was hefting a particularly heavy wrench from his tool bag and crawling under the boat seats. Båggi still stood there like a fool, ignoring his weapon.

"Båggi!" Agape called.

He looked up at her like he'd forgotten his own name. "Um?"

"Look at your cudgel!"

When the dwarf looked down, he gasped. His Telling Cudgel had gone all spiky, with bits sticking out here and there like rusty fishhooks.

"But I'm not angry," he said, surprised as he held it up and inspected it.

"Do you think there's a chance you might become angry aaafter one of those troutmuffins eats a gnome?"

As if to make her point, a high-pitched scream drew all eyes to Kirsi. One of the mermaids had wrapped slimy fingers around her leg and was tugging her toward the water, and the gnome was too stunned and smöl to do anything about it.

When Kirsi shrieked for the second time, dropping her knot of hair and clutching for Onni's hand, Båggi finally began to turn the Telling Puce that signaled his anger.

"Let. Go. Of. My. Smöl. Friend!" he shouted, his voice going two full octaves lower and his beard achieving full bush.

Agape was quite impressed, but the mermaid was not. It just

opened its mouth wider, its long tongue flapping out to wrap around Kirsi's arm. And then Agape felt something cold and moist encircle her own ankle. The mermaids were coming over all sides of the boat now, their splashes partially hidden by the boatman's whistling and the sound of Gerd's mad metal bird squawking Hurp Blep's sonnets from the sky.

"Heeelp!" Agape cried, and the thing jerked her leg, hard, making her fall to catch herself painfully on her hands.

The mermaid gurgled and a wet noise issued from its fish lips. "Ss-salllllt," it said. "Give back sssalllt."

A cold shiver thrilled down Agape's spine. "Whaaat did you say?"

"Give sssalllt. You ssstolllle."

The whole boat shuddered and splashed as mermaids flopped onto the deck.

"Let's not rock the boat, now," the boatman said. *"A butt in each seat is nicely neat!"*

"I hate gnomeric plaaatitudes!" Agape shouted, trying to reach her pack, on the seat where she'd been whittling. A hot line of pain raked over her leg. When she looked down, she saw rows of teeth serrating her skin, cutting through the wool.

A mad roar called her back to the rest of the party, and she turned just in time to see Bâggi raise his Telling Cudgel and slam it into a mermaid before kicking its wrecked body into the water, neatly saving Kirsi's life.

"Who else," he shouted, "wants a little cudgeling?"

Kirsi, now free, scrambled to the center of the boat, regained her nasty knotted hairball, and swallowed it. The mermaid nearest her began to vomit pudding, lurching and horking as its body was forced backward by the spewage. Bâggi continued bashing every beast he could find, the once-peaceful cudgel squashing and splattering until the boat deck resembled a sushi chef's garbage can. Onni managed to smash one in the gills with his wrench, and Faucon threw a star between the eyes of a mermaid from atop his gurney, slicing its face in half. Still more were coming.

Wincing through the pain of teeth in her leg, Agape stretched her fingers and snagged the strap of her pack. Dragging it to her, she asked the sort-of-talking mermaid, "Whose saaalt?"

The monster disengaged its choppers and sprayed fish goop mixed with her blood as it replied, "Bom. Bassss! Tic."

"Tommy Bombaaastic sent you? I should've guessed. Fine." She dug through her pack, pulled out a crystal saltshaker in the shape of a bear, and thrust it at the mermaid. "Here. This is Bombaaastic's saltshaker. Take it aaand go."

The mermaid's damp fingers snatched it away and it gargled fiercely before plopping back into the river, prize in hand. The other mermaids plopped and sank beneath brown waters, the attack over as abruptly as it had begun. For a few breaths, nobody said anything; they just stared at the surface of the river, waiting for a renewed nibling, up to their ankles in merpudding. When no further onslaught came, Onni sighed in relief and collapsed on a bench seat.

"Well, that was a fine infusion of nightmare fuel!" Bäggi declared. "Is everyone all right?"

Agape didn't want to look at her abraded leg. "I'm hurt."

"It is only justice," Faucon said, leading the others to gasp at his callousness, and Agape turned to find his eyes fixed on her. "I told you that stealing from a demigod was unwise."

"Yeah, you did," Agape admitted, her face hot.

"What are you talking about?" Kirsi asked, her head turning between the two of them, not really caring who answered. Faucon spoke first.

"When we were guests of Mr. Bombastic, our Vartija over there broke all laws of hospitality and stole his saltshaker. He sent the mermaids to get it back. I heard them say so."

"I'm not a Vartija aaanymore," Agape said, which was hardly the point, but for some reason being called one now stung far more than being called a thief. She *was* a thief, after all, and clearly there was no more hiding it. Everyone was staring at her, even the mechanical pilot.

She dragged herself back up to the seat and stretched out her bloody leg with a sigh. "Båggi, if you caaan do something for my leg before it's infected with fish flu, I'd be grateful. Aaand I might as well come clean with you all. Don't worry—you'll be rid of me aaat Cask-cooper." She upended her pack on the seat, revealing some chunks of found wood, a half-finished carving, and four and twenty containers of many sizes, shapes, and colors.

"I steal saltshakers wherever I go," she explained. "Aaand before you ask me why, the aaanswer is: I don't know. This isn't even all of them. I have caaaches buried in Burdell, Corraden, and Teabring. But I always leave one of my little carvings in exchange. So it feels more fair." She looked for forgiveness in the faces of her companions but saw only blank expressions. The corners of her eyes began to fill with hot tears. "I've been doing it since I was a kid. I thought nobody would ever know. I'm sorry I put you in danger. I'm glaaad I'm the only one who got hurt. Aaas Faucon said, it's justice."

Båggi sighed. "Let's clean your wound and get it bandaged," he said, laying down his cudgel and fetching his picnic basket. "And let me tell you about the time I disturbed a nest of wasps and, in my panic and pain, led them right back to my family. We were all stung as a result, and they were mad at me for a long time after that—the wasps and the Biinses. I knew very well that getting stung multiple times by wasps was sure to ruin one's good mood, so I couldn't really be angry with their reaction, but I harbored some mild resentment in my heart for a long while, and do you know why?"

Agape palmed away tears from her eyes and sniffled as Båggi applied some Hurty Howie's How About We Avoid Infection Confection to her wound. "Why?"

"They were so outraged over what I had done and so concerned with their own hurt that they never asked me if I needed any help. I was left to deal with my wounds by myself. I swore then that if anything similar ever happened to me, I would not be so insensitive. So I ask you, Agape, as a friend: Do you need any help with this problem? Not the one on your leg, but the one in your heart? Because if there is anything I can do, even if it's only to listen with a patient ear, then I will do it."

Agape felt her eyes dump down her cheeks. "Why are you being nice to me?" she whispered.

Båggi lifted a single bushy eyebrow. "You are my friend."

She wanted to believe that but couldn't. She wasn't even sure how to start.

"I . . . well." Her ears drooped. "Maybe we can work on my problems later. For now I think I'd like to rest."

"Of course! Would you like a small dram of honey-mead seed?"

"Thaaat would be perfect. Thank you." It would most likely knock her out, and if she was asleep she wouldn't have to talk with anyone about what she'd done. And it would give them a chance to leave her behind, for who would want to travel with a serial saltshaker stealer?

As the honey-mead seed warmed and numbed her at the same time and her eyelids grew heavy, Agape looked away from the circle of furrowed brows and wondered what she would do on her own.

So this, she thought, was saaaaaadness.

24.

IN A SHOP RIFE WITH SUSPICIOUSLY FAMILIAR TCHOTCHKES

"Balls! Balls! Balls! Balls! Put 'em in a bag and you can stand tall! Stinky cheese, hard cheese, as long as it's round—in my bonny ball bags it can be found!"

—POPULAR ADVERTISEMENT FOR PATRICE PLOOPENMUCH'S HUTCH OF CHEERY CHEESE BALL BAGS

Offi did everything he could to hide the shaking in his hands, which wasn't hard to do, as everyone else was too busy feeling the aftershocks of violence and revelation themselves. Surely Kirsi would know the truth now—that he was the weaker, lesser brother and not the brave, brawny Onni. She turned to him after Agape fell asleep, about to say something, then her mouth snapped shut and she turned away again. Offi looked down. A splotch of mermaid blood had marred his fine cardigan. No wonder she couldn't speak.

He was hideous.

He looked away and dug through his pack for a fresh cardigan with embroidered windmills. The blood-dolloped cardigan went in his unmentionables box, a thing he'd designed privately to turn unmentionable things mentionable again, often through washing, brushing, and occasional bleaching. Then he looked down.

Oh, no. His beard had a splotch too.

He pulled out a clean handkerchief and a bottle of beard oil, took care of that shame, and then, seeing that everyone else was appropriately busy, pulled out Faucon's contraption and set to fiddling with the toes.

When Kirsi sat down next to him some time later, he looked up from his work and gave her a tight grin, which she returned.

"Did you want to say something?" he asked. "I mean, earlier, you looked like you were going to say something, and then we both got busy with something else, so I wondered if that something was still something, you know, even if the gnomeisms suggest *not* saying such things . . . ?"

Kirsi nodded, her eyes big and sort of wobbly-looking, like an especially pretty custard. "What you did back there, Onni . . ." She trailed off and sighed, and he knew he was about to undergo a terrible buttocks-chewing.

"Oh, Onni. It was just so heroic."

Offi gulped and looked to either side to see if perhaps his brother had shown up unannounced. But no. He was the only other gnome on board.

"Heroic?" he squeaked.

"The way you grabbed your biggest wrench and crawled to the side of the boat to protect our open flank from those beasts." She sighed again and batted her eyelashes in a way that made him feel warm as a perfectly baked brûlée. "And then you stabbed one in the eye. It was absolutely smooshy."

"Well, yes," he admitted, wishing he could pop off his glasses for a good polish. "Vitreous gel can get pretty messy."

Kirsi looked down and blushed. "That's not what I meant, Onni."

"Oh." Offi gulped. "*Oh.*"

A girl had never before admitted to finding him at all smooshy.

"I mean, well, gosh, I . . . yeah, I definitely feel pretty smooshy."

They grinned at each other like loons, their noses getting incrementally closer, and then . . .

"Welcome to the non-halfling dock of Caskcooper. *Watch the ramp or your rump will get damp!*" The boatman turned to grin at them, and Offi realized they were parked at a long, crooked dock alongside all sorts of crabbit craft clearly not made by gnomeric hands.

Offi and Kirsi had already leapt apart, but Offi could see that Kirsi had stowed her smooshy self away and returned to her professional, leadery self. He understood that people had many selves and exchanged them like cardigans as the situation demanded, but Offi wished her smooshy side had said goodbye, or possibly given him a rain check.

"This is as far as you go?" Kirsi asked the automaton. "Because we'd like to go straight to the Toot Towers, if you please."

The boatman's head spun in circles. "'Fraid not, miss. My programming is limited. But please take these coupons for six percent off your ticket at Gnadine's Gnarly Gnome Gnoshery."

"That . . . doesn't sound tasty?"

A piece of paper curled out of the boatman's polished cardigan pocket and fell into Kirsi's hand. Offi looked down and read the Alphagnomeric script: GNADINE'S (GNOT ACTUALLY) GNARLY GNOME GNOSHERY: IT'S WHERE HALFLINGS DEFINITELY DON'T GO FOR DINNER. TODAY'S PASSWORD IS: PASS THE HOT NUT PUDDING.

"Well, *that's* cryptic," Kirsi said, pocketing the paper.

"I hope it's pistachio," Offi offered, trying to sound heroic.

The ramp had extended onto the dock, and Offi didn't like the look of it one bit—the dock, not the ramp. The ramp was gnome-built, a thing of strength, beauty, and perfectly straight lines, while the deck was clearly an ancient halfling construction, replete with crooked boards, gaping holes, and exposed nails red with disease-carrying rust. OUTLANDER DOCKS, a sign read.

"I doubt my gurney can navigate this embarrassingly errant embarkment," Faucon said. He was sitting up straight, and Kirsi and Offi hurried to his side as he swung his bandaged feet over the edge of the gurney. "It is clearly in violation of multitudinous building codes. Which is just as well. I would prefer to float forever, fight a phalanx of ferocious fishwives, if only I did not have to hobble into my former home like this, a shade of a halfling, emasculated and dependent upon gnomeric contraptions. Just leave me here to rot. Gerd will bring me donuts and boxed wine and I will plague the local stevedores with the dullest passages of stale political treatises."

Gerd hooted her disapproval.

"Wait!" Offi hurriedly brought the finished, wrapped contraption out publicly for the first time. Gearhands had done the bulk of the work in the City of Underthings, but he'd added a few improvements on the train and some final touches on the barge. Kneeling at Faucon's side, he touched the gauze briefly. "May I?"

Faucon looked away, his eyes screwed tightly shut. "You may, but I cannot promise an absence of tears. A halfling's toes are his greatest handsomeness, the font of his virility, the seat of his masculine power—"

"Excuse me?" Agape broke in, arms crossed. She had woken from her nap and was standing behind him on the barge, waiting to descend the ramp. "Do halfling women not haaave feet?"

"Yes, of course they do, but their toes, you see, are the blossoms of femininity, and—"

Agape bleated an angry laugh. "Do you even hear yourself? They're toes. Women and men both haaave them, so how caaan they represent both masculinity and femininity? They're toes. You fools walk around on them. And I personally think they're pretty stupid, but thaaat's just one opinion."

Faucon drew back his shoulders and opened his mouth to argue, and Offi swiftly began unwrapping his feet while the halfling wasn't looking.

"How dare you comment on a society beyond your meager ken? For eons, we halflings have focused on the merits of foot care, breeding for attractive qualities, and—"

"Sounds like a case of toxic dactylinity." Agape rolled her eyes. "Aaand who tells you feet need to be haaandsome or beautiful? Let me guess. People trying to sell you foot baaaths and powders and those oily unguents. You've been so upset about losing your precious toes, but I'm pretty sure you're the same dude you've been the whole time. You still caaare about law, right? You seemed to caaare about me breaking it."

"Naturally I do."

"And you care about halflings and gnomes living together in peace?"

"Of course!"

"Whaaat about getting these papers to the kanssa-jaarli and the king to restore the Elder Laws?"

Faucon put his hand over his heart. "More than anything!"

"Then it sounds like you're still the same dude. So staaand up and walk and show these Caaaskcooper snobs that you've still got what it takes."

The halfling hung his hairy head. "But I cannot walk without toes, even if I wanted to."

Agape smirked. "Look down."

Offi didn't know what to expect when Faucon saw the golden toe prostheses the gnome had invented. Hinged phalanges connected to the end of a foot piece that fastened to Faucon's stump via straps. The interior of the attachment was padded with beaver fur, and the straps were designed to cross over the top of his foot. Onni saw immediately that he probably should have looped the straps around the heel, but that was an easy adjustment to make. What mattered was the function and then the form, though Faucon currently prized the form over the function, and that's why Offi had spent time making the toes look beautiful. They were carefully sculpted brass digits, polished and gleaming, complete with smooth carved planes where toenails should be, suitable for painting. The fourth one on the right was specially designed to fit any specimen from Faucon's toe-ring collection, although the halfling could easily get his rings resized to fit any of his new digits.

"My gods," Faucon murmured. "Those are the fanciest toes I have ever beheld, or I am not Faucon Pooternoob of the Toodleoo Pooternoobs." He looked up, tears in his dark-brown eyes. "Yes, I can walk proudly into town on these auriferous digits."

Slowly, carefully, with Gerd hooting and humming over him like a nursemaid, Faucon stood for the first time on his prostheses. And he did wince and step a bit gingerly, causing Offi to kneel to make adjustments.

"No, no, my friend. The toes are lovely. But we must not forget that even with the benefit of talented gnomeric surgeons, I still wear fresh sutures and possess damaged nerves. If you all do not mind very much, I wish to avail myself of the benefits of the Dr. Rupert Caskcooper Super-Duper Clinic for Podiatry, where those most intimate with my anatomy might make suggestions to help me heal." He raised his owlish eyebrows. "If that is not inconvenient?"

"Not at all." Kirsi shook her head, braids flying. "We need some supplies. A few of the packs got sloshed with fish guts in the boat, and while some gnomes might like it and I'm happy for them, I don't want to eat trouty cheese."

"I've heard there are halfling artisans who specialize in making bespoke leather cheese bags," Båggi said, eyes shining. "Oh, how proud I would be, to wear a bag of fine cheese and feel it swing freely from my belt!"

"And I always enjoyed Artists' Aaalley," Agape said. "My parents used to sell their work here. It might be nice to . . ." She looked sad for a moment, but then her chin firmed up. "Shop."

I will keep watch over this clinic Faucon wishes to visit, Gerd rumbled. *I do not trust these halflings anymore. The drubs turned on you once before, Faucon, and I cannot forget such Grimme Betrayale.*

Faucon nodded his understanding and thanked her.

They began walking toward the town, and only Offi was left without a plan, outside of trailing behind Faucon to study the pros and cons of his invention. The old Offi would have just gone along with slumped shoulders and a sarcastic remark about the futility of existence. But the new Offi was half Onni, in a way, and he had Thoughts, and at this particular time they verged on the Defensive.

"Wait. So we're just going to go bouncing into a halfling town—*a halfling town!* Two gnomes and an ex-Vartija are going to waltz in, and nobody's going to attack us or swindle us or hurt us?"

Faucon turned easily in his prostheses—a good sign—and gave him a fatherly smile. "My boy, besides me, have you ever met a halfling who was not one of the Dastardly Rogues?"

Offi glared, his eyeline aching for the blackest kohl. "No. Just the ones who threw firebombs into my home. And I didn't meet them so much as dispatch them."

"I assure you the drubs do not represent my people. Before Marquant Dique and his foul cabal of miscreants from Bigly-Wicke began to corrupt the Skyr, halflings were known for food, drink, art, and merriment. Caskcooper is an old and vaunted town, and anyone wearing a medallion is pelted with old tomatoes until he leaves. See?" Faucon pointed up ahead to a barrel of . . . rotten tomatoes. Just sitting there, covered in flies. "The city elders keep barrels of Past Due Toodleoo Tomatoes on every corner for just such a purpose. You know drubs are about when everything smells of moldy ketchup."

Offi sniffed delicately at the barrel. "That's pretty serious business."

Faucon nodded. "And you'll see how clean the streets are. No one lounging under a whale-oil lamp with a tankard, selling information. Just industrious entrepreneurs politely offering buttered hot chestnut cocoa at a more-than-reasonable price. Now, shall we meet at this Dinny's at, say, teatime?"

Faucon pointed to a restaurant that did indeed look bright and inviting, with lanterns twinkling behind broad windows, displaying benches filled with happy halflings and tables groaning under grand platters of food.

"When's teatime?" Offi asked.

"After second lunch. It is roughly the same as snacksies, and the terms are used interchangeably. Right around three-ish. You will know because every halfling's stomach will grumble, and everyone will say, at almost the exact same time, *Well, I feel a mite peckish.*" Faucon grinned for the first time in a long time, obviously more at ease here, among his own kind. "Of course, we say that almost anytime we are not currently eating. Good luck!"

Faucon's walk was a little awkward at first, and Offi could see the halfling carrying himself gently and wincing with each step, but still: He was walking. Gerd leapt down from the roof and paced at his side, urging Faucon to depend upon her shoulder, should he need assistance. An older halfling gentleman stopped to enthuse over Faucon's toes, and Faucon actually preened for a moment. Pride swelled in Offi's heart as he considered the success of his first real, unique invention. Not some variation on a theme or improvement on an older model, but a true Invention. If only Seppo had been here to see it. He would've been so proud.

Offi frowned. Or would he? Who knew how his father felt about him now that Offi had defied his responsibilities and gone off on a Mad Jaunt? Seppo had always favored Onni, just like everyone else, and it was likely the old gnome would value loyalty over ungnomeric walkabouts.

Perhaps when Offi had helped end the halfling problem, his father would see him as a hero.

"Where shall we go first, my friends?" Bäggi burbled. "For I have never seen a halfling city before, and I am anxious to peruse their many fine wares and taste their famed food and drink!"

Everyone looked to Agape, who blinked at them.

"What do you think, Agape?" Kirsi asked.

The ovitaur flinched as if a mermaid still chewed on her hock. "You still want me to come with you? Even aaafter the . . . the salt-shaker thing?"

"Of course," Offi said, which was echoed by Kirsi and Bäggi. But he went on, singing, *"Everybody makes mistakes, so dust off your butt and make some cakes!"* exactly as Onni would've said it.

Kirsi gave him that look, the smooshy one, and he began to see the value in gnomeisms.

As for Agape, her face went from broken to hopeful. "Okay, we'll want to head to Artists' Aaalley first to replace your paaacks, because the smell of fish guts is pretty rank. Then we caaan trot over to the Haaalfway House, where you can donate your old stuff to orphans and rehabilitated drubs. And then we caaan hit the Halfling Market just before teatime. We'll want to get baaack to Dinny's a little earlier than Faucon suggested, though. They basically staaampede the place as soon as second lunch is cleared."

The ovitaur led the way, although she had to slow her pace as soon as the smöl folk began breathing heavily. Offi sometimes felt like everything they did was somehow an affront to the ovitaur. Were the gnomes just a friendlier, happier folk than most, or did his people learn to hide their inherent Sulkiness more than other races for the sake of getting along? Only those who had weathered a cold winter underground for months in the dark knew what it truly meant to grin and bear it. Offi once had a Grand Sulk for a week because Onni trod upon his old underpants, but of course his twin knew Offi would forgive him. Sometimes, a Sulk was necessary, much like draining pus from a fetid wound. And sometimes, a Sulk was an act. Offi wondered which it was with Agape. And which it had been with himself, before the firebombs.

An excited squeal announced that Båggi had discovered Patrice Ploopenmuch's Hutch of Cheery Cheese Ball Bags, the rafters dripping with bulbous leather bags ready-made to hold balls of halfling halfvarti cheese, and the dwarf could've browsed all day, tenderly squeezing this globe and that and making appreciative moaning noises. He selected one with a snail on it and fumbled with his coins, thanking the halfling proprietor and praising her skills so much that the shopmistress threw in a free ball of Bettera, which she proclaimed to be a better cheese than the mere Gouda of the gnomes.

Kirsi took over at the Sylvain Sagginsack Backpack and Snack Shack, deftly earning a phenomenal deal on new packs for everyone.

A few halflings greeted Agape by name, and she smiled shyly and did her best to avoid answering questions about where her parents and their golden babysitter were. So many of the halflings had firmly stated they didn't serve droids here, so it seemed they were even happier to see Agape without Piini. The more effusive the artisans were, the more Agape shied away, until at last she just stood outside as Båggi's glowing eyes led them into a shop filled with toe rings, chest-hair charms, and other hair-based jewelry.

"Do you think I'd look good with a pierced beard?" the dwarf asked Kirsi. "More . . . I don't know . . . dwarvelish?"

"I don't think a dwarf could look more dwarvelish than you, Båggi, but travel is for broadening one's horizons. I don't have the guts to pierce my beard, but perhaps you can get one of those fake rings that only goes half around?"

"Yes, yes! A halfling half ring! That's the one for me!"

As Båggi and Kirsi discussed the merits of various beard rings, Offi felt shyer about his own scraggly beard than usual and walked the perimeter of the shop, enjoying the act of perusal. All the gnome shops back home had been forced to forgo fripperies recently and dedicate their shelf space to weapons, heavy metal hatches, locks, and sternly worded signage stating NO DRUBS, BUB.

All the toe rings began to blend together . . . and then something caught his eye. Something very familiar. Something with a very, very high price tag.

He knocked on the window glass to get Agape's attention and motioned her inside.

"What?" she demanded when she entered, quite rudely, head down. "I know this place, and I don't waaant— Oh."

"These are your work, right?"

"Uh. No."

"*AF*. Agape Fallopia. You carve your initials on the belly of each piece."

"I—"

But she couldn't bring herself to deny it again, for a delicately rotating glass case held a selection of whittled wood objects, each adorned with a tuft of black wool. Small cards lined with elegant calligraphy gave each one a title, price, and earldom of origin. The prices were quite high, and the artist was listed only as *AF*. The titles were descriptive and each included the artist's initials: *Fuzzy AF, Fancy AF, Llama Is Angry AF.*

"Yeah. Fine. They're mine. But how—"

"Excuse me," Offi called to the halfling proprietress, as most of the shop owners were women. "Can you please tell me more about these beautiful carvings?"

Sensing a sale, the halfling hurried over, graceful as a dancer on her cornsilk-shiny toes.

"Oh, you've a fine eye, my good sir. AF is one of our most popular artists. No one knows who they might be, nor where the fine black wool might come from. Personally, I've always imagined AF as a handsome halfling lord, down on his luck, and his curly toe hairs bring good luck to his fortunate patrons. Which piece interests you?"

"Oh, I think I like *Bunny Is Cute AF.* But I'm wondering—if you don't know the artist, how did you come across these pieces?"

She grinned, overjoyed to discuss what was clearly a favorite topic. "Oh, it's so mysterious! The pieces filter in from all over Pell. You see how there's an origin for each? Scholars and collectors are interested in that so I make sure to label them. The story goes that this itinerant artist secretly plants them in exchange for much-needed salt. Almost like an artistic Goblin Hood!"

Agape sidled close. "So . . . so the people who find them . . . they aren't angry thaaat they've haaad their saltshakers stolen?"

The halfling laughed a deep and infectious laugh. "At the prices these pieces sell for, absolutely not! They think it a fine game. Many a halfing art lover invites mysterious strangers to dine and sets out fine sets of salt and pepper shakers, hoping that AF will visit one day and take their salt in exchange for a sculpture."

Offi watched Agape's face, and he'd never seen it so naked with honesty. Her eyes were wet and wobbly, her floppy sheep ears trembling with emotion. One finger stroked the glass case. "I imagine AF would be very graaatified to know that their transgressions haaave been so easily forgiven."

Offi put a hand on her wrist, because he felt like she was about to bolt, sheep-style. "Art is such a gift," he said.

The halfling proprietress nodded enthusiastically. "A thrice gift, we halflings say. For it gives to the artist by feeding their soul, gives to the world by making it more beautiful, and then gives to the recipient, who will always cherish it. Tell me, dear. Are you an artist too?"

Agape took one look at the halfling's kind smile, extricated herself from Offi's grasp, and ran out the door, crying.

Left behind, Offi waited for the proprietress to ask the usual sort of *well, what's gotten into her, my goodness* sort of question, but instead the woman just took out *Bunny Is Cute AF* and held it up to the light.

"She's an artist, I'd bet. A tender soul. Even if she doesn't know it. Now, shall we make a deal?"

Offi handed her a small coin and bobbed a bow. "Thank you for your time, but not today. I must stay with my friend."

The proprietress sighed, but not in a disappointed way. "That's all right, then," she called as he sprinted out the door. "I don't mind keeping this one awhile longer. It has a way of getting to people, you see. Good day, sir! Do come again!"

When Offi found Agape, she was in a busy public square replete with graceful topiaries, ancient gazebos, and a selection of statuary. The ovitaur was standing before a beautiful white marble sculpture.

"Are you okay?" Offi asked.

She turned to him, her cheeks tearstained, but now she was in a different kind of shock.

"Forget about me, Offi. You've got to read this."

She pointed to a brass plaque, and he leaned in close.

TO REMY, MY GREAT LOVE. I WILL AVENGE YOU.

And the name under that? FAUCON POOTERNOOB OF THE TOODLEOO POOTERNOOBS.

"Remy," Offi said, fascinated and horrified as he considered the subject of the statue, "wasn't a halfling at all? Faucon's dear departed Remy was—"

Agape finished the sentence for him.

"A pigeon?"

25.

OUTSIDE THE GRIMFUL
WALLS OF BRUDING

"Dry, scaly wattles offend nearly all other life forms and invite public ridicule. To get the smooth, buttery, glowing wattle you deserve—the kind of wattle young people hope they'll grow someday—you don't need to mortgage your home or sell your giblets to the Dread Necromancer Steve. Just follow the guidelines herein, collected from the lips of Qul experts in wattle maintenance."

—QARLI SYMEN, from the introduction to *The Qul Way to Care for Your Wattle*

Misdirection, Gustave thought, was still a vital skill he needed to improve. Back when he'd been a simple billy goat in a barnyard, before he'd eaten the magical boot that had made him a human king, misdirection had served him well against his pooboy, Worstley. The goose would flap its wings and hiss, because geese are jerks like that, and while Worstley was distracted, Gustave would ram the boy in the rumpus and then he would bleat and the goose would honk at Worstley lying in the mud and filth and it was all very merry. What worked in the barnyard would probably work just as well in politics.

En route to the Toot Towers from his castle in the capital at Songlen, he turned to Grinda the Sand Witch and said, "I've been thinking."

Her mouth puckered up. "That's disturbing."

"Speaking of disturbing, I think I'm developing another boil. No, don't scoot away. Aww. See, now things are awkward. Anyway, I think we should take a longish detour to drop in on Lord Ergot."

"Whyever for?" Grinda said. "That's many leagues out of our way, and I have an appointment with my wattle masseuse."

"Reschedule that wattling. This is important. All those letters I read suggested the gnomes who need help are heading to Ergot's city, so if we want to help them—and we do—that's where we should go, not the Toot Towers. I'm pretty sure he's hiding something by saying everything's fine in Bruding." He snatched a carrot stick off the tray near his hand and crunched into it with more than his usual gusto. Little bits of orange shrapnel flew out of his mouth as he continued. Human lips, he'd learned, were much flappier than goat lips. "How can everything be fine if he's being flooded with gnomeric refugees?"

"But it's days and days of delay, Gustave," Grinda said with a melodramatic sigh and a tiny shake of her head that made her healthy wattles waggle.

"I'm sure we're already saving days and days by traveling in this contraption," he countered. "It's much faster than horses and such."

Grinda raised an impeccably shaped eyebrow, conceding the point. They were cruising across the land in the spanking-new Royal Pelican Centipod and Traveling Hootenanny. They were just north of Riverhead, traveling through Corraden to Meadow Verge, and thence to the Toot Towers on the southern border of the Skyr. It was a most comfortable ride compared to a carriage: The centipod was a gnomeric invention and a gift to the crown upon Gustave's coronation. It was larger than many ships that sailed on the ocean, and it came with a galley and sleeping quarters and cargo hold and room enough for a sizable bodyguard in addition to assorted courtiers, minstrels, and professional yodelers. Musicians played festive tunes while said yodelers danced in polished boots of buttery leather, and vegetarian finger food awaited, a finger's breadth away from his hand. He even had a gnomeric oatmeal chef in the galley, who was ready to sprinkle cinnamon, apple chunks, and shaved almond slivers on his whole oats whenever he wished. But it was difficult for him to enjoy all that when Floopi Nooperkins was in mourning about exploded kin, and Lord Ergot said everything was fine. He crunched the heck out of his carrot stick and sent more of it flying by trying to speak around it, dimly aware that this was considered rude by most humans but not truly worried about that when he had an argument to win with Grinda.

"If we summon Lord Ergot to us at the Toot Towers—or anywhere else—he can continue to hide whatever he's really doing by simply lying about it. We need to see what he's up to in person."

Grinda tapped her chin. "What we need are spies."

"That too. But since we don't have those yet, we need to go there and do what we can for those gnomes."

"You know who has spies already? Lord Ergot. He'll know we're coming."

"How?"

"I am willing to bet he has spies on this very centipod. If we change course, he'll hear about it before we get there."

Gustave narrowed his eyes at his dancing yodelers. "You mean one of *them*?"

"Possibly. Or the halfling snack chef. Or one of your guards. Any of your employees could be getting paid for updates on your movements."

The king lowered his voice. "Don't you have some magic foo-foo that can do something about that?"

"My talents generally lie in the physical world. I can construct attractive sand golems to seduce people, and perhaps they would let slip something in an unguarded moment, but that would be time-consuming and have a high risk of failure."

"Ugh. I don't know why you like sand. It gets everywhere."

His chamberlain ignored this and said, "We do know someone who could root out spies with a song, and visiting her would be on our way and in no way unusual."

Gustave snapped his fingers, a practice he had come to enjoy since possessing them. His erstwhile goat trotters could never do that. "Argabella!" The bard had helped him gain his throne and she had only grown more powerful since his coronation, thanks to correspondence courses Gustave had generously gifted her after receiving ads in the mail.

"Draw Ye Thisse Foine Thatch Tortoise, and You May Be an Artiste!" the ads said, and Gustave supposed that was somehow bardically useful.

"That's right. Let us say we are on our way to visit Tennebruss," Grinda said. "We'll stop to visit Argabella and Fia instead at Malefic Reach—what are they calling it now?"

"The Songful Tower of Roses," Gustave supplied. He had granted them title to that estate after its former occupant, the Dark Lord Toby, had been killed by, ironically enough, a healer.

"A fitting sobriquet. We'll stop there, have Argabella remove our spies, then head for Bruding without Lord Ergot ever suspecting our arrival."

"I like this plan, Chamberlain. Make it so."

Grinda rose and moved to the front of the vehicle, where the automaatti pilot awaited orders. Soon the great centipod swung northwest toward Neatcamp.

"We'll head west from Neatcamp to avoid the Figgish Fen," Grinda said when she returned, "resupply in Håpipøle, and enter Borix from the south, taking the trade route north to Dower."

And it did go precisely as she said, with only a couple of days passing in between and great distances covered in very little time by the centipod. Nearly everyone asked where they were going, however, so it was impossible to tell from that who might be a spy among the courtiers and guards. Curiosity may have killed the cat, but it was not supposed to kill yodelers, according to Grinda.

The eventual stop at the Songful Tower surprised most everyone on board, who thought they were on the last leg of their journey from Dower to Tennebruss. Gustave dispatched a gregarious yodeler to knock on the tower door, warning him to beware of the UNWELCOME mat, which was a trapdoor to a widely feared cellar packed with delicious preserves and voracious vermin. The mighty Fia and Argabella the bard appeared twenty minutes or so later, for it took that long to descend from the tower's apex, but the yodeler fetched the estate's farm boy in the meantime from the barn. His name was Morvin, and during the time that Gustave had been a goat, Morvin's sister, Poltro, had tried to turn him—Gustave, not Morvin—into curry. Morvin knew nothing of this; he knew only that the King of Pell was outside in his fancy gnomeric centipod, and the young man quite likely felt unmannerly in his overalls and dung-covered waders. He was a dark-haired, dusky-hued lad, lean and ropy of limb, a smidge bowlegged and a lot besmeared with all manner of barnyard filth, but he might clean up really nice if given a chance. Once introduced, Gustave asked him if he looked after the entire estate himself.

"Yessir, I do. Ever'thing outside the tower, anyway. Dementria looks after ever'thing in the tower."

"I imagine it's a lot of work."

"More'n I can handle, sir. Can barely keep up with chores most days, much less get any work done on bigger projects. My sister used to help around, especially when it came to kicking chickens and losing eggs, but she's . . . gone now."

"Yes, I know, and I'm sorry," Gustave said, though he wasn't. Poltro was a ghost these days and he liked her better in a form that was incapable of eating him. "Tell me, Morvin, is your jam cellar easy to escape?"

"Naw. Sometimes I've forgot 'n' stepped on that mat in fronta the door 'n' then I'd not geddout until the Dark Lord Toby heard the cows talkin' 'bout not havin' milk yanked outta their pink parts. He heckin' hated moos, boy howdy. Couldn't hear me hollerin' in the cel-

lar, but if them cows started talkin' he'd shoot green lightnin' outta
the window 'n' some kinda sorta-bread would always fall outta the
sky, 'n' I got wise after a while 'n' kept some butter handy for them
times because summa that sorta-bread tasted kinda good—"

"Not easy to escape. Great. Thanks, Morvin," Gustave said.

"Oh. Yeah. Sorry 'bout ramblin' on, it's just that I'm nervous 'n'
whatnot 'n' I just sorter talk t'myself all day while I work an' them
heckin' animals don't care if I don't make sense. No, sir, they just listen and get to cluckin'—"

"Right. Thanks again, Morvin."

"Oh. You're welcome, king m'lord-liege, sire, holiness, uh . . . whatever I'm supposed to say. Maybe you can just pretend I said it—"

"No need to pretend. You said it all."

Despite the fact that Morvin possessed an immense natural talent
for prattling and babbling, Gustave instinctively liked him and supposed he would've made a decent pooboy. Then again, as Gustave
now understood it, even the king shouldn't poach pooboys from the
homes of his dear friends.

Fia and Argabella arrived at that point and saved him from any
need to continue the conversation. They looked very happy—both to
see Gustave and in general. Fia was still the tallest human he had
ever met, still the fiercest too, but she smiled often now that she had
the roses and peace she'd longed for. Her chain-mail apron barely
covered her front, and in the rear it was merely . . . a chain. Argabella
the bard used to be unsure of herself and easily frightened, in part
because she'd been cursed into a half-rabbit form, but now she was
Brimful of confidence and swagger, she might say. She had brought
her lute down with her, perhaps guessing it might be needed for
singing or possibly bashing unwanted door-to-door sales-elves and
that she wouldn't want to spend an hour on the stairs doing unnecessary cardio. After a few minutes of pleasantries, Gustave took them
aside and explained what he wanted, while Grinda called out all
hands on deck for a general announcement.

"We are all quite lucky today," the sand witch said once they were all assembled, "for one of the finest bards in all Pell is going to sing for us. Please listen carefully to Argabella."

The musicians and yodelers in the Traveling Hootenanny looked excited at this news, but many of the others, who'd had to listen to those musicians and yodelers for most of the journey, looked less than enthused at the prospect of yet more music. In truth, Gustave wasn't counting on Argabella's song to be especially fine or delightful; he was counting on it to be *effective*, for when she slung her rhymes and put some will behind it, she could accomplish surprising feats of magic.

The bard strummed a few clear chords and plucked out a sweet melody for a few measures, then opened her mouth and began to sing over the lute:

> *"We're going to play a game today*
> *To see who will go and who will stay.*
> *If you're loyal to the king*
> *Keep your hands still while I sing:*
> *But if you're working as a spy*
> *And are not in fact the king's ally,*
> *Please raise your hands up to the sky*
> *So we may now identify*
> *Who is in fact a dirty spy—"*

Two people raised their hands but also tried to make a run for it, hands still raised in the air and shouting denials. One of them was the halfling snack chef named Pierre Batterslab—Grinda had predicted as much—but the other was Hurlga, Gustave's governess, and that both surprised and hurt him.

These two miscreants were brought before Gustave for questioning and driven to their knees by Gustave's buff guards. Argabella changed her tune to one called "Tell the Truth, Forsooth, or Lose a Tooth."

Gustave crossed his arms and glared at them both. "First, you're not going to die. I don't kill people. But there's a pretty awful jam cellar underneath the tower, and we might have to throw you in there for a while to think about what you've done. It's dark and cold and possibly full of spiders and such, but on the upside it's pretty dry and you'll have plenty of jam to eat and rats to talk to. So what's the story, Batterslab? Working for the drubs?"

"Yes." The halfling's eyes widened in panic, and then he scowled at the bard, who continued to quietly burble about telling the truth.

"Were you going to poison me when they gave the signal?"

"No!" Batterslab panicked and spoke quickly. "I swear it! I'm just here to listen and report back to Marquant Dique. We want you alive, because you don't have anti-halfling sentiments and are neglecting the Skyr and could possibly be open to bribery in the form of oatmeal cookies." The halfling put a hairy hand over his mouth. "I mean . . . no poison!"

"I heard everything you said. Thank you for your honesty."

"But I meant to say nothing, and if the Big Dique finds out I squealed, he'll cream me!"

"Yes, well, Argabella's a pretty good bard and I think we have what we need. Jam cellar for you, sir. Fia will let you out in a few days and you'll be free to find employment elsewhere. I suggest you do not make yourself available to the drubs. If I see you again, I'll have you manning the walls at Fort Valiant, which the giants periodically assault to pick up a quick bite to eat."

Two guards picked up the halfling and dragged him away, howling. Gustave heard Morvin offer him some tips before he was thrown in the cellar: "If y'get angry 'n' smash all the jam, you'll just attract more bugs down there with you, and summa them critters like meat. Had my heckin' nose nibbled more'n once. The neater you are, the less chewed on you'll be. The kumquat marmalade is in the back, if you're inta that sorta thing. An' stay out of the invigorated ham jam, y'hear? That's mine."

The king's guards tossed Pierre Batterslab onto the UNWELCOME mat, and it dropped away under his weight. He fell screaming into darkness for a half second before grunting as he hit the bottom. The trapdoor swung up and cut off his last cry of "Augh, spiders!"

Hurlga was sobbing by the time they turned their attention to her, her beefy shoulders hunched up around her boulder-sized noggin. Grinda requested that she be allowed to question the governess, and Gustave waved her to proceed as Argabella's effective song continued to burble about in the background.

"For whom are you spying?" Grinda asked.

"Lord Ergot of Bruding," Hurlga replied without hesitation.

"And were you in his employ when I hired you?"

"No, Miss Grinda. And he's not paying me now either."

Gustave bleated softly in surprise at this betrayal.

"Then why are you spying for him?"

"He has my brother!" Hurlga wailed. "He says he'll kill him if I don't tell him where you go and what you're doing!"

But Grinda's firm façade never broke, in part because the magic holding her face together wouldn't let it. "Tell me about your brother."

"His name is Ralphee and he's only nineteen. He looks like me, but shorter, and with different bits in some places. He's a mason's apprentice."

"What about your parents?"

"They joined some strange cabbage cult in the Misree Hills. Ralphee escaped them a year ago. Please help me save him, Miss Grinda! He's all I've got left. Especially now that you've got to throw me in that cellar."

Grinda huffed and tapped her foot, considering. "How were you supposed to communicate with Lord Ergot?"

"Send him a letter via the postale service in every town we visit. Little yellow envelopes."

"So you did that in Neatcamp and Håpipøle?"

"I did. And Dower too. I told him we were heading to Tennebruss and there was nothing else to report, because we were just traveling."

"Do you like your job?"

"Yes! It's wonderful to see the king trying to improve Pell, especially now that he can wipe his own tushy. It feels historic. Except . . ."

"Except what?" Grinda prodded.

"Well, I'm a target now, and my brother is too because of me, which was not something I expected. Or something I like."

Grinda pursed her lips and glanced at Gustave. He thought he knew what she might be thinking. "We have to do something," he said. Grinda nodded once and turned back to Hurlga.

"Do you know precisely where your brother is being kept?"

"Not precisely, no. Lord Ergot has dungeons, I imagine. And he also has the Ping-Pong Palace and Refugee Center."

"What the Pell is that?" Gustave asked.

"It's a large space for warehousing bodies, sir. There's a housing shortage in Bruding, though I hear Lord Ergot is working on solutions. The refugee center is a temporary shelter."

Grinda narrowed her eyes. "And he might be keeping your brother prisoner there?"

"Possibly. I hope so, really, because it's nicer than an actual dungeon. Less damp and fewer rats, although an unhealthy amount of Ping-Pong, from what I understand. I don't want Ralphee to be suffering overmuch Ping-Pong on my account."

"Should we manage to free your brother, would you be loyal to me again?" Gustave asked, noting that Argabella was still playing her song. "Even if I occasionally make a very patriotic boom-boom without really meaning to?"

"Yes, of course, King Gustave." That was good to hear, and the tightness in Gustave's chest and across his shoulders relaxed somewhat.

"Very well. I'm going to ask you to stay here awhile with Argabella and Fia so that Lord Ergot will not be able to apply any pressure on you. We'll go see if we can free Ralphee."

"Oh, thank you! But . . . I won't be in the jam cellar?"

"No. Please make yourself useful in whatever way you like. Help Morvin with his duties outside the tower, or help Dementria inside the tower, whichever seems the least terrible. You'll continue to receive your full pay. When Argabella and Fia return to Songlen for their next six months of service, you can come with them and resume your duties at the palace."

That completed Gustave's icky work, and the finest warrior and bard the king knew invited him and his chamberlain to stay the night in one of the tower's many luxurious round rooms.

"We'll have a proper feast like Lord Toby used to," Fia said, but Gustave gave them his regrets. They needed to rescue Ralphee, on top of all their other business, and he didn't want to give Lord Ergot any time or a reason to hide the boy somewhere other than the usual places. So they bid farewell to Hurlga, promised to do something about Lord Ergot, had Argabella sing a "Let's All Be Loyal to King Gustave or Get Kicked in the Nards" song, and rumbled away on a hundred mechanical legs. The Royal Pellican Centipod and Traveling Hootenanny turned north to Bruding, skipping Tennebruss entirely, and kept to the western side of the Misree Hills.

Gustave did not sleep much during the night, brooding, as it were, over the necessary if temporary loss of Hurlga, who had done more to help him adjust to being human than anyone else. She was kind and considerate of him, so he'd tried his best to learn about his new body, to make her job easier. There were many features he still didn't understand, but no one had yet written a proper manual.

And he worried about what to do regarding corruption in general: how to protect his people from hostage situations like this, how to weed out the corrupt already in power throughout the kingdom, how to prevent more innocent people from being corrupted. He was having, he thought, a proper corruption conniption.

The weeding bit was going to be tough. Back when his pooboy, Worstley, used to pull weeds around the farm, it looked pretty easy to Gustave, so long as you had hands. It was work, to be sure, but there was no possibility that the weeds would win and slay the pooboy, no matter how weak and ineffective were his noodle arms. But Gustave supposed corruption, like weeds, would keep coming back and that getting rid of it would be a constant chore, as weeding was.

He left his cabin to see if Grinda was awake and willing to talk about it. The former, but not the latter, turned out to be true.

"Dealing with corruption is an excellent conversation for us to have and we should have it, but not right now. I need to concentrate," she said.

"So what are you working on?" he asked. Grinda sat on the edge of her bed, waving her wand and muttering at two humanoid shapes rising out of piles of sand that had come from who knew where. Then he realized he wouldn't be surprised if Grinda had stocked her cabin with sandbags. She paused to answer him.

"Two sand golems. I'm going to use them to infiltrate the dungeon and the refugee center to find Ralphee. Can we talk later?"

"Of course."

Gustave retired to his room and actually caught some sleep after that, able to rest knowing that Grinda had a plan—a plan she'd already set in motion by the time he woke in midmorning and was served his oatmeal and apples. His gnomeric oatmeal chef, thank goodness, was not a spy.

"The golems will enter from the eastern gate and look for Ralphee," Grinda said once he'd emerged from his cabin and they were sitting on the main deck, looking down into the wretched city of Bruding. "Meanwhile, we will sit outside this western gate and never enter the city walls, demanding that Lord Ergot come visit us on our centipod."

"Why is that?"

"We will not place ourselves in his power. He has already demonstrated that he's willing to take a hostage to spy on you. He's dancing on the precipice of treason as it is; he killed my nephew Bestley because he sensed a potential rival, and he has many, many more swords at his command than we do right now. And if we stay outside the walls, he will feel safe, believing we won't find out what he's up to."

"Wouldn't he be right about that?" Gustave asked. "How can we find out what he's up to if we're out here? I'm worried about the gnomes."

"We're going to use your musicians and yodelers to have a look around the city. I've already sent most of them in, along with the golems. And we're also going to employ your spy network."

"I have a spy network?"

"You have the beginnings of one. Your postale service." She signaled to one of the guards. "Bring the mail carrier here, please." The guard departed and Gustave gaped at her.

"You intercepted the mail? Are you insane? That's an offense against the crown!"

"You *are* the crown. The postale workers all work for you."

"Oh. Yeah."

A stocky woman with a carisak slung around her torso appeared, wearing the uniform of the Pellican Postale Service and finger gloves. She was a Qul person, with warm-brown skin and dark hair falling to her shoulders, a generous nose, and large brown eyes. One hand held a sheaf of letters.

Grinda gestured to her and made an introduction. "King Gustave, this is Qandy Liffer, a carrier in the service."

Qandy raised a hand to her heart and bowed her head. "King Gustave, it's an honor. Thank you for making the lives of all postale workers better. We'll never forget it. You have our stamp of approval." She handed him a stamp, which he accepted and stuck to his jerkin.

"The honor's mine. Thank you for doing your job so well, Qandy. I really appreciate all the advertisements for pea-za."

Grinda cleared her throat gently, in that way she had of suggesting that pea-za wasn't the current problem. "Tell me, Qandy, do you deliver anywhere else besides Borix? The Skyr, perhaps?"

"Oh, yes. I make several trips to the Skyr each month, mostly to Koloka. Gnomeric carriers take over from there and I bring back whatever's addressed to Borix."

Gustave broke in, his chin suavely resting on his fist. "Interesting. When was the last time you were in the Skyr?"

"Last week, sir."

"See anything unusual on your trip?"

"Yes, sir. Lots of gnomes on the road to Borix."

"Any idea why that was happening?"

"They said it was halflings, sir, driving them out of their homes. Firebombs and whatnot. Lots of smoke clinging to their clothes."

"That's not good for their lungs!"

"No, sir."

Gustave nodded wisely. "Tell me what else you saw."

"Well, there certainly were fires in Koloka when I got there. Plenty of smoke in the air. And there were halflings riding around on alpacas. They suggested the smoke was from a booming barbecue business hatched by the gnomes. But I didn't personally see them do anything to gnomes, sir, and they left me alone. I was able to complete my run as usual, although I never found anyone selling brisket."

"Thank you. I believe my chamberlain has some questions for you, if you wouldn't mind."

"Certainly, but I have to give these to you, sir." She held out the sheaf of letters.

"Oh, for me?" Gustave took them.

"No, sir, these are for Lord Ergot. Your chamberlain asked me to pull them out of my bag and I did, but the only people I can deliver them to are Lord Ergot and yourself."

Gustave shuffled through the envelopes and spied a wee yellow one addressed to Lord Ergot, which he pulled out. There was no return address, but this was probably the last letter sent from Hurlga at Dower. It had routed through Tennebruss and they had just beaten the mail. He kept it and returned the rest, breaking the seal on the envelope. The brief note inside read:

Still on the road to Tenebruss. Please don't hurt Ralphee, sir.

—H

Written proof of espionage and the hostage situation Hurlga described. He showed it to Grinda and she grunted before addressing Qandy.

"Does Lord Ergot send any letters into the Skyr?"

"Oh, yes."

"Can you remember to whom any of those letters were addressed?"

The postale carrier nodded. "He often wrote to someone named Marquant Dique in Bigly-Wicke, as well as others in that city. It appeared they had a regular correspondence, because whenever I picked up in Koloka, he'd get plenty of letters written on halfling stationery."

"How do you know it was halfling stationery?"

Qandy looked down at her fingertips and then splayed her hand in front of them, her voice proud. "These fingers have delivered a whole lot of mail, and papermaking isn't the same wherever you go. I can tell by touch." She lowered her hand and explained. "Halfling-made paper is rougher, with a high rag content. The ink bleeds and soaks in. Gnomeric paper is very fine, just as good as the papers you find in Qul and Teabring. It takes the ink well and is pleasant to handle. Lord Ergot also gets letters on gnomeric stationery, but the people he writes back to are almost always halflings."

"Thank you, Qandy," Grinda said. "We have delayed you long enough. Resume your route as usual, but please keep this visit a secret. It simply did not happen and you are delivering all the letters you've been given. You may rely on us not to reveal that we've taken anything from you."

"I appreciate your time and service very much, Qandy," Gustave added. "Is there anything the crown can do for you?"

Her large eyes opened fully, surprised to be asked. "I . . . am not sure. For myself, no. But perhaps for my relatives and so many people in the south: A campaign against the llamataurs to make mail and trade routes safe from Qul to Teabring? Right now everything has to go through the dank and smelly part of Kolon, and it is a dirty business. And even farther south, the seas are beleaguered by—"

"Pirates?" he asked excitedly.

She shook her head. "Oh, no. The pirates are fine. It's the POPO that's the problem."

"The Pellican Ocean Patrol Office," Grinda supplied. "The private merchant police force."

Qandy nodded. "We lose tons of mail to the POPO, sir. They do not respect your postale service one bit, and they even capture mail flamingos to sell for meat."

Gustave raised his eyebrows. "That's a serious problem. They both are. We'll look into it."

She thanked him and he smiled at her in the benevolent way that Hurlga had painstakingly taught him in front of a mirror. Smiling wasn't a thing that goats really did, so he had needed the training. He was fairly certain he had mastered it to the point that other humans thought the expression looked natural and not creepy.

His chamberlain led Qandy away and Gustave slunk into his comfy chair to consider: What were the odds that a correspondence with a lot of halflings in Bigly-Wicke, seat of the mob's power, was a completely innocent thing during a time when halflings were driving gnomes from their homes? Maybe Lord Ergot was telling them to cut it out, as in: *Hey, you rascals! You cute little scalawags! Stop with the firebombs, will you? I'm up to my knees in gnomes here!*

But that didn't match up with Ergot sending letters to Gustave saying that everything was fine or taking Ralphee as a hostage to leverage Hurlga. No, Lord Ergot was not only up to something, he was up to something with the Dastardly Rogues. And that was not only a terrible alliance for the gnomes in the Skyr, it was terrible for Pell as a whole.

When Grinda returned from seeing the letter carrier off and her eyes met Gustave's, they said it to each other at the same time: "He's a threat to the kingdom."

And then Gustave said, "Jinx, you buy me a Qoka-Qola," because he'd heard a child say it recently and thought it quite urbane.

Grinda pointed to his Traveling Icebox, although something about her manner suggested she had far-more-pressing things on her mind. "You know Qoke gives you gas. As for threats to the kingdom, you may not be familiar with the name Marquant Dique, but I am. He's the leader of the Dastardly Rogues Under Bigly-Wicke."

Gustave shook his head and said, "It doesn't look good. I'm glad we didn't go into the city. That was a good call. I'm not sure we would have come out again."

Grinda opened her mouth to respond but suddenly flinched and clutched her head with both hands. Gustave worried that she might be having some kind of episode. "Grinda? Are you well?"

"Yes, yes—no." Grinda blinked and let her hands fall back to her sides. "We have to move around to the east side of the city. The sand golems have found Ralphee in the dungeons and freed him."

"That's great!"

"They are being pursued by many armed men. They're taking fire."

"You mean they're *on* fire?"

"No, I mean soldiers are firing crossbows into them. That's what I felt and saw in my head. So far they're protecting Ralphee, but that's only so long as they can keep their shape."

Gustave's goatly instincts told him that this would be the perfect moment to drop a load of pellets out his backside, but his training with Hurlga had taught him that humans tended to say it rather than do it. "Oh, poo. Let's get over there."

"I need to focus on the golems getting Ralphee out safely. Can you think of everything else and do it, please?"

"Yes," Gustave said, though he didn't know if he really could. Usually he and Grinda decided things as a team and he liked that, because she always had some small tweak to add or a detail to consider that he hadn't thought of. He was afraid that he'd fail to think of something a human would, while remembering something entirely goaty, like where to find good socks.

The first thing to worry about was the rest of his party now circulating throughout the city, looking for information. There'd be no way to get those humans back to the centipod in time. No way

NO COUNTRY FOR OLD GNOMES

to even inform them all this was happening—unless he sent one more in.

Gustave strode to a lutist garbed in colorful tights and curly-toed shoes, the only entertainer left behind on the ship, in case the king required luting, and seeing the king coming for him, he scrambled to get his instrument in position for a festive melody.

"Never mind that. I need you for something else." Gustave plucked a purse of what Grinda called "emergency gold" from his belt and handed it to the lutist. He figured this was an emergency. "What's your name?"

"They call me Yeasty John, sir."

"Yeasty John, something's come up and we have to leave right away, but we have people in the city—your fellow musicians and yodelers. I want you to go in and find them, join them, and then settle on an inn or someplace that will accept mail in your name. Write to me in the capital from there. We will come back for you all—you have my word—but we need to know where to find you. Until then, I need you all to find employment as you can in the city and do not reveal, under any circumstances, that you work for me. That would be very dangerous. Lord Ergot is now an enemy of the crown and you'll be in a hostile city."

Yeasty John gulped. "Oh."

"Go now. Be careful. We'll see each other again in Songlen and have some proper music then, all right?"

"A-all right," the lutist said, trembling in his tights and his eyes as wide as boiled eggs.

"My thanks. Courage, man." Gustave lightly clapped him on the shoulder twice. Hurlga had taught him that men did that to indicate support for their fellows and trust in their ability to succeed. He thought it was weird and wasn't sure he did it correctly, but Yeasty John appeared mildly heartened. "You'll be richly rewarded, if you do as I say. Just keep your wits and be a musician. You can do that very well."

"Yes, sir."

"Excellent." Gustave gave him a gentle push and the musician picked up a small sack of belongings and slung it over his shoulder, clutching his lute in the other hand as he took the steps down from the centipod's deck to the cold earth surrounding Bruding.

As soon as the lutist was safely away, Gustave glanced over to Grinda, who was sitting down with her head in her hands, her eyes closed in concentration. He ordered the automaatti pilot to move around to the eastern gate as quickly as possible while staying out of range of city defenses the entire way. "Does this vehicle have its own defenses?" he asked the metal man.

"Yes, sir. *Keep it safe and your bits won't chafe!* We can encase the entire length and girth of the centipod in a prophylactic sheath. We also have several pods of antipersonnel and anticavalry automaatti that we can deploy."

"What do you mean by anticavalry? What do they target? The riders or what they're riding?"

"Either or both."

"Okay. Let's put on the prophylactic now and program the automaatti to target only the riders. No reason for the innocent steeds to get hurt here."

The pilot pressed some buttons on the conn tower and the centipod began to move as a clacking metal curtain descended from the roof to fasten onto the waist-high guardrail. Portions of the curtain could be slid open to view the outside while giving only a minimal target to anyone attempting to shoot at them. Gustave pulled the nearest curtain to the left and watched as the city's gray walls slunk past. What would Argabella call those looming walls? Loomful. Gloomful. Grimful, perhaps. Whatever they were, Gustave didn't approve.

His stomach churned, an unfortunate physical indicator of stress that he'd never suffered as a goat. They were moving far faster than they had thus far on their journey, but it still seemed too slow when he wanted to be there *now* for Ralphee. Each of his citizens was important and deserved not to get shot full of arrows or exploded by rogue halflings.

Grinda gasped behind him and Gustave whirled around. "What is it?"

"I lost a golem at the gate. But the remaining golem and Ralphee are out, running due east."

"Poo and bonus poo," Gustave said. He stalked over to the steersman. "Are we moving at top speed?"

"Yes, sir."

It wasn't fast enough. They should be there already. Hurlga would never forgive him if Ralphee died.

Gustave returned to the view slot and finally saw the corner of the Grimful Wall and, beyond it, sodden farmlands on either side of a road leading to the Skyr. Running down that road toward the gnomelands was a solidly built young man and something huge and flailing behind him, which Gustave at first thought to be a monster that wanted to eat the boy; then he realized it was Grinda's sand golem, trying to protect him. Uniformed city watchmen were firing arrows at the retreating pair, and the golem was taking the bolts in the back, allowing Ralphee to run on, uninjured.

"Cut through the farms!" Gustave said, realizing after he spoke that they had been tromping through turnip fields all along; the city needed plenty of agriculture to support it. Now that he had someone else's speed to compare it to, he saw that they were in fact moving quite fast. "We need to pick up that man running along the road. Do you see him?"

"My sensors recognize the warmth of human terror," the automaatti pilot replied, which was not the same thing but good enough. The centipod turned northeast.

"Great. Get us in front of him—no! Right behind him. We'll call him back to get on the centipod while we take fire."

He stole a glance at Grinda and saw her nod at this, though she did not open her eyes or say anything.

As the centipod gobbled up ground beneath them, Gustave saw that Ralphee was reaching the limit of bowshot range, and that was good—the sand golem took one last bolt and disintegrated. Grinda cursed softly and came to stand next to him, opening her own slot to see through. Two other bolts narrowly missed Ralphee, but no others came flying after him. The city watch had other plans.

Mounted riders charged out of the gate, perhaps a dozen of them, clanking and snorting and shouting, and Gustave knew they would catch up to Ralphee quickly.

"Pilot! Deploy anticavalry now!"

Metallic chunking noises vibrated like tuning forks in Gustave's skull, and shortly thereafter he saw little automaatti scurrying across the fields toward the horses at a frightening speed. He realized that he had not asked for any specifics regarding what would happen to the riders and feared that he may have just ordered their deaths.

He need not have worried; from the back of each spider-like automaatti, two smaller ones launched to wrap around the heads of the riders. The golden mechanical legs locked behind the skull and squeezed. The riders promptly ceased to care about chasing Ralphee; they clutched at the automaatti on their heads and most of them fell off their mounts in their efforts to get free, dropping their swords in the process while screaming, "AUGH, SPIDERS!" Once on the ground, the automaatti let go and scuttled away in search of more riders, for these weren't cavalry anymore but slow-moving men in armor, busy with panic attacks. Only two riders remained in the saddle, but neither was armed now, having dropped their weapons in an effort to get free of the automaatti.

Ralphee looked over his shoulder, wild-eyed, worried that the centipod was coming to slay rather than save him. But the craft slipped behind him, blocking the road, and Grinda ordered the pilot to open the door on the starboard side and lower the stairs for the boy. The horses of the two remaining riders veered sharply to either side to avoid colliding with the centipod, and that finally threw their riders. They thunked against the metallic prophylactic and stopped screaming about spiders, which was a relief.

"You can call off your spiders now," Gustave said, as he'd had quite enough of yelling.

"I am recalling them now," the automaatti replied. "The centipod is happiest with her spiders inside her!"

Gustave noted that some of the riders were trying to remount and might be successful eventually. But Hurlga's brother was boarding now, chest heaving and dark hair plastered to his sweating forehead, and Gustave doubted that Ergot's men would threaten the centipodial mother of spiders.

"Thanks for that," Ralphee said, "but who are you, and are you going to kill me?"

"I'm King Gustave. Your sister, Hurlga, sent us." There was no question that Ralphee was Hurlga's brother, for he really did look just like her: stout and pale-skinned, albeit flushed at the moment, same brown eyes and semi-squashed nose, same impressive hair on the forearms, sort of like an anvil wrapped in patchy fur.

"Hurlga? Is she all right?"

"She's perfectly safe."

"Oh, whew! Wait, *you're* the king who needs his backside wiped by my sister?"

"Well, not anymore, that was only at first—"

"How can you lead the country if you can't clean up after yourself?"

"I have awesome friends and cool gnomeric rides. Speaking of which: Pilot, set a course for the Toot Towers. Full speed until we lose all pursuit, then you can slow down."

The centipod lurched into movement, and they all retired to Gustave's lounge area and asked the oatmeal chef to surprise them with a refreshingly mealy repast.

"Let me ask you something, Ralphee. How did Lord Ergot learn that your sister is in my employ?"

Ralphee's face scrunched up in disgust. "I told his men when I applied for a bricking job in the Skyr. Thought it sounded mighty impressive." He leaned in. "I didn't tell him about your problematic boom-booms, though. Promise!"

Gustave and Grinda shared a look. "Lord Ergot is building in the Skyr?" she asked.

Ralphee blinked. "Well, yeah. All the housing. For the halflings and humans moving into the old gnomelands, now that the gnomes are leaving."

Grinda closed her eyes and pinched the bridge of her nose for a moment, then took a deep breath before continuing. "This is all news to us, Ralphee. Why are halflings and humans moving into the gnomelands?"

"They're laborers like me, moving there to help rebuild the gnomelands after the natural disasters."

Grinda threw up her hands. "*What* natural disasters?"

"Are you kidding me right now? The ones that drove the gnomes into Bruding!"

Gustave looked at Grinda, his eyebrows raised. "I think I might have an idea what Lord Ergot is up to with the halflings."

She shook her head and gave a short, wry laugh. "It's both a power grab and a real estate scam. First destroy their homes and then rebuild them, with halflings and humans living among them to keep control—and act as a standing army."

"But why, though? What's his end game?"

"The game is ending your reign, Gustave, and starting his own. Feeding and supplying an army capable of taking Songlen is expensive. By this time next year he'll have all the money he needs to pull it off."

Gustave made a menacing sort of sound, halfway between a growl and a bleat. "Unless we remove him first."

Grinda beamed at his understanding. "Exactly so."

"Excuse me, sir?" a guard interrupted. "There is a very large force pouring out of Bruding in pursuit. Lord Ergot is leading them."

"How large a force?"

"More than a hundred mounted."

Gustave's stomach roiled again, and he longed for the pleasant release of an emergency plop drop. A hundred riders was far more than the automaatti defenses could handle.

"It would seem that Lord Ergot is quite keen on removing you first," Grinda said.

"Oh, poop," Gustave muttered.

26.

IN THE STEAMY DEMESNE OF
DWARVELISH DELIGHT

"Different fritters for different critters."

—Låtta Senss, in *Oh, My Scattered, Covered Chunks, It Is So Dwarvelish
to Be Understanding of the Foibles of Others* (shelved in "self-help")

It was almost teatime, and bellies were grumbling. By the time they were to meet Faucon at Dinny's, no one had settled on how to broach the subject of Remy with the halfling. There was significant argument about whether they should bring it up at all.

"He never *said* that Remy was his partner or wife or anything," Båggi pointed out, "so it's not like he lied to us. There's no reason to confront him. It was a simple miscommunication."

"I don't think there's aaanything simple about it," Agape said. "The story was thaaat Remy was crushed by a staaatue, right? So in honor of thaaat, he pays to have a memorial staaatue erected of his pet pigeon? How is thaaat not a sign of mental illness?"

"It makes sense to me," Båggi said.

"How?"

"He is a halfling obsessed with justice, with balancing the scales. A gnomeric statue fell down and killed his pigeon, so he thinks it perfect to raise a statue of said pigeon and make the responsible gnomes fall down, so to speak."

"That's unbalanced, Båggi," Kirsi said.

"But it is symmetrical." Båggi hastened to explain when Kirsi's brows furrowed and her lips pursed in disapproval. "Oh, my friend! My fine bearded friend! I don't disagree with your assessment. Or with yours, Agape! I'm merely saying *Faucon* might think his response was reasonable. His behavior adheres to a code, as Gerd has pointed out to us. Please do not question his past today. He is suffering as it is."

Agape's and Kirsi's shoulders slumped, conceding, and Båggi wondered if he had done the right thing. He wondered that on a near-constant basis now. Should he have ordered the large cup of kuffee with three Teabring sugar bombs? He had hoped it would induce a state of euphoric bliss, but after a couple of sips he thought it might merely detonate his pancreas. He enjoyed discovering the taste sensations of other nations, but, as with cabbage, he'd learned that some of them were more explosive than others.

Onni pointed out the window. "Here he comes." It was easy to spot Faucon just now; he was the only halfling hobbling down the street next to a gryphon, and everyone gave them a wide berth, although many halflings stopped and exclaimed over Faucon's feet. "Hey, I think he's walking much better now."

"He has a huge bag of yogurt-covered cranberries. That's a new waistcoat too," Kirsi noted.

"Mmm-hmm. Very fancy," Onni agreed. "Possibly even schmancy. Maybe the next time I want another cardigan, I'll get a waistcoat instead." Even Båggi noted Kirsi's appreciative eyebrow raise.

They all waved through the window to Faucon and he waved back. Soon he was negotiating the hungry-hungry-halfling throng near the door while Gerd planted herself right outside the window and stared at them through the glass, her library bird perching on the shoulder joint of her right wing.

Will someone please look at the list of omlet fillings and tell me if they have ladybugges, crickets, or grasshoppers?

Båggi scanned the menu quickly and said, "I'm sorry, Gerd, they don't have any of those. They do have chocolate chips and/or mung beans."

I will settle for ten mushroom-and-bacon omlets, she said. *If you would be so kind as to order them for me and have them brought out, I will pay for them with one neck feather. Neck feathers are extremely valuable, and you will tell yon halfling waitress so. I will listen to my library bird recite Hurp Blep's* Saga of Claw and Craw *while I wait here.*

Båggi promised he would and then they all greeted Faucon and made room for him in their booth. He beamed at them.

"I feel much better," the halfling said. "The podiatrist has given me a supply of topical anesthetic while my feet heal up, which allows me to walk without pain. He had high praise for your invention, Onni, and wondered if you might be willing to either license the design or make more. I am not the only halfling with such needs."

Kirsi made a small eep of joy and Onni said, "Wow. An honest-to-goodness practical invention that works!"

"Your father would be so proud!" Kirsi said, and Onni fiddled with his sparse beard while looking supremely pleased with himself.

"It's been quite a fine day, if you don't count the mermaids," Onni said, then gestured to the ovitaur while speaking to Faucon. "Why, Agape learned that the wooden carvings she's been leaving in place of saltshakers are highly prized art. She's famous AF!"

Faucon blinked in surprise. "Truly? That is . . ."

Agape looked like she was going to lower her head and ram him. "Justice? Haaave I broken any law if the people do not feel wronged?"

Faucon pursed his lips. "Tommy Bombastic felt wronged."

"Not arguing thaaat. I'm aaasking about the people who came out ahead because what I left behind was worth way more than a saltshaker, aaand they profited."

"That is ethics, not law. By committing theft, you unequivocally broke the law. Whether it was ethical to do so is debatable."

Agape's head lowered another inch. "Let's debaaate."

At just that moment, Faucon's tummy rumbled. "Let's eat something instead and enjoy a friendly debate later."

Båggi could not stop smiling as they ordered cakes and tea for themselves and omelets for Gerd, then whiled away a pleasant hour conversing and feeling safe and cherished. It was a shame, he thought, that more hours could not be spent thus, and then he realized that perhaps they could have a few more such hours before the day ended. He inquired whether the halfling server might know of a dwarvelish inn nearby.

"Certainly," the halfling said. "It's called the Frothy Pint, and it's located across the river in the Pruneshute Forest. You can catch a ferry easily at the bank, and signs on the other side will direct you to the inn."

"Have you been there, then?" Båggi asked.

"Oh, yes. It's quite a popular drinking establishment because it's the only place you can get true pints near here. It's technically outside of the Caskcooper city limits and therefore not bound by the half-pint law. And you don't have to take a bath first."

"What?" Båggi's jaw dropped.

"Well, you can if you *want* to, but plenty of people around here don't. They have two separate service areas. One is called the Great Unwashed, and that's for folk who merely want to eat and drink, and it's kept entirely separate from the other wing of the inn, which is traditional dwarvelish service."

Båggi released the breath he'd been holding, and everyone laughed at his clear signs of relief.

"You'll be well taken care of there, sir," the server assured them, and with that endorsement, Båggi had little trouble convincing the others that they could do with some proper Pruneshute pampering.

After Faucon settled the bill, they took the ferry across the Rumplescharte River to a sturdy and much-used dock, where Båggi was delighted to see other dwarves chatting among a gaggle of drunken halflings waiting to board the ferry and stagger home. There would be no need to follow signs when friendly dwarves were ready to lead them directly to the Frothy Pint.

"Oh, there you are!" one dwarf called, waving at Båggi in a way that suggested that they had perhaps been long friends briefly parted or were long-lost cousins. "If you're headed to the Frothy Pint, I'm your guide to the perfect pour. Follow us, foine friends!"

It was not a terribly great distance to the inn, but neither was it a brief walk, especially to the panting and winded gnomes; it was at least fifteen minutes through the trees along a winding path before the Frothy Pint came into view, at which point their dwarvelish guide turned and walked backward, shouting over the many babbling conversations in progress. "Food and drink only to your left, plus the road to Nokanen! Full dwarvelish service to your right!" This was repeated several times, and almost all of the humans and halflings that had joined them on the ferry split away to the left. The only other folk headed toward the fragrant baths were a pair of halflings who swayed this way and that, arms around each other's necks. Something a bit stronger than a pint, much less a halfling half-pint, wafted from them.

"You want full dwarvelish service, my good sirs?" the guide asked, uncertain.

"Zat include a nice dwarf lass?" one of the halflings said, waggling his caterpillar-like brows.

The other halfling barked a laugh. "Got any elves, maybe? Orra nice dryad chick? Know their way around the woods is what I hear, in either case. Maybe that little gnome has three or four friends?"

Kirsi squeaked in shock, and Gerd hissed.

"Oh, my outraged outergarments," the guide said, turning beet red. "That is not—that is—please don't? I mean . . . we encourage our guests to refrain from misogyny?"

It was clear to Båggi that their guide was indeed outraged but that he also was sworn to uphold the Really Nice Rules of Hospitality and Hoedowns and that to insult his guests might cost him his job or worse—a Beard Shaving of Don't Do That Againness.

But Båggi had taken no such orders, and neither had his Telling Cudgel.

"You are drunk, *friends*," he said, pronouncing the word *friends* in such a way as to make it clear that they were not. "Perhaps you'd like to sleep it off here in the charming forest or, as the rest of your party seems to have done, take a pint in the inn?"

"Oh, yes!" the guide agreed. "Please do take these tokens for a free half-pint!" He held out two golden coins, but one of the drunk half-lings batted them away.

"We're not here for free beer, bro," he said, wobbling a little with his hand on his sword. "And we don't much like being told what to do. You'll back me up, eh?" He upnodded at Faucon, who sternly shook his head.

"I will not, eh," Faucon intoned, hand on his own sword.

The drunk halfling took a step toward Kirsi, who flinched, and Båggi's cudgel was already in his hand and swinging for the halfling's knee, as that gambit had worked in his favor previously. Right before the cudgel connected, Båggi realized that he rather hoped the half-ling didn't explode, and he also noted that he didn't seem to have as much control over the cudgel's effects as he'd hoped to have.

"Sorry!" he gulped as the cudgel connected.

Luckily, the halfling merely fell over, howling. The cudgel had no protuberances, no spikes, no coruscating beams of justified doom. It was simply a cudgel and had done what cudgels did, which was a very normal and yet annoying level of violence, at least in the eyes of someone who wasn't a half-drunk halfling lying on the ground with a broken knee.

"You bet you're sorry!" the halfling screeched. "I'll sue you! I'll tell the Dastardly Rogues about this, and your name will be grass, you see if it won't!"

"Ha ha! That is not my name! In fact, my name is—"

But Faucon put a hand over Båggi's mouth.

"What my client means is that any jury would consider what had just occurred to be an incident of self-defense, and as the Rogues are an illegal enterprise, we very much doubt that will come to pass. Now take those tokens, plus these ten fickels for your trouble, and go find another inn."

Faucon held out a handful of coins, and the halfling sneered as he took them. As for the dwarvelish guide, he, too, pulled out a bag of tokens.

"Free drinks next time you're here! But not now, ha ha! Much later!"

The halfling looked like he might reject this peace offering and start a fight, but Bäggi quietly put his cudgel up on his shoulder, and Faucon put his hand on his sword, and Gerd hissed, and the two halflings took their consolations and drunkenly wobbled off into the night, muttering about how the gnome wasn't very pretty, anyway, and any species that encouraged their women to have beards should probably go ahead and die out.

"Oh, my fluttering flutterbudgets, if that wasn't terrifying!" their guide said, exhaling in relief.

"Wasn't it just?" Bäggi responded. "Those halflings were quite the horror. I am not one to hold prejudice in my heart, but they were just quite terrifying for any species—"

"I meant you," the other dwarf said softly. "The violence in your eyes! It's been years since I've seen a young buck on Meadschpringå heft his club, and I dearly hope it'll be many more years until I see it again." He shook his head. "Control's the thing, you know, ha ha!"

"Ha ha," Bäggi said sadly, hooking his club back on his belt.

Kirsi patted his hand and said something that was meant to be comforting, but nothing could comfort Bäggi just then. At the time, he'd felt sure he'd done the right thing for the right reason, but now it seemed as if he'd done the wrong thing for the right reason and perhaps endangered the livelihood of this pleasant dwarf and whoever might own the inn as well.

The guide began walking again, and soon they looked upon the Frothy Pint. It was a charming building faced with slate and blue stones, with mosaics of shining tiles pieced together here and there depicting still lifes of food and drink with a pleasant number of fat bees. Båggi thought the surrounding forest was quite winsome and cozy too, but he couldn't enjoy any of it, not even the old-fashioned water pump that produced mead instead of water. He was all torn up inside, tender and wounded, and he felt himself slipping into a Dolorous Sulk and Skulk.

Inside the double doors—thrown wide for their entrance, with a clearance large enough to accommodate Gerd—a fountain burbled along the tiled wall and a team of robed dwarves wearing the traditional cheek tattoos of the hospitality industry greeted them, their beards oiled and braided and scented with cedar and sandalwood. Their guide disappeared, and Båggi didn't blame him a bit. Yet another dwarf awaited them, this one in a chef's hat, and it was to her they spoke first, ordering several courses from an expansive menu to be served a few hours hence. The dishes would be prepared for them while they were bathed, massaged, and groomed; their clothes would be laundered and mended as needed; and then their meals would be ready when they were all clean and relaxed. The gnomes were noticeably relieved to know their cardigans would be in good hands, and Båggi was content to let Kirsi and Faucon make all the arrangements while he himself hid behind Gerd.

Båggi was especially pleased that the chef was willing to create some "egg dishes with exotic proteins" for Gerd and that she promised they could make room for the vaunted gryphon in the dining hall, since they had few other traditional patrons that evening. They even claimed that they had the facilities to bathe and massage Gerd if she wished, and the gryphon consented to this. Båggi heard the masseuses whispering among themselves in tones of great awe, and he swelled with pride to know that he was traveling with a creature so respected by his people. If only he himself had still felt respectable, he would've been in a fine mood.

After that they were led to their respective bathing areas, where they could disrobe and send their clothing to be laundered. As Båggi was shrugging into a robe prior to descending to the subterranean heated bathing cavern, a gentle knock on the door announced the arrival of the proprietor. Båggi prepared himself for a tongue-lashing or possibly a getting-tossed-out-of-the-inning.

"Master Herbalist Båggi Biins?"

"Yes? Do come in."

A portly dwarf entered, his red beard shot through with streaks of gray on either side of his chin, his cheeks tattooed and rosy, and the corners of his eyes crinkled due to frequent smiling.

"May I just welcome you and thank you for your custom this evening? I am your host, Røkki Rüd."

Since this grand fellow was treating Båggi with esteem, he forced himself to focus on dwarvelish ways and not dwell on the halfling horror until the time came. He and Røkki beamed at each other and traded alliterative compliments and enthused about this tiny oasis of dwarvelish civilization in the midst of halfling territory.

"I don't wish to intrude, and your private time is sacrosanct," Røkki said after a while, "but I'm afraid there is a situation we must discuss."

"Yes, I suppose we must," Båggi said, his shoulders drooping, and soon enough they were in a dwarf-hewn cavern lit by dozens of candles set in recessed niches. Steam rose from the surface of a large heated pool, its bottom lined with fine sand that would squish pleasantly between the toes. A waterfall at one end brought freshly heated water into the cavern and it drained at another end, its heat to be reclaimed but the soils to be filtered out. The steam condensed on the ceiling and dropped back down into the pool, little echoing splashes providing soft punctuation to the music of the waterfall in the candlelit space. The two dwarves waded in and moved to a soap shelf lined with labeled cakes. Båggi chose a lemongrass-and-grapefruit scrub, while Røkki opted for a honey-apple soap. After they lathered and shampooed and rinsed and felt renewed, they lounged in the water up to their chins and the proprietor spoke.

"Before that unpleasantness, what have you seen in the world of late? I am bound here, with only occasional trips to Caskcooper for variety, and depend on visitors to keep me informed."

Bǻggi had certainly seen many things of late, and recounting even the least of them revealed that he was on his Meadschpringǻ.

"Yes, I had thought as much, although you do not carry your cudgel."

"I had already put it away when you arrived."

"So how goes it?"

Bǻggi took a deep breath before answering. "At first, I thought myself without violence and was quite agog at the shapes my cudgel took. And then ... er ... quite recently, I found that the cudgel retained a form of peace while I chose to mete violence to protect those in my care. I can't seem to find symmetry with my cudgel, and I fear I have done unnecessary damage."

Røkki shrugged. "Choice is important. And protecting those weaker than you is always the right choice."

"Even if it harms a third party?"

At this, Røkki chuckled and patted Bǻggi on the shoulder in a fatherly way. "My inn can do without roughhousers, be they halflings or otherwise. My young guide has not yet known his Meadschpringǻ, and so he worried more for his skin than anything else. Don't let it trouble you overmuch, although I must ask you to hang your cudgel outside before you join us for dinner upstairs."

Bǻggi inclined his head; that was quite reasonable. But he found he didn't want to stop talking to Røkki, who seemed quite wise and also worldly.

"You know, Master Røkki, I had hoped to already be on my way back to the High Mountain Home, yet my cudgel remains in an aggressive form. It had a gryphon in the grain right after I used it in anger, then a book while we were at the Great Library, and just now, I looked and it has some great lizard or salamander on it. It would seem I have much more violence ahead of me, and I confess it troubles me greatly. I worry about my fate; I worry that I'll never go home again."

"Why worry about returning to the mountains? There are many places to make a home in Pell."

"It is not the place I want to return to so much as the peace."

"Ah, I take your meaning. Still, I think your mind can take its ease."

Båggi felt his brow furrowing in a very undwarvelish way. "Why do you say that? I have no guarantee of success. My brother is a mercenary, always spoiling for a fight. He would've done much worse to that halfling tonight, and I'll admit I wanted to. How can such a life be peaceful?"

"Forgive me, Båggi, if I suggest you may be holding on to a narrow vision of peace that you see waiting for you on a pedestal at the end of a long hallway. Your Meadschpringå is not a sprint down that hall to your goal. There are rooms to explore, there are doors leading out and doors leading in, and you can take your time, take another path, and maybe find something else that pleases you besides what's on that pedestal."

But Båggi was boggled. "I am not sure I follow your metaphor. What can I possibly find in this imaginary house that surpasses peace of mind?"

"I do not think peace walks the world in only one form. It is not merely that thing on the pedestal, you see? It is a shape-shifting mystery that changes its face not only from person to person but for each individual over time. Right now you think peace is a heart-swelling return to the High Mountain Home, and I understand that. There was a time when I thought that was what peace meant too. But, strange as it may seem, I have found my peace here."

"Truly?"

"Oh, there are stresses, to be sure." The old dwarf's mustache drooped and his tone was bleak. "I miss seeing my own kind more than I would freely admit to my staff; we are the only dwarves hereabouts and we rarely get visitors like you. And there seems to be more violence these days here, near the Skyr, yet I must keep my inn open to all." He sighed, then chuckled at his own folly. He looked up at the ceiling of the cavern, his voice now choked with emotion. "But still I hear the song of the wind whispering in the leaves, and I know the voices of my brethren ride with it from the mountaintops. There are friendships and loves kindled within these walls, Båggi. And sometimes old passions, reduced to smoldering coals, reignite to full flame. Worries are soothed, raw wounds are healed, and the waters wash away all manner of troubles. My Frothy Pint is balm and blessing to many, and I am content."

"I am glad to hear it," Båggi said. "And it is certainly a blessing to me this day. But may I ask: What does your Telling Cudgel look like now?"

"Ah, you wonder how it's going to end, how you will know; I see. Well, I do not mind telling you, though this is a truth only for myself. My cudgel is mounted on the wall in my office, and it is as smooth and polished as the day I left the mountains in my youth. There is no bee ingrained at the end, telling me I may return to the lofty peaks of Korpås. Instead, there is a proud stag, at home in this forest, and the Korpåswood has been dead for many years. This is my place, Båggi, and it is no tragic end for me."

"No, not at all, to be sure," Båggi said. "Thank you for being so candid and kind with your wisdom, Røkki. You have given me much to think on."

They spoke of local herbs and the troublesome nature of geese and then they were fetched by spa dwarves, who said it was time for Båggi's massage and beard grooming. While it dangled off the massage table, his beard was expertly oiled and plaited and festooned with blossoms and an enameled bee brooch that complemented his fashionable new halfling half ring. He was relaxed and invigorated and thrilled to have clean clothes again. He felt wondrously happy to meet his friends, all shining with health in the dining room, and share a delicious repast with them and laugh and sing until they felt ready to retire. For all that Båggi had expected and dreaded the innkeeper's visit, Røkki's words had soothed him, and he left his cudgel outside with no worries that he might need it.

Agape was wearing Piini's cog around her neck with a polished gold chain; Kirsi and Onni both wore new cardigans and pansies in their beards; Faucon's hair from topknot to toes had been attractively curled; and Gerd had a bright-blue ribbon tied at the end of her tail. The bed in his room was soft and warm and Båggi enjoyed the best sleep he'd had since leaving home, and everything smelled of warm beeswax. Should they meet ruin ahead, at least they had that one magnificent day together to remember.

They met the next morning with a sunny disposition, ready but reluctant to leave the forest. When they arrived at the ferry dock they saw it would be a decent wait, and Onni wondered aloud where a path curving away to the south might lead.

"We have to go south anyway to get to the Toot Towers," he said, "and it's not certain we'll be able to book passage on a river boat anytime soon. So why don't we explore this route a little bit and see where it goes, perhaps enjoy the trees a while longer?"

No one had any objections, so they followed the path, which soon veered off deeper into the trees away from the bank, though they were still moving roughly parallel to the course of the river. It was pleasant all through the morning and the path was taking them in the direction they wished to go, so they kept following it into the afternoon after breaking for luncheon. Soon afterward they had reason to rue their detour, as they came upon a section of forest dominated by thorny bushes, sweet-gum balls, itchy vines, and a pack of the dreaded Pruneshute wolves. The toothy predators kept their distance because of Gerd, but they were clearly trailing the party behind and to either side and eyeing them for weakness and a possible fall into a stinkhole brimming with acidic marinade.

Even those over two feet tall were soon ragged and exhausted, and poor Faucon was in distinct pain and in need of a soothing foot bath, but there was no succor, no place to rest without signaling to the wolves that they were too tired to fight. To add insult to injury, it began to rain. All they could do was slog through it, arms over their heads, eyes darting to either side to make sure the wolves weren't closing in.

Agape in particular was rather worried about their presence, muttering, "Wolves don't lose sleep when there's sweet sheep to eat."

"That sounds like a gnomeism!" Kirsi said, perking up.

The ovitaur gave her a withering glare. "If so, I'm guessing the gnome who -ismed it waaas no friend to sheep."

It was nearing dusk and getting dark quickly underneath the canopy, and Båggi began to fret that they would have to make a stand and there would be much blood and no rest for any of them. After one more league and many gnomeric groans of bursting blisters, the path, thankfully, turned sharply west around an impressive fern, widening as it did so, and they saw two hand-painted signs staked into the ground alongside the path. The nearest one said: FREE EXPERT DENTAL CARE TO FOREST RESIDENTS.

"Free dental care? I didn't know such a thing existed," Kirsi said with a tiny snort.

"Who cares about dentists? I need a podiatrist!" Faucon hissed through clenched teeth, clutching a handkerchief over his head.

"Seconded," Onni moaned. "And also a masseuse specializing in dainty calves."

"There has to be a gotcha," Agape said, grimly accustomed to the perils of the outdoors and inclement weather. "Nothing's free. There's always a caaatch. What's the next sign say?"

They picked their way forward until they could make out the second sign, which was painted in a different, sloppier hand and had several lines crossed out in frustration. They had to squint to make it out.

BEWARE THE ~~SPECTRES~~

~~SPECK TREES?~~

~~FAN TOMS~~

GHOSTS!

"Bless my buttered potatoes," Båggi said, "Agape was right! That's quite a gotcha!"

27.

SURROUNDED BY PHANTASMAL APPARITIONS AND DUSTY CHIFFAROBES

"How to take proper care of your teeth: Don't. Don't stop to floss; don't stop to buy toothpaste. A Vartija's job isn't to have a nice smile; it's to keep your charge hidden and safe. And leave no dental records."

—PENELOPE FALLOPIA, in *Run, Don't Walk: A Letter to My Descendants on How to Live Long Enough to Have Your Own Descendants*

Considering she'd spent her entire life wandering the land of Pell, Agape was always surprised when she found a place she'd never seen before. The edifice firmly anchored in the forest—half hut and half castle, festooned with more cupolas than it had a right to cup—was something she surely would've remembered.

And, like she said, she suspected tomfoolery. Especially since the wolves that had been following them were no longer visible. That just meant the slavering beasts had decided on different tactics. Or were at least secure in their dental routines.

Before Agape could explain her father's foolproof method of slinking around to see if terrifying ghosts and/or wolves were in fact waiting in ambush, Kirsi just walked right up the grimly tilting cobblestones to the front door. The wet steps creaked under even her tiny boots, but she didn't slow down. Her determination was, frankly, of-

fensive to Agape. Knocking on the doors of random strangers, especially those who'd taken care to place warning signs about the
property, was a no-no, rainstorm or not.

"Kirsi, wait!" she called, but it was too late.

The gnome knocked on the human-sized (or ghost-sized or wolf-
standing-on-its-back-legs-sized) door, right at knee height, and vir-
tually howled, *Yes, hello, I'm young and delectably tender and easily
bruised by poltergeists. Please come answer the door!* Even if what she
actually said was something more along the lines of *Hulloo, the house!
We weary, most moiste travelers would be oh so glad to make your ac-
quaintance!* Agape knew what she really meant.

"If a ghost shows up to eat us, I hereby blaaame you, Kirsi," Agape
snarled.

Kirsi gave her usual competent and cheerful smile. "Oh, ghosts
can't eat you. They just tickle a bit and sometimes misplace the sugar."

Agape looked to her other fellows as she waited for a wolf ghost
to arrive at the door, but everyone seemed just as calm as Kirsi, all
edging toward the barest sliver of dryness under the eaves. Agape
had to find someone with some sense.

"Faucon, are you not concerned with the dangers in this house?
Ghosts? Aaand possibly wolves?"

The halfling gave it a moment's thought and responded, "If the
occupant is phantasmal, it cannot hurt us. If it has substance, I feel
certain that, between Gerd's menace, my sword, and Kirsi's curses, we
can best it. It would be terribly pleasant to be inside, away from
thorns and quicksand and bloodsucking insects. And this dratted
rain. And the dark, which can often be unpleasant in forests such as
this one."

"I don't hear anyone inside, and I haven't seen an apparition," Kirsi
said, on her knees and peeking under the old door, which seemed to
have shriveled away from the stone walls. "No lights, no movement.
Can we safely assume it's abandoned? Even the signs we passed
looked terribly old."

"Oh, my barmy bickering banshees! That is not the way to make a good first impression!" Båggi clutched his Telling Cudgel, which remained smooth and unblemished by murderous appendages. But that made sense, Agape assumed, since one couldn't bash ghosts, no matter how angry one might be about their existence.

This is quite foolish, Gerd said. *Faucon is in pain and requires aid. I will pummel the door down, and these ghosts you fear may Come at Me. I will give unto them the old What For.*

"Gerd, no!" Agape wailed, but did the gryphon listen either? Of course not. These citified fools thought you could just knock on the door of any haunted mansion and be invited in for cheese.

It took only one firm gryphonic headsmashing and the door swung inward, creaking in protest. Gerd performed a victory squawk, and Faucon was just lifting a golden-toed foot over the threshold, when the very apparition Agape had feared appeared. It didn't glow or shimmer or squelch with ectoplasm, which were all things Agape expected of a proper ghost. Then again, it also didn't drool and smack its lips and hold up a fondue fork, so whatever it was, it was better than a hungry wolf. It merely floated forward silently and beheld them with pitch-black eyes.

"Vhat is this?" the shadow spake, drawing a black cloak around hunched shoulders. "Who dares disturb my hallowed halls vithout an invitation?"

"Nobody!" Agape shouted. "We're just leaving."

"Ha ha! Yes! Nobody!" Båggi agreed.

"Don't be silly." Kirsi stepped forward and held out her hand to the form at least three times her height. "Greetings! I'm Kirsi, and my friends and I are so glad to meet you. I apologize for our unusual method of visiting, but you see, we thought the house was abandoned."

The figure cocked its head. "Abandoned? Vhy, did you not see the signs? They are qvite clear, I believe, regarding dentistry and ghosts."

"Oh, we saw them," Kirsi said lightly, as if they were discussing the weather. "But they looked terribly old, and we knocked, and no one came to the door, so we assumed ..."

She trailed off, perhaps hoping that the homeowner would somehow fill in the blank with a statement that didn't involve *we assumed we could trespass with no consequences*, but he did not accommodate her.

"Do you know vhat happens vhen you assume, little vun?" he asked solemnly.

"No?"

"You make an ass out of yourself."

"Pardon me," Onni interrupted, "but I thought it was *an ass out of you and me* because ass-u-me, you know?"

The figure hissed and leaned down into the scant light from outside, revealing himself to be a slender man with high cheekbones, pale skin, and black hair with a widow's peak and graying sides. His ears were the tiniest bit pointed, his canine teeth poking out over his lower lip.

"The person who trespasses is, I believe, the only ass in this situation," he said gravely. "But vhat had you planned on doing here? Looting? Searching for magical objects? Hunting for the secrets of my famed longevity?"

"Oh, my heavens, no!" Båggi burst in. "We only wanted a little space for a footbath and a moment out of the rain, you see. We are not the plundering sort, my good man! A dwarf worth his or her beard would never consider that sort of pillagy racket for even a butterfly's blink."

Agape was putting two and two and two more fangs together and determining that she liked the answer even less than ghosts and wolves. This man—or creature—had to be a vampire, or at least a vile necromancer. The waxy skin, the black eyes, the fangs. It all added up. The reason he hadn't answered the door at dusk but had arrived right as darkness had fallen—he had just awakened, hungry for blood.

"Vampire," she whispered to Kirsi.

"What?" Kirsi said, right as the figure said, "Vhat?" in that unnerving way.

"I said . . . hamp . . . hamper. I wish we had a hamper."

"Like for laundry?" the figure asked, confused. "That's vhat you're here to steal?"

"No. I just. Never mind. We caaan leave. We're so sorry to haaave bothered you, sir. Please rest assured that we're all anemic vegans who don't like pineaaapple, and our blood is terribly thin and probably full of squirrel flu, so we'll just be going."

But the figure flapped one arm out, his black cloak billowing.

"Don't be ridiculous. It is night and raining. You must stay. Join me for dinner."

"Dinner!" Faucon said, walking right in and trying not to wince with each step. "That is my favorite word, right after luncheon and dessert. Fine word, dinner. And what, pray tell, will you be serving, my good man?"

"Vhy, I vill be serving you," the figure responded.

Agape was just drawing breath for a proper scream when the figure laughed heartily. "That is a little joke. Because I vill be serving dinner *to* you, do you see? Ve'll be having fruit-bat blood pudding, raw cubes of aged thunder yak, and marinated pearl onions, so crunchy and flavorful. All delicacies from Sangvynn, you see. Ah, the old country. How I miss the Eastern lands! Do come in. Please vipe your feet on the mat."

Agape had no choice but to enter the house after wiping her hooves on the mat just inside the door, which read VELCOME. And then the door shut behind them, leaving them in the pitch dark.

"Silly me. I have forgotten the lamps. Reegor! Bring the fire!"

From somewhere deep within, a nasal voice called, "Fire!" and then, "Coming, master!" The steps that approached them went step-drag, step-drag, and Agape imagined that when the lamps were lit, she'd be met with a hideously twisted form, hunchbacked and evil-eyebrowed. But when a candle neared and lit the first lamp, there was a human girl, probably in her early twenties, wearing large glasses and sensible shoes. The dragging noise was apparently a large, fuzzy puppy that had the girl's skirt firmly caught in its teeth.

"Sorry about Frank," she said with a truly unfortunate voice. "He thinks everything is a game of tug-of-war. You guys staying at the hostel for dinner?"

"Yes?" Agape asked, utterly confused.

Reegor beamed. "Yay! Guests! And they're still alive!"

"Aha!" Agape shouted. "I knew it! He's a vaaampire, and you're his foul assistant and possible sous chef, and thaaat's ... thaaat's ... a hellhound, and ..."

Everyone went completely silent and stared. At Agape.

"Uh, is thaaat not the conclusion you were all reaching?" she asked.

"I am not a vampire!" the figure announced harshly. "I am ... a dentist! And an innkeeper for traveling ghosts. I don't understand vhy you might ever think I vas some undead monster."

"Oh, yeah. He's totally legit," Reegor said. "Dr. Murkimer is one of the best dentists in Pell. He does loads of volunteer work here in the forest. He even went to Songlen and fixed the king's teeth. We got to ride in a fancy coach with extra bidets and everything." She leaned in conspiratorially. "Worst case of goat teeth I've ever seen, but now they're sparkling white and not all scraggly. I'm one semester away from graduating, thanks to Doc Murk's mentorship."

"And now, if you're done assuming innocent dentists are monsters, I must attend to my guests," Dr. Murkimer said huffily. "If you vish to check in, ve do have vacancies. Just see Reegor at the concierge desk. I promise ve von't make you sleep in a coffin." He swept indignantly down the hall, cloak held before him, shadows capering in his wake.

Kirsi looked at Agape like she'd grown horns. "You thought he was a vampire? Seriously?" When Agape just continued to gawp, the gnome added, "Your trust issues go pretty deep, Agape."

"I'll be at the concierge desk in the parlor, polishing the doctor's humanitarian awards," Reegor said, smirking. "You're welcome to stand up here, quaking and wearing garlic necklaces for as long as you like." She walked away, the puppy still clinging to her leg. Step-drag. Step-drag.

As Agape opened her mouth to remind everyone of the pointy

ears and cape, two puffs of cloud wisped through the door, through Gerd, and down the hall, and no one reacted to that either.

"G-g-g-ghost!" Agape stammered, pointing, in case the others hadn't quite noticed.

One puff turned around, a man's annoyed face materializing in glowing blue and continuing to gain form downward in the shape of a ghostly cloak. "Rude," he muttered. "It's a ghostel and a hostel, not a hostile, if you know what I mean."

The other puff likewise materialized in glowing blue, a woman in skintight rogue's duds. "Cor, Lord Toby. Did King Gustave get together with that nanny goat he liked when he was goatly, or did some other wizard have better luck with turtlehog-type relations, because the stammering girl with the hooves don't look a bit right in the head nor hocks. A bit sheepish, if you get my meaning?"

"No, Poltro, Gustave cannot . . . I mean . . . I don't think? Gods, I hope not," The ghost named Toby cringed. "Gross. No offense."

Faucon stepped forward, holding up a hand to silence Agape. "Forget the ovitaur," he said. "Are you talking about King Gustave? Because that's the second time he's been mentioned here, and you see, we're on a quest to find him."

The ghost man grinned and smugly stroked a tiny beard that probably made even Onni feel pretty proud of his follicular accomplishments. "Why, you're in luck, traveler! For I am personal friends with King Gustave himself. Why dost thou seek him?"

"To save lives," Kirsi said, stepping forward. "We need to present a very important historical document to King Gustave to prove that Lord Ergot and the halflings are illegally waging war on the gnomes of the Skyr." She was all business, despite the fact that Ghost Poltro kept accidentally swishing her ghost cloak through the gnome's face while making boat noises. "Is he a kind sort of king? A king who would be opposed to exploding gnomes?"

"Most kind," Ghost Toby assured her. "And horribly softhearted toward people exploding against their will. I'm sure he'll try to help you."

"Mmm. Softhearted." Ghost Poltro licked her ghost lips. "And soft-haunched, and soft-gibleted. Cor, I miss curried goat!"

Ghost Toby rubbed his ghost forehead in a way that suggested he had not expected the afterlife to be quite so annoying.

"How can we convince King Gustave to see us?" Faucon asked, ever the professional. "We may appear a ragtag bunch, but the papers we bear are most legal and important."

Ghost Toby grinned. "Oh, this'll be fun. I'll give you a secret passcode. If you say it to King Gustave, he will immediately know that you are trustworthy and that your quest is a noble one. Are you ready?"

Faucon whipped out his notebook and pen and nodded, eyes narrowed. "Most ready."

"Then here it is. Simply say to him, *The Dark Lord Toby swears on a bog-frog smoothie that we are the real deal, or else may Ol' Faktri marinate me in phlegm and lemons.*"

Faucon studiously wrote that down, but Agape wasn't satisfied. "Wait. What does thaaat mean? How do we know it's not a secret code to, I don't know, throw us in an oubliette?"

Ghost Toby stepped toward Agape, forcing her to step back. He bent over, piercing her with his ghostly blue gaze.

"First of all, if I mean to throw you in an oubliette, you'll know it. I possess one, you know."

"Full of jam, it is," Poltro added. "And sometimes me own brother."

"Forget the ham jam. Child, do you honestly think that I would waste my afterlife sending people on wild-goose chases while other, more-innocent people die? No. I was a fool in life, and I've since learned that the greatest thing I ever possessed was not my tower or my grimoires or gobs of money and fine cheeses. It was the friends I made on my last adventure, and King Gustave was one of them. So use the passcode or don't, but I assure you that if you want to get anywhere useful, you've got to learn how to trust."

Poltro started to say, "Except—" but Toby interrupted her.

"Yes, Poltro. We never trust chickens. Everyone knows that."

Poltro nodded wisely, and so did Gerd, oddly enough.

"Thank you," Faucon said gravely. "Is there any favor we can do for you in return?"

"Ah! Most kind!" Toby's eyes gleamed green with ghostly greed. "If you could just bop into the Catacombs of Yore and steal—I mean, borrow—some flesh honey from this fellow named Brønsted the Buttertroll or something like that—you'll know it, as he's guarded by an ageless monk and acid leeches, but don't worry about that now. Doesn't hurt a bit. So just get a spoonful—"

"Two spoonfuls," Poltro reminded him.

"Ah. Yes. Of course. Two spoonfuls." Toby winked an eye. "Of this flesh honey, see, and then you'll need to go dig up our corpses at the Grange and part our dead, cold, worm-riddled lips—"

Faucon cleared his throat, interrupting a speech that had everyone gagging. "I was thinking more like . . . some flowers on a grave, or perhaps a pot of sugar, as my gnomeric friend assures me ghosts are into that?"

Ghost Toby sighed. "Now that I say it out loud, it does sound a bit complicated. Almost a complete quest in and of itself. But maybe . . ." He went all wistful. "Do you have some cheese? Perhaps a stout Styffi, or maybe a grand Gouda? I can't quite taste it, but I find that if I sort of waft my mouth around it, it tickles my ectoplasm in the most delicious way."

"I knew my ball bag would come in handy!" Båggi cried. "It's a bit moist just now, and I'm sure the leather has made it sweat, but the cheese is definitely most prime!"

Ghost Toby went from horrified to appreciative when he saw the halfling cheese Båggi produced, and Kirsi suggested that they check in with Reegor and retire to the dining room, where Toby could waft around the cheese to his ghost heart's content.

Dinner went about as well as could be expected, although Agape noticed Båggi didn't enjoy his cheese as much after Toby's mouth had floated around it six or seven times, making little moaning and gulping noises. The ghost lord had an entertaining trick of waggling his fingers to cause ghost croutons to fall around them like marsh-mallows, and Agape was fairly certain that several of his stories were about the king in a former life. Dr. Murkimer and Reegor joined them, which wasn't as awkward as Agape had feared. Bäggi distributed his mead to the humans and even provided a thimbleful for the gnomes and Lord Toby, who slurped at it and smacked his lips despite the fact that the level of liquor in his glass never changed.

As for Agape, she felt entirely bereft of joviality. She had always felt outside things, an observer who didn't know how to be part of the party, but now she realized . . . she wanted to be part of the party. And not as the token stranger, not as the tough-as-nails traveler, not as the mysteriously cloaked figure who looked to the horizon and claimed to have *seen things*. She wanted to laugh and tell stories and forget that the world was a scary place, as her parents had always told her it was. This ghostel—it would've terrified them both into bleating puddles. It had definitely terrified Agape and even caused her to make a fool of herself.

But now she was here, and it was lovely. Everyone was safe and happy and in a good mood. Faucon was benefiting from his footbath and Bäggi's herbal preparations. Kirsi was deep in conversation with Lord Toby regarding the practical application of magic and the production of bready foodstuffs, which could come in handy on the road through enemy territory—although the bristle witch would need to find or manufacture a wand. Poltro and Gerd had become fast friends around their common distaste for chickens. Bäggi, Dr. Murkimer, and Reegor were comparing turnip recipes and discussing the encroaching threat of cabbage cults.

That left Agape and Onni, side by side and silent.

"So this plaaace is okay," she started.

Onni chuckled. "Better than an abandoned crypt. Funny how everything on this quest goes sideways, isn't it?"

She leaned in closer. "Do you . . . do you miss your faaamily? You had a brother, didn't you?"

"Yeah, a twin. I miss him. But . . . well, he always outshone me. It was nice to be useful, when Piini was still around. I feel a little adrift now, if I'm honest. Do you miss your parents? They seemed . . ."

She could tell he wanted to say something like "awful," and she realized she did too.

But she also realized what they really were. And the mead made her tongue as loose as a ball of last year's wool.

"They're just scaaared. Being haaalf sheep does that to a person. Their entire life revolved around hiding Piini aaand me. I guess they did do that effectively, but they messed me up, and I'm just starting to see how deep that goes. I do miss them, but I'm staaarting to like being out on my own even more."

"You're Independent AF," Onni mused, and Agape laughed.

"Confused AF, more like."

The gnome boy shook his head. "Nah. You just have to figure out what you want. After we find the king and fix things, I mean. The scary part is not knowing."

"Do you know what you waaant?" she asked, genuinely curious.

He was looking right at Kirsi as he said, "Yeah, but I've always known." Then he shook his head and refocused on Agape. "But you can go back to Caskcooper, become an artist. They think you're great over there. Sell a couple of carvings and retire in style."

"Bourgeois AF," she mused, and they laughed together.

Agape looked around the table and realized . . . she'd been part of the party all along.

"I hope you get what you waaant, Onni," she said, meaning it.

"Me too. But the Skyr comes first."

As if on cue, the door banged open with an accompanying splintering of wood, and Dr. Murkimer and Reegor leapt to their feet.

"Not again," Reegor moaned. "How many locks do we have to buy for a building in which most of the visitors are incorporeal?"

Much to everyone's surprise, a giant Pruneshute boar burst into the dining room, its bristles gently smoking.

"Dooooc!" the boar squealed. "Reeeeegor!"

"Ugbüt! Vhat's vrong?" Dr. Murkimer asked. "Is it your left tusk again?"

"Forget my tusk," the boar grunted. "We're under attack! By half-lings! With bombs!" He turned around to show a singed tail and a large spot of pink broiled ham on his bare boar bottom.

Kirsi ran for the door, and everyone followed her—except for Båggi, who stayed to offer Ugbüt a dollop of Frau Thistle's One-Time Bristle & Grizzle Tonic for Hearty Hair Growth. Through the open door they saw that the boar was right on the money.

A halfling army was on the march toward them while eating their second dinner, their torches glowing in the darkness, their mouths making loud smacking noises as they ripped flesh off turkey legs and licked grease from their fingers. Forest animals fled in terror that they might be eaten next, or blown up with a firebomb, or both in any order. The halflings were chucking the incendiary devices ahead at intervals to clear the way, and Agape assumed Ugbüt had been singed by such.

"Vhy vould an army be marching through here?" Dr. Murkimer said. "They don't hate dentists that much, do they? Vhy vould anyone ever hate a dentist?" His slim black brows drew down. "Or did you tell them I vas a vampire?"

"No, but good question," Onni said. "Here's another one: Why is no one surprised that a boar just burst in and talked to us?"

"All pig species can talk," Reegor replied. "They just usually don't, unless they need to tell you where on the tusk it hurts."

"Oh, no," Onni said, hand flying to his heart. "Please, nobody tell Ugbüt I had candied bacon on my tea cake at Dinny's." He hung his head. "Oh, gods of Pell, why must bacon be so delicious?"

"Focus less on guilt and more on saving our own bacon. I bet that army is headed to Nokanen," Kirsi muttered, hiding behind Dr. Murkimer's cloak in case one of the halflings spotted a fresh target. "They're escalating."

"By traveling south of the main route through the forest, they will avoid gnomeric scouts," Faucon mused. "But . . . they do not have the look of drubs, do they? And they are marching in ranks. Disciplined." Faucon squinted, unable to make out details in the darkness. "Gerd, can you see what they wear? Is it a uniform?"

Gerd cocked her head and blinked at the torches, then reported: *Uniforms, yes. Mostly they are covered in food staynes, but underneath that they are redde with many yellö buttons.*

"Oh, no," Faucon said, his voice pained. "That's the city watch of Caskcooper. They've been corrupted too." Only when she heard the two contractions did Agape understand how this news struck the halfling to the heart.

"I think ve should all be leaving now," Dr. Murkimer said. "You kids be safe. Don't forget to floss!" He and Reegor disappeared into the old house, presumably to fetch the puppy and whatever else they could take with them, and Ugbüt emerged directly afterward, thanking Båggi for being so helpful and handy at healing his hocks.

"We've got to hurry," Agape said.

They turned to look at her.

"Are you always going to run?" Onni asked as if disappointed.

She shook her head. "Not away. *To.* We've got to get to the Toot Towers to stop all this maaadness."

Because she'd finally realized: These were her friends, and she wasn't going to wait until she was dead, like Ghost Toby, to appreciate them.

But before she could tell them so and initiate her first group hug, a firebomb detonated near the porch, setting the ancient boards of the ghostel aflame.

28.

MIRED IN THE VISCID GELATIN
OF THE FIGGISH FEN

"I'd give up three of my toes for a pudding like that!"

—OLD HALFLING IDIOM

"Them halfling folks who say they'd give up three of their toes always have ten, and they ain't never broke a bone, never gone hungry, never lost a part of themselves, or else they'd never say that. They don't know what it means to go without. Because I'll tell you right now: I'd give up pudding altogether if I could have my toes back, and I'm mad about pudding."

—TWO-TOE TITANIA TOOTENFIFE, in *Yes, I Still Love Socks: Now Let's Talk About Anything Else*

The scramble to evacuate the ghostel was somewhat less frantic than anticipated, considering all the guests were already dead. Faucon stood there for a moment, watching the ghosts puff and squeeze out of the ghostel, but then Reegor limped by, dragging the puppy and a huge suitcase, hollering, "Move it, guys! Fire: bad!" and they all surged into movement.

Kirsi and Onni were still walking tenderly, their tiny boots full of blood and blister juice, so it was no surprise when the assertive gnome girl strode purposefully to Gerd and said, "Mighty gryphon, might we beg a ride to safety? For the spirit is courageous but the legs are dainty and suffering from overproduction of lactic acid."

Gerd consented, and that gave Faucon an idea.

"Mighty Ugbüt," he asked, sweeping a bow, "my mechanical prostheses are perfectly serviceable for a leisurely stroll or even a long hike, but they have not been tested whilst running for my life amidst an ejaculation of ghosts. Would you consent to carry me to safety, if it is not against your personal code?"

"That's a lot of words," Ugbüt said, "but I suppose that could do, as long as you and your spry-fingered friends will gently rub some numbing unguents on my fricasseed nethers once we're on the other side."

Båggi and Agape would hoof it—literally, in Agape's case—but both of them could easily outpace halflings on the march. Faucon had just settled himself onto Ugbüt's back, fists clenched into the bristles of his shoulders and legs braced against the sides of the boar, when a new firebomb detonating behind them made urging Ugbüt forward entirely unnecessary.

The boar squealed and shot off into the darkness like a greased cork, and it was all Faucon could do to hold on, quickly forming a new appreciation for alpacas and ponies and saddlery in general. Praises, he realized in an excruciating moment of agony, should be heaped upon saddlers, for they were the saviors of delicate and tender bits, and such bits had little chance of emerging unscathed when riding boarback, said boar being in a panic and leaving a trail of fragrant smoke in his wake. For all that his bacon had been literally saved, Faucon couldn't help rolling his eyes heavenward in recognition that his bangers and mash were being most severely banged into mush.

Faucon heard the cries of the rest of his party, calling after him and Ugbüt to wait, but the boar was in no mood for conversation. He was in the mood to plunge through the brush and not give a tusk whether the halfling on his back got shredded by thorns, impaled by a branch, or simply fell off.

The flaying of his hide as they barreled through the brush was very painful, and the bruising punishment to his nethers was likewise painful and might be doing permanent damage to his personal pudding factories.

But none of it, he suspected, would be as painful as being set on fire by the city watch of Caskcooper, and since Ugbüt was doing his utmost to make sure that didn't happen, Faucon clenched his teeth and endured, his entire body a haze of pain anchored by the iron will to hold on. He was certain his friends would catch up with him eventually, and if they didn't, well, then he was more than capable of surviving on his own and knew, at least, where they were headed. Ever since her introduction to omelets, Gerd had possessed a nearly preternatural ability to find Faucon when she was hungry.

He attempted, at intervals, to get Ugbüt to slow down, but the boar snarled at him each time: "I still smell smoke!"

"That could be your own hind end and not the army," Faucon pointed out. "Your bristles are still sizzling somewhat. Look, it is always impossible to outrun your own ass."

Ugbüt snorted and downshifted to a more conservative if still jarring pace. "I feel like I need to try. You can jump off anytime."

Faucon assured the boar that he was grateful for the ride and would continue to hold on for safety's sake.

"Safety's sake. Yes. That's why I have to keep going. I know what happens to animals that get too close to armies. Especially delicious animals too close to halfling armies."

Gerd's mental voice spoke to them faintly after a while. *Faucon? Ugbüt? Where are you?*

Faucon turned his head to the right and looked up, seeing no stars or moon. They were completely hidden by the canopy of the Pruneshute Forest.

"Where are we headed, Ugbüt?"

"Southwest, to the Figgish Fen. No armies ever go there. And I suspect the sluggish waters will be ideal for butt dippage."

That was a long way and meant no sleep through the night, but the boar was right: There would be no danger of meeting any armies. "I'm going to shout back to Gerd and hope she hears me," he warned, then followed through. "Headed southwest!" he shouted, hoping the gryphon's sharp ears would hear him. He repeated it a couple of times until Gerd spoke again, slightly louder this time.

I hear you. We will follow. It is not difficult; your wake smells of barbecue.

The Figgish Fen was not the most direct route, but they would probably be no farther away from the Toot Towers than they had been at Dr. Murkimer's ghostel and dental practice. They would not lose time so much as lose sleep.

Faucon entered a limbic semiconscious state as the night wore on, a trance of endurance as he clung to the boar's back and the leagues bounced underneath them. The forest and the darkness ended at once: A gray dawn at first, and then a brilliant one as the trees receded behind them and Ugbüt's hooves began to make soft splashing sounds. They were entering the Figgish Fen, miles and miles of reeds and grasses mixed in with strange and exotic plants and always, always, plenty of standing water.

The boar slowed from a trot to a walk and made a series of wet snorty noises as he calmed down and began the process of recovery.

"Fair warning, I'm gonna lower my back end," the boar said, and Faucon held on as the boar sat down in the standing water and groaned in pleasure, his toasted hocks getting some relief. "Ahh, that's better. Don't mind telling you, Faucon, that was not a good night for me."

"Nor for me." Faucon ached everywhere and his muscles trembled. He doubted he'd be able to stand.

"I know where some edible mushrooms grow nearby. Join me for breakfast?"

"Sure. Until my companions find me, I will happily remain with you."

"All right, let's go. I'm hungry."

Ugbüt rose and they traveled for perhaps five minutes into the fen, until they came to a mushroom colony that had spread its spores liberally around the area. Halflings called them purple helmets, owing to their lavender color and the shape of their caps. They nestled next to some woody shrubbery on some sodden islands of black soil, surrounded by dark waters perhaps three inches deep on which floated lily pads and fen orchids. Frogs croaked and insects buzzed.

The boar had taken only a few purple helmets into his mouth before he looked up, startled. "You hear that?" he said around a mouthful.

Faucon listened. The water was gurgling ahead of them. Soft, high-pitched chirps of some kind could be heard. Perhaps a coterie of waterfowl was headed their way?

"I do," he whispered. "But said sound is unfamiliar and not reminiscent of predators."

Ugbüt grunted his agreement and kept chewing, his snout wriggling in the direction of the noises. The sounds grew louder behind an island of shrubs, and then they spied movement coming around it on either side.

Rodents of extraordinary size came into view: They were capybaras, the gentle giants of the Figgish Fen, laden with saddlebags but no proper saddles.

And riding on top of the capybaras were tiny monkeys that squeaked and chattered once they spied the boar and halfling. These wee beasties dug into their saddlebags and brandished what looked to be seedpods as if they were weapons. Faucon did not immediately recognize the seedpods, having never hunted in the Figgish Fen; he was most familiar with the flora of the Pruneshute Forest and the plains of the Skyr. The strange company of capybara calvary moved to surround them.

"Hey, uh," Ugbüt said, "that doesn't look like friendly behavior." He took a few steps back, and the newcomers stepped forward, or their capybaras did, which was far more impactful.

"I agree. But we should strive to avoid antagonizing them. We may be simply trespassing on their territory and they will subside when we exit, so I suggest continuing to back away. Do you recognize those seedpods they carry?"

"No. My eyesight's not that great. I do much better with smells. They don't smell like anything in particular, though. I just smell monkey and rat and fen. And snake."

"Snake?"

"Not surprising. Fens are full of snakes. They don't bother me."

"Nor I, my good boar. I simply do not see any snakes."

"They're sneaky. And, wow, these monkeys just keep coming. How many do you think there are now?"

Faucon counted quickly. "Twenty. And still moving to surround us if they can."

"At what point do I turn and run while squealing?" Ugbüt asked.

"Soon, I think, unless something changes."

Something changed. A shrill cry from above caused everyone to look up. A massive winged silhouette descended and the monkeys screeched and pointed.

Hello, smöl monkeys, Faucon heard in his head. *Please do not hurt my friends and I will not devour you.*

The monkeys clearly understood this, for one of them chittered something at the others and they turned their capybaras around to form a wedge behind the leader; Gerd, meanwhile, braked in the air with her wings and landed next to Ugbüt, mincing a couple of times once she touched down.

Ew, she commented, registering her disapproval of the footing. Faucon was relieved to see that Kirsi and Onni were safe on her back.

"Are the others all right?" he asked Kirsi.

"Yes, they're just catching up," she replied. "That was quite a chase you led us on. Are you okay?"

"Bruised but otherwise fine," he assured them.

"Sorry about that," Ugbüt said. "I really don't like fire."

Gerd introduced them to the smöl monkeys, her peculiar gryphon magic heard by all of them in a language they understood. The lead monkey chittered back to her at some length, and Gerd translated.

These smöl monkeys call themselves the Tym tamarins, and the leader's name is Gleek. They live with the capybaras in a cooperative community, each contributing to the prosperity and defense of the other. Gleek says we are welcome to not eat them.

"Ah! Tamarins I have heard of," Faucon said, then added, "Not this particular kind, though. What makes them Tym tamarins, specifically?"

There was some spirited explanation on Gleek's part before Gerd translated.

Tym was the legendary tamarin who forged their shared culture with the capybaras. They have lived by his ideals for untold generations. But now the Figgish Fen Wyrm threatens all of that. It wants to eat them all. Its hunger is endless.

"What wyrm?"

I was getting to that. The giant wyrm that they were trying to lead away from their village and that has eaten half their party so far. The one that's tracking them now.

"Now?" Ugbüt said. "Well, hey, uh, nice to meet you all, but I'm out. Plain old snakes are reasonable, but any reptile with that many capital letters in its name is bound to suck. Faucon, if you could get off my back, that would be great."

"Sure," Faucon said, then grunted as he slid off the boar's back and splashed in the muck of the fen, falling to all fours since he was unable to use his legs correctly after the stress of the ride. His fingers sank into the squelchy mud, and the scummy water was directly under his nose with his arms fully extended. And his golden toes—well.

"Oh, ah. This is not optimal. Onni?"

"Yes?"

"I think I'm about to lose my golden toes in the mud."

"Oh, no. Stay there, I'll come help," the gnome said, and he tumbled somewhat ungracefully off Gerd's back to land in the fen on his teeny gnomebutt, utterly mucking up his cardigan. He disappeared under the surface but rose quickly and spluttered, his entire person covered in viscid mud and remaining waist-deep in the water. "That! Was not! Sanitary!" he declared.

"Sorry about your situation, there, but I really need to go," Ugbüt said, turning around and trotting back in the direction of the Prune-shute Forest. "That snake smell is getting stronger and I want to live longer, know what I mean?" They knew precisely what he meant and bade farewell to his ham hocks as he departed. He stopped once to call over his shoulder, "Did Dr. Murkimer and Reegor get out okay with the puppy?"

They assured him that they did and were en route to their satellite location, the Spook Spa at Bicuspid Cove. The boar grunted in reply and was soon lost in the tall reeds of the fen.

Onni's tiny fingers found Faucon's right heel, and shortly thereafter he felt the golden toes braced against the stump of his foot. "Okay, you can move that foot now to get it underneath you. If we can get you on your back instead of your front so we can lift your feet out of the water, I'll see if I can readjust the fit."

With much sloshing and splashing and muttering of "gross" and even the foulest of words, "grody," they safely extracted Faucon's toes from the sucking mud. Onni pulled a set of tools out of his squelchy cardigan and set about working on the fit. In order to do so, he had to remove the toes first and wash off the prosthesis, leaving Faucon's bare stumps in the air, a sight that filled up a deep well of rage within him. Still, Faucon knew it would be as wrong to drink from that well as to drink from the fen. Either option would do him no good and possibly poison his innards.

Faucon knew his accident was just that, a matter of chance, and taking his anger out on Onni or Kirsi or indeed any gnome would be misguided and unjust, not to mention unmanly. Especially since Onni was doing everything he could to keep Faucon on his feet. The gnome was quite literally trying to restore balance to the situation— and he'd probably never be able to get all that fen out of his beard.

"Hmm. Not much more I can do with the tools at hand except reattach it snugly. But then you're in the same situation as soon as you stand up. A low-tech solution might work out, though; I should go ahead and make that design adjustment I thought of earlier." Onni turned to the gryphon. "Gerd, can you ask Gleek if they have any rope or string in those little packs of theirs, and if so, might we use some?"

I can do that. But you should be aware that the Figgish Fen Wyrm approacheth. I too smell what Ugbüt smelled, and it is Not a Good Smell.

Several of the Tym tamarins rummaged around in their packs after Gerd's request and produced spools of spun swamp-spider silk. Onni used them to fashion a truss by looping around Faucon's right ankle and then running the silk cord between the toes.

"There," the gnome said. "The cord would have to snap for the mud to claim your toes now. That should keep them on until we can craft a long-term solution." Faucon murmured his thanks while Onni repeated the process for his left foot, firmly lashing the prosthesis to the foot by twining the cord around the heel.

The wyrm is close. We should prepare for battle.

The Tym tamarins were already spreading themselves in a half circle, facing the other way and now doubling up on the backs of some capybaras while leaving others riderless.

"What are they doing?" Faucon wondered aloud as Onni hauled him to his feet out of the mire. He tested the cords by lifting one foot and then the other out of the muck. The toes remained in place, and he nodded once at Onni before drawing his sword.

Gerd consulted Gleek and then explained, *It is how they fight the wyrm. One tamarin makes a cradle of its hands and launches the other in the air at the wyrm.*

"They throw their friends to be eaten so the others survive?"

Not precisely. The leaping tamarins throw the smöl poddes at the wyrm—though I do not understand their purpose. They say the poddes are from something called the Figgish Fear Shrub. I do not know this plant.

Neither did Faucon, but the opportunity to inquire about the Figgish Fear Shrub disappeared with a quiver in the reeds, a gurgle and hiss, and the agitated shrieks of the Tym tamarins.

A sinuous shape arose out of the fen, topped with an enormous triangular head, covered in glittering green scales except for its pale-yellow belly, with spiny ridges over its eyes and down the middle of its head. A forked tongue flicked out and its cavernous mouth opened to reveal a row of sharp teeth, not two mere fangs. That was the hall-mark of a wyrm: It could tear off gobbets of meat instead of swallow-ing its prey whole, allowing it to tackle larger animals and impress its friends. It looked pleased to have found the Tym tamarins and their mounts—as pleased as Faucon probably looked when his belly hit the table's edge at Dinny's. But when it saw Gerd staring back at it, it pulled up short and made a sibilant shrieking noise, another fea-ture of wyrms: the ability to vocalize.

As if in reply, Gerd said, *Leave this place or die, wyrm,* and Faucon thought most creatures would be sensible enough to avail themselves of the first option. But the wyrm screeched a spine-shivering cry of defiance and surged forward, striking at the nearest riderless capy-bara and gobbling it whole. That set off the counterattack by the Tym tamarins, who catapulted their comrades as high as they could to throw their seedpods directly at the head of the wyrm.

The wyrm expected this and dodged many, but not all, of the pods. They exploded on contact and released a puff of white powdery seeds. The wyrm shut its eyes and reared back as the tamarins plopped into the fen and began to swim back to their fellows. Another batch of tamarins executed the same maneuver, and since the wyrm had its eyes closed, it didn't dodge in time. Almost all of the seedpods hit their target, surrounding the wyrm's head like a cloud of cotton but doing no damage that Faucon could discern. He honestly didn't know what the point of it all was.

Kirsi wasn't waiting for the seedpods to take effect. She hopped off Gerd's back and directly toward Onni, who prevented her from falling into the mire as he had, then she plucked a hair from her beard and tied it into a bow, muttering all the while. Now unencum-bered, Gerd leapt into the air and flapped mightily, circling around behind the wyrm, her claws outstretched as she shrieked, *Come Gette Some!*

The wyrm heard that, however, and much else besides, for it opened its eyes and hissed, its mouth opening for another strike. Faucon noticed that when it did so, the clouds of seeds moved directly into the mouth and eyes as if drawn there via suction. The wyrm struck again, this time taking two tamarins and their ride together. But when it raised its head to swallow them, the eyes were different, clouded over, and its mouth was too full of cotton to allow its prey to be swallowed. The wyrm dropped the full meal deal, and the two tamarins splashed down into the fen, remounted their beslimed capybara, and shrieked their victory.

As for the wyrm, it writhed and made gagging noises. Being suddenly afflicted with the loss of sight, taste, and smell would be quite alarming if one didn't know the effects were temporary—that was probably why it was called the Fear Shrub. But of course the wyrm had experienced this fear before and somehow knew it would live to take another tasty bite of the world's largest rodent and quite-nearly-smallest monkey.

Faucon couldn't let such courageous little dudes die. He charged forward as best as he could through the sticky fen, hoping to get to the wyrm before Gerd did, his sword held firmly in his hand. He surged through the capybaras and tamarins and saw Gerd swooping behind the wyrm, her head and body hidden from his sight but her spread wings seeming to give the wyrm the appearance of a winged head. The halfling tried to move faster, which might have succeeded but mostly made more noise.

The wyrm cocked its head and struck, lightning-quick, at a spot just next to Faucon, attracted to the splashing he made—it wasn't deaf. And even though it missed, the unexpected lunge also made Gerd miss. She swept on past in the air, talons empty of wyrm flesh, and shrieked her frustration. Faucon sliced down with his sword, but that bit of the snake was armored and didn't so much as scuff. Gerd banked around, and Faucon kept moving forward as the wyrm reared back. In five steps, he leapt as best he could and put everything he had into an overhead thrust directly into the center of the foul wyrm's somewhat vulnerable belly. The blade plunged in far easier than it should have but stopped at the hilt, and then Faucon's weight on the hilt—he dangled from it—dragged the blade down and opened up a gory gash from which blood and slippery bits of viscera spilled, as well as a large hairball of partially digested capybara.

The gnomeric bristle witch shouted behind him in victory. "Yes! Armor weakened!"

The wyrm cried out and tried to rear back again, which only opened up more of its belly, like a self-peeling banana, until Faucon reached the ground and yanked out his sword. He had not hit the wyrm high enough to wound the heart, but he had delivered a mortal blow. That open wound, once lowered into the fen, would quickly turn septic, and Faucon might have damaged other vital organs as well. Sure enough, tender purple things that most resembled over-sized jelly beans were plopping this way and that out of the wyrm and into the bloodied waters.

Gerd returned and raked her talons across the wyrm's neck, closer to the head, and it popped open like a magician's cane turning into a bouquet of flowers. That was the coup de grâce: The great beast died with ululations and a torrent of diarrhea. Its enormous bulk shuddered and toppled sideways, splashing into the mire. Silence settled over the fen, a silence of disbelief and wonder, broken by a capybara who let out a single wet, inquisitive poot. That sparked a raucous celebration by the Tym tamarins, who hollered and squawked and monkeyed around on the backs of their capering rodent friends.

Faucon might have capered around too if he thought his golden toes would stand for it, but he contented himself with a little shimmy and a smile at his companions. Together, despite the odds, he and a gnome had bested the beast. And he had proven that even though his life was different now and it would be inconvenient at times, he was still Faucon the hunter. He still had a particular set of skills. And snake meat was still delicious, once you rinsed off the fen muck and diarrhea.

It was at that point that Båggi and Agape caught up with them, their chests heaving.

"Oh, bless my beard, this is a very merry muddy party!" Båggi said through gasps. "What are we celebrating?" He reached his arms into the brown murky water peppered with wyrm plops and capybara guts and splashed his face, patting at his cheeks to rub it in. "I do so love a proper restorative mud bath."

29.

UNDER THE OBFUSCATED GUISE OF AN OLD ACQUAINTANCE

"Consuming the raw heart of a fallen foe is widely acknowledged to be the only acceptable form of cannibalism, since it comes with a concomitant bequeathal of powers. It is perhaps fortunate that it tastes terrible and cooking the heart first destroys the magical transfer of talents, or else we'd be routinely eating one another's hearts on breakfast sandwiches, in savory stews, or grilled and sliced atop a succulent chef's salad."

—Almont Brewne, in *Goode Fewd*

"Oh, Båggi, no!" Kirsi cried, arms out in that way that suggested she wanted to be helpful from several feet away while not touching him at all.

The dwarf looked up, confusion plain in his twinkling eyes. "Not to worry, my fine bearded friend! For there's plenty of healing mud to go around." He slapped more mud around his eyes and mouth, smacking his lips. "And a very rich mud it is! I seem to detect notes of loam and . . . is it bass?"

"Close! It's . . . ass," Kirsi said, her voice trailing off.

"What?"

"You really don't want to do that, Båggi," Onni said, trying to rid his own beard of its brown streaks with a much-abused handkerchief. "That's not mud."

"But what else is in a fen besides water and mud? The cattails decompose, making the mineral content especially rich. We herbalists are experts on . . ."

A tiny tamarin skull blurbled to the water's surface beside a nasty clot of brown and a floppy purple wyrm kidney, and Båggi's mouth fell open.

"It's the plops," Agape said with her usual lack of nonsense. "Aaand it's already in your beard, so please stop smearing it all over your face, and let's get out of here."

"Yes yes yes yes *yes*. Ha ha! That's not the kind of mud I wanted at all!" Båggi said, swiping the dripping brown glop off his face and dancing about a bit as the mud flooded his boots.

"Let's, er, find a nicer bit of swamp." Kirsi looked up at the tamarins and wished her cardigan were properly pleasant. "Dear Tym tamarins, we need to reach the Toot Towers, which are astride the Rumplescharte River. Can you point us in the right direction?"

Gerd translated, and the lead tamarin nodded sagely as all the tamarins pointed in different directions.

"So that's a no, then. Gerd, can you see the river from the sky?"

The gryphon seemed more than happy to rise into the air and shake off the muck, showering them in brown splatters as she spiraled up so high she became nothing more than a tiny black blot.

I see no river, she said. *Only more quagmire of wretched fylth entirely lacking figges.*

A light splashing signaled someone new entering the area, accompanied by a voice so beautiful and sweet that everyone stopped breathing through the mouth and sighed beatifically.

> *Perhaps I can help*
> *For well I know*
> *How to go when one needs to go;*

The river wide and the towers tall
Are all this way, beyond the wall.

Even Kirsi was amazed at the figure who had suddenly appeared in their midst. It was clearly a bard, in classical bard dress, including a floppy hat with a huge feather, a puce velvet doublet, and wide pantaloons in chartreuse with burgundy slashes. The bongos hung around the bard's neck from a silken rope were a thing of beauty, golden as honey and pitter-pattering so prettily that the capybaras purred in joy. But that's where the usual bardisms ended, because the bard was clearly a . . .

"Kobold!" Onni squawked, stumbling backward in fear. "It's a kobold!"

Kirsi's heart beat faster than the drums, and she was doing her best not to join Onni in his Fluster, for kobolds were well known for their dislike of gnomes. While the conflict between gnomes and halflings was a relatively new development, the dragon-like kobolds had always hated gnomes and delighted in eating them—and pretty much anything besides galoshes and ceramic mugs. Fortunately, the kobolds had mostly self-destructed in the Giant Wars, so rare was the living gnome who had beheld their hideous countenance. If an iguana and a hairless cat had a halfling-sized baby with lizard feet who liked eating innocent people, it would've been slightly more pleasant to look at than a kobold.

Except that this kobold wore a smile and had the voice of an angel.

Does this creature require dismemberment? Gerd asked, having descended back to their level, with the feathers around her head up defensively even as her claws clicked together along with the bongos. *For I do not sense incipient rage about its person.*

"I don't know," Kirsi said, considering the bard as she twirled a beard hair between her fingers and fought her instinctive urge to pluck it. "Do you?"

The bard played a tiny drum solo that somehow attracted a flock of beautiful blue butterflies to hang, glittering, around their heads.

Båggi laughed and danced around, the filth in his beard forgotten and drying into unsavory clumps.

"I'm more of a kobard than a kobold, if you get my drift. I was on my way to the Toot Towers to play for the kanssa-jaarli, and I thought you might need some guidance. If such is not the case, I'm happy to pretend you're not following me to the quickest way out of this swamp." The kobold, whose gender wasn't readily apparent, winked a saucy eye.

Kirsi waved her party together for a brief huddle and flapped a hand at the bard to ignore them. "We need a minute. If you'd like some wyrm meat, no one will stop you."

"Wow," Agape whispered, leaning down toward the gnomes. "That's the rudest I've ever seen you, Kirsi!"

"Well, it's a kobold." Kirsi bristled in a way entirely unrelated to being a bristle witch. "When your natural enemy shows up in a moment of need, you don't immediately fall all over its scaly feet. Point being: Do we trust it?"

"You mean *them*," Båggi corrected. "Because whatever their personal pronouns may be, *it* suggests they are not a person, which they very much are. And I say yes! Surely no one of evil heart could play such heartening drums! Why, the very bing-bong of those bongos was enough to make me temporarily forget that my face is caked in the excrement of an enormous reptile, and here we are many leagues away from a bath! Ha ha!"

"I guess so," Agape said, and if the ovitaur was surprised by Kirsi's rudeness, Kirsi was even more surprised by Agape's easy acceptance of someone new.

"What do you think is the worst that could happen?" Faucon winced and looked like he wanted to rub his boar-chafed fundament but was too much of a gentleman to do so. "If the kobold turns on us, we fight it. I mean them. We are quite adept at that."

"And if I wanted to use my bardic magic against you, I'd already be doing so," the kobold interjected loftily.

"We really need to learn to be more quiet." Kirsi sighed and turned and forced a smile. "Very well, my good bard. If you'd be so kind as to lead us, we will follow. But no funny business!"

"Oh, we kobolds have literally no sense of humor."

The crew waved goodbye to the Tym tamarins, who waved back merrily as their capybaras sang a song of many *ukka-chukka-chukkas* and *ooh-worra-worras*, and the kobold marched through the Figgish Fen, fearless and fine, pattering on the bongos and humming a jaunty tune. Soon they began to sing a traveling song that included some helpful thoughts on healing, sleeping well, and perhaps hurrying a bit away from the goopier bits of swamp, and Kirsi felt as if she were floating above the water instead of slogging through it. When the fen became less fennish and more foresty, the kobold kindly sang a song about how lovely it would be if air could clean one's cardigan and tidy up one's beard and refresh one's stank pits, and soon Kirsi was neat as a pin and grinning, as were all her companions.

"This is it!" Faucon shouted, capering about a little now that his golden toes were clean of swamp muck. He pointed at two worn ruts in the ground that suggested many wagon wheels had once packed the earth tight so that neither seed nor root could take hold. "This is the old road to the Toot Towers!"

"Why would there be a road leading into the fen?" Onni asked.

"It was not always a fen. It used to be a beautiful land that supported vast orchards of Skyr fig trees, now extinct, and the gnomes and halflings who lived there were fabulously well-to-do," Faucon replied.

Skyr figges were the best figges, my great-grandfather Funt used to say, Gerd asserted. *He claimed they were very high in fibre.*

"What happened, then?" Kirsi asked, as she knew very little about fig business.

"The land was spectacularly mismanaged by the hereditary caretaker of the orchard, a man named Skotch Figgler," Faucon said. "His family had maintained the orchard for generations, but during his time there were fires, floods, blights, trysts, twists—it's a saga in itself. They say the land grew so very tired of his mismanagement that a chasm opened up and vomited swamp water until the old coot drowned, taking his spectacular facial hair with him. And now no one can drain this swamp."

Once they were out of the fen and mostly free of swamp glop, the kobold bard sang a song to get them skipping lightly across the terrain, eating up plenty of distance with every step. Although it took them all day to cross the many leagues between the fen and the river, they still didn't quite make it before dark.

It was getting toward twilight, and the kobold suggested they should stop and make camp. Exhausted and starving, they happily complied. Bǻggi brought out his food stores, and Gerd went hunting for stoats and shrews with her library bird screeching Hurp Blep's *Tales of the Wizard of Blizzard*. Whenever Kirsi politely asked the kobold for a name, the bard brushed off the question, often with a song that made her forget she had ever asked and suggested that good deeds were more important than monikers. Kirsi was left with a round belly full of dwarvelish charcuterie over local arugula doused in a piquant vinaigrette and strange thoughts about the nature of magic.

Why could the bard create such feelings and urges with only music, while Kirsi had to sacrifice her beauty, hair by hair? Why was she limited to only curses when the bard could make up a song about anything, from killing the Dread Necromancer Steve to making tasty muffins, and expect an excellent outcome? She asked the kobold something like that, at some point, and the bard merely pattered on the bongos and sang, "I am rubber, you are glue. What bounces for me, sticks for you. It's what's in your heart, not who wears shoes."

"Enough with the riddles," she mumbled, growing sleepy as the kobold played a tune called the "Nighty Night Song," which they claimed to have learned from a bard in King Gustave's castle.

"Riddles are as riddles do. Figure out what works for you," the kobold sang.

When Kirsi woke up, she was almost angry at feeling so fantastic. She half-expected the kobold to be gone, as magical and mysterious people who randomly showed up to do good deeds didn't seem to stick around, but there the bard sat, swallowing a chipmunk whole while making gross gargling noises that reminded Kirsi of all the stories her parents had told her about how dangerous and nasty kobolds were. After a last, icky *glurk* sound, the kobold smiled at her. Two pats of the drums, and Kirsi forgot why she kind of wanted to throw up.

After a hearty helping of something Båggi called Ol' Boy Roy's Rough 'n' Grainy Honey Oaty Groatmeal, which the dwarf suggested was good for the lower intestine, they were back on the road, following their new bard in a dancing sort of way down the path. Everything was going quite well until they came to the point where the Old Fygge Road joined the road that came from Nokanen. Sitting there on an overturned bucket was a black-robed lumpy person, crying, their face hidden from view. The kobold stopped, some distance off, and hissed, but Kirsi strode bravely forward, her heart torn by the insistent sobbing.

"Maybe it's a traaap," Agape said.

"And maybe you should give people a chance," Kirsi responded.

Agape rolled her eyes toward the kobold, and Kirsi felt a wash of shame. She'd been wrong about the bard, but she felt sure that this plaintive sufferer needed help. She was almost within touching distance of the figure when it gave a great wail, and she had to speak.

"Hello there? My friend? Are you well? Have you been the victim of highwaymen, or perhaps a ravenous army of halflings, or this terrible guy named Tommy?"

The shape unfolded and flapped around a bit on the bucket but remained seated, rearranging its large and ragged cloak so that a familiar face shone down on Kirsi's.

"It's you!" Kirsi said, rushing forward for a gnomeric hug, which was a bit awkward with someone nearly three times her height and at least five times her age, but she made it work.

"Indeed, my pretty," the old witch said.

"But why are you here, so far from your cottage near Bruding?" Kirsi asked. "And why are you crying? Are you hurt?"

"No, my dear. I'm not hurt. I was merely on my way to a jousting tournament, because I follow the Bruding Boars, and—"

The witch stopped mid-sentence to gasp. Her rosy but withered cheeks and twinkling if rheumy eyes instantly went sharp and dark. As she stood, drawing her bent body up tall and straight, she focused on Båggi, pointing a clawed finger at the dwarf, who responded by gaping and looking like he wished he were the size of a bee and able to hide up his own nose.

"You!" the witch shouted, lightning arcing down around her and slamming into the ground. It was a remarkable event, since there was only a single white cloud floating directly above the witch.

"M-m-me?" Båggi stammered. "I do hope, my fine lady, that you are upset at someone else, for I'm quite sure we've never met, and unless you are related to a madman in a cabbage field or have a profound distaste for gentle herbal remedies, you shouldn't have any reason to be upset with the likes of little old harmless me, ha ha!"

"Dwaaaaaaaaaaarf!" the witch screamed, and the sky went dark as the single white cloud bloomed into thunderheads churned by swirling winds and peppered with capybara hairs and the tang of fen. Sensing a situation swiftly devolving, Kirsi plucked a hair from her nape and began to craft her curse.

Båggi crashed to his knees and tried to hide behind his Telling Cudgel. "Yes? What? I'm sorry!"

"Which one are you? Freddi? Freaki? Sneaki? Siggi? Saggi? Biggi? Or Smöls?"

"I am none of those dwarves, my lady, although I'll admit that my britches are feeling saggy at the moment and that my name is very close to Biggi but not, I swear, exactly that, because there's a crucially different vowel!"

"Listen well. Seven dwarves helped my stinking stepdaughter steal my youth and beauty—I mean, my favorite cauldron and a nice old mirror. And I am sworn to hunt for those dwarves. And I think perhaps that you are one of them." The witch strode to Bággi, imperious and cold, and kicked him with a wizened foot. "Stand up, fool! Let me see if you carry her stink. Always smelled of roses and rabbit urine, that one."

As Bággi struggled to stand, Kirsi moved in front of him. "This is not the dwarf you're looking for," she said, firm and confident, as the knotted hair danced over her tongue.

"Any dead dwarf is a good dwarf. I couldn't claim her heart, so I'll claim his!" The witch withdrew a lumpy crystal wand from her cloak and described a circle around the quivering dwarf, causing a golden ribbon to descend and truss him up like a holiday hen. As soon as the knots had tightened, she pulled a small notebook out of another pocket and flipped through it, licking a bony fingertip. "Let's see. I have a good recipe for a babka that requires a dwarf heart." She tipped his head up with a claw. "You do still have your heart, right?"

"No!" Kirsi shouted, quickly amending that. "I mean, he does have a heart, but you can't have it. It's going to stay inside of him, thank you very much. Bággi is not one of the dwarves who helped your stepdaughter. He's my friend. And as your friend, I'm telling you to back the fig off!"

The witch regarded Kirsi, her gaze so cold that Kirsi felt her own heart sputter with a sudden chill.

"We are not friends. You were merely a visitor who cleaned my oven and was reimbursed with food. Witches don't have friends."

Now it was Kirsi's turn to draw herself up proud and cold. "Well, this one does."

"You, a witch?" The old woman cackled and rocked, slapping a withered thigh. "Oh, I don't think so. Where's your wand? Where's your power?"

Kirsi drew a deep breath, narrowed her eyes, and muttered, "By the bumbling butt of Bartholomew Muckitt, may you always trip over your own dang bucket!"

"Huh?" the witch said as Kirsi swallowed the knotted hair.

But then the witch took a step toward Bǻggi and did indeed manage to trip over her bucket, which splattered something uncomfortably similar to coagulated blood all over the old woman's mangy black cloak.

"How dare you?" the witch cried, struggling to stand.

"Easily! But you can't have Bǻggi's heart! Or anybody's!"

"*Nobody* tells me what I can't have," the witch growled.

Kirsi backed up, step by step, as the witch fumbled for her wand, which had tangled up in her cloak.

"Get up," Kirsi said to Bǻggi, meeting the eyes of each of her compatriots to make sure they were ready to fight. "Look to your cudgel!"

For Bǻggi's cudgel did indeed look ready to whack some witch butt, as it had grown knobs and gnarls and had a poisoned apple engraved on the end.

"Oh! Oh, my! Yes, the violence! The unquenchable rage!" Bǻggi said, sounding more confused than angry. "Er, if someone will only release me from this magical ribbon? For it is cutting off a bit of the old circulation, you know, and it's hard to be angry when I'm this embarrassed. Ha ha!"

But the witch struck first, sending a gust of magic right at Kirsi, who barely managed to dive out of the way as it burned a hole in the dirt. At least Faucon was able to use that brief attack to slice the golden ribbon with his sword, releasing Bǻggi from his festive restraints. Again and again, the witch took aim at Kirsi or the dwarf, and they kept rolling and popping up here and there, barely managing to dodge the fireballs. When the witch again tripped on her bucket, Kirsi looked directly at the kobold.

"Some of that magic of yours wouldn't go amiss!" she said with a grin that spoke more of terror than happiness, but it did the trick. The bard recovered their moxie and began hammering at the bongos, playing a fierce staccato that sent everyone into a fighting stance. It was as if, before, they'd been frozen or perhaps watching a duel, but now the group coalesced as a battle party, taking up their weapons and preparing for a rumble. Kirsi plucked an eyelash, bidding it a fond farewell, and placed it gently on her tongue, glaring at the witch's wand and wondering how best to curse it to backfire somehow.

"Oh, so that's how it is?" the witch said, cracking her neck and doing some stretches. "All of you against an old lady?"

"The thing is, none of us particularly want to eat you, and yet you seem determined to eat one of us," Kirsi said, hands on her hips and eyelash caught between grinding teeth.

The witch looked at her as if she were dim. "Well, yes. The heart, at least. That's where all the power lies. The rest is just meat. Honestly, what did they teach you in gnomeschool?"

Kirsi opened her mouth to rebut and explain that her gnomeschooling had given her the gift of intense focus and personal confidence, but the witch started shooting off magical fireballs, aiming at one person and then the next, dancing back with unexpected agility when one of them managed to counterattack. Faucon's sword slashes missed every time, and Gerd kept getting caught in personal tornadoes, and the rocks Agape threw seemed to bounce off some kind of strange force field. The faster the bard drummed, the more agile everyone seemed to be, so at least nobody took a direct hit. Kirsi was too busy dodging fireballs to come up with a proper curse, so she prepared to skitter up the witch's cloak and grab the wand, which appeared to be the seat of her power, or at least its focusing device.

And then the drums suddenly stopped, and Kirsi could no longer cling to the witch's swishing hem. Exhaustion suffused her, and pain radiated from dozens of scorch marks. She managed to disengage and tumbled to the ground, and that's when she saw that the kobold bard had a watermelon-sized hole directly through their chest. Through it, Kirsi saw a few scraggly trees on the other side and a cavity containing one very surprised, half-digested chipmunk.

As Kirsi watched, horrified, the kobold fell over, dead.

"Fools! This is how you lose! The bard was so busy protecting you it forgot about its own safety!"

Rage built in Kirsi's chest, and she felt her hair lift and fly off her shoulders as if she'd touched a metal doorknob on a particularly cold, dry night.

"*They* forgot about *their* own safety," she ground out between clenched teeth.

The witch stared at her, perplexed. "You're correcting my pronoun usage in the middle of a fight?"

"Yes, when it needs correcting. The bard wasn't an *it*. They were a *they*, and they were a better friend than you ever were, you sorry old hag, and I hope you die!"

She swallowed the eyelash, and with all her might, Kirsi shoved the witch, and it was as if her hands were filled with the power of a plucky donkey, for the witch flew backward, knocking the bucket aside, and hit her head on a gnarled tree root.

After a long moment, the witch still hadn't moved, and Kirsi's hands fell to her sides.

"Well, that's one way to kick the bucket," she said.

"Ha ha!" Båggi whimpered. "That is terrifying!"

Everyone was staring at Kirsi as if she'd gone mad, so she hurried to the kobold's side and knelt, wishing she knew something, anything, about healing.

"Båggi?" She looked to the dwarf, but he was nervously tugging at his beard below the halfling half ring.

"I can't heal a hole in someone's person," he said. "No matter how much I might want to. Not even with Holy Hal's Whole 30 Finicky Hole-Filler Pills. Which are mainly just for mosquito bites, if I'm honest." After drawing a deep breath, he shivered and added sadly, "Ha ha."

They were the finest kobold I ever met, Gerd said solemnly. *And even if I have never met a kobold before, that is still a compliment, because I say so.*

"Ding Dang. The witch is dead," Faucon said, holding up her scrawny wrist. "No pulse, no breath."

Kirsi looked from one corpse to the other and felt like she'd aged fifty years. In the space of a moment, two people were gone. One good, one bad. One who made music, and one who made holes in people. An ebony glimmer caught her eye, and she took the witch's wand in both hands, hefting it as if it were a club, which to her, size-wise, it was.

"There's only one thing to do now," Kirsi said.

"Bury them," Agape agreed.

Kirsi looked up, shaking her head. "Oh, no. I have to eat the witch's heart and absorb her powers."

"Wait, whaaat?"

"Then I'll be able to use her wand to protect us. We'd grown so certain of our strength that we forgot how magic changes everything. If not for that kobold bard—may they be chugging chipmunks in kobold heaven—I'm pretty sure Båggi would be a small, unsightly cinder, and he's basically the nicest person I've ever met. And there would've been nothing I could do to protect him or any of you. My whole life, my parents tried to hide my ability to curse, and I always felt lesser because I couldn't bless. Gnomeric magic can only take me so far. But it seems, in the wider world, there are other ways to gain powers. So I'm going to be the best witch I can be."

"By eating aaan old woman's heart?" Agape cried, horror written across her face.

Kirsi gave her brightest smile. "Exactly. So let's get started. *You gotta get off your seat if you want to eat!*"

Agape shuddered. "I hate gnomeric aaaphorisms."

"I know!"

It was messy, and it took a while, but everyone found something else to do while the knee-high gnome carefully removed her cardi-gan, politely borrowed Agape's knife, cut the heart out of the old human woman, and ate it, bite by bite, dabbing at her mouth be-tween gulps with one of Faucon's least favorite handkerchiefs. She understood that her friends did not approve of this action, but for once she didn't care—even if it deeply sorrowed her that Onni had to turn his back. This time, she was taking care of Kirsi. Even Gerd, who was known to use squirrels like nunchucks as she juggled them into her gullet, looked disgusted.

When Kirsi was done, she burped the tiniest and most polite of gnomeric burps, barely a friendly bubble. The witch's heart tasted of darkness and forbidden fruit and burnt gingerbread, along with a whiff of Grandma's blood pudding. An odd feeling radiated from Kirsi's belly, spreading through her limbs and even out of her hair follicles. She ran a hand through her beard, pleased to feel that its fullness had returned, as if the magic had regurgitated the pain of all her old curses back to the well of her power in the form of luxurious keratin.

She stood and dusted her hands off. "Now. Let's see if it worked or if I just did something horrible and gross for no good reason."

Her first act as a witch sized the crystal wand to her hand—and painted it with cheerful bluebirds, tulips, and hearts. Her second spell created a new, wand-shaped pocket in her cardigan. Her third spell covered the dead kobold with a gentle mound of dirt and a tidy cairn of rocks. She tried a fourth spell, but nothing happened; clearly, as a beginner in the realm of real magic, or possibly as a smöl person, she was limited to three spells a day.

"Thank you, nameless friend," Kirsi said, standing over the kobold's grave. "You taught me more in one night than I learned in ten years elsewhere. I promise you: Your sacrifice will not be in vain."

Much to her surprise, a hazy blue cloud floated up out of the dirt, coalescing into a ghostly version of the bard, doublet and all.

"It wasn't a sacrifice. It was dumb luck," the kobold said.

"Do you mind terribly?" Kirsi asked.

The kobold reached a ghostly hand into the dirt mound and withdrew a ghostly set of bongos, draping the string around their ghostly neck. "I'm all about moving forward," the kobold said. "Not much I can do about it now. I did hear about a fantastic ghostel somewhere in the Pruneshute Forest, though. Maybe I'll go there and see if I can start a band."

"You've got to follow your heart," Kirsi said.

The ghost bard shrugged. "Hey, at least you didn't eat it, right?"

Whistling, the ectoplasmic kobold walked into the forest, a ghostly pattering echoing in their wake.

Kirsi looked over at Agape, who'd been watching the entire conversation. "Honestly, I'm not even surprised aaanymore," the ovitaur said.

At that, Kirsi grinned. "See? I told you. People can be nice."

30.

HIGH ABOVE A CAPRINE ABATTOIR AND ACRES OF BAD ARCHITECTURE

"Speaking in broad terms—exceptions abound, of course—those with sophisticated palates agree that goat cheese is generally superior to sheep cheese, cow cheese, and indeed most cheeses except for the rare moose cheese one can only acquire at great cost from the elves of the Morningwood."

—QELVIN QURD, in his introduction to *The Pellican Cheese Atlas* by Qermit Qoxswain

"Huh. Looks like a giant one of those things," Gustave said, looking up at whatever it was.

The Royal Pellican Centipod and Traveling Hootenanny had emerged from the canopy of the Pruneshute Forest, and up ahead, that thing was dominating the horizon, just demanding to be talked about, provided one knew what it was.

"What things?" Grinda asked.

"The things one of the minstrels was playing with before we sent him into Bruding. You blow on one end of it, apply your fingers here and there, then there's some twitching and a lot of noise."

"Are you talking about a flute?"

"Yeah. That building looks like a giant flute."

Grinda gave him the look he mostly associated with making a boom-boom in the royal carriage in his early days as a human and a king. "That's because it *is* a giant flute, basically. Both of them are. Hence the name: the Toot Towers."

"Really? Can they play music?"

"Yes. The centers are hollow and air is driven up from massive bellows in the basement. They play at the top of every hour, except for the first six after midnight. Clockwork settings move the stops to create different notes. The result is a sound many octaves below a flute, but both towers play simultaneously, creating opportunities for interesting melodies. They are called Toot Poems, and composing them is considered a great honor among composers. We're sure to hear one before we get there."

The centipod came to a whining mechanical halt and died with a bone-shaking shudder.

"Out of power," Grinda said, disgusted.

"Hey, at least we didn't have to hear another platitude from the gnomeric automaatti pilot guy, right?" Gustave said, trying to keep the atmosphere light. "If he could talk right now, I bet he'd be saying something like *We're all out of gas thanks to all of your mass!* Or *Time to get off with no time to scoff!*" He realized he was frowning. "I think I hate that guy, actually."

The road from Nokanen to the Toot Towers slashed diagonally across the map of Pell in a straight line, only several leagues of it passing through the southern reaches of the Pruneshute Forest, and two days of travel had brought them close enough to see their goal. The twin towers—the seat of the kanssa-jaarli's power—beckoned annoyingly on the horizon. All they had to do was get there. Gustave was even looking forward to the leisurely jaunt, hoping to perhaps convince Grinda to take the market road and pass an oat merchant slinging cookies from a street cart who wished to gift the king some top-notch snacks.

He was about to suggest this route when one of Gustave's guards yelped in surprise, said, "Hey, what?" and fell over dead with an arrow in his back, and other arrows began landing around them or pinging off the roof of the centipod.

Lord Ergot had never given up the chase and had obviously gotten fresh horses along the way, and his archers had impressive range and weren't nearly as drunk as a king under assault might hope.

Which meant: no oats, more running.

Gustave had never been fond of running, but he enjoyed it far less on two legs than on four. Thumbs were great, no doubt—doors and thumb-wrestling contests were no obstacle now!—but thumbs were absolutely worthless when he needed to run for his life, and he told them so between gasps for breath.

"You," he wheezed, "are bony flesh knobs of zero value."

His thumbs, numb to verbal abuse, failed spectacularly to take offense.

He wished he were a goat again. He felt frightened and hunted, which was really no different from being a goat, except that now he couldn't run away as fast as he used to. And he needed speed. Because Lord Ergot had horses. The hundred riders had been reduced significantly by their anticavalry defenses, but the spidery automaatti had eventually been destroyed and there were still more cavalry on their trail than they could handle, albeit a goodly distance behind, they hoped.

Grinda drew her wand and flicked it at the approaching cavalry. A wall of dust and sediment rose in the air, obscuring them from view and forcing the horses to sneeze.

"Harry them from the trees and reduce their number as much as possible. Slow them down!" she ordered the guard captain. He snapped more orders at his men, and Grinda tugged at Gustave's arm as well as Ralphee's, leading them off to the left-hand side of the road as the soldiers deployed.

"What are we doing?" Gustave asked. "Like, what's the plan? I feel I should know it in case it goes wrong, so that I'll know which way to run, screaming?"

"We're going to run for our lives and hope we make it to the towers before Ergot's men find us," Grinda explained. "And we'll keep to the trees to reduce the risk of an arrow plunging into our backs. Wait, wait." She stopped and her eyes drifted to the top of Gustave's head and then his hand. "You're wearing your crown? You have your ring?"

"Yes. You said to always wear them." His crown wasn't gaudy—just a golden circlet with a large ruby in the center of it, some famous stone that the dwarves had dug out of the Korpås Range long before Gustave's time. And the ring was flat on top with grooves that he was supposed to press into wax when he wrote letters or official thingies, and it was one of a kind.

"Good. We'll need them to prove who you are. Now, let's run."

That was when Gustave wished for his hooves back. Both Grinda and Ralphee were faster than he was. The old witch had a real commitment to cardio. When the sounds of battle and people dying reached his ears, he tried to go faster but couldn't. He cursed his thumbs again.

"Stupid do-nothing meat nubs! Floppity skin-wrapped mini-hams! I want my trusty trotters back!"

His thumbs remained dumb and made no comment.

Grinda stopped at one point to peek at the road behind them, once the grunts and cries of dying bodyguards had ceased and they could hear the rumble of horses approaching. She waved her wand at what she saw. Curses and coughing and whinnies and horsey sneezes followed soon after.

"What did you do?" Ralphee asked between gulps of air.

"There are only three of them now, including Lord Ergot. For the next hour or so, they will be plagued by a persistent dust cloud as long as they pursue us. Every breath they take while traveling this way equals more dust up their noses. If they stop or turn around, they'll breathe free."

"We've stopped and I still can't breathe," Gustave said. He felt as if someone were scraping a pipe cleaner up and down his throat.

"Just try to keep up. When we get into town we can blend in and lose them."

"Is it a nice town?"

Grinda shrugged a shoulder. "Of a sort. Housing for the government workers, kuffee shoppes, tooty bars, and lots of buffets on the halfling side of the river."

Ralphee blanched. "What the heck is a tooty bar?"

"You're too young," Grinda said with a scowl, and resumed running, counting on them to follow.

"What? I am not! Hey!" Ralphee scrambled after her, demanding an explanation.

Gustave lurched after them, burning lungs and noodly legs complaining as he staggered on toward some sorta-kinda-maybe promise of safety. He thought about what it must mean that Grinda had to slow their three pursuers down: His bodyguards had to be dead, and so did many of Lord Ergot's men. He had never before considered that being the king might be . . . dangerous.

He tried to think of how Lord Ergot's actions could be construed as a mistake or a misunderstanding rather than treason. He hadn't ever entered the city of Bruding or introduced himself. He'd never had his people announce themselves as there on business for the king. These were definitely not the "bro-times" Ergot had repeatedly offered in his letters. Grinda's sand golems just busted Ralphee out of the dungeon without bona fides or credentials of any kind. It was therefore plausible that Lord Ergot thought he was pursuing a criminal in an expensive gnomeric centipod who just happened to travel with uniformed soldiers wearing the king's golden-goat sigil and a sand witch who dressed in audacious shades of purple just like the king's chamberlain. Or . . . not very plausible at all.

He pushed himself to run just a little faster.

Soon they could spy other buildings huddled below the tower. In fact, once they arrived they saw plenty of construction and more halflings on the gnomeric side of the river than Gustave would have expected. They were dressed in splotched and wrinkled military livery, which looked as if it had just been taken out of storage and promptly stained with mustard, and were marching around in patrols and columns.

"Take off your crown and ring," Grinda said, "and give them to me for safekeeping. We need to disappear for a while and find our way into the towers."

Gustave did so and the items disappeared into Grinda's cloak. Shaking out his hair, he instantly felt better—lighter and less weighed down by troubles. He didn't hate his thumbs as much. Grinda led them to a street lined with markets and pulled them into Daami Perki's Herki Jerkins, a gnomeric tailor shop that catered to taller folk as well as gnomes. An automaatti took their measurements and they were able to quickly acquire some jerkins Daami Perki had in stock, with only minor alterations made to the sleeves. They also swapped cloaks with a minimum of haggling and acquired a broad-rimmed hat with a saucy feather in the band, behind which Gustave could hide his identity. It might all be for naught, since there were few other humans wandering around and they would most likely stick out regardless, but Grinda had a plan.

"Ralphee, we're going to send you to be with your sister now," she told him, and gave him directions to the Songful Tower of Roses and a small sack of coins much like those Gustave had given to the lutist back in Bruding. "You need to leave."

"But I want to see a tooty bar!"

"No, it's too perilous right now. Remember Lord Ergot wants you dead or in a dungeon, and he's on his way here. But don't return to Bruding, either, until after we've restored order."

Once the lad stalked away to the south to head for Meadow Verge and then points west, muttering about being denied his first tooties, Grinda sighed in relief.

"Now. We're disguised, we're alone, you're breathing again, sort of, and we can find out what's going on with the kanssa-jaarli."

"How are we going to do that?"

A sonorous honk blatted from the tower above them, startling Gustave. It was answered by a long, sustained note from the other side of the river, and the gnomeric tower began to grunt up and down the scale like a hyperexcited tuba.

"We're going to be tourists. If memory serves, there's a tour every hour on the toot. Come on, we can just catch this one if we hurry."

At the base of the gnomeric tower there was a kiosk bedecked with flags advertising tours; a small gaggle of people clustered around it—mostly gnomes, but also a few dwarves and humans. Grinda forked over a couple of coins and they joined the group, led by a gnome whose gname tag read Hippi Potti.

A halfling holding a mysterious chain stood before the door with her arms crossed, but Hippi flashed her badge, and the halfling gave a terse nod and let them pass, just another tour on another day full of tours.

But Gustave could not believe, once they began to ascend the gnomerically constructed mechanical tower elevator and peer through the windows at the vista below, that this was business as usual around the towers.

For one thing, there were an awful lot of halflings marching around on the gnome side and hardly any gnomes. When he mentioned this in low tones to Grinda, she ventured that they might be underground. And once they reached the top of the tower and circled around to get a good view of the bridge across the Rumplescharte River, Gustave was both awed and dismayed by what he saw.

Awed because the enclosed bridge spanning the Rumplescharte between the two towers was truly a marvel of engineering, a hallway on either side leading to a saucer-like room in the middle known as the Toot Suite, where the kanssa-jaarli met each day to attend to the affairs of the Skyr. Crescents of glass in the roof served as skylights, but the outer walls of the saucer were also windows; the view from within must've been fantastic. Gustave admired the gleaming ribbon of the Rumplescharte flowing north to the Dämköld Sea, with the tufted tops of the Pruneshute Forest on the western banks and the coiffed pastures and fields of farms stretching away like green quilted squares on the east.

But much to Gustave's horror, he also saw unnecessarily large half-ling forces on the eastern side of the river and vast herds of innocent cattle, sheep, and goats, which were obviously there to feed that army of halflings. There was even a building that clearly functioned as an abattoir, into which animals walked, screamed, and exited as butchered filets, chops, and racks of ribs. Seeing it, hearing the grinding noise it made, Gustave nearly had a boom-boom moment. But he couldn't dwell on that. The problem of exploding gnomes would have to come first.

There was an astounding amount of construction going on down below. Squat, ugly buildings dreamt up by some failure of an architect, no doubt the result of Lord Ergot working in conjunction with the Dastardly Rogues. Everything they'd heard . . . was true.

Gustave missed most of Hippi's tour patter but did hear her say that they'd get to greet the kanssa-jaarli soon. "Currently the gnomeric jaarl is Jarmo Porkkala from Luri, and the halfling jaarl is Gasparde Chundertoe of the Muffincrumb Chundertoes."

"I beg your pardon?" Grinda said. "I thought the halfling jaarl was Parnalle Peatbog of the Cheapmeat Peatbogs?"

Hippi looked surprised that a human would know or even care about the halfling jaarl. "He was, until recently. He died soon after his return from Songlen to see the new king crowned."

"How did he die?"

"Natural causes. He was very old."

"Hmm. Did Jarmo Porkkala attend the coronation?"

"No, I believe he was ill at the time."

Grinda grunted but said nothing more until they moved to enter an elevator that would take them down from the top of the tower to the bridge spanning the river.

"You might not remember meeting him, but I do, and Parnalle

Peatbog wasn't old," she muttered to Gustave. "And I bet Jarmo Porkkala wasn't ill either."

The lift opened and they exited into a foyer that led to the covered bridge. Gustave noted that there was also a broad door leading to a stairwell on the right. They lingered in the rear of the tour group, following Hippi onto the covered bridge. There were sections of thick glass in the floor, allowing one to look down at the glittering waters of the Rumplescharte and have, if one wished, a minor heart attack.

Grinda withdrew Gustave's crown and ring from her cloak. "Time to ditch that hat and reveal yourself," she murmured as Hippi burbled happily about the history of the kanssa-jaarli. "We need to ask Jarmo Porkkala why he's allowing his cities to be overrun with drubs."

Gustave noted as he donned his royal accoutrements that there were a couple of gnomeric guards but no automaatti of any kind stationed outside the doors of the Toot Suite. One would think that if they were serious about guarding anything from the taller folk, they'd have some mechanical backup. These guards did not seem particularly alert or eager to examine the tourists; instead of giving the group more than a cursory glance, they were discussing their dreams of retiring one day in the Seven Toe Islands.

The interior of the Toot Suite was a profound contrast to the exterior of steel, chrome, and glass. It was a sybaritic chamber covered in lush carpet the color of old port or older blood. A perfectly circular room, the walls to the east and west were furnished in clever cherrywood bookcases arranged to showcase iconic works of gnomeric and halfling culture. The northern and southern windows provided views of the Rumplescharte. Directly to the south lay not only Corraden but Songlen, the capital of Pell, and to the north was the Skyr, over which the kanssa-jaarli held sway. The kanssa-jaarli were seated at the northern end of the room, their thrones set upon rotating bases that were currently facing south. Behind them a couple of writing desks waited, as well as some festive potted plants drinking in the sun.

The gnomeric jaarl, Jarmo Porkkala, looked mildly interested at their arrival. The halfling jaarl, Gasparde Chundertoe, was in the midst of eating an enormous hand-rolled sushi cone and could not be bothered to look up. Behind the halfling's throne was an expansive buffet with all sorts of meats and casseroles and desserts waiting to delight his tongue. Behind the gnomeric jaarl, a more limited buffet stood ready, with twelve ceramic dishes offering variations on a theme: One could have some sort of pickled fish from the top row, a gourmet selection of muesli from the middle row, or a fine pudding from the bottom row. Gustave idly wondered if one of those was the hot nut pudding for which the Skyr was famous, but he was more interested in the muesli. He'd not eaten in some while and the run had made him hungry.

It was highly odd that both the kanssa-jaarli were guarded by halflings and that Jarmo Porkkala had not a single automaatti in sight for clerical tasks or anything. The gnome had a single gnome attendant, who looked forlorn and lost. Gasparde Chundertoe, by contrast, had five or six halflings attending him. One of them, standing at Gasparde's elbow with what looked like a golden mechanical bird perched on his shoulder, was dressed in expensive pleated fabrics in a shade of green that Gustave thought vaguely obscene, punctuated with what were either square golden buttons or pats of rancid butter.

"Remind me never to dress like that guy," he whispered to Grinda.

"You need all your regal dignity and confidence now," she replied, "like we've practiced. No bleating. Let's go."

For approximately thirty seconds things went spectacularly well. They detached from the tour group circling around to the south and approached the throne. The halfling guards perked up and moved to intercept. Gustave announced that he was, in fact, the king and here to speak to the kanssa-jaarli, and the guards moved aside. He even spoke several entire sentences unhindered!

"Jaarl Porkkala, Jaarl Chundertoe, I am King Gustave of Songlen, to whom you owe your fealty. I have come to see you on matters of grave importance to the Skyr and to Pell as a whole. I would like to know specifically what you are doing to quell the violence rampaging through your gnomeric cities at the hands of halfling rogues."

Both jaarli blinked at him twice and Chundertoe chewed once, then their heads swiveled in concert to look at the vomit-green halfling and Gustave knew that the easy part was over.

"Violence? What violence? This is nonsense," the vulgarly clad halfling said with a sneer. Though Gustave was still somewhat new to the whole governing thing, even he knew that the avocado fop should not have spoken to him out of turn like that.

"Who are you, sir, that you answer for the kanssa-jaarli? I asked them the question, not you. Hold your tongue!"

"I will not! I am Marquant Dique of the Bigly-Wicke Diques, adviser to the jaarl, and I have serious doubts that you are the king." He hooked a thumb at the automaatti perched on his shoulder. "A little bird from Lord Ergot told me an impostor might show up here, making baseless claims. I think we should postpone your audience until we can confirm your identity."

Grinda cursed and Gustave suddenly understood why it was so important that Parnalle Peatbog was no longer jaarl. Neither of these jaarli had been to his coronation and so had no idea if he was truly king or just someone wearing costume jewelry. And both of the jaarli clearly deferred to Marquant Dique, the leader of the drubs, which meant that they were definitely corrupt as a three-day-old corpse, and Lord Ergot's alliance with the drubs was confirmed by that messenger bird. Of course, all this information was useless, considering that Gustave and Grinda, for all their bona fides, were actually just two scrawny bags of meat among enemies. But Gustave wouldn't let that stop him from attempting to right the wrong in his kingdom.

"I think the infamous leader of a criminal organization shouldn't be advising the kanssa-jaarli," Gustave said, holding in a bleat. "Remove yourself before I have you arrested."

"No, I think it is *you* who needs to be arrested," the chartreuse horror said. "Guards, take these impostors!"

The kanssa-jaarli said nothing, but Gustave saw Gasparde grin with relish and take another bite of his sushi roll as the guards hastened to obey. Gustave was unarmed and absolutely incapable of fighting, so he bleated in despair as tiny, hairy-backed hands latched onto his arm and yanked him to the right. A spear pointing at his chest backed him up toward the halfling side of the Toot Suite, and the tour group made little cries of alarm and dismay that held an undeniable edge of *OMG, something is going down, and won't my neighbor be impressed that I saw it.*

Grinda was more than capable of fighting, however, and her status as a sand witch was quickly confirmed as she whipped out her wand and went to work on the guards trying to seize her, directing the soil on their clothes into their eyes and noses so that they staggered back, coughing and blinking.

"Unhand the king!" she cried, but no one obeyed. In fact, Marquant Dique sent his bird flying out of the room to fetch more guards, and a gaggle of drubs barreled in shortly thereafter, brandishing swords and half-eaten chicken wings, golden medallions gleaming on their chests. In a desperate bid to win Gustave free before the drubs could overwhelm her, Grinda directed her wand at the two guards holding him, and for a second it looked like he might escape. But they had no sooner stepped back and he stepped forward than a weight landed on his back and a line of cold steel at his throat made him stop. It was the dagger of Marquant Dique.

"Stay awhile," he cooed. His moist breath stank of olives and evil, and Gustave loathed him like no other halfling in the world. "I'm most eager to talk at length with a man who thinks he can walk in here and order me about."

The drubs were spreading out to surround Grinda, and she lifted all the foul sediment buried in that luxurious carpet into the air, blinding everyone with their own shed skin cells and castaway boogies.

"Drop your wand, witch!" Marquant shouted. "Or I will cut this impostor's throat."

Grinda ignored the halfling but quickly read the room, judged it unfavorable, and found Gustave's eyes through the vile cloud of debris she'd flung into the air. "I'll come back for you," she said, and twirled inside her cloak, flinging airborne crud at the eyes of the drubs at the same time.

They cursed, and someone in the tour group loudly announced he wanted his money back, and Gustave saw Grinda's cloak fall empty to the floor. Past that, he saw the retreating form of an opossum scampering for the exit on the gnomeric side of the Toot Suite, wand wrapped tightly in her tail. She'd pulled that trick once before; Gustave hoped she would remember how to change herself back this time. Unless she forgot him or otherwise failed to save his skinny neck, in which case he hoped she was trapped in that trash-eating body forever with a wicked case of mange.

"Where'd she go?" one of the drubs shouted.

Confusion reigned as the blinded halflings searched for Grinda and poked at her cloak, and once the sediment in the air settled back down into the carpet, Marquant ordered his Dastardly Rogues to get the tour group out of there, apply an excitement tax to their ticket fees, then secure the room and let no one in or out. He slid off Gustave's back and walked around to face him, dagger pointed in his direction. The rogue's hideous green outfit looked no better up close, and the mechanical bird that came back to perch on his shoulder did not improve it. Gustave savored that rare feeling of humanity: hopelessness. As a goat, at least, he'd felt rather more invincible, especially when divesting himself of emergency pellets, an act he'd been trained by Hurlga to never ever perform as a human, as much as he might currently wish to do so.

"Are you really him? The so-called Gustave the Great, the Goat King?"

"Yes. Are you really him? The so-called Big Dick of the Dastardly Rogues Under Bigly-Wicke? Because you're a bit smaller and more wrinkled than I expected."

Marquant's face purpled. "That is *not* my name!" He relaxed and chuckled, wiggling the knife point at Gustave. "Oh, how arrogant you are—not just you, all humans!—coming in here practically alone and thinking you can order us around. It is not merely arrogant; no, it is disrespectful."

Gustave snorted. "You're in this for respect? Being a criminal is the wrong career path to choose if you want that. Especially when you're involved in shady land deals with treasonous lords."

Marquant's eyes bugged. "Eh? What's that? What do you know?"

"I know you're plotting with Lord Ergot against me."

The halfling laughed, his cheeks growing rosy in his merriment. "Oh, you think you've discovered a plot, eh? And so you rushed over here to deliver yourself to us?"

"I wouldn't call this a delivery, no. I didn't know you'd be here. I came to see if the kanssa-jaarli were aware of what you've been doing."

Jaarl Gasparde Chundertoe belched and grinned at him before tossing the remainder of his sushi roll over his shoulder and calling for a stoup of wine. Jaarl Jarmo Porkkala blinked and said nothing.

"Oh, they're quite aware and very much in my pocket. Lord Ergot will arrive soon and we'll determine how best to move forward. You have definitely saved us plenty of time and effort by walking right into my demesne." He laughed again and shook his head in disbelief. "I really think you may have committed one of the greatest blunders in all history. They'll be calling you Gustave the Gormless soon."

"Well, that's probably true. I don't believe I have any gorms." He looked to Grinda's cloak, asking, "Do I?" before recalling that she was gone.

Ah, well. Gustave didn't care very much what people called him as long as he got to continue breathing. His window of opportunity to keep doing that would close soon after Lord Ergot stomped in, he felt sure.

He hoped Grinda came back before Lord Ergot could catch up. Not because he wanted someone pleasantly familiar to die with, but because he knew that the possum was his only hope.

31.

Near a Gourmet Selection of Hotly Contested Muesli

"Anyone can throw together some oats, fruits, and nuts and call it muesli, but gnomeric chefs employ methods that can elevate a dry collection of fibres into sublime dining experiences that not only provide explosive adventures in the boom-boom room but delight the tongue and palate as well."

—Almont Brewne, in *Deeply Moved by Cereals*

In recent times, Båggi Biins had walked on many roads. Some were beautiful and neat, like the carefully cobbled avenues of Okesvaa. Others were magical and strange, like the path through the Misree Hills, or worrisome, like the trail leading to Dr. Murkimer's ghostel and dental office. But none was so sad as the road that led away from the valiant kobold's grave and toward what the dwarf suspected would be an unwinnable fight. For although he'd been waiting to unleash his violence, he began to see what their small group was truly up against, and it made him feel tinier than a gnome toe. They'd bested the wyrm and the witch, two independent evils, but they'd suffered major losses that went eons beyond proper beard hygiene. Handily trouncing trolls was one thing, but government was rather bigger and harder to bash in the knee.

The Toot Towers were so tall, so majestic, that they were visible the moment the Pruneshute Forest dribbled away to pasture. The firmly packed wagon ruts Faucon had been so excited about merged into an altogether muckier road that had seen better days. No gnomes had been this way recently, judging by the garbage tossed carelessly aside and the definitive lack of neat rows of carrots and turnips. Nor were any dwarves in evidence, as neither bees nor thoughtfully tapped hives were visible; nary an inn could be seen. No, only the dross of halflings punctuated that dour brown ribbon, from soggy Dinny's to-go bags to discarded foot brushes bedangled with sad brown curls, and Båggi had never felt farther from home or further from the dwarf he hoped to be.

The entire party was listless as they entered the city, led by Kirsi. Since her . . . well, Båggi tried to think of it as a *fresh hemoglobin infusion* rather than an instance of cannibalism, the gnome had been even more chipper and confident than before. So perhaps she wasn't listless—she definitely seemed listy—but a palpable pall gloomed over the rest of them. The city's disgraceful ambience didn't help. As colorful and bohemian as Caskcooper had seemed, with warm lanterns and pennants and artwork everywhere, the city around the Toot Towers seemed ramshackle, older than its years, and utterly overrun with halflings in military garb with almost identical mustard stains. If Båggi remembered correctly, this area should've been a happy mix of halflings and gnomes working together for the good of their government and land, but it looked more like a military base that lacked a detergent allowance or a sense of pride. The only things that didn't droop were the weapons festooning the belts of the halflings, which was not a comforting thought.

"This cannot be. This city. It is egregious!" Faucon declared, noting the prevalence of drub medallions and piles of refuse. "And the laws against unkempt statuary are being wholly ignored!" He pointed at a bronze sculpture of a house-sized gnome and halfling holding hands, noting that it was leaning heavily and scrawled with offensive graffiti.

"Yeah, it wasn't like this the last time I was here," Agape agreed. "That was maybe a year and a half ago. It was bright and well kept then, but now it's awful. And where are all the gnomes?"

All that is quite important for the two-legged, I suppose, but personally I find the poor condition of the roads disturbing, Gerd said, fussily lifting her talons a little higher out of the muck. *Icke. I like my claws to be clean.*

"Well, at least we know where we're headed, and we're almost to our goal." Kirsi turned to face them, her tiny wand nestled in her neat cardigan. "So let's put on our smiles for the final mile. As we gnomes always say: *Brush your hair, be sweet and fair, don't overshare or rudely stare!*"

"I hate that one," Onni said. He seemed, Bàggi thought, the most down in the dumps of all, decidedly not Onni-ish. His cardigan wasn't straight, and every time he looked at Kirsi, his face kind of fell apart.

"You know what they say, Onni: *Hate is just another way to love something.*"

Onni's mouth fell open, and everyone watched him to see what he had to say about that. But he just snapped his mouth closed, shook his head, and kept walking toward the large, decorative door at the base of one of the Toot Towers, beside which a sign proclaimed that tours happened on the toot.

Behind them, the sudden slap of halfling feet on the road was accompanied by a call of "Move it or lose it, tourists!" and then three humans in the military-green cloaks of Bruding shoved past, which he recognized from his time at the Ping-Pong Palace. They marched through the very door Kirsi was aiming for, making her mutter, "Well, that's odd. And rude."

But she didn't stop slogging her way up the street, even if it took her five steps for every one a human might've taken. The road had hardened everyone's feet and bodies, their calf muscles truly tight and their blisters gone as hard and callused as a goat's knees. It must be nice, Båggi thought, to be as sure of oneself as Kirsi was. Did the magic come from the confidence, or did the confidence come from the magic?

Oh, but wait. He remembered: The magic came from eating an old woman's atria and ventricles. He hoped, for Kirsi, that it was worth it. The confidence had been there from the moment they'd met, and it didn't look like that well would ever run dry.

When Kirsi put a hand against the door, however, a giant form moved to intercept her. At first, it was as if the wall did a shimmy, but then the creature's camouflage shifted to reveal a moist, lizard-like beast too big to fit through the door. It sinuously skittered to block their passage, opening a wide, toothless maw to hiss at them. Although it had originally matched the tower's wall perfectly, it now went a sickly pinkish-white with crimson frills around its face and tiny beady eyes, like cranberries stuck in a bun. To Båggi, it looked a little like an intestine come to life and given frog appendages and a long tail, or like an angry albino sausage. Kirsi drew back, her hand on her wand.

"Sorry, miss, but the tour is closed for the day due to, uh, unforeseen circumstances," a halfling woman said. She stood a few feet away in military gear and held a long chain attached to the monster's collar.

Båggi would've been glad to find the nicest inn available and try again when circumstances were more foreseen, but Kirsi wasn't about to leave.

"What sort of unforeseen circumstances?" she said, hands on her hips.

"Um. Well. Er. The elevator is broken. Gnomeric machines are always doing that, you know." She raised an imperious eyebrow.

Båggi thought that was unnecessarily provocative and unpleasant. Gnomeric machines rarely broke. But Kirsi did not take the bait and instead responded with positivity. "Excellent! It just so happens my friend Onni is an expert in all gnomeric mechanicals and can get it running again in a jiffy. Right, Onni?"

Onni did not look so sure, especially after the tree-sized monster lizard hissed at him.

"Oh. Maybe."

"Only trained halfling personnel are allowed to tinker with official business," the woman said, throwing off that certain air that suggested she knew she was caught in an obvious lie but wasn't going to budge. "So you'd best be off."

Kirsi took another step toward the door. "I can hear the lift coming down. It's obviously not broken. So why don't you just let us in? As citizens of the Skyr, we have the right to address the kanssa-jaarli with grievances."

"Not without an appointment!"

"I don't need an appointment to register my grievance, and it says so in the rare copy of the Elder Annals we're carrying. That's kind of why we're here. So if you'll call off your frilled lizard, we can get on with it."

As if the halfling had already backed off, Kirsi again strode forward. A halberd slammed down, blocking her path, and the monster drooled on Kirsi's cardigan.

"Listen up, tadpole. I'll make it easy so you can understand. One, the answer is no, because you don't have an appointment. Two, the Elder Annals were lost; everybody knows that. And three, he's not a frilled lizard. He's a Pruneshute Two-Toed Tooting Newt, and he's been trained to protect the Toot Flutes at all costs, so you can't get past him. Oh, and four: Your attempted assault on the towers means you've been identified as an enemy of the state." The halfling dropped the chain, and the newt stood on its hind legs, towering against the tower. "Sic 'em, Glute!"

Kirsi waited too long to pull out her wand and had no choice but to launch herself backward as the newt's soft, pudgy lips slapped together right where she'd been. Faucon drew his sword and started for the newt, but the halfling retainer engaged him with her halberd, keeping him at a distance with the length of her weapon. Onni was digging through his backpack as if looking for snacks, and Gerd slashed the newt with her talons, producing little apparent effect. The wounds closed up immediately, but on the positive side, Gerd's claws came away completely scoured of muck and grime. She hootled in approval.

Agape had only her knife, but she did manage to lop off one of the newt's hands. Even as she bleated her success, a new hand grew in its place, almost like a balloon blowing up. The newt possessed remarkable regeneration abilities, and it kept snapping at Kirsi and Agape in turn. Båggi watched the scene, mesmerized. And, if he was honest, not doing a dang thing, until the situation rapidly deteriorated.

"Båggi! Help!" Kirsi cried, as the newt's new hand plucked her from the ground and pulled her in a trajectory that would end with a floppy maw and probably all sorts of unpleasant digestive waterslides. Agape was on the ground, stunned, and Onni was messing with some sort of golden box that looked more like something that would play a pleasant waltz and less like an offensive weapon to wield against large swamp newts. Gerd's slashes continued to give the newt few worries, and Faucon was still dueling the halfling guard.

Hefting his club, Båggi found that it had grown several angry-looking spikes.

"Yes. Spikes. Ha ha! I should swing this, eh?" he said, for he felt more fear and confusion than anger. Striking a government employee went against everything that he'd been taught, but he set down his cask and picnic basket anyway. As he did so, he realized that the lizard shape on his cudgel might be a representation of the newt.

"Yes!" Kirsi screamed, her tiny hands the only thing keeping her from a slide into the deep-red throat. "Swing it. Anything!"

In that moment, Båggi realized something important: All this time, he'd been waiting for the violence to arise from inside as if waiting for the muse to strike. He'd stood outside of fights because said muse had not provided any input, as if one couldn't fight if one didn't have an inner well of violence at the ready. But just now he realized that he could swing his cudgel no matter what he felt, if it would save his friend.

The violence didn't control him; he controlled it.

"Here we go!" he shouted, wrapping the leather strap of the cudgel around his hand. "Oh, yes. The good old one-two. One for each toe. Ha ha!" But this time it wasn't a sad laugh of a *ha ha*, it was a victorious sort of *ha ha!* And he liked that so much better.

He took a running leap with the cudgel high over his head and slammed it down on the newt's huge foot, flattening both the toes on its left side. In response, Glute the newt blasted a toot of pain and rage and dropped Kirsi. She landed on Onni as he was fitting some kind of huge gauntlet onto his tiny fist, and howling ensued as they tumbled to the ground and got their beards embarrassingly entangled.

The newt wobbled and struggled to stay upright, obviously waiting for its toes to grow back. Båggi didn't wait.

"So that was the one, and here's the two," he told it, swinging his cudgel into its left knee. The newt honked in dismay as it toppled over onto its halfling keeper, who had her halberd up in the air, ready to strike at Faucon. Said newt crushed her and impaled itself, and Båggi hoped it would be able to heal, for he did not wish it ill; he just wanted his friends to pass by safely. It tooted mournfully and wriggled a tiny bit, so he knew it had a chance. Other halflings in their mustard-stained uniforms, who had been betting on the fight and laughing at Kirsi's distress, now drew their swords and took a more particular interest. Gerd screeched at them and they kept their distance as Båggi scrambled to retrieve his cask and basket.

"Come on!" Kirsi yelled, extricating herself from Onni and holding open the door. Båggi joined the others in scrambling over the newt and running inside.

Once they'd reached the foyer, a very surprised souvenir salesman gasped and dropped an Official Toot Towers Snow Globe with Real Tooting Action, and Onni locked the door behind Gerd just as halfling fists began to pound on the other side. Kirsi plucked a bristle from her beard and swallowed it, cursing the salesman to fall instantly asleep on the job—it had been wise of her, Båggi thought, to save her wand's limited use for bigger fish that required frying.

"There's the lift." Onni pointed with his ungauntleted hand across the foyer to a gnomeric set of metallic double doors, all beautiful if a bit tarnished. Before they could push a button, the doors chimed and opened. Much to Båggi's surprise—for he would've bet a crock of Brother Wager's Stranger Danger Stray Animal De-Manger that an automaatti would be there to press the buttons and spout rhymes—a grizzled possum with its tail wrapped around a wand bolted from the lift, looking like it could use said crock of De-Manger.

"Ahh!" Kirsi shrieked, for the possum was nearly her size and looked a bit bedraggled and possibly rabid at that.

"Ahh yourself," the possum said in almost the voice of a cultured older woman. "You're not here to stop me, I hope?"

"We wouldn't dream of it," Båggi replied, for he wasn't nearly as frightened of smöl forest creatures as his gnome friend seemed to be. "I do fear we've left a bit of a mess, not to mention a somnambulent souvenir salesman and some hungry halflings, in our wake. You didn't happen to see three men from Bruding going up, did you?"

"What men?"

"They entered shortly before us and I do not see them here, so they must have already gone up."

"They weren't on the lift," the possum said, swinging her head to look around and cursing when she saw a door off to one side marked STAIRS. "They must have gone up that way. We're out of time."

"Time for what?" Faucon asked.

The possum squinted at him. "You're not a drub, are you?"

"Certainly not," Faucon said, lifting his chin and straightening his waistcoat.

"What a peculiar bunch," the opossum opined, which Båggi thought remarkable coming from her. "Two gnomes, a halfling, an ovitaur, a gryphon, and a dwarf. And there's a whiff of magic about you." She focused on Kirsi. "It's you. I take it you're a bristle witch?"

Kirsi returned the possum's cool gaze, her composure returned. "I was. But then an evil witch tried to eat my friend's heart and killed a kobold bard instead, so I ate her heart and took her wand. Why—are you perhaps looking for trouble?"

At that, the possum cackled, a dainty paw to her chest. "Heavens, no! Why, I think you might be just what I need. I know I don't look like much just now, but I'm the royal adviser of King Gustave the Greatest, known as Grinda the Sand Witch, and I am currently flee-ing treason by the halfling varlets who've taken the king hostage in the Toot Suite."

"Wait. You're with the king? But that's exactly why we're here!" Kirsi stepped forward, withdrawing Hellä Traktiv's sealed letter from her pack and holding it toward the possum. "We come from the Great Library in the City of Underthings with a copy of the Elder Annals and the Tome of Togethering, the founding documents of the Skyr, which our government has strayed from in the most egre-gious ways. Halflings are firebombing gnomehomes throughout the Skyr, and we are here to speak to the kanssa-jaarli to ask them to end the violence. But we also need the king's help to restore order."

Grinda did not take the letter, but her mouth did twitch in amuse-ment. "The king and I came here for much the same reason. The bad news is that the kanssa-jaarli is corrupt, merely a puppet government allowing Marquant Dique and Lord Ergot to exploit the gnomes. They have the king in their possession right now."

Faucon's face did some Rage Gymnastics. "Marquant Dique is here?"

The possum nodded. "The good news is that if we can save the king and get rid of Ergot and Marquant Dique, I assure you that a new kanssa-jaarli will be put in place and that the gnome situation will vastly improve. The king is very sympathetic to your cause. But first we have to face what's waiting in the Toot Suite and save the king before he does something unfortunate that involves bleating."

Agape, finally able to focus, gave her a sharp look. "Did you say bleating? Was thaaat a knock against ovitaurs?"

Grinda coughed into a dainty pink paw. "No, I said *beating*, of course. Now, are you willing to fight for both your earldom and king-dom?"

Båggi readily affirmed his willingness, and his friends chorused agreement.

"Good. I don't think the gryphon will fit in the lift, and if they're waiting for us, it's not a good idea to trap ourselves in a box like that, so we should take the stairs. And be ready for a fight."

The gnomes climbed on Gerd's back and Båggi led the way up the stairs, with Grinda behind him and Faucon's metal toes and Agape's hooves clacking on the steps.

Once on the landing that led to the bridge entrance, Båggi peered through the porthole into the foyer and put up a warning hand to his friends behind him. "There's a throng of halflings entering the lift," he whispered. "Drubs."

"Off to look for me, no doubt," Grinda muttered. "I have my wand, but most of my magic is based on illusion or moving dirt around. Let me cast a seeming upon you all. To everyone but our party, you will appear as motes of dust, until you break the seeming. Remain quiet and do nothing to call attention to yourselves, and we should be able to sneak into the Toot Suite and save King Gustave."

Kirsi withdrew her wand and polished it on her cardigan. "I'm ready."

Agape drew her knife and gave a soft bleat of readiness. "Saaame."

Gerd ruffled her feathers. *And I.*

Faucon had his sword out. "Bring it on."

Onni lifted his gauntleted hand, which Båggi examined a bit more closely—he decided it looked a little like a glove made out of murder. "I've been perfecting my Iron Gnome glove," he said. "So let's go."

Båggi shrugged and adjusted the straps of his picnic basket, hefted his cask, and hooked his cudgel onto his belt, nodding silently at the possum. She reminded them once more to be quiet, murmured something unintelligible, and used her tail to direct the wand over the party. Båggi felt a cold tingle settle over his skin, after which the possum pointed at the door handle. Båggi took the hint and opened it, stepping out carefully into the carpeted foyer, holding the door open for the others to pass through. There was another group of halflings there, waiting for the next lift down, but they didn't look over at the stair door. Once Gerd had passed with the gnomes on her back, Båggi gently guided the door closed so that it wouldn't make any noise. They strode past the throng of drubs unseen and entered the covered bridge leading to the Toot Suite.

Two gnomeric guards lay prone outside the doors, whether dead or unconscious Båggi could not tell. But they were able to enter the Toot Suite unobserved and reassemble in the circular room.

What Båggi saw there was chilling. The king—if the gold-crowned, terror-stricken fellow with dark-brown skin was indeed the king—was on his knees, being held at knifepoint by a halfling wearing the most hideous viridian outfit Båggi had ever seen, all while a gnome and a halfling sat in their respective thrones, watching the scene as if it were a play. The gnome seemed uncertain if it was a good play or not; the halfling was enthralled, both with the scene and with the stoup of wine he was sucking on. Beside Båggi, Faucon was shivering with rage, biting his lip to keep from making a noise that might expose them all.

Behind the halfling and facing the king but with their backs to the party, the three humans from Bruding who'd preceded them into the tower loomed over the others. There were even more drubs milling about the southern end, either waiting for orders or waiting to attack one of the buffets near either throne. Some of them looked hungry enough to eat the potted plants lining the windows overlooking the river.

Grinda silently shooed their party to the left to clear the doorway, putting them behind the rude humans in their livery. Båggi inched forward to get a better look at them. They were a grim and pale lot with identical dark mustaches that must've been in fashion in Bruding, although one was slightly fancier than the others. The green-clad halfling lightly bowed to this wastrel.

"Now that Lord Ergot's here," he said, casually gesturing to the human in the middle, who had a crooked nose and a curled lip, "we'd like to make you an offer, King Gustave. Abolish the office of kanssa-jaarli and name a single earl to rule the Skyr, like all the other earldoms."

"That sounded kind of like a command instead of an offer," Gustave pointed out.

"That's in exchange for letting you live awhile longer," Lord Ergot said.

"Great. So I can name a gnome, right? One who doesn't dress in ugly colors?"

"Nooo," the halfling growled. "You will name who we say."

"I don't know, guys," the king said, his voice far more casual than Båggi thought he looked. "Sounds like I wouldn't be much of a king if I always did whatever randos told me to do."

"You already *aren't* much of a king," Lord Ergot said.

"Well, I think my chamberlain would disagree with you there. She's a pretty good sand witch, you know. And you haven't caught her yet. I think that's going to be a problem for you, Marquant."

Båggi had suspected the avocado-draped halfling was the leader of the Dastardly Rogues, but it was good to have it confirmed. For all the whispering about him, the Big Dique was just as small and unimpressive as Båggi would've assumed. After giving the collected drubs a moment to laugh at the king's speech, Marquant looked up and scanned the room as if he required proof that Grinda was not in fact already caught. He chucked his chin at the drubs clustered in the southern part of the suite.

"You lot. Go find out what's happening with the search. Help if needed, but one of you report back on the status as soon as possible."

Most of the drubs stampeded out to the bridge, leaving only six in the Toot Suite, along with the kanssa-jaarli, Marquant Dique, Lord Ergot, and his two men.

"That's pretty good odds," Båggi said without really thinking, and the cool tingle on his skin abruptly left him.

"What the deuce?" Marquant Dique shouted and spun around,

pointing at Båggi with his dagger when he saw the stranger who no longer resembled a harmless mote of dust. "Who let that dwarf in here?" He waved at his six drubs. "Kill it!"

"Okay, that's just rude," Kirsi said, breaking her own mote spell.

With a sigh of great forbearance, she waved her wand. The potted plants standing long unwatered around the sunny windows rattled and shook, and then fern fronds burst out like vines, snaking to hold the aggressive parties in place. They reached Lord Ergot and Marquant Dique first. Ankles clapped together, arms were bound to sides, and every drub and human, to a man, tumbled over where he'd been standing, wrapped in vines of living green that seemed to hold a bit of a grudge over lack of fertilizer and repotting. A small bird automaatti similar to Gerd's chirped in alarm and fluttered about, but it resettled on the shoulder of Marquant Dique when he stopped moving. The kanssa-jaarli were left unmolested by plant life, their eyes wide and their mouths silent. Kirsi first stared at them, then cupped a hand behind her ear to invite them to say something, but they continued to sit there stupidly. Lord Ergot, however, laughed.

"Looks like the sand witch wasn't the only one we needed to worry about."

"I don't see what's so funny," Marquant Dique said, struggling against his vines. "They have us now, whoever they are."

"Relax, Marquant. It's not over yet."

Tired of listening to them, Kirsi directed the plants to shut them up, sending exploratory fronds into their mouths.

Satisfied with her work, Kirsi strode toward the king as he got to his feet, holding out her letter. "King Gustave, I bring word from the kaupunginjohtaja of the City of Underthings."

"I don't know what that is, but it sounds like you're allergic to it," the king allowed.

But Kirsi didn't even pause. "My king, we have determined that the government outlined in the Tome of Togethering has failed, and therefore the procedures outlined in the Elder Annals must be followed to restore order. We have brought certified copies of both documents." She threw a look of contempt at Marquant Dique and pointed at him. "That halfling has ordered the arson of gnomehomes throughout the Skyr and is responsible for many gnomeric deaths. Justice must be done, and we hope you are willing and able to set things right."

Lord Ergot and Marquant Dique made plant-silenced gruntings of disagreement that everyone ignored. King Gustave looked back and forth before clearing his throat and taking the letter from Kirsi's hand.

"Yes. Thank you. We knew quite a bit of that except for the huge word at the beginning and the thing about a City of Underpants. I didn't know we had one of those. I'm certainly willing to set things right. The question is if we're able. Grinda, can we do that?"

The possum sashayed forward, tapping her wand against her tiny palm. "We can. That is, after all, what kings are for. But as this earldom has long been ruled by the kanssa-jaarli, requiring minimal oversight from the king, I'd like to hear their thoughts when unencumbered by the threats of Marquant Dique." She turned to the halfling and the gnome expectantly.

Gustave likewise turned to the seated figures. "Yeah. Good call. Ruler to ruler, or co-rulers, or whatever you guys are—what's up?"

"Uh, well, that is to say," the halfling jaarl said, clutching his stoup of wine and throwing glances of desperation at Marquant Dique. "The thing you have to understand is that, um, things are very . . . well . . . the Skyr . . . you see . . . quite delicate?"

"Enough." Grinda snapped her fingers at him, and he shut up. "You're clearly an idiot and a puppet of the drubs. But what about you, Porkkala?"

Everyone turned to the gnome jaarl. Kirsi's hands were clasped against her chest in desperate hope, and even Onni managed to look like there might be something worth saving here, if only the gnome could speak his mind. Surely the jaarl cared for his people's needs and had only been kept from wise ruling by threats from these despicable traitors?

"Hurrrh," the gnome said, blinking, and shifted uncomfortably on his throne. His finely knit gnomeric hat shifted on his head and he swiped at it irritably, knocking it off entirely.

Kirsi gasped. "Are those . . . ears on the top of his head?"

Grinda skittered up his throne and around the gnome, who hissed and tried to shove her away. "Tsk. It's an illusion. I should've known." After scampering down, she waved her wand, and the gnome shimmered and dissolved, revealing . . .

"Oh, my blundering badgers! That's the most well-fed raccoon I've ever seen!" Båggi shouted. "My goodness! What a fine and robust trash panda indeed! But not," he corrected himself, "not so very good as a ruler, I suspect."

Grinda whirled about, teeth bared at Marquant Dique. "Where is the real Porkkala?" she demanded.

The leader of the Dastardly Rogues could not answer, but one of his drubs could. "Executed!" he crowed.

Grinda shook her head. "It's as we feared, Gustave. The halflings have committed treason at the highest level."

"Ergot. Marquant. You're knee-deep in metaphorical plops," Gustave said. "I do try not to execute people, but I'm going to have to dream up something really creative to make sure you can never escape or return to power." Then he turned his back on them, facing Grinda. "Well, that was easy, wasn't it, thanks to these nice meddling kids?" He yawned and stretched, his eyes rolling back and forth. "Back home, then? To write some laws? Fix this kanssa-jaarli mess, appoint some new ones until an election can be held? Definitely need to make sure they're not raccoons. I'm thinking we should confiscate that muesli, though. I'm hungry."

"No."

Heads turned in surprise to find Lord Ergot standing, unencumbered by foliage. His cloak was on the floor, revealing a hardened leather cuirass tooled with intricate patterns and runes but clearly hiding some bits of plate underneath for extra protection.

Gustave craned his neck around and blinked. "You mean no as in you really want that muesli? I think there's enough to share. We could have those 'bro-times on the town' you used to write me about."

"I mean no as in you don't get to go home. It's not really your home, after all. You made up some story about being a hero that the gullible public bought, but you are nothing but a usurper, King Gustave, and I think when it comes to usurping I can usurp better than you." He gestured to the raccoon. "You're right that the Skyr needs new leadership. But, first, Pell needs a better king. I think I'd serve admirably."

Lord Ergot drew his sword and smiled the sort of smile that makes one's bowels uncomfortably loose.

"And that muesli is mine," he added, "because Pell is mine."

"No."

Surprise bloomed again at this flat statement of denial. Eyes sought out the speaker and widened in alarm. They were all looking at Båggi. And he knew exactly why. Because he was the person who had spoken.

He had divested himself of his burdens and was holding his Telling Cudgel, which was spiked and whirring and glowing as it had never glowed before, telling everyone that this particular dwarf was imbued with a clear purpose and the magical Korpåswood was in tune with it. Båggi pointed a finger at Lord Ergot.

"*J'accuse!* You and Marquant Dique are the authors of misery and unrest in the Skyr, preying upon those you see as too weak to fight back. And you would do the same to all of Pell, seeking power when you should be seeking peace and friendship. What you have found instead is a dwarf on his Meadschpringå. Let us dance," he said, but feeling that might leave it a little too open to interpretation, he added, "With violence."

32.

AMIDST A WHIRLWIND OF BLOOD AND
VISCERA AND BEARD HAIRS

"In the moment you meet your mortal enemy, there is no speech
you can make that will be more powerful than simply breathing
after they have ceased to do so."

—KYRTIS KANDOR, noted warlord of Grunting, to his protégé Horris
Lurgoif, quoted in *The Big Privy Book of Nifty Natterings, Volume 3*

Movement tore Offi's eyes from Båggi and Lord Ergot and
toward a flash of gold. It was gone almost before he could
process it, and realization came soon after: Marquant Dique's little
bird automaatti had flown for the eastern doors of the Toot Suite,
and it was going to tell a fresh batch of drubs to come running from
the halfling tower. A second later it screeched a piercing alarm, and
the violent dance to which Båggi had invited Lord Ergot began—
albeit with more participants than two duelists.

Gerd immediately commanded her library bird to hunt the other
one down, but the first automaatti's screech must have broken Kirsi's
concentration or had some other deleterious effect on her spell, for
the vines confining the halflings and humans all disintegrated into
green dust. Everyone was looking at Lord Ergot and Båggi except
for Marquant Dique, who had his eyes on King Gustave. The nastier-
than-usual halfling picked up his dagger, and a malevolent grin split

his face even as a Cold Sweat of Horror drenched every cubic centimeter of Offi's flesh. Offi already knew what kind of governing the gnomes could expect if the halflings killed King Gustave: exploitation and oppression. And so he ran straight at Marquant Dique to intercept him, even though the halfling was probably twice his mass and three times taller than him.

King Gustave was clueless to his own personal peril, because he was glued to the standoff between Lord Ergot and Båggi. He hadn't moved far enough away from the captives, and Offi was certain that the gaping ruler was about to take a knife in his left kidney from the leader of the drubs, which is what halflings always went for when they wanted to kill a human.

As both Offi and Marquant let loose with roars, a few eyes flicked in their direction; it seemed to Offi that he could sense everything in the heat of battle, but nothing mattered except protecting the king. Gerd or Faucon or Agape would have been a better protector than Offi, their skills at martial arts no doubt exceeding his, but none of them could act in time. He sensed them beginning to move—all of them, the drubs and Ergot's guards and his friends too—but only he was in position to make a difference.

Time to see if his Iron Gnome gauntlet would work. He ran and then slid on his knees, leaning to his left so that he could reach up with his gauntleted hand and latch onto the wrist of Marquant Dique. If he missed, his body would at least trip up the halfling or force him to change course and thereby miss his clear shot at the king. That was the extent of Offi's battle plan, and for a moment it went even better than he could have wished. His fingers grasped the crime lord's wrist as Marquant tried to thrust his dagger into the king's back, but Offi yanked it down to the ground in a literal iron grip, forcing the halfling to follow. There was no way Offi would let Marquant Dique slip free of his grasp, regardless of how hard he tugged.

And, suddenly, that was less of a victory and more of a grave mistake, for the halfling had more weight and muscle, and now Offi was veritably attached to him. Offi hit the release button inside the gauntlet and learned what real failure, what real hopelessness, felt like. The glove wouldn't open. He'd been anxious to see if his first weapon had worked, and now he had an answer: No, it did not.

For all that his wrist was captured, Marquant Dique was agile and not unskilled. He growled, leapt onto Offi's back, and redirected that knife toward Offi's torso, not caring that his wrist was still clutched in the gauntlet. For his arm was long and strong and about to get some leverage on, and so even though Offi knew it was coming and did all he could to strain against it, he was helpless to stop that knife from entering his belly, a biting cold and searing heat at once, more pain than he'd ever known, and then it was gone and so was the half-ling. The gauntlet's release button had finally worked, and it was too late.

Offi's gauntlet no longer clutched any wrist: Instead, he toppled to his side, cradling his guts and trying to keep them from leaking out, his eyes wide in shock. There was so much screaming.

He saw flashes of individual battles: Agape dropped underneath the swing of a human guard's sword, turned and supported herself on her hands, and kicked him powerfully in the crotch with both hooves. The man doubled over as she spun around and slammed her knife into his vulnerable side, where his cuirass was tied.

Feathers flashed and Offi saw that Gerd had spread her wings protectively, King Gustave and the strange talking-possum lady behind the gryphon and safe for the moment. Marquant was telling Kirsi, who stood in front of Gerd, that she'd better move or she'd get the same as her brave stupid friend.

That's what he was, he realized now: brave and stupid. Just like his brother, Onni.

Faucon was pulling throwing stars out of his waistcoat and tossing them into the unprotected faces and throats of drubs, shouting, "And that is for Remy! And that is for me! And that is for Onni!" as they found home in curly hair.

Lord Ergot slashed at Bäggi as a feint, but the dwarf danced back, then twirled his cudgel with his wrist so that it passed in front of him, just in time to connect with Ergot's thrust. The impact of wooden cudgel against steel should have produced no more than a dull clunk, but Båggi's weapon was no mere length of hardwood. The coruscating energies there flashed and crackled, and the top half of Ergot's blade was sheared away with a sound like a rung bell. It flew over Offi to thunk into one of the kanssa-jaarli thrones—the one with the raccoon sitting in it, to judge by the outraged chittering. The dwarf let the cudgel complete its circuit until it was upright, and then he swung horizontally at Lord Ergot's midsection with all his strength. There was no way the human could duck under that or leap over it. Ergot had overcommitted on his thrust and would have to take the hit, and take it he did.

Offi was hoping for a meaty explosion like the time Båggi had taken down the troll, but that didn't happen. There was a flash and Lord Ergot grunted, clutching his ribs as he staggered back, but he was still in one piece afterward, his cuirass charred and smoking. That must be it: His armor was enchanted against magic. Those tooled patterns were wards. That was how he'd broken free of Kirsi's vines and how he'd survived the deadly energies of an activated Telling Cudgel.

Gerd recognized this at the same time, for Offi heard her say to the bewildered Båggi, *His head is not warded against magick.*

As Lord Ergot roared that he required a new sword and scrambled to snatch one up from the human guard Agape had slain—she was now fighting the last one—Offi blinked and refocused on Kirsi, because she was yelling horrible curses at Marquant Dique. Her right hand held a handful of hairs ripped from her chin, and he saw a pink and bleeding patch there, her face furious and red and streaming with angry tears. She finished her curses and crammed the red bristles into her mouth, chewing and darting out of Marquant's way as he surged forward, leading with the dagger already coated in Offi's blood. He missed but did not seem to care; he only wanted to get to Gustave, and now that Kirsi had removed herself, only Gerd stood between the halfling and his goal. Offi didn't think the halfling would have much luck but worried that perhaps Marquant could pull it off; both he and Lord Ergot had proven more resourceful than expected.

Like Faucon, Marquant Dique had extra weapons tucked away in his clothing. He hurled the dagger in his hand at Gerd, and it sank partway into her breast, where feathers gave way to fur. She screeched and snapped at him, but he had anticipated this and stepped back after the throw, pulling two more knives out of his chartreuse doublet and grinning as he said, "You're not invincible, gryphon."

An audible gulp above and behind Offi's head could be heard, and then Kirsi's voice said, "Neither are you, halfling."

Dull popping noises began firing from somewhere, and then Marquant Dique screamed as the pops increased into a rolling crumping noise, like the satisfactory sound of snow crunching underneath one's shoes in winter, and Offi realized as the halfling collapsed that the sound was Marquant Dique's bones—all of them—breaking into tiny pieces. And when he fell in front of Offi's vision, the halfling was rolled up like a bad sausage, every limb poking out the wrong way, elbows and knees gone backward as the leader of the Dastardly Rogues Under Bigly-Wicke died from the powerful curse.

"That's hardcore goth," Offi whispered.

But whispering seemed to break something inside him, and he shuddered and twitched on the carpet. It was so cold, and his cardigan was ruined.

He couldn't really close his eyes, so he had no choice but to watch as the battle raged on, for all that things seemed sideways and time ran strange. Agape and Faucon engaged with minions and Lord Ergot faced Båggi once more, newly armed with a dead man's sword and much more wary this time. The Telling Cudgel still glowed with purpose and Båggi advanced on Ergot, eldritch lights shimmering and playing over his beard and eyebrows, while Ergot gave ground.

"This is ridiculous," he shouted at Båggi. "Why are you even here, dwarf? The Skyr doesn't concern you!"

"If that were true, then it shouldn't concern you either. But all of Pell concerns me. High up in the Korpås Range, we dwarves hear whispers from every corner of the world. And I am certain that this is precisely where I need to be, to end your exploitation of smöl people and your treason against the king."

"You will not end me!" Ergot snarled, and he charged with sword held high for an overhead blow. Båggi had to raise his club to deflect it, and Offi worried that Ergot had some awful plan in mind, for the attack was so clearly communicated and easily countered.

As before, Ergot's sword broke at the point of impact on the Telling Cudgel. But Ergot was counting on this. He kept moving, yanked the half blade down, and then thrust it low at Båggi's abdomen.

But the dwarf's body wasn't there. As soon as the blade broke on his cudgel, he spun around to his right, away from the thrust he'd anticipated, and swung his Telling Cudgel at the back of Lord Ergot's legs as the human passed. They were not protected with magical wards, and as such they did not fare well against the explosive energies waiting to be released. A thump and a wet shucking sound sent Lord Ergot's lower legs flying toward the western door and he fell heavily on his back, a raw scream of pain and disbelief erupting from his throat.

"The end," Båggi said, and brought the cudgel down on Lord Ergot's head with a final crunch, silencing him forever. He looked around to see if any other threats were coming. Agape and Faucon were still standing, albeit bleeding from a couple of gashes, while their opponents remained on the ground.

Kirsi knelt down in front of Offi and immediately called for the dwarf. "Båggi! We need your healing skills over here!"

The dwarf's warlike demeanor slipped away from his face immediately. "Oh, my angry asparagus! I'll get my picnic basket and be right there!" He dropped his cudgel and ran for his cask and basket.

The talking possum scampered out from the protective aegis of Gerd's wings and burrowed under a pile of clothing, which soon bloomed and grew into a human woman shrouded in a cloak.

Who are you? Gerd demanded.

"I told you true: I am Grinda, adviser to King Gustave. I was the possum you were kind enough to refrain from eating. Thank you, everyone, for your invaluable help in preserving the kingdom and restoring order in the Skyr. We should probably secure the doors so we don't have to deal with a bunch of halflings until we're ready."

"Yes," Faucon said, nodding, but he cast a worried glance at Gerd. "Are you all right, Gerd?"

Wounded but in no danger, she replied.

"Thank heavens." He and Agape rushed to secure the doors leading to the Toot Towers and prevent any interruption.

Grinda glared over Offi's head at the throne area. "What'll it be, Chundertoe? Will you cooperate with us or should we have you executed for treason too?"

"I'll cooperate," he said quickly. Offi couldn't believe the laggard had never moved from his seat and had in fact soiled it prodigiously.

"Good." Grinda waved at King Gustave. "Come on over, we need to stabilize things quickly or there will be more blood." She asked Chundertoe, "You do all your official work at those desks over there facing the north windows? Ink and paper and sealing wax and whatnot?"

"Yes."

"Let's go."

The king and his adviser disappeared from Offi's sight as Båggi Biins knelt in front of him with his picnic basket and cask. He squinted at Offi's midsection and winced, then grabbed for his cask of mead. "Oh, piglet pants!" he said, handing the cask to Kirsi. "Give him as much of this as he can handle. I'll get to work on a poultice."

As the dwarf turned to riffle through his drawers of herbs, Kirsi fumbled with the cork stopper and finally popped it out with a hollow thoomp. She tilted the cask toward Offi's mouth.

"You have to drink some of this, Onni. Open wide."

Offi tried his best, and some of the sweet mead dribbled into his mouth. He swallowed a bit and it burned. He coughed a couple of times, and that inspired new waves of pain and chills.

"Not sure . . . that's helping."

"We have to try, Onni." She brandished her wand and pointed it at his belly. "For real: Heal." Nothing happened, and Kirsi frowned at the wand. "Why isn't it working? It was short, but it rhymed."

Offi took a deep breath—or tried. He failed. It was odd how his body seemed to be having a bit of a Panic while his brain had never been more calm, more quiet, more clear. There was a Great and Sparkling Clarity about the room, and Offi could tell that everything was going to be okay. Not for him, but for everybody else. For his friends, for the king, and for the gnomes of Pell. There was only one thing left to do. With shaking hands, he tried to straighten his cardigan, but his fingers were cold and shivering. He would've liked a cleaner cardigan, a black cardigan, perhaps one festooned with ravens, for what he was going to say, but this . . . well, it would have to do.

"Kirsi, listen. I have to tell you something important."

"No. Please, Onni, no. Just wait a minute until I fix this, and then we'll talk all you want. Okay? I have to fix this."

Despite the chill in his fingers, he felt Kirsi grasp his hands, and a great warmth suffused him. "You can't fix this, Kirsi. Neither can Båggi. No one can, I'm afraid."

Kirsi was crying now, her face puce and her nose just fountaining snot. She was missing a great patch of her beard, and she was covered with scrapes and a few burn marks, and her cardigan, for once, was definitely askew. To Offi, she'd never been more beautiful.

"I can fix it. I have magic. I'll give my entire beard. My braids. My eyebrows. I don't care. What's the point of having all this magic if I can't do what needs doing?"

Offi gently shook his head. "I don't think there is a point to magic. What matters is what you do with it, who you help, and how you make the world better. Just like inventing. You fix what you can and keep going. Maybe I'm a little broken, but everything else is fixed, and that's what matters."

"No, Onni! We just—"

"Kirsi. Listen. This is important." He waited until she'd stopped focusing on his wound and was instead looking steadily into his eyes. It was nice. If only he'd been wearing his glasses so he could've seen her better. "I'm not Onni. I'm Offi and have been ever since Bruding, when you told me to go fetch my brother. I'm very sorry for deceiving you—that was wrong. I just . . . wanted to go instead of staying behind. Wanted to be something more than everyone thought I could be."

"You silly." Kirsi sniffled as a fresh gout of tears sprung up. "I knew it was you."

Not much could surprise Offi now, but that did. "You . . . knew?"

"Well, not at first. But Onni never invented anything. He never fixed anything or created anything. He just shouted things, looked heroically at things, or smiled at things."

"That is . . . a pretty accurate summation of his character. But I love him. Tell him for me? That I did something good? And that I love him?"

"What? No. You're going to tell him. We just need—"

"I'm so tired. And so cold." His eyes drifted shut and Kirsi shook him.

"Offi, no! You stay awake! Båggi is making you something—I don't know what it is, but it's one of his things that's very alliterative and it's very powerful and it's going to fix you up. Open your eyes, Offi!"

He tried, but his eyelids had never been so heavy. Just a nap was all he needed.

"Please, Offi! Just hold on!"

"Saved the king," he mumbled. "That was pretty metal."

Offi couldn't stay awake any longer, even though Kirsi demanded he not sleep. He wanted to oblige her, but all the fight—all the blood—had drained out of him. He slid down into the cold and black, pleased that he had done some good and made a difference.

His grandgnome had often told him and Onni, when they were wee and whining about a skinned knee or a split lip, *If you've been stabbed in the gut and can't stand all the crying, find a cozy hole because you probably are dying.* At the time, she'd been encouraging the boys to stiffen up and toe the line. But Offi smiled. He'd finally found a gnomeism that rang true for him.

"This is goth as heck," he murmured.

And then things went black. For good.

33.

BESPLATTERED BY BLOOD AND POSITIVELY RIDDLED WITH BOONS

"This Fyne Gryphone is entitled to as many Tastee Egges and Fluffee Omlets as she can produce and eat on the Gerd's Herd of Birds Farme. No other Gryphones may call her names or suggest that she may not eat Egges, because she may indeed eat Egges, all the Egges, Really Every Egge Ever, SO THERE."

—A ROYAL BOON DRAFTED BY GRINDA THE SAND WITCH, signed by King Gustave, with spellings and capital letters insisted upon by Gerd

I n that moment, Kirsi felt, for the first time, that something broken could not be fixed. No amount of taking charge, no magic wand, no number of perfectly folded cardigans, could brighten the darkness left behind when Offi's eyes closed.

Silly boy. How could he think he'd fooled her? She'd known both twins since the day they'd all showed up to gnomeschool in their embroidered lederhosen. At first she'd been annoyed, considering she'd looked forward to indulging her smoosh on Onni. But then she'd seen Offi alone for the first time and had witnessed how he bloomed when out of his twin's shadow. If he'd ever bothered to speak up in school, if he'd ever opened his mouth without Onni stepping in front of him, chest puffed out, perhaps she would've seen it earlier. Seen that Offi was by the far the superior Numminen boy.

If only they'd been honest with each other from the start, perhaps she could've kissed Offi while he was still alive. But it was too late. Her lips brushed his, gentle as a butterfly.

"Goodbye, Offi. May your pudding be sweet, your cogs be oiled, and your cardigan remain forever as crisp as the day it was embroidered."

"Oh, my . . . my . . . oh!"

Something fell to the ground and exploded into a pile of glass shards and golden liquid and the scent of honey and herbs. Kirsi looked to Båggi, who was covered in his spilled potion, and she had never seen the dwarf so flustered or so lacking in peculiar aphorisms.

"I dropped all my wonderful stuff," he said sadly. "Ha ha."

Kirsi put a hand on his wrist. "It's okay, Båggi. It's too late. There's nothing we can do to help him now."

"Nothing? Nothing at all? Didn't those ghosts speak of some magical flesh ho—"

"No!"

King Gustave had stepped into their circle, and his royal decree was spoken so forcefully, so regally, that both Kirsi and Båggi knelt at his feet. The spilled potion soaked into Kirsi's skirt, but she didn't really care anymore. The king hadn't seemed like a king before, not that Kirsi had ever really met a king. But he hadn't exhibited Hellä Traktiv's competent confidence or even the pomp and style of the local mayor back in Pavaasik. Still, in just one word, he'd fully stepped into her personal ideal of what a king should be, and so she waited for his next kingly statement.

"No one can say that thing you were about to say, because it is totally gross, and really, you shouldn't do anything that Ghost Toby says, because he's sorta barmy," Gustave said, scratching his nethers with his head cocked to the side.

"What King Gustave means," Grinda said, sliding into their midst as if she'd always been there and had not recently been a possum and didn't still have a bit of turkey leg stuck in her teeth, "is that flesh honey is a level-three forbidden substance, and you probably shouldn't say the words either." She gave the king the sort of grin a teacher gives to a small child who won't stop scratching their bum, and King Gustave quit scratching his bum, as if he were a small child being grinned at in that terrifying way teachers had.

"Hey, so that went pretty good, right?" the king said, because he needed people to forget he'd been scratching his bum.

"By which the king means that you've all done an excellent service to crown and country and will be well rewarded," Grinda continued to translate. "You've traveled far and sacrificed much. The king would grant you a royal boon."

"I don't have any balloons," King Gustave said. "But we could possibly order some from Qul?"

"Boon, not balloon." Grinda patted him on the shoulder, and he gave a distinctly goatlike smile. "What would you ask of your king?"

Gerd was the first to respond: *Egges. Many egges. All the egges. And a special dispensation that I may feast upon them.*

Grinda and Gustave shared a look.

"How many eggs are we talking about?" Gustave said. "And, uh, who just said that in my head? This impressive birdcat? Catbird? Thing?"

"She's a gryphon, she could easily bite you in two, and she did speak in your head." Grinda turned to Gerd. "We can't promise you *all* the eggs, but we can give you many eggs," she promised.

It's pronounced egges, Gerd insisted.

"Oh, no. It's like we're in the Catacombs of Yore all over again," King Gustave groaned.

"At least we're not arguing over an umlaut," Grinda muttered. Returning her gaze to Gerd, she said, "We could build you a chicken farm, perhaps? Just name the city."

Gerd looked to Faucon, who'd been walking around the room, checking that the drubs were truly dead and collecting their gold medallions and various toe jewels.

I will go where Faucon goes, the gryphon said, almost shyly.

"Well, where do you want to go?" Gustave asked. "What's your balloon? And, hey, you're not a Dique or a Chundertoe, right?"

Faucon drew himself up tall despite his many injuries. "I would rather die than be a Dique. I am Faucon Pooternoob of the Toodleoo Pooternoobs, and what I would like best is a position overseeing the legal demesne of the kanssa-jaarli. For too long, the laws have been ignored. But we have the Elder Annals, and there are many new laws that must be made regarding building codes and statuary."

"Are you saying you want a job?" Grinda asked, one sharp eyebrow inching into her hair.

"I would like the position and power to implement laws that will help the halfling people return to their greatness." Faucon put a tender hand on Gerd's neck. "But in a place where Gerd would be welcome and well supplied with eggs."

Grinda looked at Gustave. "Are you thinking what I'm thinking?" she asked.

"If you're thinking that the muesli bar over there is mostly free of blood and probably doesn't have too many raccoon hairs in it, then yes."

"I'm thinking we need a new kanssa-jaarli, and we are in the presence of a halfling and a gnome. A halfling and a gnome who care enough about setting things right for their peoples that they'll travel across Pell for a reckoning. Not only that, but they are friends who might lead all the halflings and gnomes into a greater understanding of friendship and amity, uniting their people as one."

The room seemed to hold its breath, and Kirsi couldn't help it. She broke out into laughter, and, luckily, Faucon joined her.

"Oh, I'm just out of school!" Kirsi said. "Old gnomes will never vote for me to be the jaarl."

"And while I consider my past to be impeccable, there are many halflings who would look askance upon my adherence to the law and my loyalty to a magnificent pigeon, now deceased. I would fare poorly, I fear, in an election," Faucon said.

"But I would be delighted to be appointed to some position where I may do some good, much like what Faucon requested," Kirsi added. "An emergency appointment as acting jaarl, perhaps, lasting no more than six months while proper elections are arranged, as allowed by the Elder Annals?"

"Yes," Gustave said, waggling a finger in her direction while nodding at Grinda. "Yes, that thing, what she just said, Grinda. Let's do it."

"Done!" the sand witch said, her face erupting in a smile so brilliant that it made her wattle quiver.

"Uh, what about him?" Kirsi asked, pointing at the raccoon, who still sat on his throne as if unaware that his job was being given away. He was, in fact, emitting tiny raccoon snores.

Grinda rubbed a well-worn place between her eyebrows. "Raccoon, can you speak?"

In response, the raccoon merely rolled over, bottom in the air, and gave a whistling snore.

I could get rid of it, Gerd offered. *It will perhaps be messy, but that doesn't appear to be a problem in this room. You may have the tail, if you wish.*

"No!" Båggi cried. When everyone stared at him, he added, "My people often keep raccoons as pets. I'd rather take her home than see her, er, get Gerded. Oh, my fancy fig pies! To return home from Meadschpringå with a Cudgel of Peace and a rotund raccoon! My parents will be most proud!"

He held up his Telling Cudgel, and Kirsi felt a rush of gladness for her friend. In the last week, she'd seen the wooden stick grow violent protuberances, glow in different colors, wear different badges, and make various squishy bits explode. But now it looked as tranquil as the day she'd met Båggi, the honey-gold wood showing a beautiful grain and an intricate carving of a bee, along with a star.

"What does the star mean?" Kirsi asked.

Båggi turned the cudgel and his jaw dropped. "Oh, my juice and jam! A star indicates that a dwarf has performed a feat of extraordinary valor for the world. I've only seen one starred cudgel before, that one belonging to an ancient dwarf named Sir Gimlet, who was involved with the Fellowship of the String. Oh, my!" He hugged the cudgel to his chest, and Kirsi was very glad it no longer featured spikes.

"So you're leaving, then?" Agape asked, and it was clear to Kirsi, after all this time in the ovitaur's presence, that she was upset and hurt but trying to act tough.

"Well, the plan was always to return to my people and live a quiet life of peace, bees, and mead," Båggi said. "You're welcome to come, if you wish, but I'll warn you that my people will attempt to fleece you on the daily."

"Fleece me? Like, of money?"

"Er." The dwarf looked down and turned red. "Your wool. They'll want it for warm socks."

"Screw the dwarves, then," Agape said.

Båggi's jaw dropped, but the king's chamberlain stepped in to smooth rumpled pelts.

"You, too, are owed a boon," Grinda said to Agape. "What would you ask of your king?"

"I . . . I don't know. Nobody's ever aaasked me that," Agape admitted. "I think I'd like to go somewhere and be an artist. Work on my caaarving. But not somewhere I've been before, aaand I've been most everywhere."

"Have you been to Qul?" Grinda asked.

"Well, no. My faaather said the people were fiercely xenophobic."

"Seems like your father lied a lot," Kirsi said, but kindly.

"About this, at least, he did." Grinda nodded once and gave Agape a reassuring grin. "The Qul people are wonderful, and they always appreciate artists. The king and I would like to offer you a scholarship as the Pellican Artist of the Year, Mondo Emeritus. The grant includes travel to and housing at anyplace in all of Pell, as well as a Letter of Introduction/Forced Friendliness from the king. Will that suit you?"

"That . . . that would be amaaazing!" Agape said, and to Kirsi, the ovitaur looked years younger, as if she'd finally let go of a heavy burden. It was understandable—instead of spending her entire life belonging nowhere, on the run and frightened of people, Agape now had somewhere she could belong and something to do there. It was unlikely that anyone with the king's writ in hand would be chased on the daily, which had to be a big relief.

The smiles and hope they felt for the future evaporated once Kirsi's eye landed on Offi.

"What about him?" she asked sadly.

The king cleared his throat. "A medal of valor. A commemorative stamp from the postale service. A boon granted to his family, perhaps? He deserves so much more. The last kid we killed—I mean, the last kid who died in service to Pell—we gave his parents a newer, unmuddy farmhouse, but they did have to sign papers promising to never eat a goat again, and I might have stolen his father's boots. Did this kid eat a lot of goats?"

"Uh, no?" Kirsi said.

"Then let's offer all that to his parents."

"Their home did get bombed by the halflings."

King Gustave looked terribly alarmed. "Oh, no. He wasn't a Nooperkins, was he?"

"He was a Numminen."

"Good. I mean, not good. But that would just be a lot for ol' Floopi to take in. I just . . . I just really want to help all the gnomes who got exploded."

Kirsi smiled up at the king and finally understood what good leadership looked like. It wasn't perfect oratory or braggadocio, or a rattling saber, or military parades. It was a heart to help people and the will to do it.

"Thank you, Greatest King Gustave," she said.

After that, it was all paperwork and arrangements, with Grinda dispensing orders with the efficiency of a gnomeric automaton. She found the kanssa-jaarli's Royal Writ pad and dashed off Chunder-toe's resignation, then another writ for Kirsi and Faucon's appointments. With her great, looping scrawl, she created signs to post around town, explaining the return of law and pertinent bits from the Elder Annals. The Dastardly Rogues Under Bigly-Wicke were disbanded, and anyone found wearing a drub medal would be sent to prison on sight, where they'd receive the Great Shaving of Shame and be put to work helping clean up and rebuild exploded gnome-homes. The general idea, Grinda told them, was that very busy people doing useful work didn't have time to get into trouble. She was looking at King Gustave when she said it, but Kirsi was the only one who noticed.

When it was time for the king and Grinda to leave, Kirsi stood at the base of the Toot Towers beside Faucon, picking raccoon hairs off her ceremonial robe. In the past few days, she'd grown quite accustomed to Gustave, as he liked to be called, and his stern but fond chamberlain. Kirsi was sorry to see them go. Ghost Toby had been right: The king was okay, and they didn't even have to use the passcode.

"We're off to Tennebruss to see the Earl of Borix," Grinda said, climbing onto a centipod much like the one Kirsi's party had ridden for a time, although the king's version was much bigger and grander. "With Lord Ergot gone, we must find a new Lord of Bruding. A man who understands the people and is willing to support the retun of laws to the Skyr."

"Tennebruss?" Kirsi asked, suddenly feeling a heavy weight hanging in her heart. "That would be on the way to Bruding. Offi's family is there . . . I need to tell them what happened. And that it's safe for them to go home, because of what their son sacrificed."

King Gustave held out a hand. "Well, come along, then. We've got plenty of room and oodles of oatmeal and muesli. No one gets exploded or constipated on my watch!"

Kirsi turned to Faucon, but before she could find the words, he smiled. "Go. See your people. And tell Offi's parents that they should be proud. I shall take care of things here."

He held out his hand to shake, but Kirsi wrapped her arms around his waist and squeezed, surprising him. "I know you will, silly," she said. "To do otherwise would be against the law!"

She also hugged Gerd, which the gryphon allowed, and Agape sighed as if she didn't want a hug but knew it was inevitable. But, Kirsi noted, the offputting ovitaur hugged her back.

"Write me from Qul!" Kirsi said. "Promise me!"

"What will you do if I don't?" Agape asked. "Fine me?"

Faucon nodded gravely. "Most definitely."

Båggi was a bit too tall and broad for a hug, so to him she bowed. "I hope you enjoy your peace in the High Mountain Home, Master Biins," she said. "You've earned it."

"Oh, my tidy tunics!" he replied. "You must know I will sing of you there. Perhaps on some fine day you will hear my song in the wind."

Before she could start crying, Kirsi clambered up into the centipod and selected a cushy bench. She was worried she would have to make royal conversation all the way to Tennebruss, but it turned out the king ate a huge vat of oatmeal with maple syrup and fell asleep, and Grinda had far too much work to do, sending out official notices via postale-service flamingo and gnomeric automaatti to all halfling forces in the Skyr, recalling them to the eastern side of the Rumplescharte River. So Kirsi watched the country pass by. It wasn't as much fun without her friends, but it was rather pleasant to travel without being constantly threatened from alpaca-back. She did her best not to think about Offi, but ... well, Offi was all she could think about, really.

Once the dreary city of Tennebruss opened its gates, King Gustave and Grinda abandoned the royal centipod and let Kirsi continue on alone to Bruding, with only the oatmeal chef for company and some royal funds to arrange her travel from there back to the Skyr. She knocked on the door of the Lord Ergot Living Memorial Refugee Center and Ping-Pong Palace by herself, hoping the new lord would change the name of that place, since traitors should not be allowed memorials and refugees should not have to suffer Ping-Pong. The sadness of seeing Offi's twin and giving his parents the bad news was balanced by the knowledge that she would be leading her people back to Pavaasik and away from Ping-Pong forever.

"We're full," the human guard barked.

Kirsi was pleased to hold up the king's official writ, stamped with his official seal and bearing stains of his official oatmeal.

"Not anymore," she told him.

34.

OVER A MOIST BLACK CARDIGAN
LOVINGLY EMBROIDERED WITH BATS

"It's rare enough that someone leads such a colorful life that they get a tube of paint named after them, but Offi Numminen was the only being goth enough to get a shade of black named in his honor: Offi Black."

—Rasmus Lamppula, in *Art History of the Skyr, Revised & Expanded Edition*

"Thank you, Suppi. This hot nut pudding is delicious," Onni said, grinning winsomely at an eldergnome, who blushed and giggled as if she were wee again.

"Oh, no, Onni. Thank you. I don't know how you found the nuts or the extra sugar or even how you convinced those wretched humans to give us an entire kitchen, but you're the only reason we're not eating gruel pudding tonight."

"And look how tidy your cardigan is!" another eldergnome said. *"Neat as a pin, feed him pudding again,* that's what they always say. Your parents must be so proud."

Feeling warm down to his very toes, Onni looked to where Venla and Old Seppo sat together, heads bowed over the delectable pudding as if it were indeed the thinnest, coldest, least nutty of gruels.

Seppo had been in a downward spiral ever since their hatch exploded, but that spiral became a swan dive when Offi disappeared. All this time and still no word. As each new group of refugees entered the Ping-Pong Palace, clutching their belongings and Lord Ergot's complimentary cabbage rations and looking about at the bare walls in horror, Onni had welcomed them and helped them find their feet. But secretly, every time, he was looking for his twin, hoping for news of a black-clad loner hunching along the road, building machines and spouting adorable rage.

They'd heard nothing.

But the gnomes needed a leader, so Onni led, even as his heart felt as crumpled as an old, dirty pair of coveralls.

Suddenly, the room went silent, and Onni heard dozens of gnomes swallow their mouthfuls of pudding and drop their spoons, in exactly that order. He looked up, expecting an angry human or possibly another contingent of refugees.

What he saw was Kirsi Noogensen.

She wasn't exactly the same as he remembered her. Kirsi had been known for her neat cardigan, quick answers, and ability to get along with anyone. And surely she was that still, for all that she was road-worn and a bit dirty around the collar. But the way she stood—it was like she was taller than all the other gnomes and fierce somehow. She was also missing a rather large chunk of her beard. And when Onni looked in her eyes and saw the depths of grief there, he, too, dropped his spoon.

"Kirsi?" he said, standing from his gnome-crafted chair.

She gave him a weak and relieved smile and hurried to take his hands and perform a ceremonial nose-rubbing, which didn't bode well.

"Hello, Onni." She swallowed hard. "That pudding smells nice. But we need to . . . I mean . . . are your parents here?"

Onni walked her over to where Old Seppo and Venla sat. They hadn't even looked up at the commotion, and they still didn't look up, until Onni gently squeezed their shoulders.

"Mama, Papa, this is Kirsi, from back home. She . . . has something to tell us, I think."

His heart was sinking fast, and it didn't help when Kirsi reached into her pack and pulled out a medal. At first, Onni assumed it was somehow for him, because that's how medals tended to work in his orbit. But this one was new and shining gold, and Kirsi laid it on the table with great reverence.

KING GUSTAVE'S BEST GNOME IN PELL MEDAL, Onni read, tracing the letters with a finger. A rampant goat was stamped in the center, and when he turned the medal over, he saw his brother's name chiseled in the shining gold.

"Oh, Offi," he murmured, his eyes filling with tears. For if the medal was here and Offi was not and the ever-cheerful Kirsi was crying, that could mean only one thing.

"What's he done now?" Seppo grumbled. "Invented a machine that makes medals? You tell that boy to come home and eat his gruel pudding, by dinkus. Giving his mother fits, he is. Nobody can keep their cardigan straight anymore."

Kirsi shook her head, making her glossy red beard wag. "No, Mr. Numminen. I'm so sorry, but Offi is . . . that is, he . . ."

"He was a hero."

Spoons that had been picked up dropped again, and when Onni turned to the voice, he found a strange personage in the doorway, wearing a golden circlet and the fanciest duds he'd ever seen. The man's eyes were a little strange and his teeth had obviously required extensive oral surgery and his ears seemed far too large, but still, Onni recognized his king. He immediately knelt, his head bowed. All the other gnomes followed.

Kirsi said, "King Gustave, I'm glad you're here. This is Offi's brother, Onni, and his parents, Seppo and Venla Numminen."

"Er, hi," King Gustave said, fidgeting a bit. "Turned out the earl in Tennebruss had some centipods they use for parades, so I just took them because they let me do stuff like that now, and I followed you here to help with relocation. So, wow, y'all are intense. I never know what to do when people kneel. Should I kneel too? It's so awkward. Please stand, and do stop clutching your sweaters as if I'm going to steal them. I don't think they would fit and I don't eat them anymore. Although that one with the boots on it is terribly fetching."

Onni stood, as did his parents. "We clutch our cardigans to keep them off the ground, sir. And I feel certain someone could knit up a nice cardigan for you, if you wish." He was careful to keep his voice even and warm, for all that his innards felt colder than a shaved alpaca's tummy.

"Hey, I'd never turn down a brown sweater," Gustave said, stroking his little beard. "But that's not why I'm here. First of all, I wanted to see what's so great about Ping-Pong, which is literally nothing. Secondly, I wanted to let you all know that I have personally dissolved a corrupt kanssa-jaarli and will be enforcing new laws to ensure the safety and continued unexplodedness of all gnomes in the Skyr. You guys can go home, and we'll send help to rebuild any destroyed hatches." He knelt before the Numminens and looked deeply into Onni's eyes. "But most important, I wanted to make sure you knew that Offi Numminen saved our entire country. He saved my life, and he fought for the Skyr, and I don't know if you guys put famous gnomes on muesli boxes or what, but he was a really great guy."

Old Seppo looked up, tears streaming down his face. "Was?"

Kirsi put a hand on Seppo's shoulder. "He jumped between an assassin and the king. He knew what he was doing and why he was doing it. He died happy to save his people. And he wanted you to be proud of him."

"I was always proud of him!" Seppo roared, throwing off Kirsi's hand. The old gnome stood tall, or at least as tall as he could manage, his hands in fists and his moist eyes ablaze. "Offi was a great son, a great inventor. Sure, he was a little weird, but he knew we loved him. He knew!"

"So proud," Venla murmured, stroking the medal. "We were always so proud."

"I was cruel to him," Onni said, head down, weeping. He went for his pack and pulled out a black cardigan, neatly folded, with bats embroidered on the pockets. "I told him he couldn't wear this sweater he made. I was embarrassed that he was strange and ungnomeric. And he was so gnomeric that he died to save us. I'm an awful brother."

"Onni," Kirsi said gently, taking the cardigan from him. "Please stop making it about you. This is about Offi and what he accomplished. And as the temporary kanssa-jaarli, I'm going to ask King Gustave to rename this place the Offi Numminen Center for Gnomeric Understanding. Let those humans who wish to celebrate gnomes come here to see our work and learn from us, and let those gnomes who perhaps don't fit in come here to study, find their place in the world, and do great and possibly ungnomeric things."

"I totally rename it that thing you just said," Gustave added in a kingly sort of voice, "and I kinda wish I'd thought of it first."

Onni hiccupped a sob and looked down at his empty hands. "So we can go home now?" he asked.

"You can go—" Kirsi started.

"You can—" Gustave said at almost exactly the same time.

Kirsi bowed and gave Gustave an amused smile.

"You can go wherever you wish," the king finished grandly. "Although I wouldn't recommend the terrible places, like Yglyk or even the area around the Toot Towers, which is just jam-packed with halflings and abattoirs. Like, just stick to this side of the Rumplescharte River. And stay away from any catacombs you might find, because leeches, my gnomey. Acid leeches."

Tucking Offi's tear-damp black cardigan under her arm, Kirsi smiled at the roomful of gnomes and forgotten pudding.

"I am here to lead you home," she said, "and we'll leave as soon as you're ready. That is, when you've finished your pudding. And if there might be two more bowlfuls?"

She looked at King Gustave and winked. Two young gnomes hurried to prepare bowls of steaming hot nut pudding and presented them to Kirsi and the king with much bowing and coquettish beard-swishing.

"Hey, this stuff is pretty great," Gustave said as the rich white pudding dripped down his beard and onto his velvet tunic. "Nutty but sweet. Hot and moist. A bit dribbly. But great."

"Of course it is," Seppo said, his back now straight, his chin pugnaciously uplifted, and his eyes ablaze. "Gnomes made it."

Onni went back to his pudding, tracing his twin's name on the medal with one finger.

"He was pretty special, wasn't he?" he asked Kirsi.

She dabbed the pudding away from her beard and said, "Yeah, he really was."

"I really was," a new voice said.

With a squawk of surprise, Onni tumbled backward out of his chair, which mortified him for disrupting an important moment in gnomeric history. But no one seemed to notice. When he stood again, he found a ghostly blue shape standing quite close to Kirsi, who was grinning at the newcomer and the bat-covered cardigan he wore.

"I've been waiting my whole life to be better than you at something," Offi's ghost said, poking Onni in the chest with a spectral finger that tickled a bit. "And now I've got the biggest medal of all."

"Can anyone else see you, or just me?" he asked.

"Just you. And Kirsi. And King Gustave. There's something about magic that just makes ghosts more ghosty, you know?"

Onni swallowed hard. "N-no?"

"Oh, yeah. I'm your first ghost. But the good news is that I'm not going to haunt you forever or anything creepy like that. I just wanted to tell you something important before I moved on."

Onni sat forward, his skin all prickled over and his head and heart doing somersaults. "Yes, Offi. I'm listening."

"Oh, I already told you. It's just that my medal is bigger than any of yours and I'm a public hero and all that. It's my brotherly duty to rub it in."

Onni rolled his eyes. "Okay, Offi. Whatever. You win at dying."

Offi grinned. "I do. I do win at dying. And that is the most goth thing of all. Bye."

With that, Offi winked out of existence, leaving Onni with the feeling that he would be vaguely annoyed his whole life.

"To Offi!" Kirsi called, raising her pudding spoon.

"To Offi!" King Gustave bleated.

"To Offi!" everyone else answered before slurping down their pudding.

"To Offi," Onni said, but he couldn't be excited about it.

His entire world had changed in the span of an hour.

His twin was gone. Offi was a hero. The gnomes were free.

Now Onni just had to figure out what to do with the rest of his life that would honor his brother's sacrifice.

"Can I see that?" he asked Kirsi.

She slid the package across the table and smiled as Onni put on Offi's black cardigan.

"Let's go home," he said.

Epilogue

BUFFETED BY EBULLIENT WINDS OF
SURPASSING KINDNESS

High among the peaks of the Korpås Range, there were no elves or humans, no gnomes or halflings. There were only dwarves and gryphons and the creatures of the alpine meadows and woods. There were terraced fields of vegetables and herbs and there were lakes full of shining fish, and of course there were the Korpås trees, magic suffused in every grain of their wood.

But there were no cities in the mountains—those were for the valleys below, for the dwarves who craved other things. Here, high above the clouds, there was only what the dwarves called the High Mountain Home, a huge tract of land in which individual dwellings or sometimes warrens were cut into the rock. And outside of these shelters were shelves of granite on which the dwarves spent much of their time listening to the wind murmuring the secrets of the world, and they sang to the wind in turn.

But to make sense of the wind and to understand the bees, one's mind and spirit must be at peace. When a dwarf was young, the wind would let them read a chapter from the book of knowledge; to read more, they had to master themselves as adults.

Many never got to hear the full story of the wind but instead made their own stories in the lowlands.

Båggi Biins was going to hear the full story.

He smiled as he climbed the long and winding road from Grundelbård to the High Mountain Home, showing the sentinels the bee and star engraved in his Telling Cudgel, returning their congratulations with heartfelt thanks, and introducing them to his new raccoon friend, whom he had named Ms. Herring, after her favorite pickled fish. He often needed to dash a tear from his cheeks, so happy was he.

And when he reunited with his sister, Tåffi Biins, and his parents as well, he had so much news to share and brought them gifts of gnomeric hats woven from alpaca wool.

They feasted and drank and talked and slept, and in the morning, Båggi was led to his own personal dwelling, a bachelor's cove in the rock with a wind shelf that faced the south. On the slope of the hill above the shelf, he planted his Telling Cudgel of Korpåswood and told the bees that he would be very pleased if one day a queen came to establish a hive in the new tree it would someday become.

Then he faced east and sang of his joy to be home and of his love for Pell and its many wonders. He turned south and repeated this, then to the west and the north, and then he sat on his shelf and waited. He was ready to listen and he was prepared to wait. When the sun reached its zenith, the wind tugged at his beard and then found his ears and began to whisper in them:

A lady sleeping under a long enchantment disappeared from a tower in Borix, and no one but the wind knew where she was. Soon, the gusts confided with a chuckle, she would reappear in a distant land and Pell would never be the same.

A governess named Hurlga returned to Songlen and King Gustave's service. The king also recovered his minstrels from Bruding and there was much rejoicing of the hootenanny kind. Hurlga's brother, Ralphee, returned safely to his masonry apprenticeship but could find no one willing to explain to him what exactly went on in a tooty bar.

The City of Underthings announced it would manufacture prosthetic toes for any who needed them, thanks to a grant from the Offi Numminen Royal Memorial Toe Trust.

Somewhere in the Urchin Sea, a safe distance from the dark grottoes of the sirens, a toothy horror rose to power, and it was hungry for more than mere crustaceans and schools of shad.

Those human ghosts Båggi had met at Dr. Murkimer's were still trying to find someone who would dig up their corpses in the Grange and apply some flesh honey to their tongues, believing that this would bring them back to life. Lord Toby and Poltro claimed to know where a hive of necrobees could be found, but, no, they had not yet asked the Dread Necromancer Steve if their scheme would work, because they couldn't secure an appointment.

In the Siren Sn'archipelago, an old man sat waiting to hear the god Pellanus speak, and Pellanus did speak, and tears formed in the man's eyes as he pulled out a special leather-bound book, took up his quill, and began to write.

Båggi listened to these secrets and many more, for there was much happening in the Skyr prior to the new elections, and the wind lavished compliments on Båggi for his role in bringing that about. When the sun neared the horizon, it was time for him to sing of his peace to the wind so that others might hear and hope. He stood and stretched, slaked his thirst with a few swallows of mead, and then he sang into the breeze:

> *"I hear each of you in the High Mountain Home:*
> *Human and elf, troll and giant, halfling and gnome,*
> *Whether speaking ill or praise, at mischief or playing games,*
> *I hear you the same and know your names.*

You are all loved and here to do A Thing;
You are a verse in the Pellican song we sing.
I wish for a time when your struggles may cease
And you can enjoy a goodly measure of peace."

As Båggi sang, other dwarves on other peaks at different eleva-
tions sang as well, and their words of encouragement and affirmation
floated on the winds to become soft and gentle breezes in the lowlands someday, the breath of fresh air someone needed to deal with a
vexing relative, a troubling co-worker, or the noxious waste excreted
by the cat. The next day he would work for himself, making tonics
and salves and replenishing his herb stores, as well as purchasing
some tins of oily fish for Ms. Herring; the day after that he would
work for his fellow dwarves in the community gardens or whatever
else needed doing; and on the third day he would return to his shelf
and listen to the wind before speaking his peace to the world. Occasionally he would travel down to the lowlands, but most of his days
would rotate thus and he was content. He would like to see his
friends again, of course, and was glad there was a reliable postale
service now to keep in touch with them, but he knew he would hear
of them on the wind as well.

Several months later, with sun and careful watering, his Telling
Cudgel ceased to be a weapon and became a tree again. It sent out
roots into the mountain and sprouted branches and leaves. An extremely polite queen bee came to visit and inquired if she might have
his permission to build a hive there.

"Oh, bless my braided beard, yes!" he told her. "You are most welcome here!"

And then the wind brought him welcome tidings the very next
day: Kirsi Noogensen and Faucon Pooternoob had both won formal
election as kanssa-jaarli of the Skyr in spite of their beliefs that they
were unelectable, and his favorite gryphon was enjoying the Gerd
Herd of Birds Farme near the Toot Towers. She was often seen in
the skies and sometimes perched on top of one Toot Tower or an-

other. She would allow portrait automaatti to sketch her with tourists if the visitors promised to live in peace according to the wisdom
of the Elders. Agape Fallopia, meanwhile, now residing in Quchii
Qu, had just sold her first full-sized sculpture, titled "Happy AF," for
a barrel of gold. Bǎggi Biins could think of no better news to hear in
his High Mountain Home.

ACKNOWLEDGMENTS

Kevin would like to thank his family and friends for, you know, walking on the world with him. They can't be thanked enough for that.

And, hey, you, reading this? You are *dang* spiffy. Thanks so much for reading.

Thanks to Metal Editor Tricia Narwani and all the spiffy peeps at Del Rey for their stellar work on these books, and for conducting that one ritual in the office with the chog and the mustard and the chanting.

My deepest gratitude and a bottle of really good whiskey goes to Kathy Lord, copy editor sans pareil, for dealing with our alternative spellings, my terrible habit of misplaced modifiers, and the inevitable inconsistencies that sprout up when there are two different authors working on a story.

Turbo mega thanks to my friend and co-author, Delilah. This book has come a long way from its origins in New Orleans. I'm Lucky AF to work with you.

Delilah would like to thank her Beloved Husbande, Craig, and her two Foine Children, as well as all of her buddies in the real world and online. Thanks to everyone who lets us know that they enjoyed *Kill the Farm Boy* and then giggles when we tell them the name of this book, its sequel.

Big thanks to our beloved editor, Tricia Narwani, who groks Offi and his goth cardigans on a soul level and who embraces everything Kevin and I do with open arms. And thanks to everyone at Del Rey because you guys are family and you take great care of us and you always get me a gluten-free sandwich at conventions. And, yes, thanks to Kathy Lord for treating Gerd's spelling like something that actually makes sense instead of a language Kevin and I made up to abuse yet more umlauts and extra Es.

As always, super huge turbo extra mega gigantic thanks to my ultimate homey, Kevin Hearne, for being the best co-writer possible and for always writing the acknowledgments first so that I can kiiiiinda copy them? Kevin isn't just a Goode Egge, he is The Beste Egge.

See y'all in *The Princess Beard*!

p.s.: The authors harbor no ill will toward Ping-Pong or those who enjoy it; we just thought it would make a funny joke. Because who could hate Ping-Pong?

p.p.s.: Ping-Pong knows what it did.

ABOUT THE AUTHORS

DELILAH S. DAWSON is the author of the *New York Times* bestseller *Star Wars: Phasma*, as well as the Hit series *Servants of the Storm*, the Blud series, and the Shadow series (written as Lila Bowen and beginning with *Wake of Vultures*). Her comics credits include the creator-owned *Ladycastle* and *Sparrowhawk* as well as work in the worlds of Star Wars, The X-Files, Labyrinth, Adventure Time, Rick and Morty, and Marvel Action Spider-Man. She lives in Florida with her family and a fat mutt named Merle.

whimsydark.com
Twitter: @DelilahSDawson
Instagram: @delilahsdawson

KEVIN HEARNE hugs trees, pets doggies, and rocks out to heavy metal. He also thinks tacos are a pretty nifty idea. He is the author of *A Plague of Giants* and the *New York Times* bestselling series the Iron Druid Chronicles.

kevinhearne.com
Twitter: @KevinHearne
Instagram: @kevinhearne

Please visit talesofpell.com for more.

ABOUT THE TYPE

This book was set in Caslon, a typeface first designed in 1722 by William Caslon (1692–1766). Its widespread use by most English printers in the early eighteenth century soon supplanted the Dutch typefaces that had formerly prevailed. The roman is considered a "workhorse" typeface due to its pleasant, open appearance, while the italic is exceedingly decorative.